BLEEDING
PALM

Nancy,

Espero que disfrutes la
lectura de este libro, tanto
o más que la satisfacción que
experimenté al escribirlo!

Saludos y cariños para ti
y para Enrique, de otro gra-
duado de Villanueva,

Miguel A. Quintana

BLEEDING PALM

A Historical Novel

Michael A. Quintana

To order additional copies of this book, contact:
Xlibris Corporation
1-888-7-XLIBRIS
www.Xlibris.com
Orders@Xlibris.com
12877

To all the María Teresas of Cuba,
and their indomitable spirit.

PROLOGUE

This book was written with two purposes in mind. Its minor goal was to describe the series of events that occurred on the island of Cuba from 1956 to 1962. The main result of these events was the removal of this ill-fated country from the Western Block of democratic governments. That loss forced close to ten million people to experience a sudden shift in their lives, as their surroundings moved quickly from being the second highest per-capita income country in the Americas, in 1958, to an impoverishment corresponding only to a third world country.

At the same time, the inhabitants of this otherwise tropical paradise were turned into a slave labor force that could only be dreamed of in the political nightmares of the social engineers of a system of collectivism.

The main goal of this novel has been to depict the valiant role of the Cuban women caught in the turmoil. Even at the beginning of Castro's Revolution, the typical Cuban mother did not hesitate to send her children to live with other people. These were people that she did not know, and a country so vast that her loved ones could end up living thousands of miles away. Moreover, these children were forced to use a foreign language that they were not able to speak. With tears in her eyes and an awesome pain in her heart, she let her young children go. The only driving force was her desire that her children would be free. Operation "Peter Pan" is a witness to the relocation of thousands and thousands of these children and their ultimate reunion with their loved ones years after. We should also mention that all were not that lucky and several never saw their mothers again.

Some books have been written about the jail conditions in Cuba and the suffering of male prisoners in the bloodstained walls of the cells belonging to a penal system that intended to "rehabilitate" them. But very few books have mentioned the vexations and abuses endured by women living through that hellish ordeal. This novel intends to depict their outcry, their unswerving posture against a political and social system that insisted on limiting their role in life to acting as another soldier, another slave of the people, and the means of producing more slaves for the benefit of the few that claimed to represent the masses.

This book could be classified as fiction and rightly so. The main character and her surrounding family and friends have risen from the imagination of the author. Any resemblance to any real, living or deceased person is purely coincidental. However, on the other hand, this book constitutes also a historical novel. The great majority of events described in this book actually happened. All the places mentioned in this book are real.

Moreover, there are quite a number of characters appearing throughout this novel that are based on real persons, who are either dead or still living. Real events in these persons' lives have been linked, by the creativity of the writer, to the web of incidents and occurrences that permeated through the lives of the fictional characters in order to render veracity to the story that you are about to read.

BOOK ONE

Bay of Pigs

CHAPTER ONE

April 17, 1961 was a cold Monday morning. Normally, the temperature on the island of Cuba was already well into the sixties, even in the early morning. It was six o'clock in the morning, and the temperature was forty-seven degrees Fahrenheit, as a big Lincoln limousine traveled at great speed along Fifth Avenue, in the fashionable Miramar section of La Habana.

The black-colored automobile with burgundy leather interior was a status symbol at that time, in Cuba. It was a 1959 model that was brought onto the island at the very beginning of Castro's takeover of the government. Prior to 1958 and the reign of Fidel Castro, Cuba had been the largest consumer of Cadillacs, outside of the United States. The economy of the island was booming, and it was reflected in the number of luxury automobiles bought by its inhabitants. After World War II, the president of Cuba decided to procure a fleet of Cadillacs for his personal use and for his cabinet members. Soon thereafter, almost every politician and high ranking member of the armed forces started to buy Cadillacs. It became the car of the newly rich and a symbol of power for the habitually dishonest politician. In retribution, the old aristocracy, the high professional class and the affluent bankers decided to drive other kinds of vehicles. The Lincolns and the Chryslers became their status symbols.

The owner of the Lincoln, Don Francisco Aguirrupe, had purchased the car in Miami. He had made all the necessary arrangements for its transport to Cuba when President Batista left the island, abruptly, between the evening hours of December 31, 1958 and the early morning hours of the first day of 1959. Don Francisco was a Judge of the Supreme Court in La Habana, the owner of a large farm that cultivated primarily sugar cane, a cattle rancher, and a stockholder at the Bijagua Sugar Mill, located adjacent to his land in the middle province of the island.

These properties had been in his family for the past two generations. His grandfather had come from the north of Spain to settle in the province of Las Villas and had begun the agricultural business that grew with subsequent years. In 1955, the family had invested heavily into the farm business, starting to raise cattle in the nearby and recently purchased lands. At the same time, they had been selling, at ridiculously low prices, some of their land to the peasants that worked on the farm and the ranch for their own minor production of vegetables and fruits. They did so as an incentive plan to improve labor-management relationships that paid well for both parties.

The limousine had been originally bought with the idea of having a chauffeur to drive it. It was an issue that presented no problems for the Aguirrupes, since Jaime had always been there to fulfill that role. However, he was not available that particular morning because he had gone to Miami with some members of the family.

La Habana was a city of contrast dominated by its history. It started with The Old Citadel, with its narrow streets barely permitting the passage of one vehicle, some smooth with asphalt and some still covered with the original cobblestones. It continued with a newer area of the city, where the downtown was located, displaying all the magnificent department stores, theaters, restaurants and Chinatown. In between, spacious avenues, several parks including Central Park, the Capitol Building and the Presidential Palace exquisitely adorned the scenery. Flowing from the downtown area, suburbs bearing names such as Marianao, Almendares, La Víbora, Santo Suarez and El Cerro, had been established since the turn of the century.

By the beginning of this century, the most exclusive area of all suburbia was El Vedado. Large mansions and rich-looking houses covered the sides of its well-traced streets and avenues. Its parks contained impressive monuments and marble statues of former presidents and patriots who had died in order to give birth to the new Republic.

La Habana rested like a gorgeous and grand siren, next to the ocean, at the northern portion of the province that bore its name. A curved two-way avenue called El Malecón bordered the city, all alongside the ocean, creating a man-made barrier.

At El Malecón, just at the entrance of El Vedado, there was an impressive monument to the American battleship Maine, which was sunk in front of La Habana harbor, marking the beginning of the Spanish-American War in 1898. This cenotaph contained two of the original guns of the ship guarding two tall marble columns, on top of which a huge, bronze American eagle, with its wings spread wide, had once stood proud and defiant. The government of Fidel Castro had it destroyed.

At the end of El Vedado, there was the Almendares River. Originally there were two bridges permitting the traffic to move across the Almendares River into the beach areas of Jaimanitas and La Concha. Between these beaches and the opposite bank of the river to El Vedado, a newer, more affluent development called Miramar arose during the middle part of the current century. Huge, pretentious estates embellished and decorated its ample streets. Well-to-do families that formed the nucleus of the La Habana high class occupied most of the houses. Fifth Avenue ran across the Miramar section, parallel to the ocean line shore, tying El Vedado with the public beaches at the end of Miramar. Beyond that point, other exclusive neighborhoods were being started. They were named Biltmore and Coronela.

Fifth Avenue was a double passageway, divided by a median, covered with greens, benches and fountains. Two lanes existed on each side of the median. In 1961, it led into two modern tunnels. The most recent one was built during the last years of Batista's administration. Each of them allowed the automobiles to drive under the Almendares River at great speeds.

At the wheel, with a million thoughts in her head, was María Teresa Aguirrupe y Larrazábal, Don Francisco's only daughter.

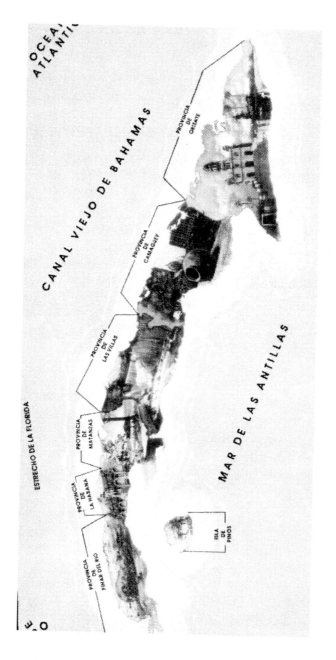

A map of the Island of Cuba, showing the six Provinces that existed
in the Island prior to Castro's regime.

A view of El Morro Castle and the entrance to El Vedado taken from the top of La Habana Hilton Hotel in 1958.

A view of downtown La Habana taken from a ship entering the main harbor in 1956.

*A detailed view of the Cathedral Church located in
the Old La Habana section of the city.*

A view of the National Hotel built during the middle thirties.

National Capitol Building. Seat of the Cuban Congress.
Picture taken in 1956

The Statue of José Martí in La Habana Central Park

The Statue of General Antonio Maceo in the park bearing his name and containing some of the cannons from the times when Spain was guarding its colonies from pirate attacks.

María Teresa was tense. Only two days before, she had spoken with her father, who had called her from Miami. She had heard over the phone the words: "I hope to see you soon, real soon," which was the countersign phrase her father told her he would use when an invasion of the island was imminent. The same day that she spoke to him there had been an attack over the airfields of the military camp of Columbia, in La Habana. The military air base was situated near the Miramar and Biltmore sections of the city. She had heard the loud sound of cannons and anti-aircraft guns, but knew very little about the details. Like so many Cubans on the island, her access to information was very limited, since all sources of news dissemination were controlled entirely by the government. Officially, they heard that there had been an attempt by the imperialist Yankees to destroy the planes of the Cuban Revolutionary Air Force on the ground, but it had been successfully repelled.

On the other hand, the Voice of America from Washington, D.C., which people could listen to only in a clandestine fashion in Cuba, was saying that pilots from the Cuban Revolutionary Air Force had managed to defect in some old B-17 aircrafts, and had landed in Miami. Before leaving the island, they had perpetrated air raids over the Columbia airfield, while the rest of the planes were stationed near the runways.

The punishment by the revolutionary tribunals for listening to the Voice of America, if caught in the act, or even if just accused of such by reliable revolutionary witnesses, was death. At the risk of getting herself involved in serious trouble, she had listened to it in the privacy of her bathroom, completely away from the servants who were still in the house. Even though she trusted them implicitly, she would not implicate them in her own counterrevolutionary activities.

María Teresa's logical reasoning could not conceive that this was merely the whole truth. She knew instinctively that the real truth was, somehow, something else. On that morning everything around her was too quiet. She could sense that something was going on.

Her brother Carlos had been missing from the house since Saturday. She had talked to Carlos on the phone Sunday, and asked him to come home. She could not tell him why over the telephone, since she knew that the government listened to conversations on certain phones. She wanted Carlos to be with her. At moments like these, she believed that the family should be together and remain together. But Carlos had gone to see his girlfriend Inés on Friday, with the expectation of spending the entire weekend at her house.

Inés was an attractive young widow, whose husband had died in an accident a couple of years ago. She had never married again, and rumors persisted that a wealthy old man who enjoyed close ties with the new revolutionary government was financially supporting her.

It was towards Inés's house that María Teresa was driving that morning. She had to get across the tunnel under the Almendares River, and to El Vedado.

The car was doing sixty miles per hour; María Teresa converted it mentally to ninety-seven kilometers per hour. She thought of slowing down, since an ominous feeling was telling her that she could not afford to be stopped that day. She brought the car speed down to forty-five miles per hour.

The time was six-thirty in the morning. She was approaching the intersection of Forty-second Street, the so called "La Copa" intersection, because the statue of an object in the shape of a huge Grecian urn was placed in the middle of it. She obediently stopped the car at a traffic light and patiently waited for the green light to come on. Green light, the engine purred, and the car accelerated until it was moving at normal speed again. Fortieth Street, Thirty-second Street, Twenty-fifth Street, she was getting closer and closer to her destination.

"Carlos is irresponsible," she said to herself. Maybe he did not deserve the big favor that she was doing him, going out to pick him up. But her father had always told her that during moments like these, moments of approaching unknown danger, a family should face whatever destiny had designed for them together. Whenever they had faced the hurricanes that usually hit the island every year, her father had always tried to keep all the members of the family together. She wanted Carlos to be with her in order to resist whatever was coming their way.

Don Francisco had four children. Three handsome boys and a glorious girl. The three boys were older than María Teresa was, and their names were Fernando, José María and Carlos, in chronological order. The youngest was the most divine creature in her father's eyes, the beautiful María Teresa. Carlos was the only one that remained in Cuba with her. María Teresa was then twenty-three years old, and Carlos was twenty-five.

They had stayed with the expectation of finishing their respective studies and obtaining their degrees from the university, before leaving the island for good. María Teresa's intention was to obtain a degree in Mechanical Engineering and Carlos wanted to complete his studies in Business Administration. Carlos had lost precious time in his earliest years as a college student, not because he did not know exactly what he wanted to become later on, but because he was too much of a playboy to give serious consideration to anything in life. Consequently, he was due to graduate with María Teresa.

Carlos would have left the island before, with his father and older brother, and would have tried to complete his studies elsewhere. His love for Inés and attachment to María Teresa had kept him there; Carlos was the brother who always came to María Teresa's rescue whenever the other two were picking on her. She knew that he had stayed in Cuba because he did not want her to remain alone, and now she felt responsible for him.

While driving, María Teresa could not help noticing the deep holes that were dug in the median of Fifth Avenue. Some government official, perhaps Castro himself, had decided, since the early days of the establishment of the Revolutionary Government, that the people should be made fully aware of the imminent attack by the United States Air Force. Therefore, they had decided to place anti-aircraft guns along Fifth Avenue. The holes had been dug, creating an atmosphere of disruption to a once resplendent boulevard. The guns were never displayed. An asinine decision from a military point of view. From a political point of view it had been the triumph of the power of the new bureaucracy over the old established higher class. It was an act of vengeance emanating from the so-called people against the so-called oppressive classes, and carried out by a government representing these so-called oppressed people. The holes were never repaired. María Teresa looked at them and thought of the futile effort that revolutions imposed upon their citizens in the everlasting name of peace. It also occurred to her that maybe the efforts were not futile at all. Maybe the real accomplishment lay in the fact that the people in power managed to make the citizens believe that an air raid was possible. It was just a big lie. Having the people busy with perfunctory work and thinking of impending attacks would keep them from looking at the real truth. This truth was that the government was leading the country directly into a Marxist path that the people of Cuba did not need, did not want and did not choose.

At the entrance to the tunnel, María Teresa increased the speed of the car. She reached seventy and then eighty miles per hour. She shot through the other side of the tunnel, facing Línea Street, and what she saw made her quickly step hard on the brake pedal. The back end of the limousine started to swerve to one side. She turned the wheel immediately against the skid momentum and straightened the car before it came to a full stop in the middle of the street. Her heart started to pulsate, and sweat began to accumulate on her temples and forehead.

On both sides of Línea, which also had a median that was dedicated, at one time, to containing the rails for the trolley cars, were tanks blocking the passageways. On either side of the tanks, military jeeps were parked with soldiers in them. They seemed to be ready to stop any approaching vehicle that might decide to avoid the checkpoint. Along the sidewalks, army trucks and army intelligence vehicles were standing by.

The entrance to the tunnel under the Almendares River dividing El Vedado from Miramar.

The street was full of soldiers in full uniform with submachine guns, officers and other people in plain civilian clothing.

Nobody else was on the street at that early morning hour, so that the black Lincoln became, all of a sudden, the focus of attention of about one hundred and fifty military and law enforcement personnel. The moment the car stopped, four soldiers and one of the officers, a young lieutenant, ran towards the limousine. The soldiers surrounded the car, rifles aimed at María Teresa. The officer, meanwhile, pistol in hand, approached the driver door and commanded her to roll the window down. María Teresa, looking at him terrified, complied with the request.

The officer placed his Colt .45 pistol through the open space and stopped only a few inches from her head. He looked at her with anger in his eyes, and said, "Stop the engine. Do it now."

María Teresa turned the car off. She looked back at the officer, and trying to appear calm, said, "Okay, I did what you asked me to do. Now, please, relax and take it easy. The car is stopped. I haven't done anything wrong. I'm only on my way to pick up my brother who went to a party last night and became too drunk to drive home."

She knew she was lying, but it was the first thing that popped into her head. At that point, she did not want to compromise him either.

"Get out of the car. Come on, do it now," said the officer while opening the door with his left hand.

"I'm not a criminal. I haven't done anything wrong and moreover I'm not armed. I'll get out of the car, but first tell those soldiers of yours not to aim their rifles at me."

María Teresa could not stop herself from protesting. Slowly, measuring every inch of movement of her body, she started to move her two feet out of the car and then finally forced the rest of her body to follow them.

Then the officer said, "Hands up. Hands up now."

She raised both arms well above her head and her long black hair. The officer advanced towards her, and jammed the pistol barrel into her stomach. She was petrified. She did not dare uttering a single word.

"Okay, you guys, come over and search the inside of the car," the officer ordered from his position, pressing his body against hers. Four soldiers proceeded to carry out his command.

His face now was very close to hers. She could smell the awful stench coming from his mouth. It was the kind of nauseating odor from a person who had not slept for a few days, did not clean his teeth and had accumulated the strong scent of tobacco, and rum. The officer, detecting her motion as she tried to move away from him, pressed even harder against her soft belly.

"Just give me an excuse, you rich bitch. Just give me an excuse and I'll have you for breakfast this morning."

María Teresa turned her body and still with both arms raised said, "Please, believe me. I haven't done anything wrong. I swear it. Let me go. Please, let me go."

The officer moved back a step, grabbed her long hair with his left hand, turned her around again and moved her against the hood of the car.

"Be still and open your legs wide apart. I want to check you for any concealed weapons. Just try to make any sudden move and I'll put a bullet through that pretty ass of yours."

Then, addressing the soldiers, he asked, "Have you found anything? Anything at all?"

Two soldiers had searched the front seating area of the car, while another climbed into the rear compartment and the last one went to check the inside of the trunk. They had found nothing that could incriminate her in any way.

The lieutenant put the pistol back into the belt holster and with both hands free went to the task of frisking María Teresa, with a grin on his face. Starting from the neck, his hands went all over the outside of her gray wool sweater. He applied enough pressure to feel her flesh under the fine garment. He grabbed her two firm breasts, and for a brief moment he touched her nipples and squeezed them hard. Then, he continued moving his hands down towards her stomach, her waist, and along her thighs and legs, stopping at her ankles. Then, he began to ascend, probing now the inside portion of her thighs, and moving his right hand into the crotch of her oxford gray flannel trousers. María Teresa attempted to make an upward motion with her body. His hand kept pressing upward, until he finally stopped and backed up two steps. He yelled to the others that she was clean, and ordered her to turn around and face him.

During the entire process that lasted no more than three or four minutes, she had been very quiet. She understood that it was not the time to complain or say anything. But humiliation and anger was creeping into her mind. When she turned around, her face was red from the surge of blood rushing to her temples, and yet, her expression was calm. Her face did not reveal her emotions, except for the two big tears running down her cheeks. Those, she could not control.

"Now that you know that I'm not carrying any weapon," she said in a calm way, without agitation, "and now that your soldiers know that the car doesn't contain anything foreign to a common automobile, would you please let me continue on my way? I'm going to pick up my brother and just plan to go to school with him after that. If I can't continue on this street, or if El Vedado is closed to normal traffic at this time, then allow me to return home."

"Where is your brother now?"

"I told you already. He went to a party last night and stayed at this house because he had too much to drink. The house is right here at El Vedado, just fifteen or twenty minutes from here. If you want to, you could follow me to be sure I'm telling you the truth."

"And why didn't he drive home this morning?" the officer inquired, impervious to María Teresa's last remark.

"He didn't have a car with him. A friend picked him up in a taxi. As I told you, he just became sick from drinking and wisely decided to spend the night recuperating."

"In that case, why didn't he take a taxi this morning?"

"Well, I guess it would have been difficult to find one at this early hour, so I decided to come and pick him up. We're both due for classes at the university by nine o'clock and now I'm running late."

"Class, eh? And may I ask where class is?"

"At the University of Villanueva."

"Well, in that case, don't worry because the university will not open for classes today. Besides, I think that you are nothing but a big liar. You are just a typical representative of the rich, Catholic bitches that attend that school. You probably know damn well what's going on, and you are the driver who is supposed to pick up some others from your counterrevolutionary cell, in order to perform some sabotage somewhere in the city. And don't deny it because I know it to be true. If not, why are you driving that big car that can carry about eight passengers in it?"

"You don't understand. I'm not an enemy of the revolution. This is the family car. We have others, but this one was parked on the main driveway this morning and was the easiest to take out."

"Do you know how many of my countrymen you people have abused in order to afford that car? Do you actually know?" Without waiting for the response, the lieutenant continued, "Well, even if it was only one, the number was one too many. Now, we will not tolerate more abuses or injustices. Your class will have to contend with people like me, dedicated to protecting the rights of the humble, of the poor people, the real people of Cuba."

The groups of soldiers next to the young officer were nodding their heads in approval.

"Look Sir, you are completely mistaken. I don't know what you are talking about, and furthermore, my fiancé is Commander Raúl Mora. Now, if you would be so kind as to get in touch with him, I believe that he could speak on my behalf. I also believe that he outranks you."

The man in the dirty fatigue uniform looked at her intensely. She could detect that he was angry. She had hit a nerve. He was angry because certain events and recent military orders had kept him from sleeping for almost two days now. Angry because he had been told, time and time again, that people like her were the primary cause for his misfortunes and the impending invasion. Angry because she was trying to shield herself behind one of the true heroes of the triumphal revolution, Commander Raúl Mora. Angry because if her last statement was true, then he really was outranked. On the other hand, he could not believe it. He thought that this girl was bluffing. He had been trained not to believe these imperialist lies and tricks.

Glancing at two of the soldiers, he said, "Arrest her and take her to one of the buses."

"Which one?" said the soldier advancing towards her.

"She came from Miramar, so take her to the bus going to the Blanquita Theater."

María Teresa could not believe her ears. It just could not be true.

"Why are you arresting me?" she said.

"What have I done? What are the charges?" she yelled.

She looked, not at the soldiers, but at the officer. One soldier was holding her firmly by one arm and another was quickly moving towards her from the other direction.

"I'm arresting you under suspicion of committing crimes against the People of Cuba and their revolution. If you are innocent, you have nothing to fear. If you are guilty, and I think you are, you filthy bitch, you will find that we give no mercy to our enemies. Go on, take the bitch away."

At that moment, María Teresa decided that she was going to put up a good fight. She was not going to walk the plank of her own volition. Screaming and kicking at the soldiers, she was still able to yell at the officer, "What about my car? What will happen to my car?"

The soldiers were trying to move her away to the parked bus about a block away and to dodge her kicks aimed primarily at their legs.

The officer, laughing at her behavior said, "Don't you worry about the car. The revolution needs it more than you do. Besides, next time I see Raúl Mora I'll give it to him with your kisses."

With irresistible force, the soldiers threw her down onto the pavement. One of them said, "You stupid bitch, if you give any more trouble, I'm gonna kick your ass so hard that I'll split it in half."

He swung his foot and landed it squarely on her behind. The kick propelled her across the street about four feet. The two soldiers then grabbed her. Each of them took her by her armpits, and without letting her get back on her feet again, they dragged her along the street and around the corner. For the first time, she saw the line of buses parked along the side street.

They reached the bus bearing a sign that read "Blanquita" and pushed her inside. There were four soldiers in the bus, two at the front end and two at the rear end. One of them signaled her to take one of the empty seats.

The soldier who kicked her smiled and said to his comrades in the bus, "Be careful with this one. She likes to give us a hard time. If she does, just give her a good kick in the ass and she'll behave. Who knows? Maybe, she's looking to have something else in her ass, besides a boot."

The other soldiers laughed with him.

María Teresa sat noiselessly. There were about one dozen people, apparently in the same predicament, some women and some men, some very young. There was one older man, old enough to be her grandfather. The men were looking down at the floor of the bus with shame reflected on their faces, not daring to look at María Teresa or the soldiers.

CHAPTER TWO

The sobs came slowly at first. Almost inaudible the first cry came out. Then the tears started and as if in slow motion, her head made a series of finite motions in the direction of her lap. By the time her head reached half of the distance, she was crying loudly. She could not remember another time, another occasion in her life, when she had cried like she did now.

The pain in her left buttock, where the boot had struck her was acute. Then she noticed that her knees were bleeding. The skin had been protected only by the flannel fabric of the well-tailored pants. Raw flesh mingled with traces of dirty skin on her knees and created a burning sensation on her legs.

María Teresa did not say another word; and no one else in the bus did either. With the exception of the four soldiers and the bus driver who occasionally made some comments, the bus sounded empty, for no one dared to emit a single word, a single sound. It was a bus of fear.

She decided to try to understand in her own mind what was going on. She was sure that somehow it had to do with her father's signal, the happenings of Saturday night at the military airfields, and what she had heard on the Voice of America news. But she still couldn't put it all together.

To have a roadblock on a street was not unusual. It had happened before when Fidel Castro had requested a voluntary general strike in support of his actions to obtain absolute control of the government during 1959. At that time, they were to have free elections, in a free political atmosphere and in a period of time no longer than eighteen months, in full compliance with the Cuban Constitution of 1940. Perhaps President Urrutia, who had been appointed by Fidel Castro, believed these original promises.

Instead, Castro resigned his position as Prime Minister and immediately the well-prepared clique appeared on the streets of La Habana demanding Urrutia's resignation, and the return of Castro as the leader of the Revolution, to command and direct the efforts of the government. Castro asked for a voluntary strike of one hour, so that he could sense the pulse of the nation, the mandate of his people in a voluntary, popular, non-written referendum. Castro's supporters then placed roadblocks at strategic places throughout the whole country, but with emphasis on La Habana where the propaganda was greater and more concentrated.

They stopped all traffic, or most of it, for a period of over one hour, so that the whole world could see that a voluntary strike had taken place. Castro himself, humbly and candidly, appeared on national television, stating that he would sacrifice himself in the name of the Revolution and return to his position of leadership, since he could not deny the cooperation, assistance and mandate of the Cuban People. Urrutia resigned, and after some ordeal, managed to flee the island. And yet, at that time, María Teresa remembered, they had not arrested anybody. They had just stopped them for a while. This time it was definitely different.

Slowly but inexorably, the buses were becoming full. There was a stream of people being brought by different groups of soldiers, all kinds of people. Some were very well-dressed, apparently having been picked up on their way to work; some looked shabby, with the appearance of people taken right out of their beds. Some appeared well-to-do, while others appeared to be poor. Some showed the expression and presence of people who were used to commanding and giving orders, while others seemed to be people used to receiving orders. Some were white, some were black, and some were Asians. From all different races, levels of social strata and faiths, people were being brought to these buses of fear. On their way to the buses, none dared to talk too loudly, and a quick blow from the butt of a rifle or wooden club rapidly silenced the ones who made any unsolicited comment.

María Teresa looked at her watch. It was nine o'clock in the morning. Almost three hours had elapsed, and it seemed like a million years.

Finally, a fat sergeant got onto the bus and told the driver to go. The bus started to move slowly towards Línea Street.

María Teresa had been pushed into a window seat, as the soldiers put more and more people into the bus. She was able to look outside without having to move her body or her head. As they passed the series of buses parked along the street, she saw them labeled with names of places where large crowds could be kept confined and controlled. Places like theaters, hotels, stadiums, arenas, convention centers and large public buildings. The government had decided to convert the city of La Habana into a large prison camp by moving thousands of people to places where they could be detained and watched.

As the bus turned onto Línea Street in the direction approaching the tunnel, the fat sergeant, chewing on half of an unlit cigar, began to talk, "Attention, attention. Listen to me all of you. You are being transported to the Blanquita Theater. When we arrive at the theater, I want all of you to leave the bus and go into the theater. Once inside I want you to occupy a seat. I want all women to go to the orchestra section. All men should go to the upper floors. When you are there, and seated, I want all of you to remain quiet and to obey all further instructions without question. In the meantime, while you are on this bus, I want you to know that I will not tolerate any disruption. Whatever you might feel like doing, you better think twice and then forget it, because I'm sure that nobody on this bus would like to meet my friend here, Esperanza." He raised his right arm to publicly show the whip that was strapped to his wrist.

"So you behave, remain silent and nothing will happen. When you are in the theater, you will remain in the seating area at all times. There will be guards posted at all doors and these will be locked from the outside. If anyone wants to go to the toilet, he will have to approach the door, and ask for permission to go. He will wait for his turn until there is a soldier available to accompany him all the way into the bathroom. One at a time. If anyone is in a hurry, then you might as well do it in your neighbor's seat, so as not to shit or piss on your own. Later on, someone will be calling on you, probably on each one of you, for your interrogation. That is all."

A very good-looking woman seated in the middle of the bus in the opposite window seat from María Teresa stood up, balancing her body by gripping the back part of the seat in front of her. She had no makeup, her hair was not combed, and she was dressed in a light blouse, wrinkled cardigan and khaki pants. She gave the impression of someone who had spent the night sleeping on the bus and had just woken up. However, under that appearance there were unmistakable signs of a distinguished and well-educated lady.

She spoke in a monotone voice and said, "Sergeant, I was dragged out of my house this morning. We were still in bed, my husband and I, when your people arrived. They have taken my husband to another bus. I do not know where he is being taken or why we are all here today. Most importantly, I don't know how long you intend to detain us. I left four children at home. One of them, the baby, who is only eight months old, is sick with a cold and has been running a temperature since yesterday.

My husband's cousin, who lives next door to our house, volunteered to come and stay with the children when she heard that we were being taken out of the house, but there are certain medicines and instructions that I forgot to mention to her. Could you please ask the people at the theater to let me make a call home? I don't want anything to happen to my baby." She started to cry.

The sergeant looked at her with eyes full of hate, revealing the kind of brutal man that he really was.

"Now you listen to me, you dirty bitch. I'm going to let it go this time. But damn it, only this time. Whenever you or anybody else wants to ask any question, you first must request from me, politely, permission to talk. Then, if I grant that permission, you can go ahead and ask me the question. But if I don't tell you to speak, then you better shut your ugly trap."

The woman became hysterical. She continued to cry uncontrollably and she started screaming, "My children. What is going to happen to my children? What about my children?"

The sergeant was getting very upset. He threw the small chunk of cigar onto the floor of the bus, and spat a black glob of saliva and crunched tobacco leaves.

"To answer your question, let me tell you that I don't give a damn about what happens to your children. To hell with your children. That's what happens whenever any one of you whores opens your legs to those counterrevolutionaries, those good-for-nothing bastards. Then you give birth to little bastards, and I don't care what happens to little bastards. Now be quiet. Stop crying. Sit down and stop crying or I'll make you."

The woman sat down, but could not stop crying. It was obvious that she was trying to control herself, but to no avail.

A man neatly dressed in a dark blue suit, with a white cotton shirt and striped blue silk tie stood up from one of the front seats of the bus. He had the look of a decision-maker, and the pose of an experienced executive. He turned towards the woman and said very calmly, "Ma'am, stop crying. Please, stop crying. You have nothing to fear. When we reach the theater I'll personally help you to get to a phone and talk to your cousin-in-law."

The woman's weeping diminished until there were only sighs, here and there, decreasing in intensity. The well-dressed man then turned around to face the sergeant.

"Sergeant, I want to speak to you," he said. "You are in command here, that's evident. I don't think that I have to ask permission to talk to you in a polite manner. We are not children, and this is not a school bus. Since no one on this bus has spoken, I'm going to volunteer myself to be the speaker for the group."

The sergeant gazed at the man. The man looked around as if requesting the consent of everybody on the bus. No one even nodded. Then, he continued as if the stillness of the people and the silence of the sergeant had given him the tacit permission he was looking for.

"Sergeant, very simply, we want to know why we are here. Why are we being placed in custody against our will? What's going on here? What's happening on the island?"

The face of the fat sergeant turned red as the well-dressed man spoke. It seemed that with every question posed at him, the tones of red on his face became darker and darker. Advancing towards the serene man, with an ugly grin on his face showing the dark tobacco-stained teeth, he said, "The fate that you are going to meet, you son of a bitch, is going to be Esperanza."

Pushing aside the people sitting in the first two rows of seats, and stepping over the ones sitting in the aisle, he approached the distinguished man, and struck the man on the head. The man immediately raised his left arm trying desperately to protect his forehead.

The short whip was made of a thin, steel rod covered with braided leather. It had a leather handle with a strap at one end, and two thick strips of leather hanging at the opposite end. The left forearm of the man received the full impact of the strike. The man emitted a loud yell and proceeded to hold his left forearm with his right hand, clutching his left arm against his chest. The second blow came right after, and the main body of the whip landed on the man's left temple, breaking the skin, and sending a streak of blood flowing down his face. He fell sideways, on top of the passenger sitting next to him, but the sergeant did not stop. Two more blows were struck on the man's head, staining his once-clean suit with blood. The man passed into unconsciousness from the blows.

The driver stopped the bus. Some women were yelling at the sergeant to stop. The soldiers removed the safety pins from their weapons and loaded the first round of ammunition into them. Then the sergeant's voice was heard, like thunder, over all the other noises.

"Quiet. Silence. I said silence. Soldiers, if anyone moves, if anyone says anything, shoot him. Silence."

The bus of fear became quiet again.

"I don't give a damn anymore," the sergeant said. "Whoever is not quiet in his seat, shoot him. Kill the imperialist son of a bitch. These are all a bunch of Yankee-loving bastards who don't even deserve the gasoline spent on this bus ride today. We should have made them walk. If any of these prostitutes gives you the slightest provocation, kill them. They don't have a heart for the real people on this island anyway. They are only good for fucking. If they make any noise, if they cry, shoot them."

Nobody moved. Nobody said another word. Even the man who had the bleeding, unconscious gentleman on top of him did not move. He simply did not dare.

"Let's get going. Get to the theater as fast as you can. This isn't the only trip that we're going to be making today, so hurry up. We're due back to pick up more scum," the sergeant told the bus driver.

The Blanquita Theater was an architect's nightmare. It was said that the original owner had participated in its design. He had built it as a memorial to his former wife.

Maybe he wanted to display his wealth, maybe he wanted to depict the size of his love for her. Whichever, he had decided to make the posthumous monument the largest theater in the world. It had a seating capacity larger than Radio City Music Hall in New York City, and yet, despite its granite floors, tiled columns, and mirrors of all shapes and sizes, it gave the impression that you were inside a huge bathroom.

The study of acoustics, seemingly, had never entered the minds of the designers. Sound did not carry well in this gigantic theater. Therefore, it had been used, before the revolution, as a movie theater and for sporadic appearances of well-known performers. After the revolution, it served also as a place for holding party meetings and assemblies. Now, the revolution was going to use it as an urban concentration camp, a detention point for would-be dissenters and potential enemies of the People of Cuba.

The bus parked in front of the main door. The two soldiers at the front end of the bus descended and stood on the concrete sidewalk, standing on each side of the front door, facing each other. Another group of soldiers came running up and formed a gauntlet between the bus and the theater doors, armed with rifles and fixed bayonets.

The driver got off and walked through the gauntlet unharmed. At the other end, he opened one of the doors into the theater.

The sergeant, moving next to the driver's seat, said, "Okay, we're here. One by one, you are going to depart from the bus and run to the main door. Once inside, you will proceed to your final destination as I explained before. If you stop or try to break the soldiers' line, you will regret this day for the rest of your life, if you live to remember it. If you try running back to the bus door, they will shoot to kill."

Grabbing the man sitting in the first seat by the collar of his shirt and pushing him to the door, he said, "Okay, let's go. Now."

Everybody stood up and started to move forward. In the front, there was a bottleneck, since only one person could fit through the door at one time, while in the back, the soldiers were pushing, and cursing, trying to move everybody forward.

The first man out inadvertently touched one of the soldiers standing in line as he was running forward and looking back to see if the next guy, who was carrying the wounded gentleman, needed any help. The soldier lifted his rifle and hit him in the back. The man fell to the ground, where the other soldiers kicked him, until he gained enough strength to crawl into the theater.

The next man, dragging the wounded man along with him, started to descend the bus steps and tripped, falling to the ground with the semi-conscious, wounded man on top of him. The kicking started again. The man closer to the floor managed to free himself from the one on top, and ran like a hunchback in the direction of the theater.

The young man who followed them was terrified by the look of the scene developing in front of him. María Teresa could see the terror in his eyes, and in his erratic motion. He ran out of the bus and made it to the door in seconds without looking at the man on the floor while he ran on top of him through the line of soldiers.

Then, two men came out of the bus almost simultaneously. They looked at each other and understood what they would attempt to do. The first man knelt down and grabbed one armpit of the wounded man on the floor, who was still being kicked by the soldiers next to him. The second man moved to the other side, grabbing the opposite armpit, and all three ran into the theater.

The first woman came down. She was in front of María Teresa. As she ran across the space between the soldiers, some of them hit her with open hands on the buttocks and made comments to each other, such as, "This one has a nice ass. I'll bet you she's a terrific fuck."

It was María Teresa's turn. She decided to run the distance, no matter what happened in between. She felt hands on her legs and on her ass, but she did not care. One soldier tried to push her sideways, so that she would fall on top of the soldier directly across from him. But she reacted quickly to the push, and she managed not to lose her balance. She heard remarks about her body, but she paid no attention. In a matter of seconds she found herself inside the theater, in the middle of the very wide and very tall lobby.

María Teresa walked rapidly across the entrance lobby and proceeded to try to enter the orchestra section through one of the center doors.

In front of every door leading to an aisle in the theater, she spotted two female soldiers dressed in uniforms, holding short wooden clubs in their hands. As she approached one of them, the militia woman signaled her to go inside with the wooden club. María Teresa obeyed without question. Once inside the area where the seats were, she stopped immediately, frozen.

The stage was full of soldiers, one or maybe two hundred of them. All the soldiers were dressed in full combat uniform, and armed with full combat gear. They were standing in three lines across the stage; the first line facing the prisoners was composed of soldiers about six feet apart. All the soldiers in the first line had vicious German Shepherds and Dobermans on leashes.

Behind them, there were two lines of .50 cal. machine guns. Each machine gun was mounted on a tripod and manned by two soldiers, one sitting behind the gun and the other one sitting next to him to feed the belt of ammunition. The first line of machine guns was aimed to cover the orchestra section of the theater. The second line pointed upwards, covering the balconies.

People were sitting all over the theater, trying to avoid the seats close to the stage.

CHAPTER THREE

María Teresa was still standing there, waiting for her thoughts to come together and to direct her to some empty seat, when the door behind her opened again. She heard a familiar voice.

"Quem Deus vult perdere, prius dementat."

The statement was addressed to the soldier who had opened the door. An old nun wearing the white habit of the Dominican Order stood in the doorway. The militia woman said, "And you too, Sister, can go to hell."

María Teresa smiled, faintly remembering the Latin. She knew that the nun had said, "Those whom God wishes to destroy, He first makes mad." The voice belonged to Sister Elizabeth, whom María Teresa knew from when she had been a high school student at the American Dominican School. María Teresa looked at the stern but lovable face of the old nun, and with tears of joy in her eyes said, "Hello Sister Beth. You're the first friendly face that I've seen today. How are you?"

For a brief moment, the nun studied the girl's face. She must have been one of her students. There had been so many in the course of the years that the school had been open.

She had taught so many Cuban girls, but there was something special about this one, and she always remembered the special ones very well. It came finally to her conscious mind like a thunderbolt. Of course, the Valedictorian of the 1956 class. It had to be María Teresa Aguirrupe, better known by her teachers and close friends as Mari-Tere.

Recognition finally came to the old woman's face. Opening her arms to the young woman, the nun embraced her lovingly and whispered, "My dear Mari-Tere, I never expected to find you here. I'm doing fine under the present circumstances, but I can see that you've had a rough time already, and I fear that this is only the beginning."

Guiding María Teresa along the aisle with an arm wrapped around her shoulders, she continued, "Please, come and sit with us. The other nuns should be here by now. They left in another bus before me. Let's find them. We can sit together and have a long chat."

María Teresa said, "I'd like that very much, Sister."

The old nun looked straight at the stage and a chill ran along her spine. The thoughts that came back to haunt her mind had not appeared for quite some time. But now they arose, and she remembered the events of long ago.

Sister Beth had been sent to Spain in 1935, to a Dominican convent in order to study and perfect her Spanish. This newly acquired knowledge would later give her the opportunity to request to be sent to Cuba. The Spanish Civil War started a year later, and the convent where she was staying happened to be in the north of Spain, the land occupied by armed forces loyal to the communist government. One day, a large group of soldiers came to the convent and asked the nuns to step outside so that they could go inside and freely conduct a thorough search of the buildings. They said they had heard rumors that the nuns had hidden General Franco's spies in the convent. The nuns protested, but to no avail. They were brought outside and ordered to stay together in a tight group with armed soldiers around them in a semicircle. Other soldiers went inside the convent to look for the enemies.

They became angry when they found no enemies, so they decided to rob the place, and removed every object of any value. Once they had loaded the truck, the officer in charge determined it would be better not to leave behind any witnesses. At the officer's command, they opened fire upon the nuns. Sister Beth and Sister Michelle were the only two foreigners among the Spanish nuns. The Spanish nuns had pushed them toward the center of the group and when the shooting took place, they were propelled to the floor where the other nuns covered and embraced them as they went down. They were the only survivors of the massacre.

Sister Beth had always believed that it was the Hand of God that had protected her on that infamous day, and she had continuously asked herself why. She was in shock for four days afterwards. A family of Basque peasants rescued them before the soldiers returned. She remained terrified of men in uniform for years to come, but by now, she had learned that her life was, and had always been in the hands of God. Her faith reminded her constantly that for God, and His Holy Name, she was ready to die many deaths, for the number and nature of each one of them would not be dictated by men, but solely by His will.

That is why, in spite of the soldiers, vicious dogs, machine guns, and rifles with fixed bayonets, she remained calm. She might have been afraid of the unforeseen, of the unexpected, but not of dying. She firmly believed that death does not exist for a true Christian.

The other nuns were sitting near the middle of the theater. They had saved a seat for Sister Beth and when they saw that she was coming with another person, one of the nuns sitting at the end of the row moved to the next row, so that María Teresa and Sister Beth could occupy adjacent seats.

María Teresa was recognized immediately by some of the other nuns, and they all greeted her with affection. She was among friends, and practically surrounded by them.

Sister Beth said, "Tell me, Mari-Tere, what happened to you today? I heard some time ago that your family had left the island and I assumed that you had gone also."

"My father had to leave because we lost everything except the house in Miramar. The only other source of money at our disposal is in a local bank. Fortunately, my family has some assets in the United States. The shock of being kicked out of the Supreme Court after so many years, and the fact that he was getting old made my father ill. Someone had to leave with him, and take care of the future of the family. It was decided that my brother Fernando should do it. Jaime, the chauffeur, also went with them. My father wanted all of us to leave together. On the other hand, I thought that it was foolish for me to go in my last year of engineering, and I finally convinced him that we would be separated for not more than a few months. That was in September of last year. If I had known then that the American Embassy was going to close its doors, if I had known then that it would become increasingly difficult to depart from the island, if I had known then that I would end up here today, I would have left with my father. Besides, I felt secure then.

"As you know, my other brother José María gave his life for the political revolution that I believe the majority of the Cuban people wanted, and not the social revolution that took its place. My fiancé is a Commander in the Revolutionary Army. His name is Raúl Mora. I love him very much, even though it is difficult to communicate with him most of the time. His reasoning has been lost to ideals. In spite of all of that, I think that we still love each other, and it's inconceivable that he would permit any harm to come my way. This morning I left the house early in the day, and I went to El Vedado to pick up Carlos, who had gone to a party and became too sick to come home last night. The soldiers stopped me as soon as I crossed the tunnel. They took my car and literally dragged me into a bus that brought me here. I stupidly offered some resistance before I entered the bus and the soldiers roughed me up a little. Look at my knees and legs. They still hurt. But you know, Sister, how tough I can be."

"Yes, I know. Tough and intelligent. But you know nothing of what is going on?"

"No Sister, I really don't know anything."

María Teresa's father had been a witness to the deliverance of more than seven million Cubans to the tyranny of communism in 1959. On the other hand, her father also claimed that this was 1961 and another government was in power in the United States.

The new government in command would never permit Castro to remain in power. An invasion was the logical solution, and he had told his daughter of the impending invasion so that she could be prepared.

The old nun got closer to María Teresa and started to whisper in her right ear, so as not to allow her voice to carry in the auditorium.

"Listen, my dear child. You came to me when you were a little girl for knowledge and education. I gave you both, and I also gave you my love and my understanding. I taught you, among other things, Latin, the language of God. I also taught you religion, the word and the love of God. It is in His Name that I must ask you not to repeat to anybody what I am about to tell you. Could you do that?"

"Yes Sister. I swear it."

"As you know, our religious order owes obedience to the Mother House, which is located in the United States. We maintain direct radio contact with this House, and do not depend on the public phone system when we want to communicate private matters with each other. On the radio, we continuously change frequency and only talk to each other in Latin. Only nuns like us or a medieval monk could really understand what we are talking about. I know that there are priests for the revolution, as well as monsignors and bishops. Nonetheless, we confide in the will of God and hope that the ones the government could request to monitor our conversations, if they actually know about them, cannot make heads or tails of what we say."

Sister Beth paused to look around them. And after she was assured that nobody was paying any attention, she continued, "Through a series of communiqués, we found out that what is going on today is an invasion of the island by an exiled Cuban military task force. The U.S. Marines and the U.S. Navy are backing this invasion force. Apparently fearing that counterrevolutionaries all over the island might attempt a series of sabotages and attacks upon the revolutionary army, the government has decided to apprehend anybody that they suspect to be an enemy of the people. The real enemies of the people are they. I believe that they are picking up hundreds of thousands of Cubans. As a matter of fact, it would not surprise me if you find that your brother Carlos is in this same theater, since they are going almost house by house, with lists of suspects. It makes sense that they would have brought Carlos here, since as far as I can see, they are holding people prisoner according to where they live."

What she told Mari-Tere about the invasion and the radio was true.

She also feared that if the invasion succeeded, they would not leave the prisoners in that theater alive. Those machine guns were not there only to keep people from escaping, but also to insure that if they were to lose the war, the invaders would only come to gather the dead bodies of their loved ones.

"Tell me, Sister," María Teresa said quietly, "do you know if the invasion has taken place, or is going to happen and where?"

"The invasion took place in the early morning hours of today. I don't know where."

"And what's happening at the University of Villanueva? Your school is close by, and I heard from an officer that the government was going to close Villanueva today."

"As far as I know, the University has been occupied by revolutionary armed forces and all the priests, teachers and students that were there this morning are being detained in the campus auditorium. I know because Sister Margaret, who is taking some courses over there, was told by one priest to leave the premises and go back to the convent. She ran across the baseball field and managed to escape as the troops were arriving at the rectory building to confront the president of the school. We then watched with binoculars from the roof of the convent and saw the line of priests and civilians marching towards the auditorium. Sister Margaret, unfortunately, made a bad choice, because shortly thereafter, the soldiers came to our convent and arrested all of us."

"If the invasion starts a civil war, we could be kept here for quite a while," María Teresa said in a sad tone of voice. She wanted to keep the private conversation alive. She realized that to some extent it was trivial. In comparison with the reality that they were facing, their talk was pure nonsense, and yet, it was that nonsense that was keeping her from facing a reality that she did not want to face.

"This conflict won't generate a civil war, because the majority of the people, the real people of Cuba, aren't in favor of this kind of regime. If a large and well-equipped force were to land on this island, even our soldiers would support the invasion. This so-called revolutionary army has never fought a real battle. Batista's constitutional armed forces were as corrupt as the government they represented, and they never really offered any type of serious fighting to Castro's guerillas. The country was presented to him on a silver platter. You should know that. Your father must have told you that at one time or another.

"Moreover, Castro's field commanders have never fought a serious battle either. As his army advanced from the mountains, through the fields of Camagüey Province and into Las Villas Province, they never encountered any resistance.

"His army is a fake, a mere figment of communist propaganda, never tested in the field of honor. Now, I would grant you that the invasion forces formed by Cuban exiles do not possess great experience either. But they are not coming alone; I'll bet you that the United States is sending the Marines with them. And believe me, Mari-Tere, the revolutionary army is no match for the Marines. I'll give them a few days, a few weeks perhaps, but that is all."

"And what about Russia, Sister? Do you think that they are going to remain as a mere spectator?"

"I think that at this time Russia will do nothing, except talking and yelling at the U.N. Maybe, they would demand to censure the United States for their actions. However, militarily speaking, they will do nothing. Cuba is too far away. The supply lines are too long and Castro doesn't have at this time any supplies or arsenals of weapons or airplanes to really talk about. There are no Russian planes, no Russian missiles and no Russian Navy in Cuba. Only a few Russian tanks and some minor armaments exist on the island. If Russia sees that the United States is definitely committed to preventing a communist base from influencing the balance of the Latin American countries and is fully applying its Monroe Doctrine, they will back down and leave Castro to his own destiny. Like our dear Mother Church, the Marxists work in aeternum. So, they will wait for another time, another country and another opportunity."

"I see your point, Sister Beth," said María Teresa, and added, "Humanum est errare."

Sister Beth smiled and whispering to herself said, "Satis verborum." She rested her old head on the back of the seat and closed her eyes.

María Teresa also felt very tired. She glanced at her watch and saw that it was two-thirty in the afternoon, and she had not eaten. Her throat was dry and she felt hungry. She wanted to go to the bathroom, but that could wait also. For the moment, she felt secure. All these nuns who loved her, surrounded her. Perspiration was running down her forehead, and being temporarily stopped by her eyebrows. Her back was sticky. The white blouse between her flesh and the sweater was getting damp.

The day might have been cold in the morning, but the strong Cuban sun bathing the mammoth concrete structure of the building had brought the temperature inside the building to the high seventies. This theater as with most public buildings in La Habana was air-conditioned. The system was probably the best design feature of the entire facility. However, the government had decided not to plug it in on that day.

She removed her sweater and placed it on her lap. She looked at her legs and noticed that already scabs had formed on her wounds.

They still hurt a little, but it was not that bad. At least the sensation from the pavement friction burns was gone. Her left buttock must be all back and blue. She could not see it, but she felt it was sore. Overall, she was still in one piece and that made her feel good.

Moving her head sideways, she rested it on top of the old nun's arm and slowly began to fall sleep. It was just an escape for her battered mind. She knew that by sleeping, she could fool reality, at least for a while. She could imagine and dream of better and safer places, and think of her father, her brothers, and of course think of Raúl. She closed her eyes and a few minutes later she was sound asleep.

CHAPTER FOUR

María Teresa Aguirrupe y Larrazábal was a true descendant of the Basque race. She was a genuine representative of that indomitable group of people, whose origins are lost in the annals of ancient history.

The Romans found them occupying the Pyrenees Mountains with their adjacent valleys, in an area that is today the southern and mid-western portion of France and the northern and mid-western portion of Spain. They soon learned how to live with them, because not even mighty Rome was able to conquer the Basques of those times.

The Moors, coming from North Africa, invaded Spain in the seventh century A.D. and remained in that part of Europe for about seven centuries. However, no mosque was ever built and no alcazar was ever erected in the northern portion of the peninsula occupied by the Basques.

María Teresa dreamed of the time when her father took her to the San Fermín fair in Pamplona, capital of the Basque province of Navarra. She remembered being with her father at the Plaza de Toros, and watching the young bull reach the entrance to the Plaza, only to be greeted by a line of young Basques, in a tight formation, just waiting for him to charge at them. It was a challenge that the bull had to take and he did.

The first man received the charge of the animal by trying to hold him at the horns with both his hands. The others just pushed forward trying to counteract the bull's trusts. But the bull threw the first man sideways, and he lay in the sand bleeding while the others tried to gain the attention of the animal and move him away from the wounded Basque. She recognized the wounded young man in her dream. It was her brother José María. She woke up suddenly and then after a couple of minutes she fell asleep again.

The strong race that resisted the conquering efforts of advanced civilizations throughout their history did not contest the persuasive philosophy or the teachings on the meaning of love of the Catholic religion.

The women of this vigorous and sturdy race of people are in general beautiful, loyal companions, clean and well-groomed, intelligent, hard workers, and also very maternal. Usually, they are very devoted in religious matters, and possess a strong will that is, at times, confused with an obstinate trait to change formulated opinions.

María Teresa was all of that.

Physically speaking, she was an extremely beautiful woman. Her hair was black and shiny as onyx. It fell in long, smooth waves on her shoulders and her back, hiding part of her ears, where exquisite jewelry frequently hung.

Her eyes were normally the pale green color of a fine emerald. This green color could change in hues according to her moods. At times, they looked like a Caribbean ocean at sunset, serene green. At times, they looked like a dangerous tropical jungle, a dark and intense green.

Her mouth was protected by well-shaped lips, hiding two symmetrical rows of milky white teeth. On top of it, there was a cute, small, straight nose.

The rest of her body was equally well-proportioned for her

weight and height. She weighed one hundred and twenty-eight pounds and stood five feet and six inches tall.

On the upper part of her chest, a long neck gave her the poise of a royal swan; while on her sides, two lovely arms culminated in delicate, long-fingered hands.

All of her was covered by an even, velvety whitish-pink-colored skin, somewhat tanned under the strong rays of the tropical sun.

Intellectually, María Teresa was the possessor of a brilliant and sharp mind. In body and soul, in flesh and spirit, in physical and intellectual parameters, she was a symbol of excellence. She was intelligent and could easily think in abstract ways. She could analyze complex situations, reducing them to simple arguments by straight logical reasoning.

Her mother had died at the moment of giving birth to her. After having three boys before her, all of them by Cesarean section, the family physician had warned her mother of the danger of another pregnancy. Her parents had tried to obey the warnings of the good doctor, but somehow, a miscalculation in her mother's cycle had resulted in her conception. Just before she died her mother had asked what kind of baby had been born. When the doctor told her that it was a girl, she had said, "Thank God, she will be a companion for Francisco. Doctor, will you tell her that her mother loved her very much for the past nine months? I'll be waiting for her at the gates of heaven. Tell Francisco to give her the kisses and hugs that I won't be able to give her in this world."

It became more difficult for her to continue talking. The doctor looked back at her momentarily and said, "Faith. Faith and hope, Doña Teresa. Don't talk like that. You're not going to die now."

Her mother had forced a smile for a mere instant. She knew better.

"Doctor," she said, "I think that you are a good obstetrician, but a very poor liar. May I see her, please?"

The doctor instructed the nurse to bring the baby to her side. However, she never saw her.

When the nurse came to the side of her bed, her eyes were closed and even though she was faintly breathing, she had not the strength to open them.

Don Francisco took admirable care of his daughter. She was christened María Teresa, after her mother, and she had a Spanish nanny who never left her side and kept her out of harm's way whenever possible. María Teresa had always called her by the affectionate nickname of Concha.

Concha had taught María Teresa everything that the rules of strict etiquette would demand of a lady.

There had been times when María Teresa had complained of the way she had to do certain things, or perform certain chores, or dress in a particular fashion. Concha's unyielding reply had always been "Mari-Tere, noblesse oblige".

On the whole, María Teresa's behavioral mannerisms were impeccable. Concha and the nuns had always imparted restraint to her spirited temperament and molded her into the fine young lady that she now was.

CHAPTER FIVE

Time marched on inside of the Blanquita Theater, and more people came in. The theater was getting full. More and more people came, until all seats were occupied, and then those who were not seated had to find a place on the floor against the walls or in the aisles.

It was becoming more difficult to maintain order with so many people in the theater. The officers in charge of the operation decided that it would be impossible to keep everybody sitting down at all times. Consequently, as long as they remained in a certain area, they allowed the people to roam around and move a little. The disruptions that these motions caused and the constant chatting were not enough to disengage María Teresa from her dreams.

Sleeping allowed her subconscious state to take over and bring illusions of safety when there were none. Unfortunately, it did not last forever and María Teresa finally woke up again.

She had slept for almost six hours. She felt a cramp in her right leg, due to the position that she had kept during these hours. She stood up to shake the leg and force the blood back into the vessels inside the cramped muscles. She now felt sweaty and sticky.

A pain started to appear on her left temple. She realized that she was starting to get a headache and she remembered that she had not eaten anything. It was already past eight in the evening. Her throat was now dry.

She stood up again, and worked out the remaining cramps in her feet. Now she also realized that she had spent the whole day without going to the toilet.

She started walking toward the main aisle, when she heard the voice of Sister Beth behind her saying, "Mari-Tere, where are you going?"

The response came without stopping the motion of her legs. "I'll be back, Sister. I have to go to the restroom."

"Wait for me. I'll accompany you. I also want to go," said Sister Beth as she also stood up and started to catch up to Mari-Tere's quick pace.

The younger woman reached the aisle door first. She knocked at the door, but nobody answered. Realizing that with the existing noise, her knocking was not loud enough, she banged the door with her feet. This time a militia woman who asked what she wanted opened the door from the other side.

"We would like to go to the ladies room."

The militia woman looked at both of them and said, "Well, I'm sorry to tell you that we have no ladies room, since there are no ladies in this fucking theater. But if you bitches want to go to the can, that can be arranged."

"Well then, we want to go to the can," María Teresa said without hesitation and before Sister Beth could utter a single syllable.

"Okay, you come with me," ordered the militia woman. Both women started to walk through the doorway. Then the militia woman stopped the old nun by placing her hand on the nun's chest and said, "Hold it, Sister. One at a time. You stay here until I come back for you."

Sister Beth looked at the militia woman and calmly said, "Look here, my child. I'm an old nun who needs help from time to time when I go to the toilet. Sometimes I faint when I stand up from the toilet seat. This lovely girl," she pointed to María Teresa, and continued, "has been gracious enough to volunteer to accompany me in case I feel weak. Please, allow me to go with her, and I'm sure that God, in His wisdom, will reward your kindness in the future."

The young woman in her olive green fatigue uniform took a second to respond. Finally she said, "Okay, you two can come with me."

Closing the door, she signaled to the other militia woman standing there and said, "I'm going to take these two to the can. You keep watch until I return."

She moved quickly across the lobby to the restroom area. She opened the door labeled "women" and ordered them to go inside.

It really would not have mattered if she had told them to go to the room labeled "men," because there were no male prisoners in that part of the theater. But that other room was being reserved for the use of the militia women only. Therefore, it contained uniforms, guns and wooden clubs that were not to fall into the hands of the female prisoners.

As soon as they walked into the restroom, they found out that they were not going to be left alone inside either. There was another militia woman sitting at the counter next to the sinks. This one had a relatively pleasant face, with slanted oriental eyes, and the color of skin that suggested a mixture of Chinese and African blood in her ancestry.

She looked at the pair entering the room and said, "Okay, the nun to the last toilet and you, pretty girl, to the first one. Leave the door open. I want to see what you are doing at all times. Okay, let's go. Move, now. There's nobody else here, but pretty soon there will be others waiting outside."

María Teresa entered the first stall and attempted to lock the door, but the door would not lock. She undressed in a limited manner that would allow her to do what she needed to do. She unfastened the zipper on the side of her trousers and pulled them down, along with her panties in one single motion. At that moment the door to her stall abruptly opened, and she looked up to see the militia woman standing there. Under normal circumstances, she would have been unable to do anything, but to her shame and amazement, she found that she was able to urinate in front of another person. When she had finished, she dressed up in no time and requested permission to wash up.

"Normally, we don't let filthy bitches like you wash up. However, I like you, so I'm going to make an exception and let you do it. Just do it fast." Reaching into one of her shirt pockets, she produced a small piece of soap and gave it to María Teresa.

María Teresa rushed in the direction of the sinks and began quickly to splash cold water on her face and neck. She washed them with soap and water, as well as her legs where the scabs were already formed. The coolness of the water felt wonderful and revitalized her body tremendously.

She did not notice at the beginning how close the militia woman was getting to her. Then she heard her voice saying in a sweet fashion, "My name is Rosa, but all my friends called me La China. You and I could become very good friends. Don't you want to be my friend?"

María Teresa looked up and just nodded at the mirror in front of her.

Dropping her wooden club on the floor, the militia woman continued, "You know, I could be very nice to you, if you were also very nice to me." The militia woman whispered at the same time as she was grabbing María Teresa's breasts from behind and fondly kissing the nape of her neck. María Teresa turned around and pushed her away with sudden force.

She landed on the floor about five feet away from the sink. La China's face changed expression and, standing up like a coiled spring, she rushed for the club and shoved it onto María Teresa's throat, holding it there with both hands. Her knee followed with a quick upward motion and hit María Teresa's lower abdomen.

"You rich whore. Who do you think you are? And after I let you wash up. Even gave you a piece of my own soap. Just move if you dare. Just give me a single reason and I'll make your life miserable."

At that moment, Sister Beth yelled from her stall, "Mari-Tere come quickly. I need help. Please, help me to stand up."

"Okay, go ahead," said La China while looking at María Teresa straight in the eyes, and then added, "I only hope that it is me who examines you when they bring you in for interrogation. You and I will have some fun together then, whether you like it or not."

La China moved aside and María Teresa went to help the old nun who, in reality, required no further assistance.

When they came out of the ladies room, María Teresa was still pretending to help Sister Beth and then she said, "Thank you, Sister. Thank you very much."

Back in their seats, Sister Beth was the first to talk.

"Mari-Tere you know quite a bit about this world and the people in it, although much of your knowledge is purely theoretical. Now, you are being exposed to the evil, and to the ugly things that are also part of this world of ours. Experience sometimes is a better teacher than abstract theory. Be careful with appearances."

Another one of the nuns then interrupted them, "While you were outside they made an announcement. Some food will be served within the hour. They forgot to mention what, and obviously nobody asked them."

The second announcement came several minutes later. It was read very loudly through the speaker system.

"We are going to serve you some food, courtesy of the Revolutionary Government and the merciful spirit of the People of Cuba. We want you to form a line in each aisle. In fifteen minutes, the door at the beginning of each aisle will open. A cup of tea and a piece of bread will be given to each of you. Only one ration per person. They have all been counted, so whoever takes more than one ration will be depriving another person of his share. We are going to give you thirty minutes to eat. After you have finished eating, you will have the pleasure of listening to some inspiring revolutionary music. At that time, you will have permission to go to the toilets. But only the number of persons that we can accommodate in one and a half hours. After that time everybody will return to their seats or places in the aisles and remain perfectly quiet until tomorrow, when we will wake you up for breakfast. Anyone making any kind of noise during the time allotted for sleeping will be severely punished. That is all."

Bread was part of the daily Cuban typical diet. It was a custom inherited from their European ancestors, mostly Spaniards. But tea was not. The typical Cuban was used to drinking coffee. Coffee was more expensive than tea, and also a commodity that they could easily export. Tea was cheaper and imported by Cuba. It was readily available.

The lines started to form almost immediately. But not everybody stood up. Some decided that what they were about to receive was food fit for no human being. Therefore, they concluded not to become part of the charade and remained seated. Two women started to make loud comments to that effect.

Two militia women accompanied by a soldier with a security dog held by a long leash came, all of a sudden, from the stage along one of the aisles. The soldier walked with the dog in front, clearing a path through the crowd in that aisle. The two militia women followed closely.

They arrived where the two women were seated, and the two militia women advanced towards them, clubbing them at least twice on their heads and their backs. Then, they grabbed one of their arms and twisted the same behind their backs. In that fashion they moved them behind the stage and ended the disturbance.

María Teresa never found out what became of them. As a matter of fact, nobody saw them again.

Finally, María Teresa and Sister Beth returned to their seats with their rations of food. Sister Beth gave María Teresa her portion of bread and told her to eat it. She protested once, but when she saw the nun's persistence, she knew that nothing else was to be said and she ate both shares. The tea was not hot but lukewarm. It did not contain milk, cream or lemon; only sugar, plenty of sugar.

Then, the music started with the revolutionary anthem, a march with music supplied by the communist "International Hymn" and lyrics by Cuban communist poets. It was played over and over again.

Some people went to the restrooms thinking that at least they would not hear the music played repeatedly. They were disappointed as speakers were installed at several places in the huge lobby and carried the sound all the way into the restrooms.

The male prisoners were located in the upper floors or the balcony area of the theater. It occurred also at that time that from the second floor, two soldiers brought down a semi-conscious man. His face was distorted and covered with blood, and he was partially naked from the waist down.

The soldiers dropped him on top on one of the stretchers near the outside main doors and told the closest ambulance driver, "Take him to the nearest hospital and tell them to sew him up. Then bring him back here when they are finished."

The orderly helping the driver to carry the stretcher commented, "Wow! This motherfucker really smells. And I have to go with him in the back of the ambulance. Bullshit! He'll go all alone. What the hell happened to him anyway?"

One of the soldiers who had brought the prisoner to the ambulance said, "This son of a bitch was taking a crap in one of the toilets and started to complain that the Revolution wouldn't let him shit in peace with the music going on. He yelled from the toilet seat that he was shitting on the Revolution, on Fidel, on Raúl and on Celia. We went in with Captain Ortega and let him have it, right then and there."

The orderly did not answer; he just went and fetched two buckets of water and some paper towels. He asked the driver to give him a hand, and placed the beaten man face down on the sidewalk. He dropped one bucket of water on the man's behind and the other bucket on top of the vinyl cushion of the stretcher. With the paper towels, he proceeded to wipe the cushion first and then the man's rear. He then proceeded to place the man back on the stretcher and the same into the ambulance. Finally, they went with the siren blasting to the nearest emergency room.

As the soldiers watching the entire scene went back into the theater, one of them remarked to the other that the poor bastard had learned his lesson for today.

"From here on", he said, "he'll shit on his own mother before he even thinks of doing it on the Revolution or its leaders."

Everybody who heard the story laughed as if it was a wonderful joke. The next morning, the incident became known throughout the entire theater.

At last, the music stopped. Everything went very quiet. Only the occasional bark of a dog on the stage interrupted the silence.

The lights remained on. The people closed their eyes, maybe sleeping, and maybe pretending to be asleep. Sporadic snoring was heard. However, most of the people could not sleep. They just remained motionless.

María Teresa was one of the persons who could not sleep at first. She had permitted her body to sink into the seat. Her knees were almost touching the back of the seat in front of her. Her sweater lay folded on top of her lap, her head rested on the back of the seat and her eyes were closed, but she was wide awake.

Sister Beth's head appeared to have fallen by its own weight towards María Teresa's seat, and her mouth was right in line with María Teresa's ear. As in the afternoon, she started a conversation whispering very softly into her ear, "Mari-Tere, are you awake? Don't answer, just nod."

María Teresa nodded slowly. Then, Sister Beth continued, "Gradually, open your eyes, a degree at a time, until you can get a full view of the stage. Then, watch them feeding the dogs."

María Teresa took her time, and opened her eyes slowly. Large, stainless steel bowls were being placed next to the dogs. They must have been full of food, because they appeared to be heavy to the soldiers that were carrying them. She could not distinguish from her seat what kind of food it was. One thing was certain, whatever it was, the dogs loved it. There was also plenty of it, because they were served seconds. After this, María Teresa thought, there should be no doubt as to whom the Revolution considered more important.

Sister Beth said, "Remember, from your history classes, that at one time the French revolutionaries had claimed 'liberté, égalité, fraternité ou la mort.' Well, there is much to be desired for freedom and equality in any revolution, and this one is no exception. Try to relax. Free your mind of ideas and think of God and His everlasting love. May His blessings bring you peace tonight. I'll be here if you need me. Go in spirit to Him, my child, and let Him carry your troubled soul for a while. Good night and God bless."

María Teresa nodded again and said, "Thank you." She tried to think about God, but she could not. Not immediately anyway, because her mind wandered restlessly from one incident to another in this day's ordeal. In a few minutes she had recapitulated fifteen hours.

Then she thought of Raúl. On a day like today, he must have known what was going on. He must have known that the government was going to pick up hundreds of thousands of people and place them in secured sites. He probably called her at her house, but when he was told that she wasn't there, he must have started looking for her. That's it, he must be looking for her at this very moment. There were not that many theaters in the Miramar section of the city; so, if Raúl was looking for her at theaters it should not take long for him to find her. Then, she realized that nobody had asked for her name, except the officer outside the tunnel that morning.

She doubted that he had passed that information along to the sergeant on the bus. Maybe her name only appeared in the list of persons to be rounded up that day. In any event, if her name was not on that list, how would Raúl find her? Suddenly, she wanted to stand up and yell her name, so that the whole world would know where she was.

On the other hand, if Raúl had looked for a 1959 black Lincoln limousine, he would have found it in no time. There were not too many cars like that one on the entire island, and definitely not with the Aguirrupe name engraved on both front doors.

Finding the car and then locating its driver should not been too difficult for someone with the pull of Raúl. He must know where she is and must be on his way to rescue her. She convinced herself of that.

But she had not examined all the possibilities. The other alternative, she concluded, was that Raúl was far from La Habana, directing the troops against the invasion forces. If that was true, only God knew where he was and in what kind of predicament he might be.

Whatever was going to happen was then unknown, and it was too early for more conclusive conjectures. Almost involuntarily, drowsiness began to take charge of María Teresa's subconscious. The quietness, maintaining her eyes closed for so long, and the rhythmical hushed sound of deep breathing all around her made her feel weary. A few minutes later she was asleep again.

CHAPTER SIX

María Teresa woke up early. She glanced at her wristwatch. It was five forty-five in the morning. She looked around her and noticed that there had been no changes. She remembered having a dream about her father, her house, the school and Concha. She had vague recollections of her dream, and could not pinpoint the details. For some hours she had managed to escape reality and that was good.

She also saw that most of the people surrounding her were still sleeping; or if not, they were pretending very well. Sister Beth, on the contrary, had her eyes open wide and in her usual low voice was the first to start the conversation.

"Good morning, my child. How do you feel this morning?"

"Fine, Sister, but dying to go to the restroom again."

"Well, I want to go too. Let's try to go together and hope that this time we have no problems."

María Teresa was worried, but she did manage to keep her fears within herself. This time La China was not there, and everything went smoothly, with the exception of the usual embarrassment. This time two guards went into the ladies room with them and they were allowed to wash themselves afterwards.

Back in their seats, Sister Beth noticed that María Teresa was getting nervous. She seemed to be relaxed whenever she was sitting down with the nuns for a while, but any encounter with a militia woman or a soldier made her tense and jumpy. The good old nun sensed that the worst was yet to come, and maybe it would be best for María Teresa to keep her mind occupied on other matters.

"Sister, I don't know about you, but I'm hungry."

"If only I could perform miracles. Right now I would love to have a big cup of rich and thick hot chocolate with some churros on the side. Better still, I would create two cups of hot chocolate and give you one."

María Teresa smiled and continued, "If I could bring you home right now, I would ask Mirta to prepare for you one of those American breakfasts with ham, eggs, hot cakes, coffee and toasted French bread with plenty of butter and marmalade."

Sister Beth looked at her with eyes full of love.

"You see, Mari-Tere, both of us have had a wonderful breakfast already. I don't know about you but I'm full. Full to the point that I might refuse whatever breakfast the magnanimous Revolution offers this morning."

María Teresa giggled, thinking that their little game had really made her forget her hunger, at least momentarily. The nun knew that she could continue sheltering this girl by not stopping the trivial talk, and sensing some sort of pause, she quickly added, "Tell me about your fiancé."

"Raúl is a good person overall, although he is also intellectually mistaken and emotionally confused. The main thing is that I still believe that in his heart he loves me and cares for me."

"I see. What does he do? Is he older or younger than you?"

"You may not believe this but he is truly a Commander in the Revolutionary Army, and he is two years older than I. You remember back in 1957, when a group of students and members of the Authentic Political Party organized an attack on the Presidential Palace. The ultimate goal was to kill Batista and bring a quick political change to the island. Well, my brother José María died on that day, inside the Palace, next to Manuel Mora, who happens to be Raúl's older brother and who also died there. Raúl was then a student at Villanueva, enrolled in the School of Law. His family decided to send him out of the country for the next summer vacation. They believed that it wasn't safe for him to be on the streets of the island. Not for Raúl, anyway, who was always talking against the government.

"He never committed any terrorist act that I know of, but the mere talking plus the stigma of his dead brother, could have provoked a feeling of vengeance that could have harmed him. For similar reasons, my father decided to send Carlos and myself, along with Concha, out of the country. We all met each other at the Eden Roc Hotel in Miami Beach. I knew who he was from school, but I had never had any serious conversation with him until that time in Florida. Carlos, Raúl and myself went swimming and boating almost every day."

María Teresa paused briefly and then continued, "In our grief, we consoled each other. Carlos, Raúl and I became almost inseparable. You know how good Carlos is with boats, so we rented a big, fast one and spent a lot of time cruising along the eastern Florida shore. Raúl and I became closer and closer friends. One beautiful night, he told me that he loved me, and that made me extremely happy. I then knew, because my heart told me so, that I also loved him very much. As I told you, he is two years older than I am, and when these events took place, he only had two more years to go in order to finish law school.

"With both my father and other brother being lawyers I knew that Raúl would be welcome in my family. At the time Raúl wasn't a member of Castro's 26th of July Movement. As you well know those people didn't participate in the attack on the Presidential Palace and there have been rumors that some of their spies forewarned the soldiers guarding the palace of the impending attack. I believe that Castro never wanted the attack to succeed; however Raúl refuses to accept that notion. Since it would not have been in Castro's best interest that the attack would have ended with the death of Batista, I do believe that there is some element of truth in that reasoning. Mainly, because it would have made heroes of the revolutionary students who were completely disjointed from Castro's wishes and socio-political views. Anyway, my plan upon our return to Cuba was to go back to Villanueva and finish my studies. I knew that my father and my brother Fernando would have helped Raúl in the starting phase of his professional career as an attorney, and we could get married after my graduation.

"Raúl had other plans. He didn't think of law school. He wanted to go back and take arms against the existing government and to avenge his brother's death. To assist in opening a secondary-fighting front in the Escambray Mountains in Las Villas Province was a faint dream at the beginning. By the time we came back to Cuba, the mission of fighting the army that had killed his brother had become an obsession.

"I tried to reason with him, Sister; I told him that our brothers had died in an attack that they had pursued to its end. It was a gallant try and a valiant plan; but the army that killed them had done so in self-defense. This army had not been the aggressor. This army or the police had not hunted two unarmed young men along the streets of the city and slain them in some dark alley. It was a very sad outcome to an unfortunate event, but we wouldn't accomplish anything positive by continuing the fight. Batista, according to my father, had to be removed from power by legal actions, such as an election, and not a revolution that promised revenge and chaos, anarchism, disunion, disorder and vindictiveness."

"Very good, Mari-Tere, you don't know how happy I feel hearing you talk like that. But please, continue. What you are saying is very interesting. Keep your voice down and tell me more."

"Well, Raúl claimed that my father was a jurist, a man of words, a man of peace, a man of the pen. In the meantime, he professed to be a man of action, a man of war and of the sword. After we came back to Cuba, Raúl left for the mountains and I never saw him again until February 1959. Castro then made him a Commander of the new Revolutionary Army, recognizing his natural fighting abilities and leadership qualities, more than his revolutionary accomplishments. During the time he had been in the mountains, roughly speaking about a year and a half, he managed to create a guerilla force that kept the regular army busy in that middle province, diverting its attention from Castro's forces. It is true that he never fought a big battle, but he did manage to stop any large transfer of troops towards the eastern provinces where Castro roamed."

"That is very interesting. Very interesting, indeed. But, tell me, my child, what happened after he returned to La Habana? Did he go back to school and finish his studies?"

"No, he didn't. Raúl came from the mountains with the ghost of vendetta that my father had been afraid of. Somehow, he had associated the armies that he had been fighting with the intellectual, professional, rich and aristocratic classes on the island. He believes that his foes are still on the loose. The fight won't be over until all these groups of people are destroyed.

"He is not the Raúl I once knew. Granted he had wanted to avenge his brother and had gone about the task in the wrong way. But, before he was an idealist without hatred for any other member of the human race. Now, behind the façade of the Revolution, I still trust that the original Raúl, the one who told me that he loved me more than anything in his life, is still there. His essence merely dormant and like a volcano ready to erupt; once the truth reaches his heart, he will become the Raúl of before."

"I see, and you're the messenger of the light and the truth. You plan to awaken him."

"Yes, I think I can do it. What's more, I know I can do it. I'm certain that I'm the only one, because in spite of all things Raúl loves me and I love him too. Love should prevail and conquer everything. You always maintained that point of view, remember?"

"You are right, my dearest child. Love always wins in the end. In the meantime, a lot of people could be hurt, suffer and perish in its name."

They were interrupted by the announcement of breakfast. It was identical to the meal they had had the night before. This time, the bread was fresher and softer.

From the balcony seats in the upper floors, some men started screaming against the detention and the food. Others seconded the few shouts of protest soon thereafter, like echoes through a high mountain range. Pretty soon, a lot of voices started chanting with periodic regularity, "Cuba yes, communism no. Food yes, shit no."

The sounds of these voices were accompanied by the sounds of feet kicking rhythmically on the lower parts of the seats in front of them. Others followed, joining the chorus.

The dogs started to bark and growl on the stage, baring their teeth to the sound that was driving them mad.

The soldiers were astonished. They could not understand what they were seeing or hearing. For a brief moment the officers appeared to have been caught completely off guard.

The soldiers at the machine gun stations reacted by sheer instinct, and automatically got their weapons ready to fire. They were awaiting orders with panicked expressions. The women in the front orchestra section became very concerned and started to yell, "Don't shoot. Please, don't shoot."

Sporadic fights started between some women. Expecting the worst, the majority of the women lay on the floor, seeking the protection of the seats. The ones in the aisles did not have that protection, and to find shelter, they tried to force themselves on top of the women lying between the rows of seats.

María Teresa crouched as close as she could to Sister Beth, who in a protective attitude threw herself on top of the girl, after pushing her down onto the floor.

No bullets were ever fired. Instead, following some officers, several soldiers who were on the stage ran into the aisles, kicking or stepping on whomever was in their way. After they reached the main doors, they went through them into the main lobby. There, they regrouped again with others soldiers who were outside, in the streets, guarding the building. The officers ordered that all firearms were to be left in the lobby to be guarded by the militia women. Armed with bayonets and wooden clubs they charged upstairs.

When the doors to the balconies opened, the soldiers rushed inside hitting anyone in sight. Some men tried to fight back, but the majority ran along the inclined steps of the few aisles, or jumped from the top of one row of seats to another. Finally, all accumulated in the front rows of seats of the balconies, and there the soldiers had their day breaking skulls, arms, legs and collarbones.

Systematically, the soldiers beat about seventy per cent of the male population in the theater. They suffered all kinds of concussions and bruises. A few, terrified at the sight, jumped into the orchestra area, falling on top of the women below. Most men spent a few months in several hospitals, due to the wounds received that day. Some were not that lucky and died a few days after. Two elderly men had massive heart attacks and died in the theater.

The lucky ones that made it back to their seats when the whole ordeal was over did not chant or protest anymore. An officer on the stage grabbed a microphone and began talking through the public address system, "Attention. Attention. Please be quiet so that everybody can hear me. Quiet. Please, be quiet. Quiet, please, ladies and gentlemen."

After a brief pause, he continued, "Attention. Listen to me. All of you listen well. Apparently, we were a little bit too crowded for the convenience of some of you. The Revolution, in its wisdom, has made a number of seats available. And now that everybody has a seat to relax in, I want everybody to remain seated and to be very quiet. There will be no more disturbances. We shall not tolerate a single outburst from any of you. I am giving the soldiers behind me the order to shoot whoever does not behave from here on." Turning around now to face the soldiers, he continued, "Is that understood?"

"Yes, Sir," was the unanimous response.

Then, he turned again to face the audience and said, "As you can see, the next time you utter a single protest about anything, you will be shot. Now, since you do not appreciate the kindness of the People of Cuba in providing you with food that you obviously do not deserve, we shall not feed you again today. You will not be able to leave your seat for any reason. Whoever merely stands up will be shot. No permission to go to the restrooms will be granted. Anything that you might want to do, hold it or do it in your own seat. But nobody, I repeat, nobody has any authorization to leave his or her seat for the time being. Now, the majority of you have been brought here because your name appeared on a list of names of probable enemies that we have. Some of you have been brought here from the streets or other places, and your names do not appear on our original lists. Those of you who believe you are not listed with us will raise one of your arms. Stay in your seat, but keep one of your arms up. An officer will approach you for proper identification. The sooner we can finish with this process, the sooner we can let you return to your own houses.

"Starting tonight we shall begin calling each one of you, by the names on our new list, and you will undergo a routine search and interrogation procedure, after which you might be allowed to go home, if you are found innocent of possible crimes against the fatherland.

"I must tell you that the Revolution is triumphant once more. Our enemies cannot succeed against our determination to protect the People of Cuba. We are the bastions of social justice and peace. Nothing can prevail against us. We shall overcome. Fatherland or death. We shall overcome."

María Teresa remembered her feelings on the bus. The multitude of people was nothing else but the compendium of many buses of fear doomed to become a theater of terror.

She started to say something. Only one word came out of

her mouth, "Listen . . . . ," for, at the same time, Sister Beth looked at her, bringing her right hand index finger perpendicular to her mouth.

After a couple of minutes, María Teresa raised her left arm and waited. It took about one hour before anybody came to her row. The young officer standing in the aisle, list in hand, signaled her to approach him. When he realized that she was hesitating, he said in a loud voice, "Come over here, pretty girl. Don't be afraid. They won't shoot you. They know that I'm here to talk to you. Come on now."

She walked along the row of seats and stood next to the officer. Then she produced the driver's license that she kept in a small wallet inside of one of the pockets of her trousers. The officer looked at the license and then at her. He then said, "You know, this photograph doesn't do you justice. You are ten times more beautiful in person. Even after some time in this hole."

She grinned and responded, "Thank you very much, Sir."

The officer staring at her green eyes, continued, "Let's see, Aguirrupe is an easy one. It starts with an A, so you go on the first page. Oh, you're lucky. You'll be among the first ones they'll be calling. How come you were not on the original lists?"

"I was picked up while driving through Línea Street yesterday morning, on the way to meet my older brother. I was given no specific reason for my detention."

"Well, in that case you shouldn't be worried. They won't hold you for too long. Now, get back to your seat and stay there like a good girl."

As she turned around to go back to her seat, the officer tapped her lightly on her behind. She stopped and became furious. Color started to accumulate on her face. She was not used to accepting that kind of liberty taken by strangers. But in those hours spent in that theater she had learned to control her emotions. With contempt and anger reflected on her blushed face and reddened eyes, she continued walking towards her seat without turning around. She sat down in silence and bit her lower lip.

Enclosed in that theater, no one could know if it was day or night, sunny or cloudy, rainy or dry weather, morning, afternoon or evening. It must have been a part of the psychological plan to make them aware of their present state only, without any external interruption. They always maintained the same intensity of artificial light. They always fed the prisoners the same type of food. Take away the usual references that allow a human being to measure elapsed time, compound it with some terror, and that person becomes disoriented, more likely to contradict himself or herself while being interrogated.

She spent her day meditating. A day of silence. She remembered the days of retreat at her Catholic high school.

That evening, they received some good news and some bad news. The good news was that they were going to be fed once more. This time they brought them a piece of bread, like a small French stick, about eight inches long, stuffed with white farmer's cheese and guava paste, and a cup of what appeared to be chicken broth. It tasted faintly like chicken, it was liquid and it was hot. They also received a tiny cup of Cuban black coffee. The bad news was that the name calling for the interrogation procedures was not going to begin for the next several hours, which meant that they were going to spend another night in these conditions.

After dinnertime ended, they were allowed once to go to the restrooms. This time they decided to let the people go by rows. One by one, whether you wanted to or not, you had to go. Most prisoners took advantage of the situation and relieved themselves. In silence, they thanked the jailers for their generosity, went back to their respective seats and went to sleep or rested until the next day.

Unknown to them, the truth was that the interrogation rooms were being erected and they were not yet ready to begin the procedures.

CHAPTER SEVEN

Wednesday, April 19, 1961. Seven o'clock in the morning. María Teresa suddenly woke up and opened her eyes. A voice from the stage inundated the building through the speakers saying, "Listen, all of you. Attention. Please, listen carefully. In approximately half an hour, we will start calling names from this microphone. Special rooms have been prepared behind us, on the stage, for the purpose of conducting the individual interrogations. After that process ends you will leave through the rear of the theater. Answer all the questions thoroughly and truthfully, and you will have nothing to fear. If we detect that you are either lying to us or concealing information that we consider pertinent to the safety of the Revolution, you will be taken to a regular prison or to the G-2 interrogation center for more questioning. I sincerely hope that further inconveniences only occur to very few of you, because as you know we are merciless with the enemies of the people. I am confident that the majority of you will have no further problems and will be allowed to go home and continue with your lives to serve the People of Cuba. When you are released, you will have to provide your own means of transportation in order to reach your final destination.

"The names will be mentioned only once. If you miss it, we will not repeat it until we have finished with the entire list and commence again from the beginning for the second time. We will call all the women first, and once we clear the orchestra seats, we will then move the men to this section of the theater and begin to call their names.

"As you climb onto the stage, you will be directed to one of the stations. Proceed quietly and do whatever they ask you to do and we will have no problems.

"Long live the Revolution.

"Long live its maximum leader Fidel Castro."

The soldiers behind the speaker cheered the two last remarks and they started promptly to move some of the dogs and machine guns backstage to clear a path to the rear portion of the stage.

María Teresa turned her head to face Sister Beth and said, "I want to wish you the very best. I hope we see each other again real soon."

The good old nun grabbed her face with both hands, smiled and gently kissed both cheeks. Then she said, "Mari-Tere, now listen to me. You have to be very strong. This is not the time to become a rebel. Agree to and do everything they ask, and get out of here. Go home and call me tomorrow. Do not say much over the phone. Limit yourself only to some small talk and I will understand if you want to see me and talk to me. We can get together if you feel that you need me. I don't understand completely what's going on here now, but this much I can tell you. Be assured that whatever was occurring has failed, and they have won. Because, otherwise, I don't believe that we would be getting out of here this easily. For now, rejoice, for the end of our present ordeal is near."

"Sister, I don't feel like rejoicing. I don't think there's anything to rejoice about."

"Oh yes, my dear Mari-Tere, there is always something to be joyful about. Be joyful in the Lord. Jubilate Deo."

"Well, as usual, you're right," said María Teresa, depositing a tender kiss on the old nun's face. "And also remember, Sister, that love shall conquer all."

"True. Give my best to that hero of yours, to Raúl. And when you see him again, tell him that your old Latin teacher said to tell him, 'Omnia vincit amor.'"

The first names started to be called through the public address system and the whole theater became, all of a sudden, dead silent.

"Sister Cristina Gonzalez y Ochoa.

"Sister Margarita Otero y Perera.

"Sister María Rodríguez y Prado."

These names were at the top of the list and were the first mentioned by the soldier who was calling them. He was a very young man, almost a boy, around 16 years old. His voice revealed lack of schooling as he was encountering some difficulties in reading the names on the roster. To compound his problems, he had to read the English names of the Sisters that followed. Apparently, some officer had decided to call all of the nuns first, and the majority of the congregation of Dominican nuns in that place and on that day were Americans.

The soldier really wanted to comply with the order given to him. However, it was becoming an insurmountable task. He felt it was an important duty, the caller of the roll. In reality he was the victim of a practical joke, conceived by an officer with a twisted sense of humor who, knowing that the nuns were the first ones to be called and that the majority of the names were in English, wanted to have some laughs by watching the problems that this uneducated kid would have in deciphering and pronouncing the names in question.

"Sister Ag-nes Mc-In-tire.

"Sister Eliza-beth Mac-Ar-thur.

"Sister Josephine . . . ." and he just could not make heads or tails out of how the Irish surname should be pronounced. So, in desperation and frustration he counted, pointing at each name remaining on the list, and said, "And seventeen more fucking American nuns."

All of the white-robed nuns moved towards the stage, amid the laughs of most of the soldiers and some of the people in the theater. The only one who seemed somewhat perplexed by the end result of his words was the young announcer who had uttered them.

The calling of the names continued without further delay, but by now the officer replaced the original soldier, with the excuse that such an important task had to be shared equally by all military personnel on the stage. The next caller knew how to read properly and it did not take long before María Teresa heard her own name spoken over the microphone.

She walked to the top of the stage. The nearest dog took a quick glance at her and emitted a sinister growl. The soldier who had him by the short leash, said, "Quiet, Satan. Quiet."

He made a motion with his left hand and placed it in front of the dog's face. The dog lay down and became motionless instantly.

A militia woman approached her and, grabbing her by her arm, directed her past the huge curtain hiding the rear portion of the stage. When María Teresa crossed the curtain behind the last row of dogs, she noticed that a series of partitions had been erected. Each cubicle was approximately sixteen feet wide by twenty feet deep.

The Revolutionary Army Corps of Engineers had constructed these temporary interrogation centers following the instructions of the Intelligence Branch and under the advice of their KGB mentors. Each cubicle was divided inside into three rooms by other partitions with doors connecting these internal rooms. Two rooms facing the sixteen-foot wall were approximately eight feet wide by eight feet deep each. At the end of these two adjacent rooms, there was a large, sixteen foot by twelve foot interrogation room. Each of the small rooms contained a single light bulb in a funnel-shaped, metallic lamp placed in the center of the room. A simple wooden chair was situated under the light. The large interrogation room had a long table, about eight feet long, placed almost in the middle of the room. Hanging from the ceiling, over the table, was a row of four potent lights facing the opposite wall. A person standing at that wall would be blinded by the great luminescense directed at his or her eyes. This room had an additional door behind the table and the chairs leading to the outside.

There were twenty-five interrogation centers operating simultaneously, designed for mass processing of potential dissenters. Each unit had a number painted on the front wall.

"We go to number seven," said the militia woman.

Just before they arrived at the left front door of number seven, María Teresa heard some quick steps behind her, and a voice that said, "Go and pick up another one, Marta. This one is mine."

It was La China. María Teresa felt like she was going to faint, but she stood still, her nerves frozen.

"Come on, pretty one. Go in," said La China, opening the door and gently pushing her inside.

Once in the room, La China walked around her, saying, "You see that chair in the middle?" and she pointed her club to the chair; "I want you to empty all your pockets and place all your belongings, including any jewelry, on top of it."

María Teresa obeyed without uttering a single word. She placed her wallet on the chair, followed by a small coin purse, her watch, and her necklace made out of 18 carat gold, from which a golden cross covered with pearls hung. Finally she took the driving gloves out of her side trouser pocket, and deposited them on top of the seat of the chair.

La China took the sweater from her hand and rested it neatly on the chair. She kept walking continuously around María Teresa, very slowly, one pace at a time. Eventually she stopped and faced María Teresa bringing her body closer to hers.

"Okay, pretty girl. Now you will stand next to the chair and undress. Leave all your clothing on the chair and stand still."

She removed her blouse and trousers and placed them folded on the chair. Then she stood up and waited.

"Apparently, there is something wrong with your hearing, my sweet and beautiful girl. Believe me, I have the cure for your lovely ears. Now, listen to me carefully. When I say undress, I mean undress. That is, you remove everything. Just tell me if you have any problem understanding me and I will gladly help you do it."

"No, no problem at all," said María Teresa and hurriedly, with rapid and deliberate movements, she removed her silk bra and panties.

She felt La China's eye all over her body and a feeling of repugnancy pervaded her.

"I knew it from the first moment that I saw you, I knew that you were a beautiful woman, but I never expected anything like this. You're truly gorgeous. You know, I could eat you up."

María Teresa did not answer. She lowered her eyes and focused her sight on the floor in shame and to avoid a direct confrontation with La China.

"My love, I said everything and that includes your shoes and knee high socks."

Without another word, the socks were put inside the shoes and these were deposited underneath the chair. Now, La China came closer to her and spoke in a soft voice, "Now, my sweet, pay attention. I'm going to find you from the identification in your wallet, who you are and where you live. I'll be good to you now, but you have to be very good to me when I go to visit you tonight. Is that understood?"

There was no reply from María Teresa's lips and La China interpreted the silence as a sign of consent.

"Okay, we don't have too much time left now, so let's finish with this search and get you out of here. Stand at the back of the chair, facing it."

The command was succinct and she followed it. Pretty soon the hands of the militia woman were all over her hair trying to catch whatever might be hidden under or in between the strands. Not finding anything, she said, "Now, bend over and grab the seat of the chair with both hands. Come on. Let's go." Sensing a hesitation in the girl actions, she patted her on her behind with the wooden club and added, "Come on. Do you're told now."

With her left hand, La China pushed María Teresa's head down towards the seat portion of the chair. Then she opened wide the terrified girl's legs and told her to maintain that position.

She removed the club from her right hand and dropped it on the floor. Then, her right hand moved upwards, almost caressing the inside area of María Teresa's thighs until it reached her genitalia. She used the fingers of both hands to open the genital lips exposing the vagina and then she proceeded to put the middle finger of her right hand into it.

María Teresa was mortified and felt defiled. In her willingness to get through her unavoidable fate as quickly as possible, she realized that she had to lower herself to that state without any resistance and that bothered her. Her instinct was to react violently against the aggression being committed to her body; but her mind fought for prudence. To feel her modesty being removed with every touch of La China's finger was an experience that she had never been prepared for. She tried to move away from the inquisitive finger that kept creeping up inside her, deeper and deeper. Abruptly, it stopped. La China commented, "You are a virgin. This has to be my lucky day. You are a fucking virgin."

She took her finger out, but her hand remained in the same general area of the girl's body.

"Now, be still, my attractive siren. I don't want to hurt you, but this is the last place I have to look into."

With one hand she opened her buttocks exposing her anus, and using the same finger as before, projected it into her rectum, producing a moaning sound from María Teresa's mouth. When La China was satisfied that nothing was concealed in that orifice either, she removed her finger from it and taking, two steps backwards, she ordered the prisoner to stand up and turn around.

When María Teresa turned around she was weeping in silence. It was becoming harder for her to control her emotions any longer.

She wanted to tell La China that she was not afraid of her or anything anymore. She wanted to put a stop to her crying, but she could not.

The militia woman had performed the routine with evident pleasure. Otherwise, it was the standard procedure for the searching of women under the communist rule of the revolutionary government.

La China looked at her, smiled, and just said, "Okay, let's go to the next room now."

The prisoner turned around to pick up her articles of clothing and start to get dressed again, but she was immediately stopped.

"No, you will go as you are now. I still have to search your clothing."

Opening the door to the rear room, she pushed María Teresa inside and quickly closed the door behind her.

The next room was completely dark as she came into it. She was trying to adjust her eyes to the new environment when four potent lamps lit up, emitting a brilliant white light. She tried to discern what was behind the spotlights, but to no avail. Her nakedness gave her a feeling of helplessness. She heard a man's voice. It sounded like a deep masculine voice. The words were pronounced in a clear monotone:

"The prisoner will move to the center of the lights, always facing them."

She then realized that it was a long room, and moving one step at a time, fearing the worst with every action of her body, she walked until she guessed that she was in the middle of the room.

She stood, covering a portion of her breasts with her right arm, and utilizing her left hand to try to hide her genital area. She stood there for a few seconds, trembling and shaking like an autumn leaf.

The man's voice spoke again:

"The prisoner will stand erect and be still, with both arms hanging loose at both sides of the body."

She did not move. By now she could see that under the spotlight there was the edge of a long table. She was picturing in her mind a row of several men sitting behind that table and all of them looking at her naked body. She had only heard one voice, but the table was too long for there to be only one person behind it.

"The prisoner will obey all orders implicitly and answer all questions without delay."

Now a soldier approached rapidly on her left side. She had scarcely heard his steps before she realized that he was already next to her. The soldier moved to her back and, from that position, he held both her arms and pulled them back with great force. He then locked his arms with hers forcing her to remain erect with her two arms pulled backwards.

That position exposed her entire body. Once more, she bowed her head in humiliation.

"Will the prisoner behave from now on?" asked the same voice.

She did not say anything but merely nodded.

"Okay, let her go."

She was freed again from the hold. The soldier remained behind her.

"And now tell me your full name."

"María Teresa Aguirrupe."

"Aguirrupe and what else."

"Aguirrupe y Larrazábal."

"Where do you live?"

"Number Five Seventeen of Forty-eighth Street in Miramar."

"Where do you work?"

"I don't work. I'm a student at the university."

"A student eh! And what are you a student of?"

"I'm in my senior year of mechanical engineering."

Another voice asked the next question, confirming her original assumption that there must be more that one interrogator behind the long table.

"What university do you attend?"

"The University of Santo Tomás de Villanueva."

"When did you start?"

"What do you mean?"

"What year did you begin going to the university?"

"In 1956."

"Why you didn't go to La Habana University?"

"La Habana University didn't offer mechanical engineering."

"It seems to me that you went to Villanueva because you are nothing but a filthy rich bitch that decided that La Habana University was only for revolutionary scum and you would not dream of dirtying your nice hands in that place. Is that not the truth, the real truth?"

The Mechanical Engineering School Building at the University of Saint Thomas of Villanova. Picture taken in 1958.

"I went to Villanueva because it was the only place that offered mechanical engineering without going abroad, and my father didn't want me to be too far away from him. That's the truth. It wasn't a planned decision, merely a practical solution to a simple problem."

"How come a girl like you wanted to become a mechanical engineer? That's a profession more proper for a man, isn't it?"

"My father and my older brother are lawyers. I didn't feel like following in their footsteps. When I graduated from high school, I wanted to modernize the sugar industry, ever since I visited an old sugar mill. I don't know why, but I always felt that I was the person destined to bring innovation to our powerful sugar industry. To accomplish it, I needed to master technology as well as the design and fabrication of machinery in general, so I decided to study mechanical engineering."

"So you plan to be the Madame Curie of the sugar industry."

"I would like to do just that."

"If you were planning to work in a sugar mill, designing new equipment and modernizing the process for that industry, then you must have applied yourself in the study of, let's say, thermodynamics. Am I correct?"

"I studied one full year of that subject on top of what they cover in general physics, and the study of the making of sugar from sugar cane."

"Good, I'm glad. Now tell me, what are the first and second laws of thermodynamics."

"The what?"

"You claim to be a senior year student of engineering. Surely, you must remember them. Just tell me now. In your own words, what are the first and second laws of thermodynamics."

"I don't know if I could do it now. What does it have to do with my presence here?"

The first voice interrupted. "The prisoner will answer all questions without delay. We are merely trying to determine whether you are really the student that you claim to be. Please, answer the question if you know it."

"The first law of thermodynamics is the conservation of energy law, which deals with the concept that the total amount of energy in this universe is constant. Energy cannot be created or destroyed by men, it just transforms itself from one form to another in the course of thermodynamic processes. The second law has to do with the fact that these processes are not a hundred percent reversible, thus creating the principle of entropy. By entropy we mean that . . . ."

"Okay, that's enough. Stop right there."

A third voice was now heard.

"How old are you?"

"Twenty-three."

"When and where were you born?"

"I was born on October 7, 1937 in La Habana."

"What is your father's name?"

"Francisco Aguirrupe."

"And your mother's name?"

"María Teresa Larrazábal."

"What is your father's occupation?"

"He is retired."

"You mentioned that he was a lawyer. Where did he practice law before his retirement?"

"He was a Judge of the Supreme Court."

"Is that so! How interesting! Which of the courts was he a member of?"

"The Civil Court."

"And when was he appointed to the Supreme Court?"

"In 1937, the year that I was born."

"Oh, I see. So Batista had nothing to do with his being appointed as a magistrate?"

"He had nothing to do with Batista's government."

"You say that he is retired. Is he living at home with you now?"

"He is in the United States of America. He has been very sick with diabetes in recent years. My older brother decided to take him to a specialized clinic for treatment in Boston, Massachusetts. He should be back in another six months, when the treatment is over. In the meantime, he is going to need some eye surgery."

"Are you sure that he is not in Miami, planning a counterrevolution with the other worms in that area?"

"No, sir. I'm sure that he is in Boston." María Teresa realized that she was lying, but she had started with the disease lie and now she could only hope not to get caught in it.

"All right, we will check your stories in due time. All shall be done in due time. Now tell me, where is your mother?"

"My mother died when I was born."

"You told one of our officers yesterday that you were not picked up from any list. Who brought you here?"

"A bus from the entrance to the Almendares tunnel on Línea Street."

"You mean to say then that we did not pick you up from your house last Monday morning."

"That is exactly what I mean. Nobody came to my house to pick me up, as far as I know. Moreover, as far as I know, my name does not appear on any list and I think that I was brought here by mistake."

"The Revolution does not make mistakes. You'd better think twice about how you answer your questions, or you might face a bigger dilemma than the one you are facing now. Is that understood?"

"You know, I'm getting tired of all of this. You people forced me to be here today, kept me in this rotten place for two days without proper food and lacking any means of personal hygiene. Then, you bring me to these so-called interrogation centers, which to me are nothing else but installations of fear and human degradation. You have a woman perform what she thinks is the glorious duty of sticking her fingers into my body, probing for concealed secrets that I do not possess, and never have possessed to begin with. Then, she shoves me into this room to appear fully naked before you, so as to deprive me psychologically of any moral shield, in a way that I'm sure that you would not have your own wife, daughter, sister or mother appear, if you have any. And now, you have the gall to tell me to be careful about how I answer your questions, because I might find myself in a larger quandary. To hell with everything. I'm not answering any more questions. Do whatever you want to do."

María Teresa no longer remembered the prudent advice of Sister Beth. Centuries of tradition, of Basque temperament, were erupting through her pores at that very instant. She remained in the same position, looking calm but decidedly adamant about not answering any other questions. Her beautiful green eyes were all reddened, partially due to having been forced to continuously face the strong light in front of her, and partially due to the tears that she was shielding.

The soldier's fist met her right kidney area. She felt a sharp pain in her lower back that weakened her legs, bending her knees and sending the rest of her body downwards into a kneeling position.

A hand grabbed her hair and pulled her up. Then another fist landed in her back and propelled her whole body towards the table. She launched her two arms forward to break the fall by holding herself on the edge of the table.

One of the interrogators stood up, and with his open hand, slapped her in the face. She fell sideways onto the concrete floor. The soldier picked her up, and now locking her right arm behind her back, made her stand up and brought her back to her original position.

A streak of blood started to flow from her broken lower lip. The pain in her kidney and back was being compounded by an ache in her right shoulder, produced by the increasing pressure of the soldier's hold.

She heard again the voice of the first interrogator.

"María Teresa, we don't like people who want to play games with us. A pretty girl like you is just asking for it. If you persist in playing with fire, we are going to burn you and burn you good. On the other hand, if you just answer all the questions correctly and truthfully, we can all go home soon. You understand, don't you? So what do you say? Are you going to behave from now on?"

"Yes."

"Okay, let her go." The soldier obeyed but remained only one step behind her. María Teresa started to rub her right shoulder with her left hand to try to circulate some blood into the shoulder muscles and tendons. She also wiped her mouth with her left forearm, feeling the broken lip with her hand. "Thank God," she said to herself, for the cut was not very large and should stop bleeding soon.

"Now, tell us how and where were you picked up Monday morning."

She related to the three interrogators the complete series of events. When she had finished, the first voice spoke again:

"You mentioned that you have a brother named Carlos and you also mentioned that you have a brother that went to America with your father. How many more brothers and sisters do you have?"

"In total, I have three brothers and no sisters. My brother Fernando is the one in the United States with my father, and my brother José María was killed in 1957 during the attack on the Presidential Palace."

"Are you telling us that you are the sister of the late José María Aguirrupe?"

"Of course, I am. There are not too many Aguirrupes on this island, and we are all somewhat related to each other. My brother and Manuel Mora planned the attack, and died in the staircase leading to the third floor, where Batista's private offices were located. I understand that a few steps more and they would have succeeded in their quest. Raúl Mora has told me that according to some friends of his late brother Manuel, two grenades thrown by José María and Manuel onto the third floor level did not explode, making the difference between the success and failure of the attack. He never found out who supplied our brothers with that defective equipment."

"And evidently, you are talking about our Commander Raúl Mora. Do you know him?"

"I am his fiancée. We have been engaged to be married for three years."

The three interrogators started to talk among themselves in such a hushed tone that María Teresa could not discern what was being said. She knew that she had played her hand extremely well, although not by design.

The first voice started to talk again in a straight military tone and said:

"We have no further questions for the prisoner. The Revolution and this inquiry are satisfied with their findings. Soldier, bring the militia woman in."

Addressing La China when she had entered the room the same voice said, when the other woman entered the room:

"What have you found on this prisoner's body or in her belongings?"

"Nothing, Comrade interrogator. This girl is clean."

"All right. You may take the prisoner to the next room. This interrogation has ended." And to María Teresa, he added, "If we need to pose any further questions in the future we will contact you. You may go now."

La China guided María Teresa to the next room and, opening the door, told her to get inside.

María Teresa stopped after crossing the doorway for a few seconds and rubbed her eyes slightly, trying to readjust her pupils to the dim light in the next room. This room looked exactly like the first one. It had a chair, and all of her belongings appeared to be on it.

La China was the first one to speak, "Okay, sweetheart, get dressed and then get out of here by that door. Another one of us will take you outside. Go home and wait for me. I'll be there tonight to see you. I'll bet that you live in a nice house and I'll bet that you have a nice room where we can play together."

María Teresa did not waste any time. She put on her bra and panties almost instantly, then her blouse and trousers. She took the sweater and threw it on her back making a one-pass knot at the front with the two hanging sleeves. She took her wallet and looked inside. Her driver's license was there, as well as her school identification card, but all of the money was gone. She was not sure, but she thought that she had had around a hundred and twenty Cuban pesos with her. She decided not to make an issue of the missing money.

Facing La China she said calmly, "You'd better not come tonight or any other night. I don't intend to see you ever again in my life."

La China smiled and approached her. María Teresa held her ground and did not move. Their faces were only a few inches apart from each other, when La China spoke, "Look pretty girl, I have decided that you are mine, and when I make up my mind about something, that is it. I could make your life miserable, or I could make you experience pleasures that you have never dreamed of. But one way or the other, you are going to be mine. I'm going to have your naked body next to mine, whichever way you want to. We can do this the easy way or the hard way. So, now, tell me, what will it be?"

María Teresa decided to gain some time and said, smiling, "Take it easy, China. All of this is new to me, and I really don't know what to say. You see, you can't come to my house. That's what I was trying to tell you. It can't be in my house, because I don't live alone. There is my brother, and other people in the house, plus my boyfriend. That's why it can't be in my house."

María Teresa stepped backwards and away from La China. She went back to the chair and picked up her gloves. She placed them in one of her pockets. Then, she noticed that there was nothing else under the gloves. Her wristwatch and necklace were missing. A quick glance at La China's forearm immediately revealed where the watch was. She then looked at La China's neck, but her necklace was not there.

"I can understand that, my lovely doll. I'll tell you what. Friday evening I'll pick you up and we can go out together. We can have a few drinks and go to a place where I will show you the best time of your life. Is that okay with you? Friday night, let's say around 8:00 P.M.", said La China, penetrating María Teresa's clothing with her lustful eyes.

CHAPTER EIGHT

A bruptly, the door marked with an exit sign was opened from the outside and the handsome figure of a bearded young man in an olive green uniform with the rank markings of Commander of the Revolutionary Army appeared.

"Mari-Tere," he said.

María Teresa turned to face the man who had spoken. She would have recognized that voice anywhere. It was the voice of Raúl Mora.

She ran towards him and embraced him. She was happy, very happy, even though she could not control her crying. Now, they were tears of joy. She felt secure for the first time in the last three days.

Raúl held her in his arms, his eyes focused across the room. La China stood at attention with a guilty expression.

Raúl took María Teresa's face into his hands and gently kissed her two cheeks and her two eyes, removing her tears with his lips. Then, very slowly, he brought his lips next to hers. María Teresa responded to his kiss by partially opening her mouth and allowing the tip of his tongue to penetrate her mouth and meet hers. After a short kiss, he pushed María Teresa away, touching her bloody lip. Looking at La China, he asked María Teresa, "Who hit you? Did this woman hit you?"

La China's reply came out before María Teresa had a chance to even open her mouth.

"I didn't hit her Commander. You may ask her again. I didn't hit her."

Raúl kept looking at La China with fiery eyes and said, "Shut up. Don't talk to me again unless I tell you to," and again he asked María Teresa, "Did this woman hit you?"

"No, Raúl, she didn't. I fell and bit my lip. She didn't hit me. Please, take me out of here. I was told that I could go home now. Please, take me out of here. Take me home."

"Of course, my love. I'll drive you home."

"Raúl," started to say María Teresa, "before we go, I must ask you for a favor. Please, would you tell this woman that it is impossible for me to go out with her to the party she invited me to next Friday night. I was explaining to her that you don't like me to go out with anybody except you or my brother."

"Listen, soldier, this is my fiancée. The only person that she goes out with to any party is me and only with me. Is that clear?"

"Yes, very clear," said La China with a look of terror on her face.

"Yes, it is, Commander. Answer properly soldier."

"Yes, it is, Commander," said La China, and continued, "If Commander Mora will allow me, I would like to tell his fiancée that I sincerely apologize for not knowing who she was when I took the liberty of inviting her, and to assure her that this will not happen again."

"That's better, soldier. That's better," and addressing his fiancée, "Come on Mari-Tere, let's go home."

"Wait Raúl, not yet. This woman has my wristwatch and I suspect that she also has my gold and pearl cross which was my mother's."

"What?" yelled Raúl, noticing the two watches on La China's left arm. "Soldier, give me that watch at once," he said, pointing at her wrist. "And if you have her cross in your possession, you'd better produce it right now, because if you don't I'm going to have you searched, and you don't want to know what will happen if I find it on you."

La China did not say a word. With trembling hands, she put the watch on top of the chair, then, reaching for the top left pocket of the olive green shirt, retrieved the gold and pearl cross dangling from the old, long gold chain. She placed the necklace next to the watch. María Teresa took them. La China said in a meek voice. "You must understand, Commander, that I didn't intend to keep those articles of jewelry belonging to your fiancée. But as you know, the Revolution has asked for contributions in gold and jewelry in order to buy arms and airplanes with which we can defend our sacred soil. I was planning to surrender everything removed from the prisoners to the proper authorities at the end of the day. "

"Liar, you were planning to profit from these prisoners, and use the Revolution as a shield for your own material or sexual gains. People like you have no place in this Revolution. Give me your full name, number and the name of your immediate superior."

La China became pale, and as a last resort, she decided to be bold. "Commander, with all due respect, I belong to the State Security, the G-2 branch of the Army, and as you know the regular Army has no jurisdiction over us. Therefore, I'm not obliged to give you any other information but the name of my commanding officer, Captain Ana Marín. "

Raúl became visibly upset, and María Teresa, trying to calm him down said, "Listen Raúl, don't bother," but was interrupted by him.

"Mari-Tere, stay out of this." And then, pointing his finger at La China, he continued, "You'd better pay attention to what I'm about to tell you, soldier. The Revolution has been fought to satisfy the needs of the People of Cuba, to bring to these people the social changes they require for the betterment of mankind as a whole. But the Revolution is not to be used for any personal purposes, and the words of our leader Fidel Castro are not to be misinterpreted by anyone for personal gain." Raúl began raising his voice with every subsequent word. "Do not play politics with me. I was fighting in the mountains when you were scheming from whom you were going to take the next dime. I earned this uniform while they gave you yours. I'm going to teach you a lesson in revolutionary values that you will never forget, because there is one thing that I don't want you to do ever again, and that's to disgrace the name of the Revolution, and its leaders."

He went to the outside door and opened it. He said, "Lieutenant Quinteros, come here on the double."

A man in his mid-thirties, with a moustache and no beard, quickly entered the room. "Yes, Commander. At your command."

"Lieutenant Quinteros, place this soldier under arrest. Take her to my division headquarters and keep a guard with her until I decide what to do with her. Under no circumstances is she to be released unless I say so myself. Contact Captain Ana Marín of the G-2 branch and tell her that I want to see her in my office at eleven hundred hours on the dot and also tell her that I'm holding this no-name soldier from her branch until we discuss the case."

María Teresa was watching the whole scene with amazement when Raúl said to her, "And now, let's go home."

Taking María Teresa by the arm, he escorted her out of the room and through the labyrinth of similar interrogation stations, outside into the back street. Behind them, Lt. Quinteros and two soldiers were escorting La China.

Raúl guided María Teresa to an olive green Oldsmobile. The car used to be one of Batista's Army Intelligence vehicles. It was one of the last of a large fleet of specially-prepared Oldsmobiles that Batista had acquired for the army, as well as for the police, to be used as patrol cars.

María Teresa climbed into the front seat of the car. She opened the window and let the gentle, cool breeze flowing from the nearby ocean caress her face. The air was clean and smelled faintly of iodine. She breathed deeply, filling her lungs with the fresh air. She felt marvelous and safe.

Two jeeps guarded his car, with four soldiers in each jeep. One jeep was standing in front of the car and one behind. The moment the soldiers saw their commander get into his car, they started the engines of their jeeps. Raúl was going to tell the front jeep where to go, when María Teresa interrupted him. "Raúl, please wait a second. We can't leave yet. What about Carlos? I don't know if he's here, but I have a hunch that he might be inside."

He did not answer, but ordered the escorting soldiers to drive around to the front of the theater and stop at the main entrance. A few seconds later, they were standing at the same spot where the bus had dropped her off two days before. Raúl got out of the car and called two of the soldiers from the rear jeep and two of the soldiers from the front jeep.

"Mari-Tere, stay in the car and wait for me. You men," he said addressing two of the soldiers, "will guard her and my car. You will come with me."

A lieutenant saw him at the entrance lobby and, standing at attention, saluted him.

"Lieutenant Ayala, Commander, Sir. What can I do for you, Sir?"

Raúl stopped, looked at him indifferently and said, "I am Commander Mora. Who is in charge here, Comrade?"

"Captain García, Sir. But he's busy at the moment organizing the interrogations on the stage. May I be of assistance to you, Sir?"

"At ease, lieutenant. Do you have a list of the male prisoners here?"

"Yes Sir, I do."

"In that case, tell me if Carlos Aguirrupe is on that list. "

"One moment, Sir." The mulatto officer went to an improvised desk in the form of a plain table standing at one end of the lobby, and came back with a clipboard full of sheets of paper. He was looking through the papers as he approached Raúl.

"Sir, I can't find the name of Carlos Aguirrupe here. He's definitely not on this list."

"Listen, if he was picked up on Monday he must be in here since his permanent address is in Miramar. Please look again. "

"No, I'm sorry to say that he's not on this list. Even if he had been picked up around here, that doesn't necessarily mean that he was brought to this theater. My understanding is that there are other places in the area being used for the same purpose, even though this is obviously the largest. His name doesn't appear on the original list of persons to be picked up in Miramar."

"Well, maybe we've detained him at some other place."

"Do you want me to check a few places by phone, Sir? It'll only take me a couple of minutes. I can see that this prisoner is important to you."

"You're very helpful, Comrade. Thank you very much."

"It's always a pleasure to serve a hero of the Revolution. I recognized your face, Commander Mora, as soon as you walked in. Wait here, Sir, I'll be right back. "

"Thank you again," said Raúl with a smile. The officer came back a few minutes later.

"Good news, Sir. I've found your man. He's at the Rodi Theater on Línea Street in El Vedado. "

"I sincerely appreciate your effort. You are an efficient officer. Keep up the good work, and the Revolution will always recognize your deeds and reward you for them."

A quick salute and Raúl turned around in the direction of the main doors followed by his two soldiers. The lieutenant came rushing behind him and, tapping him on his shoulder, said in a lower voice, "I beg your pardon, Sir. Please excuse me for delaying you, but I heard that you went south in command of the defending troops to repel the imperialist invasion. Could you tell me what happened? "

"Look, Lieutenant, as of now all of this is classified information. Evidently we won the battle, or otherwise I wouldn't be here talking to you now, would I? Unfortunately, I can't tell you much. Soon all will be revealed. However, you have been of assistance to the Revolution, and me, and I suppose that I owe you one. Confidentially, the invasion forces landed as scheduled, but we managed to maintain air superiority at all times and were able to destroy every supply line that they were going to receive. We have taken a great number of prisoners and many lie dead on the beach. The ones that escaped into the adjacent swamps are being hunted down as we speak. We won, Comrade, we won. I can't say any more to you, because I have already told you more than I should have. But you will find out all the details in due time. It won't be long now."

"I know. I understand, Commander. Thank you very much, Sir, and congratulations on your victory. Good luck, Sir."

Raúl approached his car, shouting to his men, "We are going to the Rodi Theater on Línea Street and hurry up."

The front jeep left the curb with tires screeching and the smell of burnt rubber.

María Teresa said with surprise, "What's going on? Where is Carlos?"

Raúl did not remove his hands from the steering wheel nor his eyes from the road in front of him. "Carlos is being detained at the Rodi Theater. I don't know how he got there. We are going to get him out of there now, and then I'll bring both of you to your house. I won't be able to stay with you, because I must go to the Presidential Palace to submit my report to Castro, personally. Wait for me tonight, I don't know exactly when I'll be able to see you, but I'll be there sometime tonight, and we can talk."

"Raúl, what's going on?"

"I'm sorry, Mari-Tere, but I can't tell you now. We'll talk tonight. I don't want you or Carlos out of the house today. I'll explain it to you, later."

The vehicles advanced at great speed towards the tunnel, crossed it onto Línea Street and continued without stopping for traffic lights.

"I'll stay home, Raúl, but you'd better talk to Carlos. You know how he is. I'll wait for you tonight, but please, don't come too late or Concha might never forgive you."

Raúl chuckled.

"Raúl, thank you very much for caring for me and rescuing me today. In all the excitement, I forgot to really thank you. Tell me one thing. How did you find me?"

"I came to the city at four in the morning, and immediately called you at home. I wanted to reassure myself that nothing had happened to you. I knew that a lot of people that could be regarded as potential enemies of the Revolution would be detained. Those plans were laid out months ago. I also knew that you were not an enemy of the Revolution. But the facts that: number one, your father was a Judge of the Supreme Court; number two, your family had and still has money; number three, you live in one of the better sections of the city; and number four, you go to a Catholic University, were reasons enough to make you a suspect. Magda answered the phone and called Concha right away. She told me that you had left against her wishes very early Monday morning to pick up Carlos and she hadn't heard from you since. I didn't know exactly where to look for you. I told Concha not to worry, and to stay home. I also told her that I would look for you and bring you to her as soon as I found you.

"It took me over two hours to find the places in Miramar where the people were being held. The Blanquita was one of them, and since it was the largest one, I decided to try it first. Luckily enough, you were there."

They became silent for a short while. María Teresa was going to say something, but was interrupted by Raúl. "There, two more blocks and we're at the Rodi."

It took only seconds to travel that distance. All three vehicles stopped in unison. Raúl got out of his car first, giving the same orders as before, and he went into the theater, accompanied by two of his faithful soldiers.

The Rodi Theater was a movie house, beautifully designed

and artistically decorated. Built in the mid-fifties, when the big cinemascope screen was common for modern theaters, it was one of the best movie houses in the El Vedado section of the city, spacious and very conveniently located. On that particular day, it had also become a prison.

Raúl came into the entrance hall and asked to see the officer in command at that post. A lieutenant with a dirty uniform smelling of sweat came forward and identified himself. "I'm Lieutenant Rivera. I'm the officer responsible for this place. What do you want?"

"My name is Commander Mora. I'm looking for a prisoner by the name of Carlos Aguirrupe. It's my understanding that he's being detained here. Bring him to me right now."

The officer looked somewhat perplexed but responded quickly, "I'll see if your man is here, Commander."

The shabby-looking man left and went into the theater. There, he yelled at the top of his lungs for Carlos to show himself immediately. He came back with Carlos a couple of steps behind him.

"Is this your man, Commander?"

Raúl did not answer him but directed his first question to Carlos. "Tell me your name," he said.

"Carlos Aguirrupe."

"Do you have any form of identification with you?"

"Yes, Sir, here's my driver's license," and Carlos extended his plastic card to Raúl, who examined the same with attention.

He returned the card to Carlos and said to the officer, "I'm relieving you of the task of guarding this prisoner. From now on, he is mine." Raúl turned sideways to face one of his assistants, "Soldier, escort the prisoner to my car and put him in the rear seat."

Before the soldier had a chance to react, the dirty lieutenant interjected, "Not so fast, Commander. You have no authorization to do this. I don't see any written order here."

Raúl looked at the repulsive officer with a gaze that could

puncture holes in a steel plate. "Lieutenant, I don't need to present you with written orders or consent from anyone. I told you that from now on I'm responsible for this prisoner, and that's all you need to know. Moreover, I would advise you to go to the nearest phone and call your commanding officer and inform him that Commander Raúl Mora took one of your prisoners and released you from your duty of guarding him. What we are going to do with this particular prisoner is no concern of yours. Do you understand me?"

"Yes, Sir, Commander, Sir, I do."

"And furthermore, you can tell your superiors, while you're at it, that if they want to get in touch with me, I can be reached at Fidel Castro's private offices this afternoon."

Carlos remained very still during the entire conversation. His face was serene, as a submissive prisoner's should be. The soldiers, following Raul's next command, took Carlos by his arms and pushed him outside. Raúl left right behind them without looking back.

María Teresa tried to get out of the car to greet her brother when she saw him coming, but Raúl told her to stay inside. Dutifully, the soldier next to her pushed her gently into the car and closed the front door.

Carlos was ordered to climb into the rear seat. Raúl went to the driver's seat and the soldiers to their respective jeeps.

The olive green Oldsmobile made a U-turn at the next intersection of Línea and C Streets, proceeded along Línea Street in the opposite direction towards Miramar.

At the Rodi Theater, the filthy officer sat on a wooden chair next to a table and glanced at the telephone resting on top of it for a few minutes. Then, picking up a pencil from the table, he used the eraser to eliminate the name of Carlos Aguirrupe from the list in front of him. "To hell with everything. This bastard did not exist," he said to himself, and reaching for a bottle of rum, he took a full swallow from it.

In Raul's car, Carlos was the first one to speak. "Hey, Raúl, thanks for everything. That was very nice of you. I owe you one."

"You owe me nothing. We've known each other for years, and you're Mari-Tere's brother. Besides, I'm sure that you may be many things, but I'm positive that you're not a counterrevolutionary and never will be. Believe me, if I had suspected that you could do damage to the Revolution, I would have left you there to rot, Mari-Tere's brother or not."

"Well, brother, or should I say Comrade, you know I love you anyway, Mari-Tere's fiancé or not. So, what's new, dear sister? Were you worried about me? Where I was I just couldn't go to the nearest phone and call you."

María Teresa turned around to face Carlos and said, "Listen, you ass." She was visible mad at her brother for the worries and aggravations that his actions caused her. Raúl laughed as he drove, and María Teresa continued, "I left our house Monday morning to try to come and pick you up from Inés's house, so that we could be together either back at our house or at school. I cared for you and came, knowing that you had no other means of transportation, and suspecting that something was going on, since there were military trucks moving along Fifth Avenue in Miramar, in both directions, very early in the morning. I was stopped at the exit of the tunnel, dragged onto a bus, taken to the Blanquita Theater and have spent three days in terror. And all because of you and your desire to spend the weekend with a woman that has decided to sell herself to a repugnant old man for financial security."

Carlos was mischievous, but he had a lovable disposition and appearance. He loved María Teresa above all else and she knew it.

"I'm sorry, I truly am. I never intended to put you through any kind of ordeal. You shouldn't have come for me. They took me when they came for Inés. I wasn't on their list, but you're right, I was at the wrong place at the wrong time, as usual. As far as Inés is concerned, I can't believe that you could be mad at her, since she is a wonderful woman and I like her. In my own crazy way I also love her a lot. Another man, who by the way is now working with the government in spite of his capitalistic background, supports her economically and spiritually. Two very important functions that wealthy and powerful men well into their early seventies can only perform. I, my dear sister, provide sustenance to her insatiable and gorgeous body. Something that only a man of my age can do properly."

By now Raúl was laughing loudly. Carlos, somehow, always made him laugh.

"Raúl, stop encouraging him. If you believe that all his deeds are funny, and play up to his buffoonery, he will bury us with his jokes." After a couple of minutes, even María Teresa started to smile and after a while she was also laughing loudly, for the first time during the past three days, and it felt good.

"Listen Carlos," said Raúl, "this is serious now. When I drop you at your house with Mari-Tere, I want you to do me a great favor. Stay with her at the house; don't go out. Don't call any of your friends. Don't make any plans for anything like a party, or a dinner or anything. Just stay in the house and wait for my return tonight. Would you do that?"

"Sure, Raúl, you know I will. I'll stay in with Mari-Tere, but in the meantime tell me, what's going on?"

"I really can't tell you now. I know it but I can't say anything at this time and I won't. Trust me and I promise that I'll tell both of you later."

"Mari-Tere, have you noticed," said Carlos, "it is early afternoon and there are almost no cars on the streets, and the few businesses that we have passed are all closed. Isn't that odd?"

"I'm sure that Raúl knows why, and he will tell us tonight as promised."

Raúl tried to change the mood and subject of the conversation by saying, "You said that the other day you were going to pick up Carlos. What car were you driving? And what happened to that car?"

"Now, that you remind me, I was driving the Lincoln. The soldiers and a young officer took it from me when I was arrested. They claimed that the Revolution needed it more than I did and I have no idea what they did with it."

"Bastards," exclaimed Raúl, "I have a hunch as to where they probably sent it. These abuses in the name of the Revolution really burn me up."

"Naughty, naughty, I heard you say 'bastards' when you referred to your comrades in arms, and I have Mari-Tere as a witness."

"Shut up, Carlos, and don't be an ass as your sister said. Be quiet, I'm going to call the military camp on the car radio."

Raúl called the supply headquarters on the two-way radio that was installed underneath the standard car radio. He called several times before getting an answer.

"This is Army Supply Headquarters. Please identify yourself. Over."

"This is Commander Mora, Code number, 51071017, and code word Pandora. Over."

"Please, wait a couple of seconds, Commander," said the voice on the radio, and after a short while he added, "Identification process completed and satisfactory. What can we do for you, Commander Mora? Over."

"Give me the transportation supply officer. Over."

"Hold on, Commander. Over."

"This is Captain Mendoza, the transportation supply officer on duty. How can I be of help to you, Commander Mora? Over."

"Captain, a young officer picked up a black Lincoln limousine on April 17, in the early morning hours, at the El Vedado exit of the Almendares tunnel. I want to know if you have that car. Over."

"This might take some time to find out. May I call you back? Over."

"No, I'm in my car now and will be out of it several times in the next few hours. Go ahead and check it now, as fast as you can. I'll wait. Over."

"Affirmative, Commander. I'll be back with the information as soon as I can. Over and out."

They were driving along Fifth Avenue in Miramar, when the radio came on again.

"This is Captain Mendoza. Are you there, Commander Mora? Over."

"This is Commander Mora. What is the password to reach me today, over."

"The password is Pandora's Happiness and my code is 44406308. Over."

Raúl stopped the car momentarily and spent a few seconds looking in a small, black book full of names and numbers that he took out of his right breast pocket.

"Affirmative. What are your findings, Captain? Over."

"I found the car. It is here. Over."

"Good. I'm formally requesting that car for my personal use. I'll send Captain Albacete under my command to pick it up late this afternoon. Over."

"I'm afraid that it would be impossible to do so, Commander. Over."

"Explain yourself. Over."

"There are papers and forms to be filled out and properly documented. It'll take us at least a couple of days to prepare everything. I'm sure that it will be all right, but why don't you come and pick it up next Friday? Over."

"Because if I wait until Friday, I stand a chance of losing the car. You don't need to do a lot of paperwork with me. The car just goes in and out of your place, and if anybody asks you anything, I will take full responsibility. Just give the car to Captain Albacete today, and I'll go Friday to sign the release form and any other papers that you require. Over."

"You have a point, Commander. Well, I guess it would be all right, since you are the one requesting it. Let me tell you that the car is really a beauty, one of a kind. By the way, may I ask you how you knew it was here today? Over."

"By the same means that I find out everything. Over."

"I see. Could you tell me where you can be reached today? If, by the time your Captain is here, I have any other pertinent questions to ask you, where can I call you? Over."

"You may reach me at Castro's private offices in the Presidential Palace. I'll be there most of the afternoon. Over."

"Enjoy the car, Commander. By the way, I don't think it will be necessary to bother you on Friday. I'll ask your Captain to sign the release in your name. I won't have time to get new government plates, but if you bring it back next week I'll give you the right plates according to your rank. Over."

"It won't be necessary. I won't use the car for official business, but for my personal use, and I don't want to draw any attention to it. Leave the present plates on it. Over."

"As you wish, Commander. Over."

"Thank you, Captain. Over and out."

When they pulled up to María Teresa's house, Carlos said, "Raúl, my friend, they can say whatever they want about you, but I'll always say that you're a good egg, for a communist."

"Carlos, please, don't call me a communist, because I'm not one. And for your information, this isn't a communist revolution either. As Fidel says, this revolution is not red, it is green like our Royal Palm tree, the Cuban national tree, the one appearing on our coat of arms."

"This revolution has no similarity with any national tree, Raúl. On the other hand, it does resemble one of our simple fruits, the watermelon," Carlos said, and then added, "I'll see you tonight and perhaps we can talk some more." Opening the rear car door, he closed it behind him, started walking along the horseshoe shaped driveway and disappeared through the main door to the house.

"What does he mean by a watermelon?" inquired Raúl of María Teresa.

"He meant that it's green on the outside, but red on the inside," she replied.

"The son of a . . ." exclaimed Raúl.

"Don't say it, Raúl. I know that you really don't mean it, and it is only an expression, but don't say it. Remember that my mother is dead."

"I'm sorry. You know that I wouldn't be disrespectful to your mother."

She felt sorry for having cut him off. She leaned over to him and Raúl responded by kissing her on the cheek, since it was daylight, they were on the street, and more importantly, he was in full uniform.

"I shouldn't be kissing you, here and now. Besides, I'm running late. I'll bring you the car later on, when I see you tonight. I'll give you a great big kiss then."

María Teresa left the car. She looked back at Raúl, tenderly, and said, "Thank you, Raúl. Thank you for everything. I'll see you later."

His car took off at great speed. She stayed on the sidewalk until she did not see him any longer. Then, she ran into the house.

A typical house in Miramar during the late fifties.

CHAPTER NINE

Concha was the first one to greet her. Mirta, the cook, who had been with the family for the last twenty-five years and had known María Teresa since her birth, came running to the front door, followed by Magda and Esther, the two younger maids.

María Teresa embraced all of them with equal warmth. Concha was hugged the longest, and she was the first one to speak, "We were all so worried for both of you."

She held María Teresa's head in her hands and kissed her gently on both cheeks, and added, "Especially you, my treasure. I was so worried about you." Noticing the cut on her lip and her torn trousers she added, "What happened to you?"

"It's not important anymore. Don't worry, I'll tell you later. Let me rest for a while. I'm tired and I feel very dirty," María Teresa said.

Carlos was watching the whole scene with interest. "Hey, how about me? Don't I get hugs and kisses also?"

Magda and Esther obliged. It was not customary for household servants to take liberties like that with their employers, but Carlos was special. He was jovial, a practical joker and the type of character who would welcome them with open arms and embrace them fondly.

"Now, all of these kisses have made me very hungry. I don't know about Mari-Tere, but I haven't eaten a decent meal in the last two days. So, what's cooking today, Mirta?" he said.

Mirta was caught off guard by the comment.

"Oh, my God," she said, "both of you must be starving and I have nothing prepared, because I didn't know exactly when you would be coming back home. You know how difficult it is getting any decent food anymore. But, I do remember that there is some skirt steak in the freezer, so let me make you some white rice, with fried eggs and fried plantain bananas, and ropa vieja. It will take about two hours. Time for you people to shower and rest a while. I also have some custard made for dessert in the refrigerator."

"That sounds delicious to me, and I'm sure Mari-Tere will agree. I'm going to take a hot shower and relax a bit. I'll be back by the time the food is ready. Also get some rosé wine from the wine cellar and chill it well." He looked at the two maids standing next to him and said, "Which one of you is coming to brush my back while I'm in the shower?"

Magda and Esther were used to Carlos's suggestive remarks and did not respond. They went into the dining room to fix the table for the late afternoon meal, and then to the kitchen to help Mirta.

Concha said, "My dear, dear Mari-Tere, where have you been for the last few days. I've been very alarmed. Some friends called to warn us that the police and the army were taking prisoners left and right, without any reasons or proper charges. Many people are missing from their homes. On the other hand, the radio, the television and the newspaper have all been very quiet. They're not telling the people anything."

"Not now, Concha. I'm just too tired. I'm going to take a long, hot bath, and then after we eat I will tell you everything I know up to now. Raúl is coming tonight to visit me and maybe I will find out some more from him."

Concha took María Teresa's hand and started to walk to the second floor where the bedrooms were located.

"While you get undressed I'll start to prepare your bath with bubble bath and cologne. It'll be ready in a few minutes."

María Teresa put her watch and necklace in the leather-covered jewelry box that had once been her mother's. The rest of her attire she just threw at the foot of the bed, including her shoes. She slipped on a robe and walked towards her private bathroom. María Teresa submerged most of her body in the relaxing hot water and rested her head on a folded towel. The hot water soothed María Teresa's nerves. The effect of the hot bath began to permeate all of her senses. She closed her eyes and her mind became detached from her surroundings. She felt good. She was once again with her family, her friends and, most importantly, in her home.

The Aguirrupe's estate was larger than the typical house in Miramar, while still maintaining the flavor and Old Spanish architectural lines of the adjacent properties. It had been built in 1935, and remodeled twice after that. The main structure was a two-story house built with concrete walls, concrete floors and a concrete roof. A combination of mahogany and wrought iron adorned the windows and doors, adding to the security of the house. The floors were covered with exquisite white and black marble that came from the quarries at the Isle of Pines, south of La Habana Province. The main staircase was a combination of marble and rich woods leading to a hallway along which were seven huge bedrooms, four of them equipped with private bathrooms.

The house had a huge, covered, horseshoe-shaped entrance that allowed visitors to get into and out of their cars without getting wet during the frequent Cuban rainstorms. The first floor had a big foyer, a living room with fake fireplaces, a formal dining room, a family room, a kitchen and a combination studio/library. The servants' quarters were at the side of the main house with a separate street entrance but also interior doors leading to the pantry area, next to the kitchen. The enormous garage, on the other side of the house, could harbor four automobiles comfortably.

The swimming pool with its adjacent patio and guest cabanas, as well as the tennis courts, had been added in 1952 and 1953. The entire dwelling was air-conditioned.

María Teresa remained in the bathtub for a long time. She then took a warm shower, ending with a blast of cold water. Some of her body still ached, and unfortunately this would last for some time. Her split lip was a little swollen on the inside, but she had no broken bones and no loose teeth. She decided that she felt fine. She felt she could go and try to conquer the world again, after she ate.

When she came into her bedroom, she found that Concha had laid out fresh clothing on top of her bed.

Downstairs in the dining room, the table had been set for two people. Carlos was already seated, sipping rosé wine from a fine baccarat glass, when María Teresa entered and sat down.

They ate in silence, devouring every morsel of the splendid fare, as compared to the meager sustenance they had received the past days.

After the meal, María Teresa and Carlos informed the servants of what they had experienced during the last seventy-two hours. Concha and the other servants sat at the table and listened attentively. They could not believe their ears, except for Concha, who had undergone similar experiences during the Spanish Civil War. María Teresa purposely skipped some of the details, like the incident with La China's and some parts of the interrogation procedure.

Carlos told them of his experiences at the Rodi Theater, which were, to a point, very close to María Teresa's: the same treatment, but with no machine guns on the stage; the same type of food; some sporadic protests and similar beatings given to restore discipline. The only difference was that in Carlos's case the beatings had been selective. They were directed only against those who were shouting or suspected of shouting. In the end, Concha told them about some of her own experiences in Spain, pointing out the similarities and parallels of both situations.

Carlos left the dining room after a small cup of strong Cuban coffee, and lit a cigar. He usually smoked American cigarettes, but they were very scarce in Cuba at the time. He recently had been able to purchase a few packs on the black market and was saving them for special occasions.

With the cigar in his hand, he lay in the hammock that hung next to the pool. He started to rock himself, feeling guilty for all the things that had happened to his sister on his account. She should not have done it. After all, he was twenty-six years old and not a little boy anymore. María Teresa was stubborn and at times charged with the impetus of a raging bull. He knew that, but he also knew that she did it for love. It was true that Carlos was her closest brother. They were barely three years apart, and they had always been the two who had played the most together when they were younger.

The servants went to resume their daily chores and María Teresa remained alone with Concha in the dining room.

"I'm going upstairs to take a nap. It's almost four in the afternoon. I'll be up again around seven. Please, wake me if I'm not up by that time, and tell Mirta to prepare some soup and sandwiches for tonight. How is the food situation?"

"The food situation is getting worse, because of the recent events, whatever they are. You know Mirta, she does wonders on the black market, buying whatever we need for essentials and then some. She also exchanges food with the adjacent houses. But recently, we have not been able to do anything, and therefore we are running low on many things. We could make you some soup for tonight with the meat broth from the skirt steak, maybe some onion soup, but I'm sorry to tell you that we have no cold cuts to make sandwiches. In the freezer, however, we should have some hot dogs, and we could cook those for tonight."

"That sounds delicious. It will do."

"Mari-Tere, why don't you go now and rest like you said. Gain some of your strength back."

With the excitement of being in the safety of her own house,

María Teresa had forgotten the problem that was starting to occur in most Cuban households, and that was to be able to obtain enough food to feed the family properly. It was not the only thing that her memory had forgotten to bring into focus. Two big balls of red and blond fur came running into the dining room. Their attention was concentrated on María Teresa, their one and only master. They were Samson and Delilah, the two Chow-Chow dogs that María Teresa had raised from pups.

She knelt on the floor and hugged them and kissed them. With their tails, in the upward spiral characteristic of their breed, moving from one side to the other frenetically, the dogs showed their approval. Their blue-black tongues licked María Teresa's hands and arms.

"Oh, my God. I forgot about my children. Where were they, Concha?"

"At the kennel, outside the house, when you came in. They huffed and barked when you went into your room, but you were so tired that you probably didn't hear them. I told Magda to bring them over after you finished eating, so you would be able to eat in peace."

"Okay, Chows, that's enough, let's go to bed now."

She ran upstairs with the two dogs pursuing her. As soon as she took off her shoes and lay in the spacious bed, the two dogs went to rest at the foot of the bed. It gave the appearance of two Chinese bears guarding a temple.

María Teresa fell asleep in no time, a sound and deep sleep, the kind that she had not been able to enjoy for some time.

CHAPTER TEN

Carlos and Raúl were two young handsome men, but that was the full extent of their similarities. Raúl was of fair complexion, with hazel eyes and auburn hair and beard. Carlos was of dark complexion, with dark brown eyes, dark brown hair and a clean-shaven face. Raúl was an idealist, with a sense of fairness, honor and duty. He was also a warrior. Carlos was a pragmatist and a playboy, with what some might call a weird sense of humor. He was witty and intelligent, and a lover of ironies and sarcasm. María Teresa loved both of them deeply, each in a different way.

Raúl arrived at nine o'clock. He parked the Lincoln limousine in the driveway, and walked towards the main entrance of the mansion, passing between the two huge, red clay pots that adorned the vestibule in front of the house. These pots, which matched the color of the Spanish roof tiles, were typical in some Cuban houses.

He rang the front door bell. María Teresa knew some seconds before that he had arrived because Samson and Delilah started growling, announcing the presence of someone who was not a regular member of the household, and was definitely not to their liking. Raúl was very fond of the dogs, but Chow-Chows are innately aloof, independent and one-person dogs with a deep sense of their own territory. Samson and Delilah only tolerated the people that lived in the house. Anyone else was a stranger, even if he or she visited the house frequently, as Raúl did.

Esther opened the door and told Raúl that María Teresa and Carlos were waiting for him in the studio room. María Teresa had asked Concha not to remain in the room that evening. She sensed that Raúl might want to say something confidential. Concha had agreed since Carlos would be with them. She had also told Concha to make sure that the cook and the maids retired to their quarters early that night. She wanted to be left alone with Carlos and Raúl.

The studio was a beautifully decorated room with its white marble floor, in contrast to the dark mahogany bookcases covering most of the wall space. There was an ample wooden desk at one end of the room. Leather chairs and sofas provided comfortable seating arrangements toward the front end of the desk. At one side, there was a rosewood chess table, on top of which ivory carved, Chinese-style chess figures proudly stood. On the other side of the room stood a bar with a black marble countertop, brass railings, brass foot stand, and brass and leather stools that could accommodate up to six persons. The shelving space behind the bar contained all kind of spirits, liqueurs and wines. Underneath, a refrigerator kept the beer, champagne and sparkling wines well chilled. Next to it, an ice machine was constantly producing ice cubes. A mirror, which ran the full length of the bar and covered the wall over which the crystal shelving was hung, gave an illusion of amplitude to the enclosed corner. Other pertinent gadgets and appliances were there, ready to satisfy the demands of any customer.

When Raúl entered the room through the massive double wooden doors, María Teresa was sitting at her father's desk with a glass of No. 43 liqueur in her hand. Carlos was behind the bar preparing a Golden Cadillac—a mixture of Galiano, brandy and milk, shaken in a blender with crushed ice—for himself, and

Concha was standing up ready to depart with the two Chows, who were still huffing and growling.

"Good evening to all of you," Raúl said.

"Hello, Raúl," Carlos replied.

"Good evening, my love," said María Teresa, and she stood up to meet Raúl halfway across the room and gave him a short kiss.

"Good evening, Commander," said Concha, and after that she disappeared with the dogs. María Teresa sat on one of the sofas and invited Raúl to come and sit beside her, which he did. Carlos finished making his drink and poured it into a large cocktail glass. Then he went to rinse the blender.

"Raúl, how about something to drink? The Revolution is not allowing us to be too generous with our food anymore. But drinks we do have galore. At this rate, it will be at least another year before our drinking supplies are somewhat depleted. So what is your pleasure?"

"Very funny, Carlos, as usual. Give me some aged Cuban rum on the rocks."

"Okay, Old Bacardi Special Vintage coming up. You'd better enjoy this one. Bacardi made it before Castro took the business from its rightful owners. The people running the breweries and distilleries nowadays may know quite a bit about revolutions and politics; however, they don't know how to make a decent bottle of beer or rum."

"You mean, when Castro gave it back to its rightful owners, the People of Cuba. And as far as quality is concerned, you have to realize that traitors with the know-how abandoned this island, and those who remained are still learning. Give me the rum and shut up, Carlos, for you know nothing of what you speak."

"Oh, stop it. Stop it, both of you. Stop it right now," said María Teresa with visible frustration. "What is the matter with both of you? Carlos, bring the rum, sit down and be quiet. Let Raúl talk. He came to tell us something and not to discuss foolish things with you."

Carlos and Raúl were somewhat startled at María Teresa's outburst, and decided not to continue with the argument. Carlos came from behind the bar and gave the glass full of ice cubes and golden rum to Raúl.

"What's happened in the past few days?" inquired María Teresa.

"There has been an attempt to invade the island using Cuban counterrevolutionaries. We met them at the beach and won the battle. The so-called invasion is over. I was in command of the Free Cuban Armed Forces who repelled the invaders. The United States, who backed the invasion with planning and military support, is now trying to see how they can disavow any knowledge of it. Castro is pressing them, through diplomatic channels, to admit their complicity. It is a day of triumph. Castro told me so himself. He said, 'Commander Mora, your name will be recorded in the annals of history as the military genius who defeated the imperialist invasion. You are the bastion of the Revolution and a true hero. It is a day of rejoicing for you and your men, for all the Cubans on this island and for all the freedom-seeking and peace-loving revolutionaries throughout Central and South America, and the rest of the world.'"

"Is that all?" said María Teresa.

"What else do you want to know?"

"The details, Raúl, the details. What really happened? You're giving us a compendium of the official version that will appear in the Gramma Newspaper probably tomorrow. Please, don't give me a military communiqué, because I think that I deserve better."

Carlos sat and sipped his drink in silence.

"I'm sorry, Mari-Tere, I guess it sounded like a soldierly report. Well, let's see, I think I'd better start at the beginning. But before I do so, I must ask you to keep in strict confidence what I'm about to tell you. Is that clearly understood?"

María Teresa and Carlos both answered affirmatively.

"Intelligence told us about the invasion several months ago.

You see, not every Cuban in Miami is anti-Castro. There are some Cubans like your family that moved there to salvage whatever is left of their fortunes. They feel that they will do better by staying abroad. They aren't politically inclined, and all they want to do is to be able to work and increase their capital in a land that still allows them to exploit the working class. We have been able to place some of our agents amidst the Cubans counterrevolutionaries, whose main desire is to overcome the present government of Cuba, and therefore the first true government representative of its people since the inception of the Republic back in 1902. And also we have been able to buy out some of those Cuban patriots in exile. Between our own agents and the ones that we have bought along the way, we have managed to establish a spy ring that has intercepted information from the very leaders of the counterrevolutionary headquarters. Through these agents we have befriended CIA agents and, consequently, we knew that the CIA had developed invasion plans during the latter part of the Eisenhower administration. Now Kennedy had given his approval to the plan and it was being carried out, full speed ahead. Cubans were trained under American military advisors in places like Florida and Guatemala. We also knew that Somoza had agreed to allow Nicaragua to become an attack base.

"The CIA's plan was indeed very clever. They initiated two air raids over Cuban Air Force landing fields, with the purpose of destroying our airplanes while they were sitting ducks on the ground. The success or failure of the invasion plan actually hinged on that achievement. When our planes were destroyed on the ground, they planned to launch an invasion force whose main objective would be to occupy Cuban soil, let's say a beachhead, and secure it for 48 hours. Their chosen landing point was Playa Girón in the Bay of Pigs, next to the Zapata swamps.

"As you can see, without air cover or a suitable navy, the only way that we could counterattack and try to repel the invasion would be on land. Now, because of the nearby swamps, there is only one road tying the mainland with the beach. If they could succeed in either mining or occupying that road, our troops wouldn't be able to mount a serious attack force, since everything that we could deploy in doing so had to reach them via this route. Moreover, with just sporadic air raids on that road and with their rear end protected by the vast sea behind them, they could have easily maintained a beach head that would allow them to stay in that territory for as long as they would have wanted to.

"In order to insure that no attack would come from the ocean, the U.S. Navy only needed to park one aircraft carrier a few miles from the shore. Then, after a period of time, the Cubans on the beach would have established another government on Cuban soil. The United States would've recognized them as the legitimate Cuban government, and as such, the invasion force would have enjoyed the same privileges as any national government, including diplomatic relationships with a foreign country. This would have included the right to sign treaties between them. Obviously a military aid treaty would have been requested by the new government and granted by the super power. After that, the United States would have had the perfect and legal excuse to invade the island without international embarrassment.

"At the same time, Commando groups trained in Florida under CIA and Special Forces supervisory personnel would have landed at several spots on the island with the mission of sabotaging power plants and information bases to disrupt lines of communication throughout Cuba. The invaders also expected to be supported by their friends on the island.

"Yes, as I said, a really clever plan indeed. And yet, in their arrogance and stupidity, they never conceived or thought that we knew about it. We knew as much as the Cubans in the streets of Miami knew, and then some. It's true, we didn't know the exact location of the landing, and that's why we made plans for various possibilities. It's also true that we didn't know when, but the air raids that were going to take place before the invasion would forewarn us, trigger the alarm system, and put us on full alert.

"The first air raid occurred last Saturday at dusk. Cuban pilots dressed in fake Cuban Air Force uniforms, departing from Nicaragua and flying B-17, World War II aircraft, carried it out. The planes were painted like our own, with the same insignias and labels. The plan was to pass as defecting Cuban Air Force pilots when they landed in Florida, because the long trip would have consumed all the gasoline they had in their tanks, and they only had enough to make a couple of bombing passes over our airfields, and then continue to the Florida peninsula. The first strike really caught us by surprise, and they managed to destroy most of our airplanes that were on the ground. We were able to save two training jets and two of the British jets that Batista had purchased toward the end of his regime, when the Americans would not sell any more weapons to him.

"I admit that one or two more air raids would have obliterated our air force and, if that had happened, we would have been fighting in the streets by now. But after the first air raid, the Russians accused the United States at the Security Council of the United Nations of being the perpetrators of the attack. Stevenson, the American ambassador, tried to deny everything in such convincing terms that we suspect he might not have been told by his own government of the plans. Nevertheless, with the Soviet Union backing us, we exerted enough diplomatic pressure to make the United States cancel the other attacks. That fact, from a military point of view, was their biggest and first mistake. The second was to proceed with the invasion as originally planned, but now without proper air cover. Maybe they thought that the presence of their aircraft carrier in the nearby waters would constitute enough of a deterrent.

"We have been on red alert since last Saturday. That's why I told you, Mari-Tere, that I was going to be occupied with military exercises for a while.

"The invasion force landed on Playa Girón in the early

morning hours of April 17th. We left for the area as soon as we had been told of the landing. Trucks carrying the foot soldiers, jeeps with officers and two small helicopters for reconnaissance were the first units to be mobilized, followed by the slower tank column. I was in the first jeep. Some of the enemy ships were at the landing points trying to land supplies to the invaders on the beach. Our jets destroyed all of the supply ships, and their B-17 planes were no match for our faster aircraft. They were blown out of the sky during the first hours of the battle. The ships were all sunk without being able to unload their cargo of tanks, military vehicles and ammunition. With air superiority, we began to push them back towards the sea. They took defensive positions at several points on the beach and the adjacent swamps, but without the supplies they couldn't last too long. Two U.S. Navy jets from the nearby carrier flew twice over the beach. They were never engaged in battle. They only flew overhead to ascertain the progress of the troops on the beach. They never bothered us and we never bothered them either. We intercepted some of the radio communications between the leaders of the invasion troops and the U.S. aircraft carrier. For all practical purposes it was a one-way communication. The invaders were demanding, then pleading and finally begging for help and military assistance. The commanders on the carrier always had the same answer. I don't remember the exact words, but in essence they told them that they had no orders to comply with their request, that they were on their own, and that they wished them good luck. The forces on the beach kept calling on the radio for help and supplies. At one point, they were crying on the radio for the aid that would not come.

"By Tuesday evening, it was all over. As I returned to La Habana, I left quite a number of them lying dead on the sand. The full count of their casualties is unknown as of now, but I will find out soon. There are some who fled into the swamps and are being chased by our men. The final operation will not take long, and I expect the balance of my troops to come back to headquarters by the end of the week. If anyone remains alive, I would not give him too much of a chance for survival. Between the quicksand and the alligators, I doubt that they would live long. The others were taken prisoner. They are being counted and interrogated. Castro plans to parade them next week so that everybody can see the kind of swine that attempted to take control of this island. They called themselves the 2506 Brigade. By the way, there were several Villanueva alumni among them. I recognized the names and some of the faces. What we finally will do with them has not been decided yet.

"And talking about Villanueva, don't go there anymore. Our forces have occupied the university and all the priests are being kept under surveillance at the auditorium, along with some students and professors that were in the school when we took it over. The priests will be expelled from the country in the near future. The school will be closed forever and another center of political dissension will cease to exist. One less worry for the Revolution. I'm sure that the government will find some good use for the buildings eventually.

"So don't you worry about final exams next month because there will be none. I'm sorry for you, Mari-Tere, because La Habana University still will not offer mechanical engineering, but maybe they will allow you to transfer your credits to another branch of engineering. In any event, at my side, as my wife, you are not going to need a college degree.

"And finally, I will tell you that the United States is trying desperately to save face, when in reality they are in it up to their necks. It's like being immersed in a pool of shit up to their chins, and Fidel is making waves and the Americans have no choice but to swallow bit after bit. It will probably cost Kennedy his reelection three years from now, if he doesn't find himself impeached in the process."

"Oh my dear God! Then all is lost! Now and forever," said Carlos very seriously. "I think that I'm going to make myself another cocktail. A triple one this time. Anyone care for another drink?"

"Yes, bring me another rum. What do you mean when you say that everything is lost? We won, Carlos, can't you see that?"

"My dear friend, Raúl," said Carlos as he was walking towards the bar. "I like you a lot. In spite of your naïveté in comprehending what is really at stake here."

"Hold on a second. I'm not naïve, and I don't know what are you getting at."

Carlos did not answer immediately. He served the next round of drinks and brought one to Raúl. After sitting down again in the other sofa across from Raúl, he looked at him and said, "I've listened to you without interrupting a single time. Please, have the same courtesy with me and allow me to finish before you say anything. I'm not into politics. In reality, only two things motivate my existence: money and women, and in that order, since you need the former in order to have the time to procure the latter. The only other reason that I'm breathing is sitting right next to you on that sofa. The rest of the world and their activities interest me up to a point.

"However, not being interested in politics does not mean that I must be blind or impervious to the events shaping this world in which we live. Let us face the truth. The truth is, we are all responsible for kicking Batista out of the presidency.

"My brother José María and your brother Manuel were responsible when they gave their lives trying to kill Batista. You were responsible when you went to the mountains to fight for your brother's beliefs. I was responsible, because I did nothing about it."

"Come on. Batista was not good and you know it," interrupted Raúl.

"Please, let me finish," said Carlos.

"Raúl, let him say whatever is on his mind," interjected María Teresa.

"Thank you, Mari-Tere," said Carlos and he continued, "Let's agree for a moment on the overall principle that Batista was not good for Cuba. One could argue against this point with very intelligent and valid reasoning, only to lose the argument because of the stigma attached to the coup d'état of March 10, 1952 when Batista took over the government. But, let's agree that his government and his army were corrupt to the core. Nevertheless, he represented the only legitimate government on the island. Because you know as well as I do that in 1954 Batista gave free elections, and although he was supposed to be hated by the people of Cuba, the truth is that he won fair and square, when his opposing candidate renounced his candidacy the very day before the election. That candidate did that because he knew damn well that he didn't have a chance of winning against Batista. Batista should have been ousted then, by political means, by the electoral vote. My father was right on that point. Batista's political party should've been voted out of office when he offered the next free elections in 1958, after the customary four year term. All of this could have happened in accordance with the Cuban Constitution of 1940. Do you remember that this was the election that Castro opposed so violently because it didn't serve his own purposes? Well, that was the election in which I didn't vote, because I considered myself above the filthy politics, and because I was afraid to be killed by rebels just like you, while waiting in line for my turn to cast my vote. That event, along with others that followed, paved the way for Castro's free ride into power.

"So, we can concur on the point that we all got rid of Batista, and, in his place, we got Fidel Castro, and with him a worse form of tyranny and repression. You know what I think? I think that if we were to compare Batista with Castro, we might reach the conclusion that on the one hand we have Batista, who is like a low ranking angel, and on the other hand we have Castro, who is an abominable demon of the worst class.

"In this world that we live in everything is relative. Batista used the island as his own and, no doubt, he profited personally from its riches. And yet, it is also true that at the same time he expanded our economy to provide us with the most abundant wealth that we had ever experienced. During the last eight years, our rate of economic growth surpassed even the wildest expectations. This was not done at the expense of the People of Cuba. That is a lot of bullshit communist propaganda, and you know it, because you were in the countryside. You were next to the peasants. You saw how they lived and you saw it with your own eyes.

"Sure enough, we had and still have poor people on this island. What country doesn't? But in 1958, before Castro came into power, we enjoyed the highest per capita income in North, Central and South America, after the United States. Higher than Canada, mind you. The Cuban peso was equal to the mighty American dollar. Can you name another country where this happened? I'm sure you can't.

"Castro, in contrast, is destroying the entire economy of the island. Whether he himself denies it now or might admit it later, the truth is that he is serving the whole island, on a silver platter, to the Soviets. Now, you may ask, and why to Russia? We have nothing in common with the goddamned Bolsheviks, neither traditionally, nor philosophically.

"To be honest with you, Raúl, I would've liked the invasion forces to have won, and kicked Castro's ass all the way to Siberia, where it belongs. I would never have wished you any harm, Raúl, you know that. But without Castro, maybe this country of ours could find a path to democracy again, with happiness for everyone. With Castro in power and in all his glory, this dream becomes impossible. That is why I said that all is lost now, and probably forever."

Raul's face was matching the color of his beard. He stood up, and advancing toward Carlos, said, "Carlos, for the sake of our friendship I must inform you that you are stressing it beyond the breaking point. For Mari-Tere's sake, I'm going to pretend that this conversation never took place. I have not heard anything but if, by any chance, you do one iota of activity against the Revolution, I'll personally come for you, apprehend you and leave you in jail to rot with the rats."

Changing his mood completely, Carlos rebutted, "Hey, what is going on, brother? This is the second time that you have threatened me today. Are those the latest orders from the Party? When you can't argue intelligently with your friend, then menace him with jail? Come on, relax, sit down and drink your capitalistic rum."

"No, the Party does not give me any orders. However, this is the latest one from the Revolution." With one swift motion of his hand, Raúl tossed the contents of the glass of rum at Carlos's face. The rum along with the ice cubes splashed on his light brownish skin and came down, staining the pink sweater that Carlos was wearing. María Teresa moved between the two men.

She looked at Raúl intensely and gravely said to him, "There was no need for that gesture. I think that you owe an apology to Carlos." She then turned to Carlos and continued, "Carlos, after Raúl apologizes, I want you to leave this room. I want to talk to Raúl in private."

"I will not apologize to any worm," said Raúl.

Before María Teresa had a chance to say something to Raúl, Carlos covered her lips gently with one hand. Then he took some of the droplets of rum from his cheek with one of his other hand's fingers and licked it with his tongue.

"You know, this is really an excellent rum. Thank you, Raúl. You did not have to go to that extreme to let me try it. Well, anyway, I needed another shower before going to bed. I bid both of you a very good night." And as he was walking away in the direction of the doors, he said to Raúl, "If you were expecting me to challenge you to a duel or a fist fight, I'm sorry to have disappointed you. Again, I love you too much. In spite of everything you said and did tonight I cannot harbor violence in my heart. I only hope you understand someday. Good night." And he disappeared from view.

María Teresa took Raul's hand and pulled him to the sofa next to her. She held his hand in hers and started caressing it with gentle strokes. Then she said, "Raúl, why didn't you apologize to Carlos?"

"Because your brother has revealed himself as an apparent enemy of the Revolution, and I don't wish to apologize to that kind of person."

"Raúl, Carlos isn't your enemy. He isn't the enemy of any Revolution either. You know that he would not do anything to hurt anybody, especially you. All he was doing was stating an opinion. I believe that everybody is entitled to have their opinions, and express them in any place. Especially in his own house. Don't you think?"

"Mari-Tere, please don't start confusing the issue. The issue here is that he voiced his feelings against the Government, the Revolution, and Fidel Castro. When he said that Fidel was selling Cuba to the Soviets, he sounded just like the echo of the imperialist propaganda. That isn't true and you know it."

"Raúl, I wish you could hear yourself. You said that the issue is that he voiced his feelings against your Revolution, and I say, so what? Are we not in a free country? Does your Revolution aim to establish a free government, or does it want to establish some form of totalitarian regime?

"You know, one of the differences that I'm noting between Batista and Castro is that Batista never forced anyone to see things his way and never imposed his views on anybody. In other words, you were free to have a different opinion.

"Now, under Castro, you may be able to think in opposition to his goals. But those thoughts cannot be expressed either in public, or in private. Because the so-called Revolution for the establishment of the freest society in the world is going to follow you wherever you may go and effect whatever pressures they deem necessary, just to guarantee that in the end you will think exactly as they want you to think. And you start living the life of a zombie. Let's face it, anybody who does not comply with your way of thinking is an enemy of the people, is he not?"

"No, everybody who is against the Revolution is an enemy of the people."

"Ah! But you are the Revolution, Raúl, and you think and

react at most times like the Revolution wants you to. Ergo, anybody who is against you, is against the Revolution, and hence an enemy of the people. Is he not?"

"Mari-Tere, you're trying to entrap me again. Stop it."

"I'm not trying to make you mad, my love, I'm just trying to see if you realize the fact that you are being used by people who are filling your head with fallacies."

"Fallacies! What fallacies?"

"For example, Raúl, you claim to know for a fact that Castro is not giving Cuba to the Soviets. In order to believe that with such assurance, you choose to ignore other verifiable pieces of information. In April of 1948, the Eighth Conference of the Organization of American States was going to open its doors in Colombia, and to begin its meetings with the main purpose of recognizing and strengthening that body for its future fight against the menace of international communism and its imperialistic ideology. Then, the Soviet Embassy in La Habana recruited a group of students to be sent to Bogota to create an atmosphere of chaos and to disrupt the meetings.

"Among them was Fidel Castro. True or false? The others were Enrique Ovares, student of the School of Architecture and President of the Student Federation, Rafael del Pino and Alfredo Guevara, the senior member of the communist cell within La Habana University and the contact with Gomer Bashirov, Cultural Attaché of the Soviet Embassy and a member of the KGB. All four went to Colombia well-armed, and with lots of money. Later on, they participated in the revolt that killed the Colombian political activist Jorge Eliecer Gaitan, and almost toppled the existing government of that nation.

"You must remember Father John Kelly, the President of Villanueva University, warning us at the university a few years ago about the strong possibility that Castro was a communist. You know that Father Kelly is a learned man and has nothing to gain by lying to us. While Castro, by lying now and showing his true colors later, can definitely gain the precious time needed to ensure the success of the Revolution, and to have the necessary control of the masses.

"I know you are aware that his brother Raúl Castro was educated in countries behind the Iron Curtain. That is extremely unusual for a Cuban. You should know also that his other lackey, the infamous Ché Guevara, is internationally well-known as a communist militant. And, isn't it a fact that General Bayo, who trained Castro and his original guerillas in Mexico, is also a well-known communist from the Spanish Civil War?

"I'm sure that you must know that Castro is reestablishing diplomatic relations with The Soviet Union, which had been non-existent since the Korean War. Also, that he personally received Anastas Mikoyan when he came here, and you must have listened to Castro whenever he decided to give one of his classic four to five hours long speeches. He always takes pleasure denouncing the Yankee imperialists as the enemies of the Revolution in Cuba. On the other side of the coin, you do choose to claim, implicitly, that the United States does have the imperialist desire to thrust itself upon people and territories, and to occupy them forever. That is something that can be easily, categorically and historically disproved.

"At the same time you claim that the communists, who have enslaved, tortured and killed millions and millions of people in their efforts to impose their atheistic ideology, have no imperialistic wishes whatsoever. Do you see, now, why it is so hard for me to understand you?"

"Mari-Tere, listen, I came here tonight to bring you the car. I came to see you, and to tell you about my triumphs, so that you could rejoice with me in my revolutionary endeavors for the betterment of mankind. I don't want to argue with you, but I must tell you that I will not tolerate either you or Carlos making fun of this government and its accomplishments."

"Raúl, believe me, I'm very glad that you could come tonight. I wanted to see you and I wanted to hear what happened in the past few days. Mainly because I knew that you wouldn't lie to me. Now, bear in mind that I'm not making fun of anything. I only want to help you understand, so that you can see what these people are doing to your way of thinking. I love you, Raúl."

He removed his hand from hers and was showing visible signs of anger on his face. "No, I don't believe that you love me. If you did, you would love the Revolution as I do. You know, I sometimes think that you only love your money and class status."

María Teresa paused for a minute before responding to his last remark. She was getting frustrated with his attitude, but managed to remain calm, as she said, "You know, Raúl, that statement really hurt. It disappoints me more coming from you, because I thought that by now you would know me better. Several times in the past few days I've been called a filthy rich bitch. Apparently it is a cliché of the Revolution. Are you going to call me that also?"

"Mari-Tere, I'm sorry for whatever they did to you. But only a month ago, maybe two weeks ago, you were not like this. We have never argued like this. You have never said the things that you have told me tonight. What the hell did they do to you to make you behave like this?"

"Do you want to know, Raúl? Because I must confess that I was not planning to tell you anything, mainly to spare you the pain and the consequences of your reaction. Still, if you insist on knowing about these events, I will tell you.

"I was stopped and searched without probable cause by a man, one of your army officers, who touched me all over, in front of everybody. When I merely offered some resistance to that kind of treatment, I was kicked, dragged through the street and thrown into a bus like a piece of meat. I was taken to the place where you found me. For the next three days I was detained there against my will. The fact that I was innocent bore no significance whatsoever. I was forced to go to the toilet in front of a woman who admired my body, with lust in her eyes. I was search by that lesbian, who took pleasure in inserting her dirty fingers into every possible cavity and lustfully touched every inch of my body. I was forced to appear completely naked in front of a panel of men who asked all kinds of questions. I was beaten with a closed fist and slapped with an open hand for giving an answer they did not want to hear. I still have the marks on my body that only modesty keeps me from showing you, so you'd better take my word for it, because it is the truth. I was not properly fed in all that time, which in retrospect was the most insignificant detail of the entire ordeal. I witnessed men being beaten half to death, merely because they were saying 'Cuba yes, communism no.' I felt terror for the first time in my life. I felt terror for over fifty consecutive hours, and that is, my dear Raúl, the result of your Revolution."

"No, you are mistaken. Excesses occur everywhere. In reality, we are fighting for the well-being of everyone. It's pitiful that some people might have to suffer a little bit in the meantime. I repeat I'm truly sorry for what happened to you, and I will take care of that lesbian, personally. In the end, the majority will benefit from the changes that we have to make."

"I don't think that you understand. Don't be a naïve fool, Raúl. The ends never justify the means."

"So now, all of a sudden, I'm also a fool. What else, Mari-Tere? What else do you think I am?"

"You are a visionary, a castle builder with utopian ideas. You have to understand that the state of political and social perfection that you are seeking does not exist in reality. It was a figment of the imagination of Sir Thomas More, and that is all. It cannot exist, because man himself is not a perfect being."

"Well, yes, I guess that you are right. I'm a dreamer, a castle builder. I'm going to make my dream come true and I'm going to build my castle. The only problem is that, as I see it now, you will have no place in either of them."

"I'd love to share your glory with you, Raúl, such as we discussed it some years ago. Now, if your goals have changed and your present objectives are to create a race of human robots, dominated and directed by imperfect, devilish creatures, then I must agree with you, and admit that you are one hundred percent right. I shall have no place in your life under those circumstances, because I don't want to belong to the robot race and refuse to be a part of the programmers."

Raúl stood up from the sofa and started to walk towards the thick wooden doors. María Teresa followed him in silence. When he opened the door and went into the hallway leading to the nearby foyer, he paused and said, "For a moment, I really thought that you and I were above all of this. But since I'm a dreamer, I was probably dreaming again."

"No, Raúl, don't leave sad. Our love shouldn't end like this. I probably said many stupid things tonight. I was tired and frustrated by the impotence of my position during these past days. If I have offended you in any way, please, forgive me, for I'm truly sorry. I love you, Raúl. I love you very much. You know that I'm yours."

She put her arms around his neck and closed her eyes. She wanted to kiss him, but his hands grabbed hers and pushed her away from him. He moved rapidly to the front door, and just before he opened it, he turned around to face María Teresa standing in the middle of the foyer. He threw his ring at her and said, "There, you keep the engagement ring as a memento of this fool. I shall keep my heart."

María Teresa almost emitted a laugh, but managed only to say, "Your heart, Raúl? It's not yours any longer. Maybe you don't know it yet, but Fidel Castro has it."

Raúl slammed the door behind him and walked through the front patio in the direction of his own car, where a chauffeur was dutifully waiting.

María Teresa bent down to pick up the ring, switched off the lights and started to climb the stairs, very slowly, a step at a time.

Love shall conquer in the end. She was taught to believe that, at one time in her life. She had felt that she could have persuaded Raúl to see the light and the truth in the name of their love for each other. Unfortunately, Raúl had changed lately. He appeared to have been possessed by some demon, which was slowly poisoning his intellect and spirit, thus brainwashing him.

In blatant opposition to that evil force was her love and her reasoning. Somehow, she was losing the battle, and maybe the whole war. Tears appeared in her weary eyes. This is the last time that someone will make me cry today, she thought.

END OF BOOK ONE

BOOK TWO

*Universidad Católica De
Santo Tomás de Villanueva*

CHAPTER ONE

The year was 1956. The month was June. It was a magnificent summer Sunday, and the guests were starting to congregate in the patio adjacent to the pool of Don Francisco's house, to partake in the big party that would surely last into the early hours of the following day. The occasion was María Teresa's graduation from high school.

It had been a very happy day for her. She had graduated the first in her class, with the best and highest academic record in the annals of the American Dominican school. The honor of delivering the valedictory address to the graduating class was hers. She had prepared an essay on individual human rights and values, with poetic overtones, that was recited beautifully, thus receiving a proud nod of approval from her father and a well-deserved standing ovation from her peers and faculty.

The patio had been exquisitely adorned with white, wrought iron tables, red tablecloths and gold colored napkins. The orchestra that was hired for the affair started to play soft and harmonious Cuban bolero-type music. The servants circulated among the early guests, offering all kinds of hot and cold appetizers that were served with glasses of very chilled and bubbling Spanish hard cider. An open bar at the end of the patio, near the orchestra, also prepared delightful Caribbean concoctions, such as frozen daiquiris, mojitos and Cuba Libres. The list of guests included the Assistant to the Archbishop of La Habana who had presided over the graduation ceremonies, several nuns from the school, and the Minister of Justice and the Minister of Education, both of whom were old friends of Don Francisco's. There were also five other members of the Supreme Court, prominent professionals and businessmen, as well as some close friends of María Teresa and her brothers'.

Sister Beth was the first nun to embrace her. "Mari-Tere, congratulations. That was a beautiful speech at school. We are all very proud of you."

"Thank you, Sister," said María Teresa, returning the embrace and kissing the nun's cheeks, "my dear and beloved Latin and history teacher. Should I say, carpe diem?"

"Yes, well said. I shall enjoy the present day."

The nuns proceeded to congratulate Don Francisco and other members of the family, who were, more or less, in line, forming a welcoming committee for the arriving visitors. Their presence had been requested between two and three in the afternoon, but they started arriving between three and four. In accordance with typical Cuban etiquette, it was considered impolite to enter the host's dwelling at the time specified on the invitation.

By early evening, everybody was having an extremely good time. Some young couples were dancing to the tune of the latest cha-cha-cha. The dancing music intermixed some danzones and boleros for the older generation, with some sones, guarachas and mambos for the younger group. Some Spanish pasodobles, waltzes, sambas and tangos were played from time to time also. Fewer people, but usually people who knew how to dance very well, danced them.

Another view of a typical house in Miramar in 1956.

Enough alcohol had already been consumed to remove any inhibitions from shy or spiritless guests. Some boys, mostly friends of Carlos's, were asking María Teresa to dance with them. She did not have a chance to sit down for almost two consecutive hours. She was happy, but also tired, since many of the dances and especially the tango were quite demanding. Concha watched her from a corner of the patio with joy in her heart.

A few minutes before seven o'clock, the orchestra took a well-deserved break, and Don Francisco took the opportunity to announce that dinner would be served momentarily, kindly requesting everybody to occupy their seats. At each place, there was fine bone china along with elegant silverware, baccarat goblets and wineglasses, and on each table a floral centerpiece containing a combination of red and gold carnations. The Assistant to the Archbishop of La Habana recited the benediction over the food giving proper thanks to the Lord. A famous restaurant in La Habana, called El Centro Vasco, had catered the dinner and Juanito, its main chef, had excelled in the preparation of the delightful dishes. Toward the end of the dinner, while dessert and champagne were being served, Don Francisco stood up and asked respectfully for everybody's attention.

"Monsignor Lasaga, respected American Dominican nuns, eminent Ministers of Justice and Education, honorable colleagues in the Supreme Court, distinguished guests and friends, members of my family, ladies and gentlemen, on behalf of my family, and especially my daughter, in whose honor we are congregated here today to celebrate her scholastic achievements, I would like to express our gratitude for your presence. Your company is welcome in this house. We thank you so much for coming and partaking in our joy. Your generosity has been revealed in the multitude of presents that you have sent to my daughter or brought to her today. Of course, I'm sure that you understand that there was no need for you to do so. However, your personal signs of affection are greatly appreciated.

"I, for one, have been waiting until now to ask you to join me in giving María Teresa the toast that she deserves, and a gift that I know she has been wanting for a long time. Now the gift will be first."

With the cue, Jaime came into the patio holding both a male and a female Chow-Chow puppy, one in each hand. The female had a pink bow around her neck and the male a blue one. María Teresa did not wait for Jaime to reach the main table where she was seated. She ran towards them and, grabbing them in her arms, she started to kiss them and with them she went to face her father. To him, she gave a bigger kiss. Then she went back to her seat, next to the Assistant to the Archbishop, and placed the puppies on her lap. They were very playful and were constantly biting her hands, her arms, or biting each other.

The Assistant to the Archbishop said, "They are indeed very cute. Enjoy them Mari-Tere. The male looks like the lion that Samson killed."

"That's perfect, Monsignor Lasaga. You just gave me a great idea. I will name them Samson and Delilah."

"Very good, Mari-Tere. I'm honored to have been the provider of the idea for their names. If that's so, then I'd advise you never to cut his hair, and he will grow to be the judge and the king that will defend you against all evil."

In the meantime, Don Francisco continued, "And now, my friends, the toast. I will ask you to please stand up and join me, glass in hand. To María Teresa, whose dedication and labor have culminated in casting the first cornerstone of her intellectual base. For being the wonderful person and the lovely daughter that you are, we all here congratulate you on this day, and merrily drink to your health and wish that you reach the goals that your heart desires."

Don Francisco drank his glass of champagne with a chorus of "here, here" from all the guests. María Teresa went to her father and kissed him again and again, still holding the dogs in her arms. Delilah took the opportunity to bite one of the buttons on the front of Don Francisco's jacket. He gently opened her mouth to release the button and said laughing, "Hey, this isn't going to be a good start, if you're trying to win me over to your side."

Concha approached the table and said, "Mari-Tere, let me have the dogs. You have to take care of your friends. I'll feed them and keep them for you."

"Okay, Concha, but don't feed them. I want to do that myself. I'll do it before I go to bed."

The party resumed with the same impetus as before. The young people started to dance again. The mature crowd formed small groups at the tables and began to discuss recent events and the latest gossip.

Don Francisco went to the library to enjoy a refreshing pause in the air-conditioned room. The lights of the patio were dimmed to the point of being lit almost by the candlelight at each table. Fernando followed his father into the room, accompanied by Monsignor Lasaga and the two Cabinet Ministers.

After the customary offering of a glass of excellent Spanish cognac, for example, Gran Duque de Alba or Cardenal Cisneros, as well as hand-made Cuban cigars, they sat down on the comfortable leather furniture to enjoy a few minutes of solace and tranquility.

Monsignor Lasaga was the first one to start the conversation. "Don Francisco, I must congratulate you wholeheartedly for a very nice party and for such a magnificent daughter."

"You're most generous in your assertion and truthful when you refer to my daughter. Mari-Tere is any father's pride."

"Father, how about your sons? How about me?" said Fernando jokingly.

Fernando Aguirrupe was the eldest of Don Francisco's children. Among them, he was the one who physically resembled his parents the least. With the face of a renaissance cherub and a slightly overweight body, he reminded Don Francisco of a mixture of his older brother and his father-in-law. Brown hair and hazel eyes were the distinctive characteristics of his face. He was twenty-eight years old and already a senior partner in a prominent law firm that handled most of the legal affairs of the U.S. Embassy and American investors in Cuba.

"Fernando, you should be content, because of all my children, you are the one that I've loved the longest."

"Francisco, there you go again with your quick diplomatic mind. I tell you that you should have practiced international law. You could have made a great diplomat," said Dr. José Luis Rodríguez.

Dr. Rodríguez was a brilliant lawyer, whose studies and books written on the subject of international law had won him the respect of his peers along with several awards from the International Law Commission in The Hague. He had an emeritus position at the University of La Habana, where he lectured whenever his other various commitments allowed him the time. During the late forties and early fifties, he had been the Cuban Ambassador to the United States, which was the most prominent position in the Cuban Foreign Office. In 1954, Batista had asked him to become the Minister of Justice during his next four-year administration period.

José Luis, better known to his closest friends as Pepe, knew that Batista was probably not the best President to serve under. It was true that in 1954 Batista had won an election that legally made him the President for the next four years, according to the Cuban Constitution of 1940. But it was also true that the opposing party nominee, Dr. Ramón Grau San Martín, had resigned his candidacy before the national election, thus leaving Batista as the sole candidate running for office. Batista ran unopposed, after an approximate eighteen-month period in the office that he had usurped through a coup d'état on March 10, 1952.

Batista in his sincere wishes to try to be fully accepted by the Cuban people had wanted to surround himself with prestigious, capable and uncompromising professionals like Dr. José Luis Rodríguez. Pepe had accepted the position thinking that his presence could not bring any harm to either the government or the people. On the contrary, he would always do his best to attempt to perform fairly, and to bring some equanimity to a period in history that he feared could become bloodthirsty.

"Pepe," said Don Francisco affectionately, "If I would've decided to practice international law, you wouldn't have had a chance to win all those awards."

"Not true, because you wouldn't have been that good!" Everybody laughed.

Dr. Juan Alberto Gómez, was another friend of Don Francisco's and the present Minister of Education. He, Don Francisco, and Pepe, had studied law together at the University of La Habana. Juan Alberto also had a doctoral degree in education, and in time became the Dean of the Law School at his old alma mater. Pepe had recommended him for the position of Minister of Education when his predecessor had died of a massive heart attack. Batista had appointed him gladly. Juan Alberto had accepted the position somewhat reluctantly, under the pressure of his old friend Pepe, who convinced him of the historic role he could perform in that office.

The Assistant to the Archbishop of La Habana, Msgr. Miguel Angel Lasaga, was another friend of Don Francisco's. The two ministers were not as close to him as they were to Don Francisco. However, they only needed to know that Don Francisco trusted him, and that was enough evidence to indicate to them that they could talk freely in his presence.

"You two remind me of our school days whenever you get together," Juan Alberto said. "When are you both going to stop teasing each other?"

"Who's teasing whom?" said Don Francisco with an expression of innocence on his face. "Am I teasing you, Pepe?"

"Me? Not me. No, you aren't teasing me. That's for sure. I really think that we are both teasing Juan. Can you see it, Juan?"

"Oh, stop the comedy routine," said Juan. "And let's talk of something more serious."

"Such as?" said Don Francisco.

"Well, how about the construction of the new Palace of Justice in the new Plaza de la Republica. Is that coming along all right?"

"Yes," answered Pepe. "It's coming along fine. The budget was approved. Francisco and I are members of the recently appointed supervisory board, and we can tell you that the plans are just grandiose. Construction is already scheduled to begin within a few months. We expect to have it completed by 1958."

"It is going to be quite something when it is finished," added Don Francisco. "All the glass and bronze work is coming from Austria, and it's quite impressive according to models and drawings. It'll be a magnificent structure that will have no parallel in Latin America."

"Tell me, Msgr. Lasaga," said Juan, changing to an even more serious theme, "What's the Church's position concerning the events unfolding in Mexico and pertaining to Fidel Castro, who is apparently planning a full scale revolution for this island?"

"At this moment, the Church, officially, as you all know, is saying nothing. We aren't making any statements at this time. We are waiting to see how these events develop in the future. Unofficially, we're divided among ourselves into two major political groups. There are some among us, mainly Jesuits and some priests of Basque origin, who are sympathetically viewing the outcome of an impending organized revolution by Fidel Castro. Their support within the Church itself rises well up to the higher echelons of the Catholic Church, including several Cardinals. Others, like myself, more traditional and conservative priests, aren't happy with the idea of a revolution. Spanish priests who lived through the barbaric acts of sacrilege committed by the communists during the Spanish Civil War, and American priests, especially the Augustinians attached to the University of Villanueva, believe that Castro is a communist. They claim his so-called revolution is nothing but a Marxist-Leninist takeover. In the event that this revolution hits in full swing, and the Church has to make some public statement of position, it is my belief that we would officially condemn Castro and his followers.

"It's a fact that we do have a bunch of leftist Cardinals, but while the Pope is Pius XII, I can't foresee that he would yield to internal Vatican political pressures against his own views. On the other hand, the Pope is an old man and his wishes, I'm sure, do not include leaving behind him a divided Church. Consequently, he might also compromise, and choose to order his flock to remain silent, neither consenting in full, nor dissenting. I, for one, would do my utmost to try to find a peaceful solution to the Batista problem. One that paves the way for a political change without fighting, and without a political takeover by a group of fanatics."

"Batista undoubtedly has a problem, politically speaking," said Don Francisco, "because the people in general have never accepted the fact that he is our legally-elected President. I can't understand why we need a revolution to get rid of him, when all we have to do is wait another two years. Two years aren't a long time in the history of any nation. Then, vote his political party out of office. He can't be reelected, since our own constitution says that no elected officer can run for a second consecutive term."

"We don't need a revolution of any sort. All we need is a good political conscience in the minds of the electorate," said Pepe.

"But, what if Batista decides not to offer free elections again," Fernando said, "and simply declares that he'll uphold his position for another four years, with the backing of the Armed Forces and the recognition of foreign governments?"

"It is unlikely that he would choose that path, because it's in complete contrast with his previous behavior. I will grant you that a revolution as a means of carrying out political change could be justified. But you are a lawyer, and you should know that the implementation of a sentence in a hypothetical situation isn't allowed. You cannot kill a person because you think that he or she could harm you physically or psychologically. Your personal life has to be in real danger before you can act and claim self-defense. Revolutions, normally, are nothing but the corruption of logical thinking by twisted minds in their quest to achieve power through the only means they can employ. Means such as deception, treachery, chicanery and murder, always acting under the assumption that the end result justifies whatever must be done to achieve it," interjected Don Francisco.

Msgr. Lasaga then said, "You are the closest to Batista, Pepe. What is his reaction concerning Castro?"

"Well, the situation concerning Castro is a complex one. Allow me to recapitulate some of the primary events involving this issue, so that I can bring my answer to your question into a more meaningful perspective.

"First of all, let's remember that Fidel Castro's first act of violence against the government of Batista was a truly criminal and sadistic action. I would describe it as an act of cowardice, if you ask me. I'm referring to the attack on the Moncada Army Post on July 26, 1953. You all know the propaganda that the international presses, and in particular the Cuban press, gave to this action. A great military feat, said some journalists, while the liberal American news media applauded it in a very convenient fashion in order to portray Castro as a local folk hero.

"The truth of the matter is, there are very serious doubts that Fidel Castro himself even participated in the attack. Sure, he may have planned it, or been one of its leaders. But, I've heard enough evidence to believe that he only entered the infirmary, which was the first and the only building taken by the guerrilla forces, after his men had already secured it. And then he joined his forces in the butchery of the soldiers who were sick, bedridden and unarmed. When the group of revolutionaries advanced towards the army barracks thereafter, they were restrained and captured. Amazingly, Castro was not among them. He had somehow gone into the streets and taken refuge in the Archbishop of Santiago de Cuba, Monsignor Pérez Serante's residence.

"You'll forgive me, Msgr. Lasaga, but the Church should never have granted sanctuary to a criminal, and furthermore shouldn't have negotiated his surrender."

"In the eyes of the Church, there are no criminals, just repentant sinners," Msgr. Lasaga responded.

"I agree. But I do not believe that he was truly repentant. This was the act of a coward, not the act of a glorious military savior of a nation." Without waiting for an answer, he continued, "After the trial that found Castro guilty, Batista decided to send him to the Isle of Pines Prison, under pressure from the Church, public opinion agitated by the media, and personal favors owed to his old communist friends like Juan Marinello, Blas Roca and Carlos Rafael Rodríguez. The latter, as you all know, interceded personally before Batista in favor of Fidel.

"At the prison Castro was treated with the utmost courtesy and respect by Batista's police force. Fidel was given a private cell with a library at his disposal and spent most of his time reading and writing. Castro was released from jail after the political prisoners' amnesty of 1954. Castro should never have been considered a political prisoner, but the common criminal that he really was, from both a legal and humanistic point of view. Batista not only chose to pardon him, but also to give him ten thousand pesos out of his own pocket, so that Fidel could leave the island in style and go to some other country to start anew."

"I heard that before, but didn't believe it. Is that really true? Did Batista give Castro the money when he left the prison?" said Fernando.

"Don't interrupt. Please, Pepe, continue," said Don Francisco, looking at his son with some reproach.

"I don't mind. And, yes, it is true. You see, in Batista's mind at that time, he truly felt that Fidel could be bought in that fashion. Even though some evidence was presented to him to inform him of Castro's Marxist background, he didn't choose to see it as the complete truth. Between us, what politician doesn't think that he can buy another politician? It is like the thief who thinks that other people are always stealing from him. Now, in giving Castro that money he was underestimating Fidel's ulterior motives. What's even more dangerous is that this action on the part of Batista created resentment in the Army, which already had a morale problem, to say the least.

"And now, getting back to your question, Msgr. Lasaga, Batista can't believe what is going on in Mexico. The Army Intelligence Branch has presented to him undeniable proof that Castro is receiving money from the deposed Ex-President Carlos Prío Socarrás, now in Miami, as well as from the Soviet Embassy in Mexico. And to think that Prío was the first Latin American president to break diplomatic relations with the Soviet Union at the beginning of the Korean War, a decision that he'd always claimed was based on his deep, personal, anti-communist feelings. Indeed, it happens that in history sometimes necessity, and sometimes hatred towards a common enemy and sometimes plain ignorance can make strange bedfellows. The Police Bureau of Revolutionary Activities informed Batista that Castro had joined forces with a well-known mercenary, Marxist-activist and soldier of fortune by the name of Dr. Ernesto Guevara, better known to his close friends as 'El Ché'. An old Spanish communist general from the Spanish Civil War is training his troops in Mexico, by the name of Bayo. I also know that diplomatic pressures have been exerted upon the Mexican Government to attempt to stop these activities. After all, Mexico is considered a friendly country. But every time that the Mexican Police has performed a raid and imprisoned Castro and his gang, requisitioning enough arms and military equipment to start another war, the extreme leftist Mexican Ex-President Lázaro Cárdenas has intervened and obtained their freedom after a few days. And to think that Batista and Cárdenas were close buddies in the forties, when Batista was allied with the Cuban Socialist Party and their communist leaders.

"So, Batista is waiting. He's perplexed by the nature of the events, but calm, for he firmly believes that Castro could never be such a fool as to try to launch an armed insurrection against him and the Cuban Army.

"My honest opinion is that he's being misled by a group of inept and corrupt military officers that unfortunately possess the highest ranks within the Armed Forces. He doesn't see the long reach of international communism, which is determined to gain some ground in Latin America. It's obvious to me that they are aiding Fidel, but Batista doesn't want to admit it. If I were in his shoes, I'd have much of my intelligence force concentrated in Miami and Mexico, in order to find out when and from where Castro is leaving Mexico to attack Cuba. Then, I'd send my Air Force to meet him on the open seas and sink him and his attacking force to the depths of the ocean, before they could ever reach Cuban soil. I've said this to Batista himself, and do you know what his reply was? He said to me, 'Pepe, devote yourself to solving legal problems, make sure that legal procedures in Cuba are being carried out with justice for all, and leave the military tactics for those in the Armed Forces.' I'll tell you one thing, I'll admit that I've never attended West Point. However, I'm sure that I know more about strategy than that bunch of inefficient parasites in uniform that he's surrounded himself with, and that are only good for building his ego."

"Well, Pepe," said Juan, "the problem, so far as the possibility of political unrest is concerned, doesn't only arise from outside the island. There is disenchantment among the students at the universities, but especially at La Habana University. There, the faculty members and the intellectuals who lecture from time to time have incited the students into believing that the way of the revolution is the only way to solve what they consider to be the Cuban political predicament. This feeling is being transmitted also to the journalists and to some professionals and businessmen. All of these groups of individuals that I've mentioned are engaged in some clandestine way of collecting funds for Castroesque activities. The biggest contributions are coming from the wealthy owners of large industrial complexes and the rich landowners."

"Yes. You're one hundred per cent right. I only hope that they realize in time that they are only feeding a fire that could flash, and burn their faces along with their castles."

The doors were opened abruptly, and a young man, twenty-six years old, came into the room. It was José María Aguirrupe, the second son of Don Francisco.

José María had graduated as an architect from La Habana University two years ago, and had just finished his graduate studies at Harvard University in Cambridge, Massachusetts. He was a promising designer of multi-level and single-level dwellings even at his young age. He was working for a large architectural firm in the construction of his first design. It was a new, condominium-type building, with one apartment per floor, a towering skyscraper that was going to be erected at the entrance of El Vedado, with all the main balconies opening to El Malecón, the ocean avenue in front of the building. He had already purchased the penthouse for himself. Physically, he was very much like his father, tall, lean, handsome, with dark eyes and dark hair. His older brother Fernando liked him a lot. With only two years between the brothers, José María was always Fernando's closest companion in the games that they used to play as children. Fernando's only resentment was that, unlike his younger brother Carlos, José

María had grown up to be an introvert who never allowed anyone to see his inner motives and emotions. He was a full-fledged member of the political revolution against Batista, having been recruited at the university by some faculty members due to his contacts and access to important sources of information. This fact was not known by anyone in his family.

"Father, you're being missed at the party. Some guests who are leaving early wish to say good-bye and are asking for you."

"Talking with old friends, I lost track of the time. Let's go in and join the others."

Don Francisco stood up and started to walk towards the massive doors, accompanied by the others in the room. When he reached the knob, he opened the doors and stepped aside to let his friends and sons depart from the library before him, and then, after closing the doors, followed them down the hallway, through the glass French doors and onto the patio.

The graduation party was now in full swing. The majority of the couples were dancing and everybody was having a great time.

María Teresa came up to her father and said, "Aren't you going to dance with me today?"

"But of course, Mari-Tere, you know that I'd love to dance with you on this or any day."

When Don Francisco and his daughter approached the dancing area, the other couples stood back, leaving them alone in the middle of the floor. The orchestra quickly concluded what they were playing and started with the well-known melodic bars of an old and traditional Cuban folk song. Its lyrics began, "On the trunk of a tree, a young girl carved her name . . . ." and they danced amidst the applause of the surrounding couples.

"Father, thank you so much for the Chows. How did you know I wanted them?"

"How could I not notice? You've been giving me lectures on the subject of the Chow-Chow breed for almost a year. Besides, don't I always know what's in your heart?"

"Yes, you do know me well. Then you must also know that I love you a lot."

"On that account, I'm pretty sure of your feelings. I love you in a very special way, and I'm extremely proud of you. Be happy, my sweet girl, for you deserve it more than anybody in this place."

"Oh, I'm so happy. I'm terribly happy to have a family like mine and a dear wonderful father like you."

María Teresa rested her head on her father's shoulder and continued dancing with him to the soft rhythms of the melodic song.

CHAPTER TWO

The Universidad Católica de Santo Tomás de Villanueva was the proper name under which the Augustinians from Philadelphia, in the State of Pennsylvania, in the United States of America, decided to create a new Catholic university in La Habana, Cuba, in 1946. It was the same year that the same priests also chose to found Merrimack College, in the community of the small town of North Andover, in the State of Massachusetts. The Cuban educational endeavor was primarily the culmination of great efforts that were exerted by a most dedicated priest, the Reverend Father Lorenzo Spirali, O.S.A.

The university, simply called Villanueva by most students and faculty members, was located at the end of the Miramar suburban zone, only a few blocks from the ocean. It was flanked on its east and west sides by two of the most prestigious social clubs in the city. These two clubs, namely the Havana Yacht Club and the Biltmore Country Club, were at the oceanfront approximately seven miles from each other.

The main chapel with the rectory and main classroom buildings comprised the first attempt at a scholastic campus. Later on, a library, plus other classroom and laboratory buildings, were added, as well as a huge parking lot, tennis courts and baseball fields. Overall, the architectural design was massive, modern and impressive-looking, although simplistic in its lines, drawing elegance, grace and beauty from its ornateness. It was not fully air-conditioned. As a matter of fact, only part of the rectory and some of the offices benefited from that refreshing experience. The main classrooms and courtyards were pleasant and quite livable due to the constant and cool ocean breeze.

Reverend Father John J. Kelly, O.S.A. was the President of this institution of learning when María Teresa went to register as one of its students, on a hot September day in 1956. Registration days were always hectic times at the university. A large number of disoriented students were trying to get their class schedules straightened out and were having difficulty locating buildings and classrooms.

María Teresa and Carlos were in two separate lines waiting for their turn to talk to their counselors and administrative personnel. Behind María Teresa, a beautiful girl with blonde hair and blue eyes was also standing in line. Her color hair and eyes might have been uncommon characteristics for a Cuban girl, but her full body, small waist and shapely legs, reflected the traits and attributes of a woman native to that tropical paradise.

"Hello, my name is Inés Pidal y Aspuru. You must be María Teresa Aguirrupe. Am I right?"

"Yes, that's my name. I'm very pleased to meet you," said María Teresa, quickly turning to face the person who had spoken in the smooth, seductive voice, and accepting the extended hand she continued, "But, how do you know who I am?"

"I saw your photograph some two months ago in the Society Section of El Diario de la Marina. I believe you were at your high school graduation party, and I have a photographic memory for all those things. If I remember correctly, it was also mentioned that you graduated with the highest honors, so I hope that you don't become one of my future classmates, because in that case the competition is going to get very tough."

"Well, I don't know about that. You look very intelligent to me. Anyway, I'm going to become a mechanical engineer, God willing. How about you?"

"I'm going into my third year of architecture, so I don't think that we're going to have too many courses in common. In fact, I was just joking when I told you that. I knew that with you being a freshman, there wasn't much of a chance of being in any classes together. But, watch out about engineering. That's a school that in many of its different branches is supposed to be very hard. I hope that you really like mechanical drawings and drafting, because you're going to see quite a bit of it. I understand that there is a professor who teaches those subjects, as well as machine design and advanced mechanical analysis, by the name of Professor Blanco. I heard that he is a brilliant designer, with a deep, unusual knowledge of mechanisms, who is also very tough with the freshmen."

"Well, I guess I'll find out soon enough about Professor Blanco. I must tell you that I enjoy challenges, especially intellectual ones, and have never been afraid of hard work. Maybe I'll drive him crazy with my questions. By the way, Inés, are you related to the Aspurus of the sugar empire family?"

"No, I'm not. The name of the major patriarch of that family is Manolo Aspuru. I know of him, but there is no relation whatsoever between him and my mother's side of my family. There is also another Aspuru, José María Aspuru, who owns the largest industrial supply house on the island and whose son Carlos is also a student here, but again, no relation to my family. Maybe, if our lineage was traced back to the Basques in Spain, we'd find that we are all related somehow. Who knows?"

María Teresa's eyes wandered lazily around the room and suddenly they stopped to glance at a boy who was standing in another line, three rows away.

"Tell me, Inés, since you've been in the school now for a couple of years, who's that boy with the auburn hair standing in line over there? I think I know him, but his name escapes my mind at the moment."

"That's the row of students enrolling in law school. I don't know him personally, but I think his name is Raúl Mora, and I should add that you don't have bad taste in men. Do you really know him?"

"No, that's not the name. I have him confused with another person."

"Well, do you want to meet him?"

"Not now. Maybe at some other time."

"Well, as you wish. Listen, María Teresa, I hope that I don't sound fresh to you, but my car is being serviced today, and I came with some friends that would like to go to the country club afterwards, and I really have no desire to do that today. I'd rather get back home early and attend to some chores. If you don't mind, I would appreciate it if you would give me a ride to some place along Fifth Avenue where I can get a bus and go home."

"Where do you live?"

"I live in Miramar, on Thirty-second Street between Fifth and Seventh Avenues. If you could take me home, that would be a big plus. Do you think it would be possible?"

"After I register, I'd like to see where my classes are located. Now, since you already know the school, you can guide me a lot quicker than if I go alone. I really don't see any problem in taking you home, except that we would have to wait for my brother, who came with me and is now in another line."

"No, it'll be no problem at all waiting for your brother. I'll be glad to show the school to both of you. Believe me, I sincerely appreciate the ride. After you finish with the registration paperwork, please wait for me in the main courtyard, next to Father Spirali's statue. You can't miss it. I'll be there as soon as I can, and thank you very much."

"All right, I will."

María Teresa's turn finally arrived and she made the first payment toward her tuition fee while enrolling in all the courses the university required for a freshman in the mechanical engineering school, namely physics, chemistry, mathematics, drafting, English and religion.

Carlos took his time, since the girl from the administration office happened to be very cute. Finally, after some protests from the people who were waiting in line behind him, he proceeded to go outside to look for his sister.

"Well, well, well. Hello there, Mari-Tere. Here stands in front of you a duly and formally registered student in the School of Business Administration. Shall we go home now?"

"Carlos, before we go, I want you to meet my new friend, Inés. Inés, this is my brother, Carlos."

"A real pleasure, Carlos."

"With those blue eyes and that figure, believe me, Inés, that the pleasure is all mine."

"Carlos, stop it. Look Inés, I should've warned you about my brother. He believes that he's the reincarnation of Valentino."

"Don't worry, I think I can handle him."

"That would be what I'd enjoy the most," said Carlos with a big smile.

"Inés has promised to show us the buildings where our classes will be held, and afterward, I told her that we would drive her home."

"Inés can show me anything that she wants, and as far as driving her home, she shouldn't have any fear, since I'd drive her to the gates of heaven and back if she so wished."

"Be serious for a while, Carlos. Okay? Let's go now, Inés."

The three young students started to make the rounds through the buildings. María Teresa and Carlos found out that all of their classes were going to take place in two buildings that were located across from each other. These were the Hickey Building and the Tarafa Building, where the main auditorium was located. It did not take long, and soon enough they were standing in front of Carlos's Jaguar, which bore the classic green color of the British racing cars. The automobile possessed a rich, beige-colored, leather interior and a genuine rosewood front and door paneling.

"You sure know how to pick your cars," Inés said.

"I'm glad that you like it. Between you and me, I know even better how to pick my women."

Carlos opened the front passenger door of the car and signaled Inés to get in, but María Teresa gained access to the seat before Inés even had any time to react. Carlos did not utter a single word, and opened the door to the rear seat for Inés, who climbed inside laughing. Then he proceeded to climb into the driver's seat and start the engine. The 2.8-liter engine responded instantaneously, with the typical purring sound of the wild cat it represented.

María Teresa caught Carlos looking in the rearview mirror and said, "Watch the road, Carlos. I want to get home in one piece."

Carlos did not reply. He just started to look forward.

"I'm sorry," María Teresa said. "I didn't mean to be rude. All I really wanted was for Carlos to pay his undivided attention to the road, and not to you, especially considering the way that he usually drives this car."

"Oh, don't worry, María Teresa. I took it as merely a joke, anyway. He won't scare me, I can assure you, because my fiancé loves to drive very fast cars. Faster than this one, for sure."

"I knew you couldn't be perfect. There you go with the fiancé. But before you tell me who the lucky guy is, let me know where I'm taking you."

"It's easy. Just continue on Firth Avenue until you reach Thirty-second Street and then make a right turn. The lucky guy is José Miguel Font-Vachon."

"You sure know how to pick your men, if that happens to be the heir to the Font-Vachon fortune in cattle, in Camagüey Province."

"Yes, he is the one and I'll tell you, it's not a matter of money. We really love each other a lot."

"I'm very happy for you," said María Teresa. "You can't pay any attention to Carlos, as I told you. He's always kidding everybody and half of the time doesn't mean anything."

"Yes, but the other half of what I say I do mean, and this half now is asking you, Inés, how come this glorious man didn't take you to the university today to wait for you? You can be certain that if you were my girl, I wouldn't let you go alone, so that a fresh, good-looking fellow like me could start making all kinds of passes at you."

"José Miguel is past the university age. As a matter of fact, he graduated two years ago with a degree in law. I think he should've studied business administration, since he'll end up running the family business. However, his grandfather always wanted him to become a lawyer, and he did it to please the old man. Right now, he's more interested in racing cars than anything else, and he's in Italy training and learning how to run his first Ferrari Formula One. He says that Juan Manuel Fangio, from Argentina, is the world racing champion now, but that he'll be the next champion in a year or two."

"That's very interesting," said Carlos, "but I'll tell you that I would never leave you for the most beautiful Ferrari. Since he's in Italy now and you are here, how about going out with me tonight to celebrate registration day?"

"Carlos," said María Teresa, "how can you say that? You must forgive my brother. If he offended you, I apologize for him."

Inés could not control her smile from turning into a giggle and then to a sincere laugh. María Teresa looked at her and had no choice but to accompany her in laughter. Carlos took immediate advantage of the development and said, "You don't have to apologize for me, dear sister. In reality, I said what I said as a compliment to her personality and beauty. She knows very well that I would never offend her."

"All right, Carlos. I took it as a compliment and thank you very much for the invitation that I have no choice but to decline. José Miguel is a very jealous man, and besides, I'm very much in love with him."

"You see, the main difference between him and me, is that he's a very jealous person, but I'm not. Therefore, I'll forgive and forget the fact that you are his fiancée. Now, about tonight, we can go to a movie where it's dark so nobody will see us and afterwards, I'll invite you to El Recodo, where we can eat something in the car, and again nobody will recognize you, unless you are a close friend of all the waiters. See, I just feel that if I don't see you again tonight, I'm going to die tomorrow with the anguish in my heart that I met the most beautiful woman in my life, and let her slip through my fingers without even holding her in my arms at least once."

"Oh, cut it out. Inés is engaged to be married and she's not going out with you, so stop clowning and let's talk about something else."

Carlos did not reply. Inés did not say anything either. He looked through the rearview mirror of the car instead and noticed a sensual expression on Inés's face.

María Teresa switched the radio on, and the notes of the latest American music broadcasted by CMOX, a radio station, began to fill the car. Carlos produced a pack of cigarettes and offered one to Inés who accepted it in silence.

A short while after, the car made the expected right turn and parked in front of a pleasant-looking house. Inés said good-bye to María Teresa and promised to look for her when the regular classes started. Carlos went out and around the car, to open the door for Inés. He offered his hand to her, to assist her in getting out of the automobile. They walked to the entrance door while María Teresa waited inside the car. Just before they arrived at the front doors adorned with black wrought iron work, he whispered, "I'll be here to pick you up at seven."

"Seven will be fine."

At that precise moment he felt like the luckiest man alive. Nothing else was said. No other words were needed.

CHAPTER THREE

Thanksgiving was definitely an American holiday. It did not exist in the Cuban tradition, even though the proximity of the island to the North American continent had brought many other American habitual celebrations into the Cuban social practices. However, for the Augustinian priests that governed Villanueva, it was certainly a major holiday, and a day without classes, which the students enjoyed by participating in various activities in the pleasant atmosphere of the spacious campus.

The day started with a beautiful Mass, celebrated in the roomy and modern chapel, which was located at the main gateway to the school. Most of the student body and faculty members attended the ceremony. The Mass lasted longer than usual, due to the long lines of participants waiting to take Holy Communion. The day continued with a long list of festivities, among which were the annual softball game, with the staff and faculty versus members of the student body. There were tennis matches, vaudeville shows given by some talented students, and, of course, a turkey dinner offered by the administration to everybody attending the celebration. The turkey dinner was offered at noontime.

For María Teresa and Carlos, it was the first of such occasions. They had driven in together that morning, and they had attended Mass together. María Teresa had gone to church with the fervor and devotion imparted by her upbringing and previous education. Carlos had gone mainly to accompany his sister. It was not that he did not find solace and peace in the church, or that he had lost his faith in God, but merely that he could not picture himself lying to the only Being Who could read into his heart through the fog of hypocrisy. "Why tell God how good I'm going to be from now on," he used to reason, "if tomorrow I might do things which are sins, but which I shall do anyway, if the occasion arises."

After Mass and after dinner they separated, each seeking their own group among their peers.

During the show, Carlos spotted Inés, and upon its conclusion he went directly to where she was sitting.

"Inés, how are you?"

"I'm fine, Carlos. Let me introduce you to these friends and professors."

When the customary greetings and salutations were over with, Carlos grabbed Inés by her arm and requesting politely "to be excused" pulled her away from the small group.

"I've have called you numerous times, but you were never home and never returned my calls. I've restrained myself from going over to see you, because I don't wish to cause you any embarrassment at your house or with your family. In school I hardly see you, so I must talk to you today. Even better, now."

"Please, don't talk like that in here. Let's go outside and watch the ball game."

They walked together out of the Tarafa Building, smiling at the known faces that they were passing by, and continued to the field like mere acquaintances strolling side by side. They sat apart from the main crowd, between first base and the right field area. The ballpark, unfortunately, did not have seating arrangements for the spectators, since it was used mostly for practices by the university baseball team and for some softball games by the different school teams for intramural competitions that were attended by few spectators.

"Listen to me," Inés said, "I went out with you one time, because you aroused some curiosity in me. Somehow, I liked you and was taken by your manners, the way that you handled yourself, as well as by your looks. That was then. Today, believe me when I tell you that there will not be a second one. I'm engaged to be married and besides that, just like I told you at the end of that lovely evening, I have a lot of work to do. It's not easy to meet the requirements of each of the courses that I have to take this year. Even if I wanted to see you, and José Miguel were not a part of my life, it could only be on sporadic weekends."

"I can only buy part of what you're telling me. A normal girl just doesn't go around kissing curiosities the way that you kissed me that night. Maybe it was the full and clear moon shining over the ocean, or the soft music on my car radio, but I believe that somehow there must have been something else that had to do with me. Could it have been what I told you that night?"

"I bet you say the same things to all the other girls."

"Perhaps, I do. But let me tell you that they never sounded the same way as when I said them to you, because in truth, I did mean them."

"Well, I grant you that you sounded quite honest in revealing your feelings to me that night. I kissed you the way I did because I believed you. But, I tell you now, it's over."

"I can't conceive that it can be over. You're telling me today that you have a lot to do, and I respect your decision concerning the placement of your studies ahead of me. What the hell, everybody has his or her own set of values. I also know that if you wanted to see me you would find the time to do it. Not every day, and maybe not every week, but a weekend here and there. Because I doubt very much that you don't have the time to see José Miguel either. Now, this is what really brings us to the crux of the matter, is it not? I hear you when you say that you're engaged to him, but the words sound empty to me. Do you want me to tell you the truth? The truth is I don't think that you really love him."

"You don't want to listen, do you? Now I know why Basques have the fame of being stubborn. When I say that I'm engaged to José Miguel, I'm telling you that I do love him, and fully intend to marry him early next year. He doesn't want to wait any longer, and neither do I. I'll finish my studies afterwards, even though he told me that I don't have to do it if I don't want to. In the long run, I know that he will respect my feelings and allow me to pursue my own career."

"I'm going to tell you something that I have never told anybody. I think that I'm in love with you."

Inés tilted her head backwards and laughed. "You're confusing love with infatuation. I'm the one who gave you a taste of what I can be when I fully surrender to a man, but I didn't let you find out the rest. I'm slipping away from your life, and you can't tolerate losing the siege. I think that you really desire me, and that you would love to add me to your list of amorous conquests. Love, no, I don't think that you love me."

Carlos felt hurt for the first time in his life. Inés was the first woman he had actually fallen for. For once, he had tried to open himself to a lovely girl, and she had promptly shot a poisonous arrow into his heart. Now, the more typical, frivolous personality of Carlos emerged ready to counterattack.

"Well, perhaps you're right. I did desire you from the first moment that I saw you. It's a sentiment that is easily aroused in me whenever I see a beautiful and accessible girl. I made a mistake in judgment. Now, let me ask you one question, and please be honest with me. Do you really love José Miguel, or do you love what he represents?"

Inés suddenly stood up, and standing next to Carlos, who remained seated, she said, "I hope that what I'm going to tell you sinks deep into your brain, or whatever it is that you have underneath that thick skull of yours. I do love my future husband and whatever he is or represents is of no importance to me. I wish that you would consider me as a friend, because that's all I can be to you. A good friend."

Carlos stood up and replied, "Oh, well, let's say that I take your words at face value. I also want to be your friend. Besides, some of my best girlfriends go to bed with me, anyway."

Inés smiled. Carlos undoubtedly had the charm and the ability to bring joy into her life.

"I just aspire to be your friend, and not precisely your girlfriend," she said.

"Wasn't it Molière who said that the main aspiration of a woman is to inspire love? I should add, blessed be the one who inspires lust."

Inés walked silently in front of him, approaching the main crowd seated near the players, and rooting for their favorite team. At that moment, a young man in his early twenties, dressed in black flannel trousers, a light pink cotton shirt and a herringbone light gray silk and wool sports jacket was also walking towards them. His black, straight hair was nicely combed and parted on the left. His dark eyes revealed an acute and sharp mind determined to obtain whatever he set his intellect on procuring. His height was average and his actually athletic body was concealed under a very slightly overweight condition. He resembled a football player more than a real businessman or a daring car driver. Inés ran towards him when she recognized him and kissed him tenderly but fully on his mouth.

"I've been looking for you for the last half hour," he said, and continued, "I finished with the racing practice and came to pick you up and take you home."

"Oh, I've been talking with some friends and didn't realize the time. Let me introduce you to Carlos. Carlos, I want you to meet my fiancé, José Miguel Font-Vachon. José Miguel, this is my friend Carlos Aguirrupe."

Carlos was the first to offer his hand. "It's a real pleasure to meet you. Inés is always talking about you."

"The pleasure is all mine. Are you by any chance the son of Supreme Court Justice Aguirrupe?"

"Yes, I'm the youngest son."

"In that case, it's indeed a great pleasure, for some time ago your father saved my family from going into bankruptcy."

"Is that so? Well, it's a small world after all. I'm glad that my family was in some way instrumental to your well-being. But I must confess I have no recollection of the incident."

Inés, looking very surprised, said, "José Miguel, you never told me about that. What happened?"

"Some time ago, about eight to ten years ago, members of the family of the President in office at that time put a claim against my family's land and possessions, based on some questionable documents dating back to the last century. The paperwork was obviously fake and the witnesses had been bribed. When we fought the case in the lower courts, they won the decision of the judges. We appealed several times until the case finally reached the Supreme Court. The political pressure on the magistrates was great. We really thought that we were going to lose again. Fortunately, your father was the Supreme Court Justice in charge of studying and presenting his findings to the Civil Court. I know my father called on your father, and begged him to allow us to present our side of the story for his consideration. My father later told me that your father said that it wasn't necessary. Your father added that if my family wasn't in the right, he would have no choice but to recommend sentencing against us. If, on the contrary, we were right in our assertions, then he shouldn't worry, because no outside pressure, whatever the source or force exerted, would make him sway his decision. We won the case because your father is a just and fair man. He's a credit to his profession and to his position. Wait until I tell my family that I've met one of you, and that you're a friend of Inés's. They are going to be very happy. You know, at one time, my father sent six Arabian horses that he bought in Andalusia to your father as a Christmas present. Your father returned all of them, expressing his gratitude, but declining the gift. After that incident, my father never dared to offend him by sending him any other present. Please, give my very best to your father."

"I'll do that this evening. It was a really fascinating story. Now, changing the topic of conversation, I understand that you just bought a Formula One Ferrari."

"Yes, I did, and I intend to race it next year in some of the European circuits, mainly in the Italian Mille Miglia and in the Monaco Grand Prix. I don't expect to win the first time. You have to consider that I'll be racing against people of the caliber of the Marquis of Portago, Sterling Moss and of course Fangio. For sure, I'm going to give it my very best though. By that time, I'll be married to Inés, and she'll bring me all the luck that I need. The rest is skill, and I'm acquiring that every day that I practice."

"It must be very exciting to drive one of those cars. I hope that you'll give me the opportunity to ride with you during one of your practices. That is, if you practice in a two-seater."

"Sure, I can arrange that. We'll also invite your entire family to our wedding. I do hope that all of you can come and share that happy occasion with me and my family."

"Don't worry. I wouldn't miss your wedding for anything in the world. When is it?"

"Inés and I are still working out the final details, but I'd like to make the formal announcement by the beginning of next week, and celebrate it on January first. Then I'll never forget our wedding anniversaries."

Inés wrapped her arm around José Miguel's waist and said, "That's a nice surprise. You said early next year, but I had no idea that you meant that early."

"Well, congratulations to both of you. I hope that you will be very happy together. Any plans for the honeymoon?"

"With Inés's schoolwork, the honeymoon trip can't be a long one. We'll manage to go to Europe for a week or two. I'll have to go to Modena and check on my car, which should be ready by then. Wherever we go, we'll have a super time."

"Of that I'm positive," said Carlos.

After the customary good-byes, Inés and José Miguel walked away, hand in hand, and Carlos went to look for his sister.

He found her in the lobby of the library, where a small group of students, mostly girls, had gathered to listen to a youthful priest from Holland playing the Spanish guitar. He was entertaining the small gathering by giving them an introduction to old Dutch folk songs intermixed with some Spanish and Cuban melodies.

Carlos bent down to speak to María Teresa. "It's about four o'clock. The games are just ending. I think we should be leaving. What do you say?"

"Let's wait until he finishes this song. It would be impolite to leave now."

Carlos smiled to himself. To offer any resistance to María Teresa's statement was useless. He waited patiently standing next to her.

Finally, they said good-bye to the people congregated around them and left the library in search of his car. They were walking through the main courtyard, when he noticed that María Teresa kept looking in the direction of an auburn-haired young man. He was leaning against an outside column of the Hickey Building, and laughing loudly at jokes that were being told by other students.

Carlos stopped and tapped María Teresa on her shoulder. She turned around to face him.

"Do you like that fellow?"

"Be quiet. People are going to overhear you. Let's go home."

She tried to resume walking, but Carlos stopped her again.

"No, we stop right here. I'll ask you again, in a lower voice this time. Do you like that fellow standing over there? The one with the reddish hair?"

"I don't know what you're talking about. I just glanced at him for a brief moment."

"Come on, Mari-Tere. I've noticed that you haven't taken your eyes off him since you spotted him coming out of the library. Just tell me, honestly, do you like him or not?"

"All right, I admit that I like him, but that's all. I have never met him, and only saw him once before, on registration day, while waiting in line."

"I know more about these things than you do. It's okay, Mari-Tere. It had to happen to you sometime. I understand. Now, if you like him, why don't you talk to him and find out whether he likes you or not?"

"Carlos, you're crazy. We've never been properly introduced. A girl just doesn't go around talking to men she doesn't know."

"Oh, don't be so old-fashioned. Those are Concha's last century standards and the medieval customs of those nuns that ran your high school. Listen, if you want to meet him just leave it to me. As a matter of fact, let's go and meet him right now."

María Teresa blushed all over. "Don't be a clown. I won't move from here except to go to the car."

"Okay, you stay here. I'll bring him to you." Carlos turned to face the group of people who were having a good time interchanging jokes with one another. He walked towards them and, addressing the one with the auburn hair, he said, "Excuse me, may I have a word with you?"

"What can I do for you?"

"My name is Carlos Aguirrupe and I wanted to meet you. You see, I was told that you're in your third year of Law School, and I just started this year in Business Administration. Next year I'll have to take a course in business law with Professor Iznaga. I believe that you had Iznaga already in some of your classes and I was wondering if you could give me a few tips on how to study for his classes. I'm really sorry to have interrupted your conversation with your friends, but since I've always seen you very busy between classes, I thought this would be a good moment to catch you. I hope you don't mind the intrusion."

The student moved closer to Carlos and further apart from the group.

"No, not at all. My name is Raúl Mora. Are you by any chance related to José María Aguirrupe, the architect?"

"Sure, he's one of my older brothers. Why do you ask?"

"He comes to my house very often. He and my brother Manuel are very close friends. Wait until I tell José María that I've met you."

"Well, don't tell him that you have only met me, but also tell him that you have met his sister. Please, come with me over there for just a moment."

Pulling Raúl by the arm, Carlos brought him next to María Teresa.

"Raúl, I want you to meet my sister, María Teresa. Mari-Tere, please meet Raúl Mora. His brother is a close friend of José María's."

"It's very nice to meet you," said María Teresa.

"Delighted, Miss Aguirrupe."

María Teresa's eyes met Raul's squarely for the first time. She felt a sudden bolt of electricity rushing through her. She kept her composure somehow. Raúl could not conceive how he could have missed her before. In his eyes, at that very moment, he was contemplating not the face of just a pretty girl, but a perfect face with the natural beauty of an angel. He tried hard not to reveal his emotions. In reality he was elated.

"Well, Raúl, about Professor Iznaga?"

"Oh, yes, don't worry too much about him. He has the reputation of being very tough with the students. He's more fair-minded than anything else. Just come prepared, because he has a knack of surprising students by asking questions and giving unannounced test cases to solve. He usually bases the final grade on these tests and class participation. With your father to help you, I'm sure you'll have no problem in his class, and you can always count on me to give you a hand in preparing for the case studies. I've already taken similar courses with him. Hey, any brother of José María's is also my friend, and what are friends for?"

María Teresa couldn't contain the remark. She did not know how or why she said it. She just did. "And the sister of José María. Isn't she considered a good friend also?"

"Of course, María Teresa. I didn't mean to leave you out of

my circle of friends. I honestly hope that we'll become very good friends. Can you forgive me for my lapse?"

"Yes, you know I was only kidding, anyway. What's strange is that José María has never mentioned your brother's name. Although he usually keeps to himself, and is the only member of the family who keeps an apartment in the city, where he spends most of his time."

"Now that you mention it, it's true that José María is very reserved in his opinions. He seldom talks much, and my brother Manuel, is very much like him. Maybe that's why they get along so well."

"It's really getting late and we'd better get going Mari-Tere," said Carlos while he shook hands with Raúl. "I'll see you around in between classes."

"It's been a real pleasure meeting both of you, especially you, María Teresa. I'm sure that we'll see each other again."

"Very happy to have met you, Raúl," replied María Teresa, giving him her hand to hold for a brief moment.

When they arrived at the car and Carlos started the engine, he said, "You see, it wasn't that difficult, was it? And, may I add, he said that it was a real pleasure to meet us, but especially you."

"I know that you're trying to make fun of me now. With all my heart, I sincerely forgive you, because you're the best brother any girl could ask for."

Carlos chuckled and, putting the car in first gear, sped along the road. Happiness tends to precede euphoria, and María Teresa was extremely happy at that moment. Everything in her life seemed to be shaping up in the best possible way. Little did she know that already fate had set in motion events that would strangely bring tragedy to her life. Events that had been forged by destiny, sometime in the past, and that she could not control, stop or reverse.

CHAPTER FOUR

"Mirta, are you sure that everything is going to be ready on time?" said Concha, approaching the kitchen where Mirta, assisted by Magda and Esther, was preparing the Christmas Eve dinner for the Aguirrupe family and their guests.

"Don't worry, I have everything under control."

Concha was very nervous. Usually the Aguirrupes enjoyed a quiet and typical Cuban Christmas Eve dinner. After dinner they would attend Midnight Mass. Upon returning from Mass, the family would gather together to exchange gifts and have some sweets and drinks. The tradition was not intrinsically Cuban. The inhabitants of the hospitable island had inherited that tradition from the Spaniards.

On that particular year, Don Francisco had invited his friends José Luis and Juan Alberto to partake of his hospitality with their respective families. The head of the Aguirrupe family had also decided that it was only fair for his children to invite their friends, if they wished to do so. Fernando and José María had decided to attend by themselves, while Carlos had invited Dolores Santa Cruz and her family, and María Teresa had asked Raúl Mora, who had declined due to a severe cold. Dolores had been Carlos's selection since he had been trying to incite some sort of jealousy in Inés. Dolores was a friend of Inés's from the university, and he was sure that the affair would reach Inés's ears somehow. Besides, Dolores was one of the most beautiful girls in the school.

The choice of dishes for that evening's menu was the easiest task of all for Concha. Don Francisco had told her to prepare the same dinner that they enjoyed every year. He also told her to make sure that a place was set at the dinner table for her. Concha had participated in that celebration since she had come to work for the family.

As in previous years, Concha had made sure that enough food was prepared, not only to satisfy the appetites of all the family members and their guests, but also for the servants to eat and to take home to their families.

At the beginning of the dinner, when all the attendants sat at their places around the table, Don Francisco stood up and said, "Lord, on this happy day when we commemorate once again the coming into this world of Your Son, Jesus, Whom You sent into our lives to expiate our sins and deliver us unto Your Kingdom, we ask You, humbly, to bless the food that we are about to receive. We give You thanks, our God, for all the blessings and all the graces that You, in Your magnanimous way, have bestowed upon us during this year. We are grateful, Lord, for allowing these good friends to celebrate with us the birthday of Your Son and to rejoice together in Your Glory. We beg that You accept this offering of love in the name of Your Son, Jesus Christ. Amen."

"Amen" was repeated by all present at the table in unison. María Teresa was seated at the right hand side of her father, who was presiding over the table at one end. José Luis said to her, "How do you like the university, Mari-Tere?"

"Very much so, Dr. Rodríguez. There's a lot of work to be done in this first year. I've been told that only half of the students make it to the second year of engineering. There's a lot of pressure, but I'm enjoying every minute of it."

"I see. Just like your father. The harder the courses, the more he seemed to like them. You know, Mari-Tere, Dr. Rodríguez is too formal for such an old friend of the family. You aren't a little girl anymore. Why don't you call me Pepe, like your father and all my closest friends call me?"

For a second María Teresa's eyes moved to meet her father's who agreed with a quick and almost imperceptible gesture.

"Well, all right. I'll call you Pepe from now on."

"That will make me very happy."

"In that case, don't call me Dr. Méndez anymore either. If you are going to call him Pepe, then you must call me Juan. Let's say enough to formalities. How about it, Mari-Tere?"

"You're also a very good friend of my father's, and I've always remembered how you asked to play with me when I was a little girl. I'll call you Juan."

"Ladies and gentlemen, I would like to take this opportunity to announce to everybody sitting at this table, including my two older brothers, that you may call me Carlos from now on. With the only exception being Mari-Tere, who may also call me Carlyle, and Dolores, who may call me her sweet guava pastry anytime," said Carlos with such a serious face that everyone laughed out loud.

"There goes the court jester," said Don Francisco.

The conversation went on to more mundane and banal matters. The typical small talk took place and subjects such as the weather, professional achievements, the latest gossip of high society circles and other trivial topics were discussed.

After dinner, Carlos took Dolores and her family aside to show them the rest of the house. María Teresa went to the kennels with Concha to feed the dogs and to play with them for a while. Fernando and José María played the latest music on the modern stereo system to entertain Pepe and Juan's respective daughters. And Don Francisco entertained his friends, Pepe and Juan, and their wives.

Pepe's wife, Magaly, said, "Francisco, where is that beautiful chess set that you told us about?"

"I had it placed in the library. Let me take you over there and I'll be glad to show it to you."

"So when did you buy it?" inquired Magaly.

"I just bought it about a year ago, from an art collector, who travels frequently to the Far East. He acquired it in Hong Kong. It's all hand-carved in ivory."

Don Francisco had been leading the way into the library and specifically to the area where a rosewood table, handcrafted with oriental motifs, sat, with the standard chess pattern of 64 squares made out of highly polished magenta and light beige squares."

"Here it is."

"My God, the pieces are extremely beautiful."

"I know that I shouldn't ask this. Nevertheless, curiosity is killing me. Forgive me for the indiscretion, but how much did you pay for it?" said Mariana, Juan's wife.

"Mariana, how dare you?" exclaimed Juan, visibly upset.

"You're too much, Mariana," said Magaly holding the white queen in her hand and admiring the delicacy of the artwork.

"Oh, never mind, Juan," said Don Francisco. "Look, Mariana, art like this can't be measured with money. Let's say that I paid what I believed it was worth, several thousands of pesos to tell you the truth. However, the main thing is that I'll not sell it for any offer that I might receive, no matter how large it might be." And, turning to face Pepe, he added, "Now, tell me, Pepe, what do you know about Castro? What have you heard lately? We have a few minutes to ourselves. My other guests seem to be preoccupied with other matters, at the moment anyway."

"Well, what I told you some time ago that I feared was going to happen, has happened. As you all know, Fidel finally landed with an invasion force in Oriente on December 2nd. I sincerely believe that the Navy betrayed us, since it's very curious that the greatest interest in preventing Castro's plans came from the Army, and not from the Navy, when in reality the expedition came by boat and not in an armored vehicle. I think that there are enough grounds to suspect this. You must remember that the naval base at Cienfuegos revolted against the government last September 3rd with an insurrection that didn't last long. However, I'm afraid that the safe voyage of the Gramma, the boat used by Castro for the transportation of his troops, has been our Navy's major contribution in its rebellious activities.

"In the meantime, a fellow by the name of Frank País had been organizing a group of students and revolutionaries in Santiago de Cuba. When this group was alerted that the force was leaving Mexico, they took to the streets and nearby mountains to commence fighting. Little did they know that the revolutionary expedition was not coming for three days. When the Gramma arrived, there was already some resistance going on in that region. The person in charge of organizing the aid to Castro and his forces at the landing point was a woman by the name of Celia Sánchez-Manduley, assisted by a local farmer named Crescencio Pérez. It is my understanding that Señorita Sánchez's family has several members with extreme leftist tendencies.

"Something went wrong at the very beginning when Castro's boat landed. The Cuban Coast Guard started to fire its guns against the Gramma when it was approaching the coastline. Castro decided to launch the boat at full speed towards the shore, and caused a shipwreck when he was about fifty meters away from it. The members of the expedition jumped off and, carrying whatever they could on their backs, reached the shore by swimming. The Cuban Navy took possession of the boat, where they found some anti-tank guns and .50 caliber machine guns. They should have destroyed them in the open seas.

"Army troops from the nearby towns of Manzanillo, Niquero and Pilón rushed to meet the invaders. The first battle occurred on December 4th in Alegría del Pío. It was a defeat for Castro. Of the eighty-four men that formed the original task force, only twelve remained, including Castro. They escaped, running for their lives into the nearby mountains, where, because of the inaccessibility of the terrain for a large number of troops, the mountains became a haven to hide in."

"I don't like what's going on," said Juan. "Castro is like a cat with nine lives. It really seems as if destiny is playing a role in keeping him alive. For what purpose, I don't know as yet; but I'm sure it won't be for anything good. There was an article in the New York Times on December 7th where it was mentioned that the head of the Soviet Diplomatic Mission to the United Nations, Vasily Kuznetsov, in a speech addressed to the General Assembly, made an open reference to the desperate situation facing Castro at this moment, and requested openly that the United Nations help him in his quest. I mentioned it to Batista the other day, and asked him to express his discontent at the UN, as well as to the United States, for this blatant act of meddling in Cuban affairs. He's done nothing about it, and the United States hasn't given any importance to this act, which is clearly the first official demonstration of Soviet interest in Castro's Revolution."

Don Francisco looked at both of his friends. "Has either of you seen Batista after that? What is he saying about the fighting in the mountains?"

Pepe said, "Absolutely. Juan and I attended the cabinet meeting last week at ten o'clock at night. Batista still likes to rest during the morning hours, and work throughout the night. He conducted the meeting as usual, wishing each of us a very Merry Christmas, and inviting us to the New Year's Gala Party at the Presidential Palace. I'm sure he's invited you also, Francisco. He always invites all the Supreme Court Justices. Are you coming?"

"Yes, I'll definitely attend this year."

"Well, in that case, we'll make plans to go together. Now, getting back to the meeting, the Minister of the Interior asked him point blank what his plans were concerning Castro's landing and his success in escaping into the Sierra Maestra. Do you know what Batista said? He said his plans were to dispatch a small group of soldiers to attack the invaders, that such a task force was sufficient because these revolutionaries would die by themselves anyway in the mountains.

"The Minister retorted that, so far, the Army had failed in

eliminating these traitors. What assurances would they offer now that they would fulfill their goal? Batista's reply was typical of his ego. He told the Minister that he should leave the military matters to the professionals who knew how to deal with them, and to dedicate himself to more important matters within his jurisdiction.

"The Minister kept pressing the point. He said that whatever happened on the island was unmistakably his responsibility. He claimed to have access to intelligence sources that had told him that Castro was at the point of receiving monetary and personnel assistance from a number of undisclosed sources, both inside and outside of the island. Then he added that he would like to know what the plans of the Army and the Air Force are for preventing that aid from reaching Castro's hands. Batista became furious. He ended the meeting right then and there, and asked the Minister in question to meet him in his private office the following day at four in the afternoon. I don't know what happened at that second meeting."

"Ah, but I do," said Juan. "When the Minister arrived, he found out that Batista had invited General Francisco Tabernilla, his Army Chief of Staff, Admiral José Rodríguez-Calderón, his Navy Chief of Staff, and Dr. Andrés Rivero-Aguero, his personal political assistant, to participate in the encounter. Batista tried to convince the minister that everything was under control. They wouldn't do anything for the time being, due to the Holiday Season and the fact that, according to him, it would constitute a bad political act to separate the soldiers from their families at this time of the year. Moreover, a large number of troops being sent to Oriente Province at this time would echo the Cuban leftist press, confirming that something was really wrong in that zone. He has decided to wait until after January 6th, when his wife Martha will spend the day giving toys to the children of poor families, thus commemorating the celebration of the Epiphany. Then, the Army will launch an attack upon the meager rebel force and capture them, dead or alive. The Minister appeared to be satisfied with the explanation when he left the office. Yet, my source told me that he had remarked that this was the first time in his life when he had heard that the Army didn't fight on holidays, granting the enemy time to recuperate and obtain reinforcements."

"It's a sad situation. I only hope that the New Year will bring better news, because a revolution or a civil war isn't conducive to political stability, and God knows that this blessed island and the people on it deserve better. I think we should go and rejoin the other guests. Shall we?"

With everybody's consent, the group marched towards the doors. Before reaching the hallway, Pepe took Don Francisco's arm and, pulling him behind the others, said, "Francisco, can you give me a couple of minutes of your time, in private."

"Of course, Pepe, let's go back into the library."

He asked the rest of the group to proceed to the living room and told them that he and Pepe would join them shortly. There was a mixture of music, voices and laughter coming from that area of the house.

Magaly said, "For God's sake, Pepe, don't take long. I know how you are sometimes when you get going. Promise me you'll keep it short."

"Don't worry, Magaly. We'll join all of you in a few minutes, I promise."

Once they were back in the library and the massive doors were closed, Francisco said, "What's happening? I rarely see you with such a serious face."

"We've known each other for many years. I hate to talk to you on a day like today about this matter. But you must know that I accepted your invitation to come here today because I wanted to have the excuse of seeing you alone. We're living in hectic times and we seldom have time for each other in private."

"My God, come to the point, man, what's going on?"

"It's about your son José María."

"What about him?"

"You know that, due to my position, I have frequent meetings with high ranking officers of some of the branches of the police force. I attend some of their meetings where heads of different departments exchange pertinent information. The day before yesterday, in one of these meetings, I found out that the police has information about a group of students from La Habana University, lead by some of the former alumni and faculty members, who are planning a massive act of rebellion against the government. The police still don't know what it is, but they are making great efforts to find out. They're gathering names of possible suspects and as much information as they can by trying to infiltrate the revolutionary cell. They already have some names of people that they are sure belong to that subversive group. They haven't seized them, because they feel that if they do so now, then a great number of their comrades will go into hiding. They aren't quite sure, at this point, whether the names of the people they know about are top members that could, when captured and questioned, reveal a complete list of associates. Right now, they're giving themselves a six month period to complete the investigation in full. For certain, by next summer they plan to have everybody in jail. Under the present circumstances, I fear that the leaders won't arrive at the court alive. The police don't want any more Castros, not in the city, anyway. One of the suspects on the list that I saw was a young man by the name of Manuel Mora, and among the list of Mora's friends, at the top of it, was the name of José María Aguirrupe."

"Oh, my God. I can't believe this. José has always been a very reserved person. He seldom talks about himself or his feelings to anybody. Not to me, and not to his brothers or his sister. He never liked politics. He's so dedicated to his work. Perhaps he's a friend of that fellow Mora, but I would doubt very much that he's involved in Mora's activities, whatever they are."

"Please, Francisco, be very discreet with this information. When they mentioned his name, I immediately told them that I knew him personally, and that I was an old friend of the family.

You know that right or wrong I will vouch for him, and, that if it becomes necessary, I'll go to Batista himself, so as to keep him out of harm's way. Unfortunately, you must also be aware that the police mean business, and won't take very lightly anything that, according to them, constitutes an illegal act."

"Yes, I know and I'm grateful to you, Pepe." Don Francisco pulled Pepe towards him and gave him a strong hug.

"I thank you for the information, and rest assured that I'll act upon it without getting you involved in any way."

"I wouldn't have told you about it if I didn't have complete confidence in you."

Don Francisco grabbed Pepe by his arm and escorted him out.

One by one, all of the guests left. Don Francisco remained alone with the children and Concha.

"Mari-Tere, have you fed the Chows?"

"Yes, and they're in my room already, father. They are resting and waiting for me to go to sleep with them. Is anything bothering you?"

"No, why do you say that?"

"Somehow your expression is different from before. You have a sad look on your face."

"You're imagining things, Mari-Tere. I'm just tired."

"Does that mean that we're not going to Midnight Mass this year?"

"Oh no, my sweet girl. I'm never tired for the Lord. Besides, I have a lot of praying to do tonight. Fernando, get the sedan ready and drive us to Mass. Is everybody ready?"

Everyone was ready to go except José María, who said that he would like to be excused since he had another party to go to. Don Francisco looked firmly into his son's eyes.

"What party is that?" inquired Don Francisco.

"It's at my friend's house."

"And what friend is that?"

"You don't know him, father. His name is Manuel Mora. We met several years ago at the university."

"Are you going there now?" María Teresa interjected. "Then give my very best to his brother, Raúl. We met at Villanueva and I invited him here tonight, but he's home sick."

Don Francisco was flabbergasted. "Look, José María, I'm serious. Call your friend and present your apologies for not attending the party tonight. I want you by my side at church. When we return, I also want to talk to you. There are a few things about your work that have come to my attention lately. I do believe that they are very important and merit a careful discussion between you and me."

"Can it wait until tomorrow?"

"No, I don't think it can. I don't think it should. I would rather talk to you tonight. You can sleep here afterwards. There is no need to go to that apartment of yours at such a late hour. So, after Mass, we open the presents and then we talk."

José María did not offer any more resistance. He went to make the phone call, and climbed into the car where everybody else was waiting for him.

"Did you lock the front doors?" asked María Teresa.

An affirmative nod was all that came from José María as a reply. Then, Concha said, "Thank God. We're all going to church together like a good Christian family to praise the Almighty on the birthday of His Son."

"We're really a close-knit family. Aren't we?" expressed María Teresa.

"Yes, we certainly are," said Don Francisco, resting his hand for a brief moment on top of María Teresa's head.

She looked back at her father and said, "What do you think we should ask God to give us for the coming year? We have almost everything that we want."

"Pray for peace, Mari-Tere. Pray that the next year will be full of peace for all men of good will."

CHAPTER FIVE

José María's apartment was located on the top floor of the recently built, square, cross-section structure, that, protruding from the ground straight as a needle, was erected at the beginning of Línea Street. From the huge L-shaped balcony that surrounded the apartment, one could see a magnificent view of the ocean dominating the scenery, which included the American Embassy building, along with the El Maine Monument to one side in front of the famous National Hotel. He had bought the apartment with his share of his mother's inheritance. He had received that money as soon as he had graduated from the University of La Habana.

A plush, light gray, wall-to-wall carpet covered the floor of the living room/dining room area. In the bedrooms the floors were a rich, highly polished, off-white granite, which was unexposed only in the areas around the beds. There, a shaggy, dark-gray carpet provided some comfort to naked feet, especially in the early morning hours.

Chrome, glass and leather were the basic materials of the furniture in the apartment. It provided a very modern look with its advanced Scandinavian design. Some ultra-modern paintings, including two genuine Modiglianis, one Klee and one Dali, decorated the walls.

March 10, 1957 was the anniversary of Batista's coup d'état, and the army as well as the other law enforcement agencies would be too busy celebrating to bother with the task of persecuting revolutionaries. It was the perfect day for a general meeting and that apartment was the best place to hold it. Nobody would suspect José María.

Before long, Manuel Mora found himself in front of the door to the apartment. He gave the agreed upon signal: two knocks, followed by three quick consecutive knocks and finally two more knocks. It was a signal that José María knew well. Any other person would have used the electric doorbell. José María answered promptly and said, "How are you Manuel? Please come in. You're the first one to arrive, as usual. It's good that we're going to enjoy a few minutes to ourselves before the others arrive."

"I'm fine, and ready to discuss the final details of the plan. I think we should make up our minds today."

José María signaled his friend to sit down, while he quickly went to the kitchen to fetch two frosted glasses. He filled them with beer, and placed one in front of Manuel. He sat across from him with his own glass in his hand.

"I wanted to talk to you about that before the others arrive. I think that we have some serious problems. I haven't told you, but my father said to me last Christmas that some friendships are dangerous. He added that they only lead to situations that become disastrous and that most of the time one is so close to the danger itself that he may not see it coming. He also mentioned that he had heard that I was associating myself with a group of people that were no longer thinking about my well-being, but about my death. No matter how justifiable their thoughts were, it was my life that they were playing around with. He asked me to stop seeing you. When I inquired why, and also who had been filling his head with all these worries, he wouldn't answer. He told me that it was sufficient for me to know that he knew, and that other concerned parties were also aware of the situation. You must understand, Manuel, he's my father and he's a very stubborn person. I had no choice but to tell him that I would abide by his wishes. I didn't tell you about this conversation back then, because I wanted to find out more for myself. I wanted to be sure of what I was going to tell you, and not to fill your head with conjectures that would lead us nowhere.

"First I thought it was my sister who told him, since she's becoming more interested in your brother Raúl with each passing day. I thought that he might have overheard you talking, and told her. That's why, if you remember, I asked you last January after our meeting not to get Raúl involved in our affairs. When you made me aware that Raúl didn't know of your activities, I believed you and no longer suspected Mari-Tere of being our informer.

"It was unlikely that my father had known for any length of time, because his volatile character when anything concerns his family would have prompted him to tell me much sooner. He must have been told that very same night. But if that was true, then who told him? It could only have been Fernando or one of my father's friends attending the dinner party. By a simple process of elimination I could discard Fernando right away, since he was with me the entire evening. Furthermore he would've told me directly if he'd found out something that concerned me. He might have talked to my father, but only after he'd talked to me.

"It had to be one of my father's friends. Of the two that were there that night, the most likely would have been Pepe. He's the Minister of Justice, so he must have access to police information. It took me a while to come up with a good pretext to see him in private. I finally managed to do so a week ago. It confirmed my suspicions. In our short encounter, I mentioned to him that my father had asked me to stay away from you, and that I obediently had done so. I also told him that if you were in any kind of danger, I would like to know, so that I could be of help to you and your family. He said that he was very glad that I had obeyed my father's wishes, and that he was sure my father knew what was best for me at any given time. He also said that I could count on his assistance if you should get into trouble some time in the near future. He would not say anything else pertaining to you, although he didn't have to, for I already had the information that I was looking for.

"You see, Manuel, that conversation revealed to me that some government officials are definitely after you, and that they know about our friendship. The fact that he said 'some time in the near future,' means that we still have some time, but not much. If we're planning to kill Batista, we should do it now."

"I'm glad that you told me that story. That confirms the feeling of persecution that I've experienced for the past few months. You see, I've been thinking that someone is following me at all times. Lately, I've gotten into the habit of changing routes, switching from my car to taxis to public transportation, to try to shake loose these pursuers. I'm glad to know that I was right after all. For a while, I thought that I was going nuts.

"I agree with you one hundred per cent. When the group arrives today we'll take care of the final details, and, if you're ready, we'll kill the bastard as soon as possible. By the time they react, they'll find Batista dead, and a new government in power to offer our people the democratic government they deserve. Even Castro is going to be pissed at us, but so be it. Fidel will have to take his chances at the polls like everybody else when we give free elections according to our Constitution."

One by one, the other leaders arrived. Mainly they were members of the FEU (La Habana University Student Council) and the DR (Revolutionary Directory). José Antonio Echeverría, student leader, better known as "Manzanita" for his baby face, and Dr. Pelayo Cuervo, ex-senator of Cuba, arrived together. Rolando Cubela came as the liaison between these revolutionary cells and Castro's July 26th Movement.

When everybody was seated comfortably around the oval-shaped table, and more glasses of cold beer had been served, Dr.

Cuervo, being the eldest member of the group, called the meeting to order.

"We're all aware that the purpose of this meeting is to coordinate the final details of the plan to eliminate Batista and declare a political take-over by a new government headed by me, that will call for national free elections in a period of time no less than three months, but no more than eighteen months in accordance with the Constitution. I have also mentioned that I won't participate in that electoral process. I will merely supervise it and ensure its fairness and legality, so we can return to the democracy that we all desire. Now, I'll ask Manuel to inform us of his plan and preparations."

"Thank you, Dr. Cuervo. We're already prepared to stage an assault on the Presidential Palace. We have acquired a large commercial truck and we have two old sedans ready. They're parked at the construction site of one of José María's projects, hiding under huge tarps, looking innocent. In these three vehicles we can carry forty-six men to the glorious task of deposing the dictator once and for all. We plan to break in through the gate leading to Colón Street, when we know that Batista is within the building. We believe that gaining access to the interior of the Palace should be an easy task, since the few guards at this entrance will be caught off guard by the element of surprise. This unexpected attack will give us enough leverage to rapidly dispose of them, and gain access to the interior courtyard. Once inside, we'll rush our way in to the second floor, where Batista's private offices are located. We're positive that in the mid-afternoon he'll be there reviewing papers and attending to his daily appointments. We'll throw grenades into each one of the rooms and then we'll use machine guns to kill anyone that might remain alive to offer resistance. A group of twelve, selected, suitable men, with me leading the attack, will be the ones proceeding to the upper floors. The main bulk of the platoon will remain in the courtyard to repel any counterattack from the defending forces trying to keep us from gaining access to the upper floors. They'll wait until we return, and then, as a group, we will retreat to the vehicles and leave the Palace in a complete state of disorientation, confusion and shock. The entire operation shouldn't take more than ten to fifteen minutes according to our calculations, and we won't be inside the Palace more than eight minutes. They won't know what hit them, and Batista will be dead."

"The plan is a fine one," said José María. "I can vouch for it, since Manuel and I have been discussing and preparing for it for almost a year."

José María reached under the table for a large box and placed it on top of the table. He then reached for its content and said, "This is a scale model of the Presidential Palace, cut away into sections to expose the interior." José María proceeded to explain the details of the attack. At the end of his explanation, he said, "There is only one question that remains unanswered. Who is going to supply us with the heavy artillery? I mean the grenades and the sub-machine guns. As far as I can report now, we only have some rifles, shotguns and several pistols."

"Ah, that's my department," said Rolando Cubela, "and the task of the July 26th Movement. They have given me their word that they will supply you with eighteen sub-machine guns with five clips of ammunition for each of them. They are made in Czechoslovakia, and are supposed to be very reliable. A special envoy will bring them to you, as soon as I give them the word. They will also give you three dozen Garand rifles, three dozen Colt .45 pistols and thirty-six grenades, plus plenty of ammo for the rifles and the pistols. I know that they are all hidden in one of the mansions of the fashionable country club area, but I don't know which one it is.

"I would also like to take this opportunity to tell everyone that Castro sends his best wishes to all of you, and that you can count on his cooperation after the attack takes place. As usual, I'll communicate with him by radio, and inform him of the results of this meeting today."

"We have the plans, the transportation and the armaments

ready. Now, what about the propaganda? Can you bring us up to date on your activities, Echeverría?" inquired Dr. Cuervo.

"Thank you, Sir. I'd like to inform all of you that we are also ready. We have weapons hidden at La Habana University. Within minutes after the success of the attack, we'll drive in three cars towards the CMQ Radio and Television Station, which is only a few minutes away from the hill of the university. By that time, we will also have some armed men at strategic points surrounding the station. When they hear the approaching cars, they'll move to quickly neutralize any opposing force. I'll then deliver a message over the radio that will be transmitted to the entire island. In that message I'll report that Batista is dead, and that the Revolution is alive, that we have placed the reins of the government into the hands of Dr. Pelayo Cuervo, who will address the people as soon as the operation is complete, and everything is under control. I'll urge all sympathetic members of the police and armed forces to show their allegiance to the People of Cuba, and take over specific Police Stations and Military Posts, and wait for further orders. To the Cuban population, I'll say that it's the request of the Revolution that they stay home and participate with us in a general strike that will paralyze the country until we can consolidate a temporary government and safely return to a stable situation. We will keep full control of the station, and send the portable TV units to the Presidential Palace to broadcast live Dr. Cuervo's speech to the country. The units will be accompanied by a large group of students that have already been alerted to participate in our endeavors at any moment. Obviously, these people don't know anything else. The students will march in front of the caravan of trucks and cars bringing Dr. Cuervo to the Presidential Palace, and Manuel and José María will meet them at the Maceo Park, and provide an armed escort in case of any problems reentering the Palace. We can place all these gears into motion the moment Manuel gives us the go ahead on the day and the time."

"Then everything is ready. The next question is when. Are

we prepared to discuss that issue at this meeting?" said Dr. Cuervo, looking at all the faces around the table.

Manuel said, "Dr. Cuervo, I must tell you that for some time now I've had the premonition that I was being followed. Well, today I almost had that notion confirmed. The government's investigative agencies are following me. If this is true, it won't be long before I'm captured, and to tell you the truth, I don't know how long I could stand torture. If they break me, I know too much about all of you and the plans. So, I consider it very important that we don't delay any longer. I propose that we carry out our plans as soon as possible."

"Rolando, how soon can you have the weapons ready?" said José María, trying to reinforce the importance of Manuel's urgency.

"They could be ready the day after tomorrow, if I let them know today after I leave this meeting."

Pelayo Cuervo said, "Okay, let's review." They went over the proposed plan a few more times. José María suggested launching the attack on March 13 at three in the afternoon. They all agreed.

José María said, "I think, Manuel, that you should go into hiding until that day. We'll find you a safe home to stay in. You'd better call your family and tell them that you are going to spend a few days at Varadero Beach. Tell your father that you've met this wonderful woman. I'm sure he'll understand."

"Well, I'm sure that three days from today we will have the immense pleasure of serving our country, and being remembered by history as the heroes of the decade. Our children and grandchildren will be proud to bear our names. This meeting is adjourned."

They all left, one by one, at ten minute intervals. Manuel was the last one to leave. Before he left, he told José María, "You've done enough already for the cause by supplying us with information, giving us your monetary support, and allowing us the use of your apartment for our meetings. What I mean to say is that you don't have to go with us on the 13th. Nobody will reproach your final decision. I'll make sure of that, and I could find someone to replace you."

"At the beginning, when you asked me for my cooperation in this matter, I told you that you could count on me all the way. I'm doing this because it's something that I truly believe to be my duty. I'm going with you inside that building. Besides, I know the place better than you do. I've been in it, and you've always looked at it from the outside. I may not be the adventurous type, but I can also handle a gun better than you can. Therefore, my dear friend, come and pick me up at two in the afternoon, that day. I'll be waiting for you, and if you don't show up by that time, then I'll go alone and attack the fucking Palace at two-thirty, and kill the son of a bitch myself."

"Well, maybe I'd better take you. I need a crazy daredevil to cover my ass, and I think that you're mad enough for the job. I'll be here on time to escort you to destiny."

"In the meantime, where are you hiding?"

"If I'm going to tell my family about Varadero, I think it's best that I go there. I'll be at the International Hotel, under my own name. If the police are after me, it would be best to spend a couple of days there with a real woman. They'll probably think that I'm just having a good time, and they won't bother me over there."

"Yes, I think that you're right. But where are you going to find a girl to go with you like that?"

"Well, I was thinking about your sister, but I couldn't do that to my brother."

"Go to hell, Manuel. Be serious."

"Think it over, José. What do you think I'll do? I'll go to the Mambo Club and grab the best-looking whore in the place and pay her to come with me."

"Do you need money?"

"No, thanks anyway. I'll have to go home first and pack. I have some money hidden away for a rainy day, and I think that tomorrow it will pour."

"In that case, so long, Manuel. Take care and have a good time."

"Good-bye, José. Until the 13th."

The Statue of General Maximo Gómez at the park containing the entrance to the tunnel under the Bay with El Morro Castle in the background. The Presidential Palace stands at the opposite end of the avenue. Picture taken in 1958.

Cuban Presidential Palace.

CHAPTER SIX

March 13, 1957 started as a normal day in the city of La Habana. The weather was perfect for a revolution. The deep blue tone of an almost cloudless Caribbean sky revealed the presence of a bright, sunny, warm and dry day.

María Teresa had gone to the piers with a group of students from the school, escorted by Professor Blanco, to see and study the engine room of a merchant marine ship. The captain of the boat, that navigated under the United States flag, had found it very hard to say no when the American Embassy had telephoned him with the request from the American Augustinian priests. That afternoon, seventeen students had showed up aboard his vessel. He had given orders to the mess hall to prepare a little snack for the visitors, consisting of hot dogs, apple pie with ice cream and Coca-Colas. She was inside the engine room when the attack on the Presidential Palace started.

Carlos had not had any classes on that afternoon and had gone home early after lunch. He was taking a siesta when Concha woke him up with the news of the attack.

Fernando was in the American Embassy, discussing with one

of the Consuls a legal problem involving an American citizen who had a large portion of real estate in the city.

Don Francisco was working, as usual, in the Supreme Court building, located in the old section of La Habana.

José María was seated in the front seat of one of the cars. He had an automatic pistol attached to his belt. Two fully loaded extra clips were in his upper shirt pocket. In front of him, on the car floor, was a sub-machine gun ready to be fired. Four additional magazines were in his trouser pockets. From a long belt slung over one of his shoulders, six grenades hung.

The caravan of vehicles approached the side entrance to the Palace very slowly. From the front vehicle, two men came out and walked towards the sentinels on duty, shouting out that they were looking for information on how to get to the Fine Arts Museum, which was only a few blocks away from where they were. When they got close to the sentinels, they took out their pistols and hit them on the head, knocking them out. These two men then turned quickly around and yelled to the rest of the group that were still inside the truck and the cars to follow them. In an act of valor they ran charging against the interior gate, which was guarded by three more men. In order to prevent this second tier of guards from closing the Iron Gate, they had no choice but to fire their weapons. The sudden attack took these other guards by surprise, and before they had any time to react, they were on the ground, fatally wounded.

The first burst of gunshots should not have taken place until the majority of the task force was inside the courtyard. But now, as the entire group was running into the Palace, the other soldiers on duty regrouped to try to repel the invaders. What was even worse was that those shots were heard on the second floor where Batista was at the moment. He immediately ran to seek refuge in the private bedrooms of the third floor. A select number of bodyguards and soldiers remained on the second floor to prevent any access to the upper floors.

José María took possession of the main floor, and dispatched his men in a way that he could maintain his position and cover

Manuel's daring charge to the second floor. The battle was fierce, with lots of bullets flying from one side to the other. From his cover, behind a thick concrete column with a large square pedestal, José María tossed three grenades against the enemy, and saw that two failed to explode. The only advantage gained from the grenades was that their mere presence on the floor next to the soldiers made them run into the open, where he quickly killed them with his sub-machine gun. The invading force suffered some casualties, but not enough to merit a retreat.

In the meantime, Manuel with his group of selected men had climbed the stairs to the second floor. They found very strong resistance as they moved into the office area. Two of Manuel's men were killed when they attempted to cross the wide hallway, to take cover behind the doorframes. These two men had run in front of him, and their guns had jammed. They could not fire while running, and became easy targets for the defenders. When they fell on the cold marble floor, Manuel opened fire, running and jumping over them. He managed to kill the guards inside the room.

Manuel took two grenades from his belt and rolled them down the hallway towards the doors leading to the main offices. Both exploded, launching the bodies of several soldiers into the air. He then yelled to the rest of his men to follow him and the small platoon entered the main offices, shooting anything that moved. Manuel reached the main door to Batista's private office. He shot the lock with his sub-machine gun, and, kicking the door open, he threw a grenade inside the room while taking cover behind the wall adjacent to the door.

That grenade didn't explode. He then moved in with two men behind him. They emptied the entire magazine of their automatic weapons. In the end, they realized that they had walked into an empty room. Batista was not there.

It did not take long for Manuel to realize that he had to continue to the third floor if he was going to dispose of his target. Coming out of the office, he found more resistance coming from nearby rooms. His men fought them with courage, but they were pinned down. The noise of the shooting and the radio communication must have alerted the police. Soon enough, these forces would mobilize and cut off their escape route.

In desperation, he started to call José María for help. José María had his hands full by that time, just trying to maintain his position. However, when he heard Manuel yelling, he rushed to aid his friend. He looked at his wristwatch and noticed that twenty minutes had elapsed since they had begun the attack. They were already out of time, according to the original plan. He then told the men next to him to take over the operation on the first floor and to wait five minutes for him and the rest of the men.

"If we aren't here in the next five minutes, get the hell out of here with whoever is alive."

Then he took five men who were positioned closest to the staircase, and, marching in front of them, began the climb to the upper floor.

José María managed to make his way to Manuel's position. Four more men were lost in the attempt. When he arrived next to Manuel, he said, "Did you kill Batista? Is he dead?"

"No, he wasn't in his office. I think he's run with his personal bodyguards to the third floor where his private bedroom is supposed to be. I hate to say it, but I think that we've failed. All that's left is to try to get out."

"The hell we've failed. We're now on the second floor. One more floor to go, and we can get the bastard. I say we go up first and then we leave."

"You have more guts than I ever imagined. I'm glad you came along. I'm with you. Let's do it."

José María tried to put a smile on his face and said, "You might find a hard-headed Basque, but never one who is a coward. You men cover us. Let's go, Manuel."

They ran up the staircase in a matter of seconds. Two men were standing on the third floor landing armed with rifles. They took aim the moment they spotted Manuel and José María climbing the stairs, two steps at a time, but they were not fast enough. José María fired his weapon, and they fell backwards as the leaded impact ripped the guards' bodies almost in half. As soon as the two invaders reached the hallway on the third floor, they moved as close as possible to the heavily defended doorway. Manuel threw a grenade that exploded right in front of the thick wooden doors, destroying them and disposing of the guards inside at the same time. Both comrades advanced to the opening, and standing on either side they threw their last grenades into the room. Batista was inside the room. Neither of the grenades went off.

Manuel did not have any more ammunition for his sub-machine gun. He pulled out his pistol and ran into the room ready to fire when a shotgun blast ripped his chest wide open and he fell backwards in front of José María.

José María loaded the last magazine into his sub-machine gun and entered the room with his finger on the trigger, but his gun misfired. He looked with a surprised expression on his face at the two men standing in front of him. One had a pistol in his hand; the other was holding a 12-gauge shotgun. Batista was behind them with a .45 caliber revolver in his hand. The pistol shot first. The bullet entered José María's forehead, pushing his head backwards, and exited from the top rear portion of his head, sending bits and pieces of his brain in all directions.

Shortly after the agreed hour, Echeverría and his men had taken possession of the radio station and he was transmitting to the whole country the news that Batista had been killed. The Chief of Police dispatched his forces to regain control of the main radio and television station. He had also had information that an attack had been launched against the Presidential Palace. By the time his men arrived at the broadcasting studio, they knew that the main attack had been a failure and that Batista was alive and well. They stormed the station with fury and violently disposed of anyone who resembled a revolutionary. Echeverría ran for his life towards his car, which was parked two blocks away. He was recognized climbing into the vehicle, and he died under a barrage of bullets. When they searched his clothing, they found a paper with his next speech on it, the one that would mention that Dr. Cuervo had taken control of the provisional government.

An order to arrest Dr. Cuervo was issued. He was found at his home, half an hour later, where he had been waiting for someone to take him to his glorious destiny. The police took him to the nearest station, and after obtaining all the information that they could out of him, he was escorted to the Laguito, a small pond in the Biltmore section of the city, and shot. The government officially disavowed any knowledge of his death.

When Don Francisco heard the news, he was in session with the other magistrates. The first reaction of the other magistrates was to call the Presidential Palace to see if the information was true. Don Francisco's first impulse was to contact his house to find out where all his children were. He told Concha the news, and commanded her to tell Carlos to stay put in the house and to wait for him. He found out the whereabouts of Fernando and María Teresa, but he did not know where José María was exactly. Don Francisco thought that he might be able to locate José María through his office.

Fernando came to the phone immediately, and said, "Father, what's going on? Have you heard the news? CMQ is saying that Batista is dead, and they are calling for a general strike. Other radio stations are saying that they don't know anything about it. The Embassy has tried to contact the Palace, but can't get through."

"Listen, Fernando, I don't know at this time what's true and what isn't. María Teresa is at the pier visiting some vessel with a group of students. I'm going there right now to bring her home. I want you to stay at the Embassy. Talk to the Consul, he's a friend of mine. Ask him if he could take you home. Under no circumstances should you take your own car. If you have any problem with transportation, let me know and I'll pick you up as soon as I get Mari-Tere. I have the Supreme Court official plate on my car and that will make the vehicle safe. Now go and ask the Consul if he will do it. I'll wait for his answer."

A minute later, Fernando was back on the phone, "Father, the Consul said that it would be no problem. We're going to leave in about fifteen minutes, so I'll probably get home before you do. Is there any other thing that you want me to do?"

"Try to locate José María. Call the office, the construction site or the apartment. Wherever he is, tell him to stay there. Tell him that I'll send Jaime to fetch him later on. Thank you, Fernando, and take care."

"I'll see you at home. Don't worry about José María. I'll find him one way or another."

Don Francisco hung the black robe that he wore whenever he was in session. He had sent for Jaime, the chauffeur, who came rushing into his private chambers and found him already wearing his own coat.

He then proceeded to call Villanueva to find out which boat his daughter was visiting. He climbed into his car and told Jaime to take him to La Habana harbor.

When he arrived at the pier, he found confusion everywhere. There were a few cars on the streets, but a lot of police and army security vehicles were on the roads, traveling at incredible speeds. They were stopping some of the cars and making all the passengers get out for searching and questioning.

He told Jaime to park at the entrance to the pier. When the security personnel came to tell him that he could not station the car at that spot, he simply told them that he was there on official business and proceeded to the ship without waiting for a reply.

All seventeen students were inside the cargo ship with Professor Blanco. María Teresa came forward when she saw her father. "Dad, we're all worried. We don't know what's going on."

Don Francisco did not answer his daughter. Instead he looked around and asked, "Who is in charge here?"

Professor Blanco took a couple of steps forward. "My name is Ernesto Blanco and I'm responsible for these students."

"Delighted to meet you, although I would have loved it to have been under a better set of circumstances. My name is Francisco Aguirrupe, and I am María Teresa's father. How did you come here today?"

"We came in three cars. One is mine and the others belong to these two students here. They all wanted to leave the moment they heard the news, but I've been telling them that three cars full of young people will constitute a very dangerous proposition at this time. I've advised them to remain calm until I find a way to get them home safely."

"You've done right, Professor. I agree with you wholeheartedly. Now, who is in charge of this vessel?"

"I'm Captain Johnson. You must realize that I can't keep all of these people here overnight. I just don't have enough room for all of them."

"Please to meet you, sir. I'm a Supreme Court Justice. Don't worry, because I intend to take these people off your hands right now. But first, let me give you my thanks for allowing them to remain here safely." Then, addressing the entire group, he continued, "Now, listen to me, all of you. I can take seven of you in my limousine, including my daughter. That leaves ten of you and Professor Blanco. I suggest that Blanco take four of you in his car. The remaining six students will go equally divided, in two groups of three, in each of the remaining cars. Those of you who live the closest to each other will go in the same car. We shall leave together and continue in a caravan very close to each other. My car will be in front, and anyone experiencing any problems or anyone who may be stopped by the authorities should stop right away and blow the horn. All the other cars will also stop and everybody is to remain seated in their own car. I will do all the explaining."

"Let me make a list of addresses and plan a safe route," Professor Blanco said. "I think we should leave as soon as feasible and try to reach home before dark. Don't you think?"

"I quite agree, Professor. Let's go now."

The whole trip took over two hours to make, but it went without incident.

When Don Francisco reached his home, he was glad to find Fernando and Carlos in the house. However, José María was missing. He inquired about his other son, but all he could get out of Fernando was that the latter had tried every possible place. He then went into his library alone, and closing the door behind him, sat at his desk and phoned Pepe.

"Francisco, how are you?" Pepe said when he came on the line.

"I'm fine, Pepe. Most of my family is here with me, but I can't find José María, and to tell you the truth, after what you told me last Christmas Eve, I fear the worst. Do you know what actually happened today?"

"There was an attack on the Presidential Palace by a group of rebels with the intent to kill Batista. I've been told that they reached the living quarters where he was hiding. They didn't succeed. Apparently some of the rebels' weaponry misfired or were defective. Most of the assailants died in the assault. Others died in the streets adjacent to the Palace. At the same time, another group took over CMQ and started to broadcast the news that Batista was dead. They all died when government forces regained control of the station. I haven't been able to talk to Batista. Another minister told me that he's extremely upset, swearing vengeance to anyone associated with the attack. In a sense, you can't blame him, for his entire family was with him when it occurred.

"I don't know anything about José María. I'll start making some inquiries, and call you back the moment I have some news. Stay calm, my friend, you know how young people are. Maybe he's at another friend's house and has decided to spend the time there, without thinking of calling you. I promise you I'll call you back within the hour."

"Give my very best to your family, and thank you very much. I'll wait for your call."

Don Francisco prepared a double brandy for himself and sat

in one of the big leather chairs. Concha came in about half an hour later to tell him that dinner would be served in fifteen minutes. Don Francisco replied that they should all go and have supper without him. When asked if he wanted something to be brought to him in the library, his response was negative. Then he poured a second double brandy and lit a cigar. He could not get José María out of his mind.

Another half an hour went by, and this time María Teresa came into the library. "Father, there's a Colonel Rojas at the door asking to see you."

"Please, bring him to me, Mari-Tere."

A tall, deeply tanned, handsome man in the uniform of a Colonel in the Cuban Army, with dark eyes matching the black color of his well-groomed hair, walked into the room.

"Are you Magistrate Aguirrupe?"

"Yes, I am. What can I do for you, Colonel?"

"I'm afraid that I'm the bearer of bad news, Magistrate. I come directly from President Batista with a letter that he has asked me to deliver personally into your hands. Here it is, Sir. I'll wait while you read it, for your reply, if there is any." He handed Don Francisco a white envelope.

"Please, Colonel, have a seat. I have to find my glasses first."

Moving towards the desk, Don Francisco opened one of the drawers and took a pair of wire-rimmed glasses from a leather pouch. Then, grabbing a letter opener, he slit the top part of the envelope with one stroke.

La Habana, March 13, 1957.
Dear Supreme Court Justice Francisco Aguirrupe:
    I regret to inform you that your son, José María Aguirrupe, has died while attempting to take my life in the unsuccessful attack on the Presidential Palace today. It is my understanding that he was part of a revolutionary cell that has been planning this feat for some time. I do admire

courage and valor in a man, and I must tell you that he died bravely, fighting for his misguided beliefs. I do not wish to burden your soul with more worries than the ones that I am bringing you in this letter. It is necessary then that I tell you that I am fully aware of the innocence of the other members of your household, who should not fear any consequences derived from José María's actions. There are no words that I might say to console you at this moment. It must suffice then for you to know that, as a father myself, I join you in your grief.

With deep sorrows,

> Fulgéncio Batista Zaldívar
> President of the Republic of Cuba.

Don Francisco dropped the paper on top of his desk, as it was unbearable for his hands to support it anymore. He held his tears with the strong will of a man determined not to let his emotions surface in front of strangers.

"Colonel, please convey my acknowledgement to President Batista. You said that I could reply to it, didn't you?"

Colonel Rojas stood up and said, "Yes, I shall tell the President anything that you want me to say to him."

"Would you please tell the President that I insist on having my son's body brought to my house, so I can arrange for a proper funeral. I don't want him to be buried in a common grave."

"Yes, Sir, I'll convey your wishes to the President. May I also tell you that, due to the wounds received by your son, he's not in the best shape? You have other members in your family, and it could be quite a shock to see him in his present condition."

"Colonel, bring my son to me, even if he is in pieces. Let me worry about my family. They shouldn't be any concern of yours. Is that clear?"

"Yes, Sir. I understand you perfectly. I'll do as you ask. Please accept my condolences. Good night, Sir."

The Colonel turned around with the martial etiquette of his military training, and left the room without waiting to be escorted out.

Don Francisco fell on top of his chair. The withheld tears came profusely from his weary eyes.

María Teresa entered the library, and, seeing her father in a way that she had never seen him before, started crying also. "What's happening, Father? What did that man say to you?"

"Mari-Tere, please hold me. Hold me tight, for I've just lost another piece of my heart."

CHAPTER SEVEN

The President of Villanueva University called a meeting to be attended by the priests responsible for the administration of the school, the members of the Board of Trustees, and the deans representing each of the different faculties. The agenda was simple and brief. It limited the discussion to the question of whether the university should remain open for classes or close its doors for an indefinite period of time.

La Habana University had already decided to cancel classes as a sign of lamentation for the death of the students and former alumni that were involved in attacking the Presidential Palace. The decision was not uncommon, since that school had a long history of political unrest. On many occasions in the past, it had opted to cancel its classes as a sign of protest against the establishment, and a means of conveying to the general public that it was unsafe for students to attend classes. Villanueva, on the contrary, had never undergone a similar experience. The administration was completely opposed to the idea of telling the students to remain at home.

But some of the professors, who were mostly Cubans, argued that not only might it not be safe for their students to attend classes, but that the decision of making them come to classes could very well place them in a controversial position. That position could entail political as well as personal repercussions in the future professional lives of the young men and women after their graduation.

The members of the Board of Trustees assured the administration that, according to their own experience in affairs of this nature, the time period would not have to be more than several weeks, maybe a few months at the most. In the meantime, they claimed that Villanueva might not be the safest place to move around, especially if you were a young student. The police could expose students in the streets to attacks if they suspected that they were part of the conspiracy to overthrow Batista. Other students from La Habana University, who might be upset that they had not joined them in their grief, could also assault them. Furthermore, they could be killed by revolutionaries dressed as military personnel, in search of another torch to light the flame of anger and the sentiment of revenge in the hearts of the people. One of the members of the Board concluded, "Cuba does not need more martyrs."

Nevertheless, at the end of the meeting, the affirmative votes carried the motion. The university was not to be closed for any period of time and classes would continue without further interruptions.

José María's funeral was a private affair. Don Francisco had decided that, in view of the circumstances surrounding his son's death, it was for the best to have a very simple burial and Church service, with the participation of the immediate family members only.

A few days later, he allowed his friends to visit him at his house to offer their condolences. The outcome of his wishes was a long parade of many different people, some of whom he hardly knew, that lasted over two weeks. Among these people, there was one person that he had never met before. His name was Luis Mora, the father of Manuel Mora.

Luis showed up last. He appeared at the door of the Aguirrupe's house one Sunday afternoon, and asked to see Don Francisco. He gave his name to Mirta, who answered the door. She told him to come in and to wait in the foyer, while she went to look for Don Francisco. A few minutes later she reappeared and asked him to follow her to the patio where Don Francisco was resting in a lounge chair. Detecting a hesitation in Luis to say the first words of salutation, and seeing the expression of entanglement on his face, Don Francisco decided to extend his hand to Luis and said, "My name is Francisco Aguirrupe. I understand that you are Señor Luis Mora, and that you wish to talk to me. I'm glad to meet you. How do you do?"

Taking the offered hand and shaking it firmly, the man answered, "I'm fine, thank you, considering what we've been through in the past weeks. You are very kind, sir, in receiving me. I'm very happy to have this opportunity to meet you. I've always heard that you were a fine gentleman."

"Well, thank you so much for your kind words. Nobody will bother us here. You can talk freely, for nobody else is in the house now, besides the servants. May I offer you something to drink while we talk? What would you like?"

Luis asked for a soft drink, and Don Francisco went to the bar at the other side of the pool. He returned with two frosty glasses filled with crushed ice and two bottles of Materva. He placed the drinks on top of the glass surface covering the wrought iron table. Then he sat again in one of the comfortably cushioned chairs and signaled Luis to do the same.

"Señor Aguirrupe, you have a very beautiful house. Your son José María described it to us at one time. You know how he liked to describe structures and city dwellings. However, it's hard to visualize the charm and elegance of something like this from words. One has to see it to actually appreciate it."

"Thank you very much. My wife, who died many years ago, also liked this house a lot, even though the patio and the pool weren't here then. José María, as a student, worked very hard in designing this area. Later on, if you wish, I could show you the inside."

"Yes, I'd like that if it's possible. How is work?"

"I haven't gone to the Supreme Court for the past three weeks. All of my cases have been postponed. Tomorrow will be my first day back on the job, God willing."

"I'm sorry. How stupid of me! I shouldn't have asked that question."

"No, don't worry about it. Tell me, Señor Mora, what do you do for a living?"

"I'm the department manager of the Salón Imperio, where they make the hand-made suits, at the J. Vallés store on San Rafael Street."

"How interesting! Do you purchase the fabrics?"

"Yes, as a matter of fact, I do. Twice a year I travel to England, Germany and Italy to study the latest styles and fashions in men's clothing, and to purchase the latest weaves. My assistant goes to the United States with the same purpose. We usually purchase about 70% of our raw material in Europe. The Italians are great at working with pure silk, and this year we have just received a shipment of silk, and also a combination of silk and wool, that will make good-looking sports jackets. These rolls of material won't be on display until the end of August, but if you care to take a look at them, I'll gladly put aside whatever you like."

"That's very kind of you. I usually dress very conservatively, in three-piece suits, but my sons Fernando and Carlos might be interested in your proposition. Now, tell me, Señor Mora, what do you really wish to say to me? I'm sure you didn't come here today to discuss our professions."

"You're right. How clumsy of me! I came to talk to you about our children. But first, you must forgive me for intruding in your sorrow. I'm also carrying in my heart the loss of my son, Manuel." Some tears started to show in Luis's eyes. He swallowed hard and continued, "I know that Manuel and your son were conspirators in that attack. I also know that they were very close friends, to the extent that my son might have involved yours. And in so doing, he brought your son to his death. I apologize for my son, and beg you not to hold a grudge against him for his actions. Let his soul rest forever in peace, and give my wife and me the serenity of continuing with our lives without any additional burden on our consciences."

"My dear friend, Mora," said Don Francisco, looking the white-haired man squarely in the eyes, with an expression revealing compassion as well as empathy, "May I call you friend?" Without waiting for a reply, he continued, "You and I have experienced one of the worst things that can happen to a father. Believe me, I have no grudge whatsoever against your son, or your family. I must confess, I told José María not to get involved with Manuel. You see, I heard news at that time that something bad was going on. I didn't know any details and neither did my source, but the overall picture was sufficient evidence for me to warn my son. I'm sure that he acted on his own volition. He was the type of person that, if he didn't want to do something, no one could convince him to the contrary. What he did with your son he did on a voluntary basis. So, don't apologize to me, for apologies are not needed. I also want you and your family to know that I'm deeply sorry for your loss."

"I shall be honored that you call me your friend. May I embrace you, Francisco?"

"Of course." The two men stood up and held each other in their arms.

When they sat down again, Luis said, "You bring a great sense of relief into my heart with your kind words. José María always spoke very highly of you. I'd like you to know that we also loved him dearly. Now, we only have one more son left. His name is Raúl, and my wife and myself are both very concerned about him, because he has expressed wishes to avenge his brother's death."

"Yes, I've heard about him. Mari-Tere, my daughter, and Carlos, my other son, knew him from the university. But don't worry too much about his feelings at this moment. It's a natural reaction for a younger brother, especially if he was attached to his older brother. What you should do, if you allow me to advise you in this matter, is to tell him not to try to perform what he might consider to be a heroic act. At his age, heroism and foolishness are easily mistaken for one another."

"That's exactly what I've been telling him. I also told him to think of his mother. She can't take any more suffering. We're really living through difficult times, don't you think?"

"Difficult? That's an understatement. Sometimes I think that the entire world has gone mad since the beginning of this century. When historians write about these times, I'm sure that they will refer to the twentieth century as the Era of Madness, the period of time in which civilization advanced technologically and scientifically in leaps and bounds, and at the same time regressed philosophically and politically to the age of darkness."

"Why do you say that?"

"My friend, Luis, just look around you. Airplanes, submarines, automobiles, television, nuclear propelled vessels, stereo sound systems, refrigerators, air conditioning systems, washing machines, etc., etc. We're enjoying realities that were only dreams in the last century. At the same time, we've undergone a ridiculous World War I, the overtaking of a religious country by proponents of an atheistic philosophy that have decided to impose their will onto mankind. They convert every country they control into a huge prison, and deprive its inhabitants of their basic elements of freedom. We've also had an insane World War II, carried on by lunatics on both sides, who decided after it all ended to deliver into slavery the very population for whose freedom the war had been fought in the first place. On top of all that, there is a lack of moral values in today's society. Societies sanction and praise the shrewdness of the criminal, and admire his intelligence for evil, while they just feel sorry for the victim. Justice has been eradicated from this century, and all that matters is the cleverness of lawyers in winning legal points. Maybe other times have been similar to these, but I always wanted to believe that men, in their quest to become civilized beings, would try very hard to overcome previous mistakes. Unfortunately, that is not true."

"I guess you're right. With my limited knowledge of history and philosophy, I wouldn't dare argue with you. But, if you permit me, I'd like to get back to my other son, Raúl, and ask you for a personal favor."

"By all means. If it's in my power, I'll grant it to you. What is it?"

"I've been thinking, that is, my wife and I have been thinking, that with the approach of the summer vacation in just two more months, it could really be a very bad time for Raúl to be around the house with nothing to do. Idleness can easily be the source of very bad thoughts in a restless young mind that is harboring notions of revenge. What we have thought would be best is for him to be out of the country for a while. Miami seems to us a good place to send him. It's close by, and he can learn some English, which is going to be helpful in his future professional activities. We aren't a rich family, but we have some savings, and we can afford to put him in a hotel over there for a couple of months. I understand that to procure a tourist visa from the U. S. Embassy will take approximately a couple of days, but to obtain a passport from the Ministry of the Interior might take months. We can't wait that long. Could you help us to speed up that process?"

"Of course, Luis. Give me the particulars of your son and his photograph, and I'll have my eldest son, Fernando, take care of it. It should be ready in a week or so, including the visa."

"We shall be indebted to you forever."

"Oh, don't mention it. I'm glad to be of service to the father of the friend of my son. I also think that your idea of sending Raúl to Miami is a very good one. I wish I had thought of it concerning my children."

"But, Señor Aguirrupe" Luis said, overwhelmed by Don Francisco's generosity.

"Please, call me Francisco."

"Very well, Francisco. I think that it would be a very good idea if your children were to go to Miami with my son. You see, they do have a lot in common and I know that they will be a good influence on Raúl. I also know that my son might be reluctant to take this trip on his own, even when ordered to do so, but if I could tell him that your children are also going along with him, I'm positive that he will go without an argument. What do you say?"

"I really have to think it over. Let me discuss it with Carlos and Mari-Tere and I'll let you know. Why don't you bring me your son's papers for his passport sometime next week and I'll give you my decision at that time."

"That's fine. I'll be here next Thursday after supper. And now, I must go. I've taken too much of your time. It's been a real pleasure to meet you, sir. You can count on me for whatever you wish me to do for you."

Luis offered a firm handshake that was gladly accepted by Don Francisco. After a brief tour of the house, he accompanied Luis to the front doors and bid him good day.

The idea of sending Carlos and Mari-Tere to Miami became more appealing to Don Francisco with the passing hours and, by the time Fernando returned with them, his mind was made up.

During the evening meal, Don Francisco told them about the afternoon visit and then revealed his plans for the immediate future. Carlos, Mari-Tere and Concha would leave for Miami the first week of June with Raúl Mora. They would remain there until asked to return. He argued that it would be good to distract their minds with other matters for the time being. A lot of sad events had occurred lately, and the change would do them good. At the same time, it would be less worrisome for Fernando and himself to have them in a safe place, away from potential problems.

Carlos accepted right away. He welcomed the change. Inés's wedding at the beginning of the year had been a sad experience, compounded now by his brother's death. It was definitely a good idea to get away from it all.

María Teresa said yes, trying desperately not to reveal her emotions when she heard that Raúl was also coming along. Her only concern was the dogs, but Don Francisco assured her that he would take care of them personally in her absence.

Fernando offered to procure all the required paperwork, plane tickets, as well as the hotel rooms. He mentioned that there was a new hotel opening in Miami Beach by the name of the Eden Roc. The owners had other investments in Cuba that his law firm was handling.

When Luis Mora came to bring his son's papers, he was informed that everything was settled. They would all depart from La Habana's José Martí International Airport the morning of June 1st. The management of the Eden Roc had offered to provide them with two two-bedroom suites for as long as they needed them. One was for María Teresa and Concha, and the other for Carlos and Raúl. They would be at no cost for the Moras. Luis was elated, and thanked Don Francisco no less than ten times before he made it back to the street.

CHAPTER EIGHT

O n June 1st they landed at Miami International Airport. The flight on the Cubana de Aviación's British Canberra Jet-Prop airplane, in which the customary sandwiches and daiquiris were served, had been smooth and delightful. Despite this, Concha had been praying to all the saints during the whole trip that only took about forty-five minutes. The hotel sent a limousine to take them to their final destination. Carlos hired a taxi to follow them with the luggage that did not fit into the trunk and the other available space inside the limousine.

The Eden Roc was one of the latest additions in the long line of luxurious hotels on Collins Avenue in Miami Beach, catering mostly to the tourist escaping from the colder, northern temperatures during the winter months. Like its closest neighbor, the Fontainebleau, it offered its guests a private beach area, swimming pools, several lounges, restaurants, a nightclub, coffee shops, a shopping area for immediate needs, and spacious suites decorated in an exquisite and elegant art deco fashion.

Carlos made arrangements to rent a speedboat. A 26-foot Chris-Craft was delivered to a nearby marina. He knew that it would be a good way of getting María Teresa to be with Raúl, since Concha was terrified of the ocean and fast boats.

The trio went out into the ocean almost every day during the first two weeks in Miami. Carlos was a natural with boats. Every time that they went out, the conversation almost always veered toward politics. Carlos, inexorably, tried to lighten up the exchange of political arguments between his sister and Raúl; and with his usual charm, he always managed to end the discussion with a touch of humor.

Toward the beginning of the third week, they started to do some inland sightseeing, and Concha decided to tag along with the group. All four of them went once to an Indian village located along Route 44, the Tamiami Trail, that ran east to west through the Everglades and joined Miami with the cities of Naples and Fort Myers. The main event of the visit was seeing live alligators and watching the people from the village wrestle with them. Concha became very scared when an Indian struck a large reptile, about 1000 pounds in weight, on his ears with a long pole. The animal jumped, thrashing his tail at thin air while fully opening his jaws. She jumped at the same time as the animal, about a foot in the air. She then asked María Teresa to go with her to the ladies' room and they left the men laughing. Carlos noticed how Raul's eyes had followed María Teresa as she walked. When they were alone, he said, "Raúl, if it weren't for the fact that we're good friends, and that I know you mean no harm, I would tell you that I resent the kind of looks that you give my sister."

The statement embarrassed Raúl. "I wasn't looking. I mean, I wasn't trying. I mean, it's not what you think. I didn't mean anything bad. Believe me, I like your sister, but I would never dream of thinking about her in that way. I mean, I wouldn't dare to do anything to her. My God, this is a mess. What am I saying?"

"You're just saying that you're in love with my sister. But stop right there. Stop and relax. Don't get nervous. I know what's going through your mind, and it's very natural. I just made my comment as a joke. You should know how I am by now. Relax, relax, man."

"You're always putting me on. I should know by now."

"Raúl, if you've noticed, most of the time you have an answer for my quips, except now, because now we're talking about Mari-Tere. Tell me, do you like my sister? Man to man, give me your honest answer. I just want to know."

"Yes, I admit I like her a lot."

"So there. Now let me ask you another question. Do you love her?"

"I think I do. I don't know. I've never experienced these feelings before. Does she love me?"

"Come on, Raúl, even if I knew the actual answer to that question, would I tell you? That's something you must find out for yourself."

"Yes, I agree. But how? I never have a single moment alone with her. If it's not you, it's Concha, or both of you. So how can I ask her?"

"My dear, poor Raúl. For someone who has a brilliant legal mind, you aren't too sharp when it comes to dealing with women."

"Oh, no! You're completely mistaken. I can easily deal with situations concerning any woman. It's Mari-Tere who makes me feel uneasy."

"Do you mean her clever mind, her acute responses to your arguments or her physical attributes?"

"All of it."

"In that case, I really pity you, because you're obviously very much in love. However, I like you, so I'll help you to see my sister alone."

"How? When?"

"Well, let me think about it for a moment." Carlos paused as he was walked with Raúl at his side towards the small shop at the entrance to the village where he knew they would find María Teresa and Concha browsing. He stopped before reaching the store, in front of a big cage containing two huge parrots, and turned around to face Raúl, saying, "Listen, next Sunday after Mass, I'll propose to take a long ride in the boat. I'll drop the anchor some place near the shore, by Crandon Park, with the excuse of going diving to see the reef. I'll leave you alone in the boat with her. I'll give you as much time as I have oxygen in my tanks. Then, when we return to the hotel, I'll feign sickness and I'll ask Concha to stay with me. That should be very hard for her to swallow, but let's see how good an actor I am. Anyway, you take the opportunity to invite Mari-Tere for dinner. Let me warn you, my sister is extremely romantic. She appears to be cool and logical, but I know that she can be really emotional when her feelings are touched. Be very imaginative with her. She likes poetry a lot. Make the best of it."

"Carlos, thank you very much. You are a true friend. I'll never forget it."

"Believe me, I'm a still a better brother. Let's go and join the ladies, shall we?"

That day, driving back to Miami, they stopped for pizza at the Red Diamond on LeJeune Road. Raúl ordered the food, four large pizzas with all kinds of different toppings. Carlos ordered the beer. María Teresa was surprised over the sudden appetite that had overcome Raúl. Even Concha made some unobtrusive comment to that effect. Carlos laughed openly and sincerely, realizing the explosion of happiness in Raúl.

The following Sunday, events developed according to plan. María Teresa chose to wear a one-piece, black swimsuit that exposed, in magnificent contrast, the delicate tone and texture of her skin. A short, white and black cape completed the outfit. Carlos's first thought when he saw his sister in the hotel hallway waiting for the elevator was about Raúl who was still in his suite getting ready. He chuckled when he came to the conclusion that, if Raúl had been shy with his sister before, today, after seeing her dressed like that, he would not be able to utter a single sound. Taking advantage of the fact that he was alone with his sister, he said to her, "I don't know how good a swimmer Raúl is, so when we arrive at the reef, let me go diving alone first, so that I can feel the strength of the undercurrents. I don't want to take care of you and Raúl at the same time if anything goes wrong. Is that okay with you?"

"Yes, I guess so. You go down first and then Raúl and I can take turns or go together with you."

"All right, here comes Raúl now. Let's go."

In the boat Raúl helped Carlos put on the diving equipment. Before putting on the facemask, Carlos winked at Raúl, and with a swift motion, he plunged his body into the warm, crystalline waters. María Teresa was rubbing the exposed portions of her body with suntan lotion when Raúl said, "Can I get you a beer or a soft drink from the cooler?"

"No thanks, not before diving, and if you take my advice you shouldn't have one either. Wait and we'll enjoy them even more later on."

"Well, as you can see, I'm not the best at aquatic sports, so let me follow your instructions and wait until later for the drinks. The only thing that I know how to do is to swim, and that's because my father threw me into a swimming pool and said to me 'Either learn how to swim or drown.' I don't know whether he was kidding or not, because I never found out. That day I didn't learn how to swim properly, but I did manage to stay afloat and make it to the edge of the pool. You're a terrific swimmer. How did you learn?"

"My father never threw me into any pool. He had the instructors at the Miramar Yacht Club teach me. I learned the right way. I guess if you want me to teach you style, I can do that. You already have the basics so it would only be a question of polishing the rest."

Raúl sat next to her and his naked leg rubbed against her thigh. She did not make any move to avoid the touch. The feeling of her soft and oiled skin against his was very pleasant. He wanted to hold the gorgeous girl in his arms and kiss her endlessly. Raúl had met other girls before, but he sensed instinctively and rationally that María Teresa was the woman that could fulfill all of his desires, and all of his fantasies. She should be the mother of his children. At that moment, he had to exert a lot of will power to overcome his particular shyness with this wonderful creature.

"Mari-Tere, I have wanted to talk to you for some time now."

"But Raúl, we've seen each other at school many times, and we've gone out to movies on several occasions. What's so special now?"

"I've always seen you with somebody else. At school there have been groups of students around us. The two times that I took you home, Carlos was with us. Whenever we've gone out, Concha has been with us. I haven't been able to be alone with you until now."

"And what do you want to tell me? What's so secretly important that you have to tell me when we're alone?"

"Please don't be cute with me, not now."

"I'm not being cute with you. But you must admit that to talk to me alone, you've certainly picked the right spot."

"You're joking. I know that you're kidding me. I can tell when you're serious and when you're cynically humorous. Is that a trait of the Aguirrupes?"

"Now, now, don't get my family involved in my petty vices. When you're right, you're right. I was just trying to make a little bit lighter what I thought was becoming a very serious conversation."

"Does that mean that you only want to joke with me?"

"No, Raúl, I've learned to admire you too much to try to make fun of you, if that's what you mean. Now, tell me, kidding aside, what is it that you wish to tell me privately?"

"Let me start at the beginning. I want you to know that I'm extremely sorry for the fate of your brother, José María. I understand that over the past year my brother Manuel was heavily involved in the revolutionary process. Sometimes I took phone messages from unknown people who didn't leave their names, and just asked my brother to meet them at prearranged locations. Manuel never admitted it to me, perhaps because he didn't want me to get mixed up in it. Perhaps, because he didn't wish me to tell my parents about it. Nonetheless, I knew. Now, what I didn't know, and probably never will, is to what extent Manuel influenced your brother into becoming a part of that deadly game. But, for what happened in the end, that brought grief and sorrow into your heart, I'm deeply and sincerely sorry. I need to know that you understand my sentiments, and that you accept my apologies."

"Raúl, I'm moved by your words. Your apologies aren't neccessary. If it makes you feel better, I'll accept them wholeheartedly. I knew José María to be very independent and idealistic. If he acted the way he did, it was really of his own volition. Manuel might have been his partner in an ill-fated adventure, but never his mentor. After the funeral, I overheard my father talking to some friends of the family and they were saying that they had heard strong rumors that both of them had been recruited by some professors from La Habana University that used to belong to the Orthodox Political Party. My brother could have been one of the most brilliant architects that Cuba had ever seen. Instead, he died a dreamer, giving up his life. I've always heard that he was my mother's pet, so maybe, if she would have been alive, he would have chosen a different path."

Her eyes turned glassy. She removed her sunglasses and Raúl could see redness forming around her green irises. Two big tears started to roll down her cheeks. She hid her face between her hands, bending her head toward her knees. Raúl took her hands into his, away from her face, with a gentle but persuasive command. He placed her hands around his neck and let her head rest against his shoulder. He never let go until María Teresa stopped crying completely.

"I'm afraid that I've gotten your nice shirt wet with my tears, and stained it with my suntan lotion."

"Don't worry, Mari-Tere. I didn't mean to make you cry. Please forgive me."

"There is nothing to forgive. Sometimes I cry just thinking of unhappy events, and I think that I've needed a good cry for some time now. Thanks for giving me a shoulder to cry on. I feel much better now."

"A shoulder to cry on is nothing. What I want to offer you is much more. If you let me, I want to give you my arms to defend you against all your enemies, my legs to follow your footprints wherever they might lead, my mind to perceive your most intimate desires, and to conceive ways to fulfill them, and finally, my heart to love you with infinite and everlasting passion."

"Raúl, I don't know what to say!"

"Just say that you love me. Just look at me with your beautiful, green eyes, and tell me that you want me as much as I want you. Offer your lips to me, to consummate our secret pact of love."

He grabbed her by her shoulders and firmly pulled her towards him. Their faces were getting closer by the passing seconds. He moved his mouth slowly to meet hers while closing his eyes. Raúl did not see her hand, placed like a partition in between the two pairs of approaching lips. Finally, he kissed her hand tenderly instead of her mouth.

"Wait, you're going too fast for me. I've never kissed a man before in my lifetime. Not the way that you want me to kiss you."

"I understand. When I get going on something, I usually build up steam like a locomotive and start to move faster and faster. I'll give you the time that you want. You have until tonight to think it over."

María Teresa let her head roll backwards and started to laugh, exposing her long, seductive neck. Raúl wanted to cover it with kisses, but he sat back and laughed with her. Whenever she laughed like that, loudly and openly, two dimples formed on her cheeks. He found them divinely attractive. So far, he could not think of anything that she had that could not arouse him.

"Now, who's kidding who? What do you mean that I only have until tonight to give you an answer."

"I'm serious." He told her about Carlos's ploy to feign sickness in order to allow them some time alone later on. "Would you dine with me tonight? Say yes, and make me the happiest of men."

"Well, I say maybe, and hope to make you the most curious of men."

The boat swayed to one side as Carlos, emerging from the water, tried to climb into the boat. Raúl stood up to lend him a hand. María Teresa helped her brother remove the diving gear.

"Thanks," Carlos said. "Boy, am I ready for a cold beer." He went to the cooler to fetch one for himself and two more for his friend and his sister. "The sight down there is beautiful, but the currents are strong here and there. Do you people want to dive today."

"No," said María Teresa. "It's getting late and I think that we should go back. Besides, you don't look too good to me. You seem pale and somewhat weak to go down again. Are you by any chance getting sick or something?"

Carlos was caught by surprise, and he glanced at Raúl before answering. "You know, little sis, you're right most of the time. I think that I'm coming down with something because my legs feel weak, my arms and my back hurt, and I guess my body temperature is on the rise. Let's go back."

"Yes, let's go back right away. The minute we get to the hotel, I want you to go to your room and stay in bed tonight. Concha and Raúl can order some dinner to be brought to the room, and I'll personally take care of you."

"No, that isn't necessary. I like you to stay with me when I'm bedridden, but Concha is better when it comes to giving someone back, chest and arm massages. Don't order any food for my suite. I just know that I won't be able to stand the smell of food tonight. Raúl, why don't you take Mari-Tere out for a nice dinner?"

"I can do that, if she wants to come."

"Well, Raúl has already invited me to go and have some dinner with him tonight. Apparently he had a premonition that you were going to be sick. Some kind of psychic power, if you know what I mean. The truth is that I told him that I didn't know whether to accept or not. You know, Raúl and I going alone. I know that this is Florida and not Cuba, and yet, we might run into some tourists. Word can get back to our father. And then there are you and Concha, in the same bedroom and alone. What will you both think of me? And what will the people in the hotel think of the both of you? I really don't know what to do."

The anchor was again tucked safely inside the boat, and the engine was spinning the propellers once more. Carlos climbed into the driver's seat, and before starting to drive the boat back to the marina, he turned to face his sister. "You can cut the bullshit and just say a simple yes or no."

"Mind your mouth," María Teresa said. "Since you put it in those terms, I guess I'll simply say yes." And now, facing Raúl, she added, "Where should we go?"

Carlos started to turn the boat to the right, when he heard Raúl saying, "Wherever your heart desires. I'm ready to take you all the way up to heaven, if that's what you want."

"That's a very promising offer, but I think Miami will suffice for tonight. Pick me up around eight. That will give me enough time to buy some rubbing compound for my dear brother, and to prepare Concha for the shocking news."

"No, just some light moisturizing lotion will do. I think that it's only the strong sun. Too much exposure."

"And don't forget to put some on your head," said María Teresa, "because that's the most susceptible part of your entire body, since it is practically empty."

At eight o'clock sharp, Raúl knocked on the door to María Teresa's suite. She and Concha came out into the hallway. Before entering Carlos's suite, Concha told both of them that she expected them back in two or three hours.

"Oh, my God, Concha. I'm twenty years old," María Teresa said.

"No, you will be twenty in October, and even if you were fifty, as long as I am responsible for your well-being, I'll tell you what to do. I know what is best for you. And I'll also tell you this in front of Raúl. The only reason that I'm letting you go is because I know Raúl to be a decent and honorable man."

"And what about me? Am I not a decent and honorable woman?"

"Get out of my sight, both of you. Raúl, please take good care of her."

"Don't you worry. I won't let anything happen to her while she's with me," Raúl said.

The doorman called a taxi, and Raúl told him to take them to the Robin Hood Restaurant on Biscayne Boulevard and Thirty-sixth Street.

Raúl ordered for both of them after a brief conversation with María Teresa. The waiter took the order of lobster meat cocktail, prime-rib medium rare with au-gratin potatoes, Caesar salad and cheesecake, and suggested a red French Bordeaux to go with the dinner.

María Teresa was wearing a light yellow, silk, short-sleeved blouse, accompanied by a wide, pleated, navy blue skirt. Raúl had a two-piece white suit with a Mediterranean blue shirt and no tie. The top button of María Teresa's blouse kept coming open, seductively revealing the top line of her lace and satin yellow undershirt. She kept putting the stubborn button back on in its proper position, until another move of her body opened it once more. It was like a game that lasted the entire evening.

"You know, that is the sexiest blouse that I have ever seen you wear. I think you wore it tonight on purpose," Raúl commented.

"No, I took this one in a hurry without realizing that it doesn't stay buttoned properly. Now, if you really are the decent gentleman that you told Concha you were, then you shouldn't even look, and avoid all temptations. They will only invite sin, and I don't want to be responsible for your sins, since that would also be a sin on my part."

"To sin is to imply that you are doing something against God, something against nature, something evil, something wrong, and nothing that you might initiate in me could be sinful. If that were true, then I would've been living in mortal sin since the very first day that I laid eyes on you at school. For I've always wanted to feel you very close to me. A meeting of our souls, an encounter of our bodies, and their surrendering to our desires."

"Take it easy, Raúl. People might hear. Let's eat in peace, enjoy some small talk, and later on you can continue what you were saying."

María Teresa became a bit nervous and she dropped her steak knife to the floor. Raúl went to pick it up and banged his head on the table as he was retrieving it.

"You see, God is already punishing you for being so fresh with me," María Teresa said in a good humor.

The waiter came with another, clean knife and the rest of the meal continued uneventfully. The taxi driver who took them back to the hotel was a funny character. He was an old Jew from New York City, and never stopped telling them jokes about the Jewish people in Miami. Raúl and María Teresa did not understand the punch lines of some of the jokes, but they laughed with the old man as a gesture of politeness. When they arrived at the hotel, and while Raúl was getting the money out to pay for the fare, the old Jew told María Teresa with a wink in his weary eyes, "I hope that you have a very good night."

María Teresa smiled and left the car as soon as the doorman opened her door. She knew that, this time, he wasn't joking.

They decided to take a walk through the gardens. A clear sky showered them with light from a billion shining stars. The bright, full moon was giving its blessing to the soon-to-be lovers. The smell of fresh flowers moistened with the evening dew, the nice cool breeze coming from the nearby ocean, and the rhythmic sound of its waves against the sand formed the perfect setting for romance.

"Well, what do you say?" Raúl said.

"I'm still a little bit confused. Do you really love me, or are you just infatuated with me?"

"I like you a lot, but I don't think that I'm infatuated with you. I know deep in my heart that I love you. I love you like the sun loves the trees, like the birds love the air, like the fish loves the water that supports its life, like the lioness loves and protects her cubs, like the prisoner loves freedom, and like God loves and forgives the sinners. Love of loves. My love for you is the combination of all loves. I'm sure that I love you with all my heart. I love you now and I shall love you forever."

"Raúl, this has been a day of surprises. I never realized that you were capable of such words. I never thought of you as a romantic poet."

"I must confess that what you say is true. Normally, I don't think and speak in those terms, but to become a poet at your side is very easy, because you're poetry itself."

"Tell me more. This afternoon you were talking about a kiss."

Raúl stood in front of her and looked deeply into her eyes. He squeezed her upper arms with his hands and started very slowly to move closer and closer to her. At the same time, he whispered, "A kiss? Yes, Mari-Tere, we were talking about a kiss, when I kissed your hand instead of your lips. A kiss is the ultimate sign of affection between friends, between parents and their children, between the bees and the flowers and, of course, between lovers. Like the wind, it could be gentle, caressing the stone and turning it into small particles, or it could be tempestuous, conquering everything in its path. It's the beginning of a wonderful love affair and the end of a romantic interlude. It is said that God granted man His soul by breathing into him His own breath. I believe that He did it with a kiss. The first kiss of everlasting love by the Creator to the man that He was making in His own image.

"Yes, I want to kiss you, and with this kiss, I want to give you all my love, my heart and my soul. From now on, they are all yours to do with as you please. Treat them carefully, for they are all that I have to give you at this moment."

This time, María Teresa did not stop Raul's lips from approaching hers. Raul's lips swayed from side to side in a very seductive manner, and brought a tingling sensation to her lips that started to fill her entire body.

She parted her lips slightly, allowing the tip of his tongue into her mouth, where it enjoyed pursuing and trying to make contact with her own. The moment they touched and started caressing each other, she felt a spark of electricity running up and down the entire length of her body. She placed her hands around his neck and held him as close to her as possible.

Their lips separated long enough for her to say, "Raúl, I love you. I love you with all my heart." And their lips met again with increasing force.

CHAPTER NINE

In spite of attempts by the opposition forces to circumvent and disrupt the normal living conditions on the island, the economy flourished during the year 1957, bringing prosperity to all sectors of society. They tried to stage a general strike, and announced it throughout the entire island. They asked, as well as demanded, that the people unite in demonstrating to Batista that he was no longer wanted. It failed completely when the working classes and the small businessmen decided that they did not want any part of it. The Cubans were ready for a political change if offered, but not at the cost of losing all or part of their capital gains.

With the exception of some sporadic fighting in the Sierra Maestra Mountains, where Castro was hiding, most of the island resumed its carefree lifestyle by the summer.

The summer months of that year were of reasonable tranquility in the capital, with life continuing as usual in the western portion of Cuba. For the first time, the Cuban Grand Prix was held. The event attracted all sorts of international jet-set figures and the best of the racing establishment. The event was a great propaganda success. As expected, the Argentine, Juan Manuel

Fangio won the main event with Font-Vachon coming in a distant tenth place.

Meanwhile, the political climate started to decline, and the guerrilla warfare in the eastern mountains continued.

On July 30th Frank País-García died in the streets of Santiago de Cuba, in a gunfight with the Armed Forces. According to some historians, País-García had the charisma and the leadership to challenge Castro's role as the leader of the Revolution.

The unrest was also slowly moving west, and sometimes members of the Armed Forces rebelled against the established government. Such was the case on September 5th when the naval lieutenant Dionisio San Román and José Gonzalo-Brito staged a revolt at the Navy Base of Cienfuegos, on the south coast of the province of Las Villas, situated in the middle of the island. The whole act of insurrection lasted only a few days. Superior forces that descended upon the military installation from the city of Santa Clara suffocated it. Another maritime expedition came to Cuba's northeastern shore with thirty men under the command of Calixto Sánchez-White. The boat's name was the Corinthia, and they landed in Lengua de Pájaro with the purpose of establishing military positions in the Sierra Cristal Mountains. Ultimately, they were to link with Castro. Before they could reach the mountains, they met the troops of Colonel Fermín Cowley and lost twenty-five men in the ensuing battle. Only one member from the expeditionary force managed to make contact with Castro. There was no doubt in their minds that Col. Cowley had known exactly where to find them. They had been betrayed.

And so, anyone who could become a future headache for Fidel Castro's supremacy was mysteriously disappearing. Either fate was paving the destiny of Cuba in obscure ways, or there were already forces in motion, acting to reach their unquestionably concealed goals.

Official press releases tried unsuccessfully to diminish the importance of these tragic events that were eroding the position of the government. The people, in their ignorance of the truth, assumed the worst and began to lose confidence in the official sources of information. Batista, in his obstinate reluctance to recognize the truth, was living in a world of fantasies where reality was whatever he wanted to believe, but never what it really was.

Toward the end of the month of August, Don Francisco called Concha on the telephone and requested that his children come back to commence their studies at the university. Carlos resented his father's decision, but obeyed anyway. He was having a good time. After his sister and Raúl became secretly engaged to each other, he started to spend more and more time alone at the Eden Roc lounges. In doing so, he started to meet young American girls who frequented these establishments, and he did not miss an opportunity to invite them to take a boat ride with him. Therefore, the customary number of passengers in the boat increased from three to four. Raúl and María Teresa became more adept at water sports and diving in particular. They usually spent a long time underwater. This situation provided Carlos with a clear stage to woo these young women. Soon enough he exchanged the rented speedboat for a cabin cruiser. His excuse was that it was more comfortable to have a boat with a toilet and a small eating area. His real reason was the convenience of the cozy sleeping quarters in that kind of vessel.

María Teresa told her father about Raúl as soon as she was back home. Concha felt relieved to know that Don Francisco received the news happily. She had been afraid of his disapproval. María Teresa's eyes sparkled like two highly polished emeralds when her father consented to the engagement and told her that he wanted to further discuss the matter with Raúl and his family.

The Mora family came to the Aguirrupe's house for dinner the last Saturday in the month of September of 1957. As it was customary on these occasions, the future groom's father had to formally ask the bride's father for his daughter's hand in marriage.

After the dinner, when both families gathered in the living room to partake of some fruit, coffee and champagne, Raúl stood up and, raising his hand, said, "Don Francisco, would you please allow me to propose a toast?"

"Yes, by all means, go ahead young man."

"Gracious host, dear family members and friends. I ask you to join me in offering this toast to María Teresa, the most intelligent and beautiful woman that human eyes have ever seen."

Everybody drank, and Carlos said, "Well, I'm not so sure that I completely agree with that, but a toast, is a toast, is a toast. Here's looking at you, Sister. Bottoms up."

As usual he sparked a round of smiles on all faces, with the exception of his father, who said, "Behave Carlos, and spare us your gags tonight."

Luis Mora said, "Don Francisco, I would like to make a statement, now that we are all here. May I?"

"Of course, Luis. Attention, everybody. Attention, please."

"First, I would like to express my family's gratitude, myself included, to the entire Aguirrupe family for inviting us to your house this evening, and permitting us to share with you on this happy occasion. It is a gesture of friendship that we would like to return in the future. Secondly, I want you all to know that my wife and I received, with great satisfaction, the news that our son Raúl is deeply in love with María Teresa and vice versa. As the eldest member of my family, I would like to formally request that you grant me, Don Francisco, your daughter's hand in marriage, for my son Raúl. We would consider it a great honor if you would consent to this wedding, and it would make us all very happy, especially Raúl."

Don Francisco, receiving his cue, stood up to face Luis and said, "My dear friend, Luis. It gives me great pleasure to hear those words coming from you. María Teresa has told me that she loves your son, Raúl, and has assured me that he loves her too. Her word is enough evidence for me in this case. I accept your proposal, and gladly consent to give my daughter's hand in marriage to Raúl. The honor is mutual, Sir."

Raúl went to embrace María Teresa. Luis and Don Francisco

hugged each other. Fernando and Carlos applauded and whistled. María Teresa asked her father's permission to bring the Chows into the house. Don Francisco complied. Samson and Delilah were brought in to participate in the festivities.

Toward the end of the celebration, Don Francisco announced that an idea had occurred to him. He had decided to give María Teresa an engagement soirée along with a birthday party next October 7th. She would then be twenty years old. He mentioned that he had hesitated at first, due to the fact that his family was in mourning. However, this new set of circumstances was important for María Teresa, and she deserved to be duly recognized by society. It would be the biggest event of the year.

"Yes, on October 7th at the Miramar Yacht Club, I shall give a birthday and formal engagement party," he said. "Raúl and María Teresa will exchange engagement rings and announce an approximate wedding date of, let's say, three years from now. That will give Raúl the time that he needs for his graduation and establishing his new practice. Fernando and I will take pleasure in helping him to achieve his goals as a lawyer. The party will spare no expense. We shall bring Beny Moré and his Orchestra as well as Celia Cruz and the Sonora Matancera. I'll take care of sending all the invitations."

Everybody started to engage each other in semi-private conversations about the coming party, and Don Francisco took advantage of the situation and asked Luis to come to the library with him for a few minutes.

"Francisco, about the cost of the party," said Luis, "I would like you to know that I'm ready to use some of my savings to contribute to María Teresa and Raul's happiness."

"Luis, are you crazy? I didn't bring you here to talk about money. Don't worry about the party. It's my decision, and I'll pay for it. Thank God, I can do that and more for her, if necessary. It's my pleasure, so forget it. Besides, you're going to have enough expenses in buying the engagement ring."

"María Teresa deserves the best there is. I'll make sure that Raúl buys her the very best."

"Many times, the most expensive or the biggest is not the best representative of intentions. I know my daughter, and she will be delighted with whatever size, shape or monetary value the ring has."

"I realize what you're saying, but I also know what I'm saying. I'll leave the party to you with the agreement that you leave her ring to me. Agreed?"

"All right, I agree."

"Now, if it wasn't the money that was on your mind when you asked me to join you here, then what was it?"

"The invitations. I'm going to need a list of the people that you and your family want to invite."

"I'll prepare the list with María Luisa and Raúl, and I promise that we won't abuse your generosity."

"Don't take it the wrong way. Invite all the people you want. That isn't the problem. Let me come to the point. What I want to talk to you about, in private, is that there is a person that I will have to invite, and I want your approval now."

"My approval? It's your party more than mine. Obviously, you can invite whomever you want."

"You don't understand. I'm talking about President Batista and his family."

"But Francisco, how can you do that?" Luis asked with an expression of disbelief on his face.

"I knew that I'd have to convince you. It came to my mind after I proposed the party. Look, Luis, the question is how can I not do it? You must realize that I'll have to invite other members of the Supreme Court, some members of his personal cabinet who are also personal friends of mine, some members of the Armed Forces whom I have known for many years, some members of the hierarchy of the Catholic Church, industrialists, bankers, landowners, learned scholars and highly-skilled and notable professionals. How can I single him out? I must invite him and his family. I have no choice in the matter."

"And if he refuses the invitation?"

"Well, I have no control over that. It's his decision, not mine.

But even if he comes, he'll show up and stay no more than one hour. Enough time to pay his respects on the occasion, and say hello to everyone at the party. After that, he'll depart, and we can enjoy the rest of the party in peace. While he's there, I can't tolerate, and will not allow, any incident that would provoke a bad situation and embarrass my family. It's my party, and the people attending are my guests. Even more important, it will be a very special time for both María Teresa and Raúl, and I don't wish anything to happen that could spoil their evening."

"I understand your feelings, but what are you implying, that my friends are all a pack of troublemakers?"

"No, I'm not implying anything. I'm just asking you to be careful when you generate that list. People will be drinking that night and God knows what someone might say to him or to one of his aides under the influence of alcohol."

"It's a real problem. I'm tempted to tell you to forget the whole idea. It might be better to have a more private, family type, formal engagement party and then you could give Mari-Tere a birthday party of her own at another time. I'll tell you now that you can invite Batista to your daughter's birthday, but leave my wife and me out. Raúl can do whatever he pleases on that matter, but I warn you about him. His feelings concerning his brother are very strong."

"I'm sorry to have offended you so much. I really thought that to have the party would be a good idea. It would please María Teresa a lot. I'm certain of that, and it would give Raúl the exposure that he needs in order to become a successful attorney in one of the large and important law firms on the island. In that sense it would be an excellent investment towards the future lives of these kids. Why can't you see it my way?"

"Oh, I can see it all right. That's not the point. The point is, how can you stoop so low as to invite the man who is responsible for the death of our two sons? I always thought that Basques were so hot-blooded, but you must have ice in your veins."

"Listen to me, Luis. Try to understand. A man in my position has to go through life making many compromises. Some are harder than others, some are more painful than others, but protocol and etiquette dictate norms that we have to follow in life. I will not compromise with evil and injustice, but I'll bite my tongue hard and do what I don't wish to do, but must. At this point, I have to invite him, and I will. If he declines the invitation that is another matter. On the other hand, if he accepts, then I'll receive him like any other guest. In any event, he will be invited.

"Now, let me make one other point. If your son or my son had been shot by a firing squad under Batista's personal command, or if Batista himself had pulled the trigger of the gun that killed them in a premeditated fashion, and not in self-defense, I would be the first one to tell you that, whatever the repercussions my action might bring me, I wouldn't invite him to my party. However, that hasn't been the case, and you and I know it. Your son and mine are dead because other sinister and malevolent minds filled their heads with utopian goals and the wrong ways to achieve them. They should've been told that the only way of accomplishing the expulsion of Batista from the Cuban Presidency is by votes and not by bullets.

"It was Cuban blood that was spilled on our land over fifty years ago by other heroes, so that we could have a democratic form of government and a Constitution. Those well-intentioned men did not die so that we could continue fighting every so often to place someone else into power, if the present government doesn't suit us. We have in hand a democratic avenue to get rid of Batista. Let's use it.

"Damn the intellectuals who, behind closed doors, injected evil notions into our children, such as socialism, fascism, communism and atheism, for they have killed our sons. Damn the professors who conceived the plans, and then enrolled these idealistic students to carry them out, for they have killed our sons. Damn the political activists that provided the money, the weapons and the resources for the task that they chose not to participate in, for they have killed our sons. Damn the revolutionaries of yesterday and today with their insistence on rocking the boat, for they have killed our sons. Damn the false prophets, the renegade priests, the atheistic wolves dressed in lambs' wool, nuns' habits, monks' robes or cardinals' gowns who, with their twisted, theological reasoning, clouded the intellect of our youth and pushed them away from the true and only God, for they have killed our sons. They all killed them, Luis. Batista did not."

Luis was appalled at the long series of arguments from Don Francisco. He let his entire body collapse on top of one of the leather chairs.

"Francisco, you definitely have a way with words. I had never been aware of those things, and I still don't understand fully some of your reasoning. On the other hand, I trust you to be right, since I know that you're an honest man and that you wouldn't lie to me. We will do as you wish, I just don't know how to explain the whole mess to Raúl. My God, sometimes I wish I could talk like you."

"Thank you, Luis. Thank you for coming to my side on this issue. If you want me to talk to Raúl on the subject, I will do so. Now, let's go and join the others, shall we?"

Don Francisco prepared and personally mailed all the invitations. His old friend Pepe called him on the telephone the moment he received his. During the course of the conversation, he told Don Francisco how happy he was for María Teresa and asked his friend to convey to her his congratulations. He also inquired, respectfully, if he thought that this was the most suitable person for his daughter, given the circumstances that he was Manuel Mora's younger brother. When Don Francisco told him that he had no desire to interfere with María Teresa's wishes, and that he would respect his daughter's decision, Pepe warned him that sometimes decisions are made based on feelings and emotions instead of logic. By the end of the conversation, Don Francisco convinced his friend that there was nothing he could do, or would do, except to try to make his daughter as happy as he could.

CHAPTER TEN

The party took place as announced. Security was extremely tight from the early hours of the afternoon. Many members of the social club were asked, politely, but firmly, to vacate the premises a few hours before the party started, so that bomb experts could search for explosives. Admittance was restricted from then on to those with invitations only. Photographers, reporters and other members of the press from newspapers such as "El Diario de la Marina" and "El Mundo" came earlier to set up their equipment to cover every detail of the party.

María Teresa and her father made their entrance at 7:30 P.M., and remained in the main lobby to greet their guests as they arrived. She was wearing a long, white, pure silk evening gown that left her arms and shoulders exposed. A blue fox stole covered these parts of her glamorous body. A pair of long white gloves covered her hands and arms up to her elbows; a gorgeous necklace of diamonds and emeralds set on white gold with matching earrings adorned her neck and face; and a small, white, spangled evening purse completed the attire. Her father wore the customary black formal tuxedo.

The long parade of personalities and dignitaries started to arrive around eight and continued for about an hour. Batista showed up with his wife, Martha, at the tail end of the caravan. At nine, Fernando, following his father's instructions, went to the microphone placed near the orchestra's stage and requested that everybody take his or her allocated seat.

The party was held outside, in the area adjacent to the huge swimming pool. There was a long, curved, main table at one end of the dance floor. The Club used its best china, glasses and silverware for the occasion. There were at least two dozen red roses on each table, in beautiful and different arrangements. A massive, silver-plated candelabra containing seven long, white candles on each table gave a sense of intimacy to the tables with the glow of their warm light.

Father John J. Kelly, O.S.A., President of Villanueva University, was called to the microphone by Fernando and gave the benediction. The gala affair started soon after. The exquisite and elegant dinner with nine different courses pleased the guests, while Beny Moré and his Orchestra played their latest compositions.

While dinner was being served, army security personnel checked all the presents that had been brought and left at the two large tables in the main lobby. Again, they were looking for any kind of explosives.

A huge rum and whipped cream, vanilla birthday cake, in the shape of a three tier heart, with twenty edible Cupid sculptures surrounding it, made its entrance, on top of a large, wheeled cart. A red candle protruded from the right hand of each Cupid. When these candles were all lit, everybody joined the background music in wishing María Teresa a happy birthday, singing the traditional American song. She blew all the candles out at once, and proceeded to cut the cake, which was served along with dishes of tropical fruits. Afterwards, Don Francisco slowly advanced across the dance floor to the microphone podium.

"Major General Fulgéncio Batista y Zaldívar, President of

the Republic of Cuba, and his charming wife, Señora Martha Fernández de Batista; Most Reverend Father John J. Kelly, President of Villanueva University; the Honorable Dr. José Luis Rodríguez, Minister of Justice, and Dr. Juan Alberto Méndez, Minister of Education, and their respective wives, Señora Magaly Gómez de Rodríguez and Señora Mariana Ramírez de Méndez; Honorable members of the Diplomatic Corps; distinguished colleagues of the Supreme Court; dear friends and relatives; ladies and gentlemen:

"It is indeed a great pleasure, as well as a great honor, for me to be able to address you at this festive event. In accepting our invitation to come here tonight, you have demonstrated the sincere and particular affection that you have for my family and especially for my daughter, María Teresa. For your presence, and for the gifts that you have brought my daughter, we thank you very much.

"A man should consider himself fortunate to be surrounded by well-wishers throughout his mortal life. Tonight, you have given me the satisfaction of being able to look all around me and feel blessed by God, for allowing this humble man to count so many friends.

"Twenty years ago my lovely wife was recalled by her Creator to be with Him in paradise. Before she went, she left me a present, a wonderful girl who has been my pride and my most beloved possession ever since. On this day, we are gathered here to celebrate her birthday. Now, there is a second celebration that is occurring tonight and that I must tell you about, so that we can all share in my daughter's happiness. I take pleasure in announcing to you the formal engagement of María Teresa to the handsome and intelligent Señor Raúl Mora, and in doing so, I pledge her hand in marriage to this gentleman.

"I will now ask that you welcome this young couple with a heartwarming round of applause."

Every person stood up and gave them a standing ovation. When María Teresa and Raúl reached the spot next to Don

Francisco, Raúl made a solemn promise of his love to her and placed on María Teresa's finger a 3 carat diamond solitaire ring set in platinum. She made a similar pledge and put on his finger a thick, yellow and white gold, geometrically-carved ring.

Don Francisco continued, "This happy couple is especially dear to me, and I would like to be the first one to wish them a love-filled, and rewarding life together." He then kissed his daughter and embraced Raúl. "Now, I would like to reiterate my personal gratitude to each and every one of you for being participants on this joyful occasion and I would like you to remain with us and to have a good time. Before I end, please allow me to introduce to you a man who really requires no introduction and who asked me to permit him to say a few words. Without further ado, please welcome our President, Fulgéncio Batista."

Batista approached the podium while the people applauded and said, "Thank you very much, Justice Aguirrupe for allowing me the opportunity of expressing my feelings to your honorable friends. Members of the Catholic Church, Cabinet Ministers, Honorable Ambassadors representing their respective countries, distinguished Magistrates of the Supreme Court, and dear fellow Cubans:

"I feel honored to have been invited to participate with you in this jubilant celebration. To María Teresa, I want to extend a double congratulations. One for her birthday, wishing her the health and longevity to enjoy many more of these anniversaries. The second, for selecting to join in holy matrimony Señor Raúl Mora, a young man that I just met for the first time tonight, but whom I long to remain friends with in years to come. It is my belief that these two young people exemplify the characteristics of the next, brilliant, Cuban generation that will enable this great country of ours to continue on its path of glory and fulfill its destiny among the free and civilized nations of this world.

"To Raúl, I want to extend my congratulations for having chosen as his fiancée Señorita María Teresa Aguirrupe y Larrazábal. In her, I am confident that he will find the dear and loyal companion of a lifetime. She is not only a beautiful woman who will bear him adorable children, but also the possessor of a keen intellect who I am sure will make important technological contributions to her fatherland.

"In conclusion, I would like to clearly indicate my apologies to all of you for leaving early, but State matters demand my attention elsewhere.

"Wishing you good health and a pleasant evening, I bid you farewell.

"Salud. Salud. Salud."

Batista always ended his speeches, whether long or short, with the same three words. Before he departed he stopped to say good-bye to his host and his family, who were back at the main table with the Moras.

"Señor Presidente, allow me to introduce to you my future in-laws, Señor Luis Mora and Señora María Luisa Aguirre de Mora, the father and mother of Raúl. Of course, you already know my son Fernando, my daughter María Teresa and Raúl."

"I'm happy to meet you, Señor and Señora Mora. I congratulate you for a wonderful son and a lovely future daughter-in-law."

"Señor Presidente, we are honored," Luis said. María Luisa just smiled and nodded her head.

Turning to face Raúl, Batista said, "I brought an envelope for María Teresa as a birthday present. Now that I've heard the news, permit me to present it to both of you as an engagement present." He extracted a white envelope from his breast pocket and gave it to Raúl. Then, he said to María Teresa, "I will send you a more personal gift first thing Monday morning."

María Teresa quickly answered, "Thank you, Sir, but honestly, you need not do it. One present is enough."

"I understand, but it will be my satisfaction to do so."

Raúl took the opportunity to reply, "Thank you very much, Sir. I'm sure that María Teresa and I can use this for a good cause. It's a pity that my older brother couldn't be here tonight to say hello to you also. I'm sure that you have seen him before, for he was at the Presidential Palace not too long ago."

Don Francisco looked at Fernando with sudden desperation reflected in his eyes. María Teresa grew pale. Luis could not accept as truth what he was hearing. María Luisa just smiled again.

"And how come your brother is not here partaking in this great party? Where is he?" Batista said, expressing concern.

"He's dead."

"Oh! I'm very sorry."

"I'm sure you are."

At that point Fernando interrupted, "Well, let's not talk of sad events on a day like today. Don't you agree, Señor Presidente?"

"Yes, I quite agree."

"Tell me, Sir, have you seen the latest models of the new Palace of Justice?" Fernando asked.

"Yes, I have. It should be finished shortly and is going to be a fantastic building. Of course, you're on the building commission with your father, are you not?"

"Yes, I am. Before you depart why don't we go and find the Minister of Justice. I'd like to discuss a couple of minor points with him and your opinion on these matters is very important. Please, Señor Presidente, come with me."

"All right, and after that I must go. Good night to all of you."

Fernando moved away from the group with Batista. Don Francisco looked at Raúl with reproach. No other word came from his mouth. María Teresa asked Raúl to dance with her. Walking on the way to the dance floor, he opened the white envelope that he was still holding in his hand. It contained twelve thousand Cuban pesos.

María Teresa and Raúl danced endlessly throughout the night. She had decided that she wouldn't explore the subject of the conversation between Raúl and Batista. Nothing was going to ruin the best night of her life, she had said to herself when she had asked Raúl to dance with her.

Carlos went to the table where Inés and José Miguel were seated. He congratulated him for his good showing at the La Habana Grand Prix race. José Miguel told him that he was not so impressed with his own performance, and Carlos responded that in that league of international racers, to be able to cross the finish line without any broken bones and with an undamaged car was already quite an achievement. Furthermore, he said, to come in 10th from a list of 42 top drivers was a miracle in itself. José Miguel finally admitted that he did not do too badly, considering that it was his first year in that kind of sport.

"Do you mind if I dance with your wife?" Carlos inquired.

"I don't mind, but don't ask me, ask her," José Miguel replied.

"Inés, would you grant me the immense pleasure of dancing with you? It would be a great honor for me if you simply said yes."

"How can I refuse?" Inés said, in a frivolous voice.

They headed, hand in hand, to the dance floor. When they arrived, Carlos took Inés in his arms and pulled her body towards his. She resisted the motion and kept dancing at a convenient distance away from him.

"If you keep moving away from me, I'll have to send you telegrams to talk to you while we dance," Carlos said.

"There's nothing wrong with my hearing. Just keep talking, and I'll answer you. You'll see."

"It's hard for me to dance this way. I'm not used to a woman being so far away from me."

"You're doing fine. Besides, this is the appropriate distance for a married woman dancing with a man who is not her husband."

"Talking about weddings, I'm sorry that I missed yours. I just couldn't watch you getting married to another man. I'm sure that you understand."

"No, I really don't. I told you once that I could be a good friend, that I want to be a good friend, and that's all I intend to be."

"Well, someday you might change your mind on that subject."

"Don't count on it, Carlos. I'm happily married."

"That I do believe. You see, Inés, you haven't had anything to compare José Miguel with."

"And I won't have to. I know that I'm married to the best man in the world for me. Now, just to satisfy my curiosity as an inquisitive woman, are you that good?"

"Absolutely. Are you ready for some casual sex?"

"No, thank you, that notion hasn't crossed my mind."

"I thought so. That's why I came dressed formally tonight."

The remark brought a big smile to Inés's face. She kept swaying to the melodic rhythms of the romantic tune.

"You have a fitting remark for everything, don't you?" she said.

"Not really. As a matter of fact, I'm at a loss for words when it comes to talking to you."

"I can't imagine you lacking words where women are concerned, particularly me. Are you going to tell me that I don't arouse your intellect?"

"Quite a bit below my intellect."

"Carlos, you have a one-track mind."

"And it's all set for a one-way ticket to heaven."

"Well, you'd better find another suitable angel to guide you, because I already have all my tours booked solid."

"Maybe the future might bring some cancellations, and then you and I could visit paradise together."

"And in the meantime, you'll date all my female friends."

"If that'd make you jealous, as I think it would, then definitely yes, I would do it."

"You're wasting your time, my dear. As far as I'm concerned, you can date all you want."

"Then, there's no problem. I'm glad that you have that kind of attitude, because, like a professional boxer, I'll keep myself in shape by training all that I can, until I get to you, my main bout."

"And if your main bout never comes?"

"Well, in that case, they will bury me when I die and will

write on my tombstone: Here lies a man who died with a smile on his face."

"In that case, I do wish you a very happy life."

"I only hope that I don't have to wait too long for my chance at the title fight. I want to reach it while I still have my guard up."

"That problem should never worry you. I can't imagine you ever with your guard down."

The music ended and they stopped to applaud. Inés told Carlos to escort her back to her table. At the table, José Miguel said, "Carlos, you once expressed some interest in trying my race car. I'm going to run some practice laps next week. Would you like to join me?"

"I'd be delighted. Where shall I meet you?"

"I'll pick you up at your house next Saturday afternoon around 3:00 P.M. Bring a change of clothing. You can change at my house afterwards, and in the evening we can all go to the Tropicana. I'm eager to try a new system that I devised for roulette in their casino. Don't worry about money either. That night will be on me."

"That's splendid, and very generous of you. Thank you very much," Carlos said.

"Good. That's all set for next Saturday, unless Inés has other plans."

"No, that idea is fine with me. I'll even find one of my friends to come along so Carlos won't be alone. Do you approve?" she asked Carlos.

"Yes, I do. I'm sure that you'll find the right kind of girl for me. I'll leave it in your hands."

Carlos excused himself by telling them that he shouldn't be impolite to the other guests, and went to mingle with the crowd.

The man-made beach was some hundred and fifty yards away from the huge patio. María Teresa and Raúl took their first break around 1:00 A.M. and walked, with drinks in their hands, slowly, until the soft sand touched their feet.

The ocean breeze helped dry the sweat from their faces. It was a very nice sensation to feel its coolness all the way through their hair.

Raúl kissed her eyes, her cheeks, her ears, her neck, her shoulders and finally her lips. She emitted tender sounds of delight every time that his lips met some part of her body. These subtle moans drowned in her mouth when his lips pressed hard against hers. The nip fresh air was not a fair match for his kisses. She felt as hot as an ignited coal briquette.

"I have to talk to you," Raúl said.

"What do you wish to tell me, my love?"

"Listen, I have something to tell you. Ever since my brother was killed, I've tried to make contact with the revolutionary cell that he was operating with. My main purpose was to try to find out what really happened that day, and also how I could help in avenging his death.

"It took me a few days to make contact. As I went through my brother's belongings, I found hidden in a shoebox, inside of a brand new shoe, carefully taped to the front part of the shoe, a tiny notebook. It contained pages of numbers, no words or letters, just numbers. I deciphered the code after a couple of days. It was the same one that we used to employ as children when we played spy games. Then, I was able to identify the phone numbers written in it. I started to make phone calls stating who I was and what I wanted. At first all I got was hang-ups. But finally someone gave me an address to go to. The day before we left for Miami, I went there.

"There are three ways in which I can be of help. The choice is mine, and depending upon what I decide to do, I'll be working for a different group of individuals. The student movement that our brothers belonged to is out of the question. They have disbanded, and what was left was absorbed by Fidel Castro's forces. If I were to join them, then I could do one of two things in the city. I could go around collecting money to send to Castro in the mountains, or I could be part of the team that is dedicated to disrupting all kinds of normal activities by placing bombs in strategic locations all over the city. My third choice is not with Castro, but with Eloy Gutierrez Menoyo. He has formed a second front to combat government troops in the Escambray Mountains, in the province of Las Villas. His idea is to get control of that zone and eventually the entire province, thus cutting the island in half and protecting Castro's western flank.

"Ever since I returned from Florida, they've been after me to join them. I really wanted to do it then, but with school, and above everything else, with you in the picture now, I needed more time to think it over. By now, I have given it serious thought, and I've decided to go to the mountains with Menoyo. I'm sorry to have to break this news to you in this fashion, and on this day, but believe me, Mari-Tere, there is no other way. Now, there's a group of people leaving next week, and if I don't join them, I'll have to wait until the next caravan is organized. That might take several months. I was informed of this fact yesterday, otherwise I would have told you before."

There was disgust expressed on María Teresa's face, and there was contempt in her mind.

"I think that you're making a grave mistake. First of all, you have to realize that there's nothing you can do that will bring your brother back to life. I understand that you want to avenge his death. I imagine that this is a normal feeling considering the situation, but the logical conclusion to that premise has to be to inflict punishment on the people who actually killed him, and you don't know who they were. To say that I'm going to kill soldiers because soldiers killed my brother is pure nonsense. Now, if you wish to tell me that you want to go because you're looking for a way to fight Batista's government, that I can comprehend.

"If you go next week chances are that you'll be engaged in military operations for some time, and that will delay your graduation. I'll be honest with you and tell you that I wouldn't have minded, except that it would also delay our wedding, which is the event that I consider most important in my life. I'd rather that you stay here, in the city, with your family and with me. That'll give you the opportunity to continue your studies, and in the event that you get caught, my father could protect you and make sure that you could leave the island without being harmed. Conversely, the price to pay for that luxury is that you become an extortionist or a terrorist, and I would never marry either of these. So, if you want to fight, if you wish to pursue your course of action into what you might consider your military glory, if you desire so much to avenge your brother's death, then go to the mountains and become a rebel. I don't know what your parents would say, but I guarantee you that my father will never forgive you, and that my brother Fernando will consider you an irresponsible fool. Carlos will laugh about it, and I shall wait for you."

"I knew that somehow you would come through for me. Believe me, it's not my intention to upset anybody. I just consider this a tour of duty."

"No, be honest with me and with yourself, your brother's death is just an excuse to do what's been in your heart for some time. I don't know what you're trying to prove. I only know that I love you immensely."

"I also love you, Mari-Tere. I don't think that I'll be gone for too long. The news from these people is that the situation in the countryside is far worse than what official reports would have you believe. They claim that the end is very near, and that we'll manage to get rid of Batista in a short time. When I return, I'll continue my studies, and we'll marry as soon as you finish yours. Maybe even earlier if you want to. I'm longing to hold you in my arms forever, to feel your naked skin against mine, and to melt our bodies in a fusion of passion until they become only one."

"Hold me in your arms now, Raúl. Hold me as tight as you can, and kiss me. Kiss me, darling, in a way that its remembrance and the taste of your moist lips on mine will stay with me until you return."

CHAPTER ELEVEN

Political unrest increased in Cuba during the year 1958. Normal living conditions all through the island deteriorated at a fast pace, with the exception of La Habana. The capital of the island still experienced an influx of tourists seeking to have a good time in that Caribbean paradise. The native Cubans who lived in La Habana, with their natural good sense of humor and their ineffable carefree characteristic of wanting to party at any and all times, always enjoyed the ebullient life of an international metropolis that seldom slept.

La Habana had, at that time, great spacious hotels with luxurious casinos and gourmet restaurants. This fabulous capital city displayed a wide variety of entertainments, catering to all possible tastes. A ballet and opera season during the winter months featured top billing performers. The Philharmonic Orchestra of La Habana presented guest conductors who were at the pinnacle of their musical careers. There were also small theaters performing classical and modern dramas and comedies, and a vast myriad of ultra-modern movie houses, showing not only all of the latest American films, but also a large selection of foreign movies.

Musical plays in the form of operettas or Spanish "zarzuelas" had always been a traditional and well-liked form of entertainment for the Cubans. This taste was not acquired but rather inherited from their Spanish ancestry. There were also plenty of nightclubs and lounges, whose doors usually closed around four in the morning. The three most famous nightclubs that presented sumptuous shows with internationally recognized stars were the Tropicana, the Sans-Souci and the Montmartre. The latter had closed its doors during the previous year due to the murder, on their premises, of Colonel Antonio Blanco Rico, Chief of the Military Intelligence Service. Castro's agents had killed him while he was sitting at the bar enjoying a night out with his family. It appeared to be just another act of terrorism by the revolutionaries. In reality, he was assassinated because he was a decent and well-informed army officer who could have challenged the leadership of Fidel Castro by making an exposé of his Marxist affiliation.

In the meantime Castro was maintaining his fake democratic posture at the eastern mountain range, and sending from that region the message that all he wanted to achieve was a mere political change. He claimed that he wanted a simple replacement of Batista with an interim form of government that would offer free elections in a period of time no longer than 18 months in accordance with the Cuban Constitution of 1940. That political process should then place the country on the track of successive, democratically elected, ruling administrations every 4 years. This image of Castro as the main representative of the political force that would save the Republic and eliminate the tyranny of a supposed dictator was created and presented to the world by Herbert Matthews. Mr. Matthews was a reporter for the New York Times who went to the mountains to interview Castro. This newspaper called Castro "The Savior of Cuba and the Robin Hood of the Americas." Coincidentally, Mr. Matthews was also the foreign correspondent who went to China in 1948 to interview Mao-Tse-Tung and reported that he was merely an agrarian reformer.

That year saw Fidel Castro emerge as the leader of a

Revolution that was growing more and more in intensity. The deaths, under all kinds of circumstances, of all other possible people associated with the opposition to Batista paved the route free of obstacles for Castro to become the leader of the Revolution.

The Cuban youth was being recruited and trained to perform revolutionary activities. They became familiar with weapons and explosives, and were trained to commit all sorts of assassinations and terrorist acts. Sabotages occurred in some industrial facilities; bombs exploded in some theaters, bars and public places throughout the countryside and in some of the most populated cities. Some of these revolutionary cells dedicated themselves to murdering policeman or soldiers that were alone or in small groups. Law enforcement agents and military personnel retaliated by disposing of these revolutionaries and terrorists when they were caught. The total number of these civilians found murdered by Batista's forces may have reached a few hundred by the time Batista left the country, but it never reached the twenty thousand deaths that the revolutionary propaganda reported. Fidel Castro's guerrilla forces never surpassed one thousand in number.

Peasants in the countryside were forced to join the guerrillas at the Sierra Maestra and Sierra Cristal in Oriente Province, as well as the Sierra Escambray in Las Villas Province. These honest and hard-working men usually lacked the cultural background and strong ideological principles required to withstand the brainwashing techniques that were inflicted on them. In due time, they were convinced that the country needed something more than the expected political change. Notions such as agrarian reform, death to anyone associated with Batista's regime, socialism, hatred against the upper classes and American imperialism were implanted into their heads and nurtured by continuous indoctrination.

Most of the people in government positions, including Batista himself, miscalculated the revolution that was evolving in the areas outside La Habana Province. They treated it as a fight launched by an opposing political force wishing a plain change in power, and never as a well-organized movement desiring the takeover of the government in order to firmly take control over the people, and with time to implant a Marxist-Leninist form of regime. To this end, it was fully backed and financed by every international and conspiratorial group that existed and that used communism as a controlling tool for the society that they wanted to create. They were recognized and supported by all the press and communications media, both national and international. At the same time, the U.S. Government looked the other way while all sorts of money and weapons were being flown from U.S. shores directly to Castro.

Of course, not all Cubans fell into the trap. Some businessmen, industrialists, landowners, educators and professionals forecasted the gloomy future. Unfortunately, they were in the minority and their voices were not heard beyond their closest relatives and friends. Besides, it was easy for Castro's forces to overcome any verbal or physical opposition to their mission. They only had to accuse that particular individual or group of being associated with the government of Batista, whether it was true or not, to finally disqualify their statements as biased and untrue.

Negative propaganda was also issued by the leftist inspired "free press" outside the Iron Curtain. Nevertheless, despite their premonitions, and the fact that during the decade of the fifties no Cuban was in any way restrained from leaving the island, not more than a few hundred Cubans chose to enter into self-inflicted exile.

La Habana University remained closed during 1958, while Villanueva University continued offering classes as usual during most of its academic year. Several attempts were made to disrupt the normal activities at this learning institution. At one point, a group of students tried to stage a student strike with the backing of a few professors. It failed when the priests running the school were not convinced of the legitimacy of the students' actions or their intentions. Finally, on one evening of classes, the same group succeeded in planting several bombs in the school. The first bomb exploded in an empty classroom. Police bomb squad units found the other bombs that same evening. One of them was in another classroom and the other was found in one of the restrooms. This time, the administration, fearing for the safety of the student body, had no choice but to close the school temporarily. It reopened after a period of approximately eight weeks. The main student body and the majority of the faculty members never agreed with the small dissident group.

The military situation during that same year eroded almost to the point of high treason. The Cuban Army was corrupt and led by unscrupulous men who lost their ground to the enemy time and time again by not engaging in real combat, and selling their positions and sometimes their weapons for money. This information was normally concealed, as much as possible, from the people, by the press, which was at times deprived of the freedom to report the truth. The rebels started to gain confidence in themselves after the various skirmishes with the regular Cuban Army in places like La Plata, El Uvero and Alegría del Pío. In July of the previous year, at Jigue, the rebels had surrounded the battalion under the command of the officer, José Quevedo-Pérez. The battalion had surrendered with two hundred and forty-one men, and the rebels had captured all sorts of military firepower. A year later, in July 1958, at Las Mercedes, the revolutionary troops, under the command of Fidel Castro himself, suffered such a large number of casualties that Fidel sought and started negotiations with General Cantillo. He claimed to look for some form of settlement that never took place. Cantillo should have been wiser and realized that the Revolution never wanted an armistice. They were only trying to gain the time needed to topple Batista's regime from the inside.

Castro's agents outside Cuba were acquiring all kinds of armaments that usually reached the high mountains without major difficulties. At the same time, the U.S. Government was issuing more and more restrictions on the sending of armaments to Batista, even though the Cuban Government was paying for them and they were part of previous treaties between both countries. This policy of intervention into the internal affairs of the island by the U.S. Government culminated with the weaponry embargo issued by John Foster Dulles, the Secretary of State under the Eisenhower Administration, who yielded to the attacks formulated by the press and several members of Congress who declared themselves sympathetic to the Cuban Revolution.

This was the last straw that broke the moral backbone of the regular Cuban Army. This Army still had some officers who fought back, displaying courage and great ability for military strategy and tactics. Men such as Jesús Sosa-Blanco, Merob Sosa and Angel Sánchez Mosquera were examples corresponding to this last statement. Regrettably, they were few and it was already too late to reverse the cycle of events.

Encouraged by the recent gains and the demoralization of the opposing forces, Castro sent a task force to march and try to overtake La Habana. Camilo Cienfuegos and "Ché" Guevara commanded this invasion force. They moved across Camagüey Province without engaging in a single combat or being harassed by a single airplane. Camagüey Province was a large section of the island without a single mountain, just a large vast area dedicated mostly to raising cattle and agriculture. From a military point of view the crossing of this land without a battle was a strange and unheard of feat. It was not fear that made the regular Army avoid any type of contact with the rebel forces; it was dirty money that bought the revolutionaries the right to pass uncontested through the province. Castro's forces reached Las Villas Province, and made contact with the guerrilla forces at the second front in the Escambray Mountains. Eloy Gutierrez Menoyo, Fauré Chomón and William Morgan were in command of these troops. Among them a young officer was getting inured to war, and starting to distinguish himself as a clever tactician. His name was Raúl Mora.

In the midst of these events, La Habana was getting ready to celebrate its second annual Grand Prix Race. As in the previous year, this race attracted a great number of international Formula I drivers for the 500 mile long course, comparable only to the Monaco Grand Prix, in the sense that it ran, like its European counterpart, through regular city avenues. This acclaimed race started in the afternoon hours; the morning was devoted to other types of racing through the same circuit using different and lower-powered vehicles.

The Argentine World Champion, the great Juan Manuel Fangio, who had won the same race in the previous year, was in La Habana ready to defend his title. This year, like last year, one Cuban was going to challenge him as well as the other well-known racers. His name was José Miguel Font-Vachon.

From the apartment that once belonged to José María Aguirrupe, the race could be seen quite well. Suitable binoculars could place the spectators gathered there close to the cars and their drivers. The apartment had not been used since the death of its owner. Don Francisco had removed all of his son's personal belongings with the exception of the original furniture. Then, he had locked the doors and never let any other person in, not even himself.

The race was of special significance for Carlos, who had enjoyed tremendously being the copilot of José Miguel in his practices for the last few months. Besides the excitement of handling the fast car, it had also been an excuse to see Inés. He begged his father to let them use the apartment on that day.

His son's request was not the only reason that Don Francisco had told Carlos to go ahead and organize the festive event for a large group of friends. Pepe and Juan had already asked Don Francisco if they could impose on their friendship to see the race from the vantage point of the apartment's large balcony.

A cleaning crew was sent to prepare the place and from El Carmelo, a local restaurant, all kinds of succulent dishes and delicacies were brought to stock the dining area. Cold beer, sangria and champagne were on hand to celebrate José Miguel's victory if it happened.

El Vedado during 1958. The avenue running along the seashore is called El Malecón. The tall building on the left is the La Habana Hilton Hotel. On the right there is the FOCSA Apt. Building.

Jaime drove María Teresa along with Concha and Fernando to the apartment early that morning to help with the arrangements. Don Francisco arrived later with his friends and their wives. Carlos had volunteered to escort Inés until José Miguel could join them later.

By noon, lunch was served. Concha was assisting Jaime with the drinks when the phone rang. Jaime answered the phone and shortly thereafter said, "Don Francisco, someone wants to talk to Dr. Rodríguez. He says that it is urgent."

Pepe went to the bedroom to answer the phone, and a few minutes later he emerged from it with a sad and worried look on his face. Don Francisco noticed it and he said, "What happened?"

By this time, the other guests and family members had congregated around Pepe waiting to hear some ominous revelation.

"Fangio has been kidnapped by the 26th of July Movement. A group of men, I don't know how many, entered the hotel where he was staying and abducted him, at gunpoint, this morning. They said that he's well and alive and that he'll be released unharmed after the race. They've done it for political notoriety and propaganda. The government has been trying to keep it a secret with the expectation that they'd find out where he is being held and storm the place in order to free him before the race. They were forced to make the story public since they have not been able to locate him. Evidently, he will not race today. The Argentine Ambassador has presented his concerns, and is demanding his immediate release. It is indeed an embarrassment to allow a personality like this to be taken by a bunch of criminals."

Juan Alberto said, "It's shameful that something like this can occur. On the other hand, I'm sure that nothing will happen to him, except losing some points toward the world champion position. It wouldn't be in the best interests of the abductors to harm him in any way. I agree that the main, and possibly only, motive behind this act of terrorism is to humiliate the administration of Batista internationally. They have succeeded in this, because by tomorrow the whole world will know about it."

María Teresa said nothing, and Fernando did the same. Carlos was the one to utter the next words. He said, "Well, everything has its bad points and its good points. You've only mentioned the bad ones. The main good point is that this enhances José Miguel's chances of winning. Let's face it, with Fangio racing today, José Miguel's only possibility was to finish in second place. Inés, are you sure that your husband didn't plan the whole caper and manage to blame Castro as well?"

"Don't be an ass," Inés simply said.

"Now, now. Such language! It's most inappropriate for a lady from Villanueva who's married to one of our most prominent scions and my good friend," Carlos replied.

"I'm sorry, Don Francisco. I didn't mean to call him that. I apologize to all of you."

"Don't you worry, my dear, no need for apologies. My son isn't an ass in reality, even though he persists in behaving like one, most of the time. I think that this kidnapping is a bad omen. The officials should cancel the race for this afternoon and postpone it for a better occasion."

"No, they can't do that," Fernando interjected. "Traditionally, these types of races are never cancelled or postponed. No matter what happens or what the weather conditions are they are always carry on."

"Well, I still think it should be cancelled. Let's watch the news on television, and see if they have anything else to say."

No further information was given in the succinct broadcast. The race was on, and it was going to start on time.

It was time to relax until it started. The young people went to the balcony to observe the preparations. Jaime and Concha went to the kitchen to clean and collect all the leftovers. Don Francisco with his friends and their wives, sat in the living room to have some coffee, rest and exchange a few ideas.

Magaly opened the conversation by saying to her husband, "Pepe, why don't you tell them what the Cuban Ambassador to Mexico told you the other day?"

Pepe looked around him first, and ascertaining that they were alone in the room, at least for the moment, said in a low voice, "Well, our Ambassador to Mexico told me last week that he had heard that the new American Ambassador to Cuba, Mr. Smith, was being sent here to preside over the fall of Batista. If that's true, it seems that the U.S. State Department has already made up its mind that Batista has to go."

"That's preposterous," said Mariana. "Who the hell do they think they are to dictate Cuban policies from the White House?"

"Come on," said Juan Alberto. "The United States has been

mingling with Latin American governments, and forcing their will onto them for a long time. You only have to look closer at the history of Mexico to realize that. And mind you, that is only one example of many."

"Juan is quite right," Don Francisco said. "They are who they are. It's not going to be the first time that they promote a certain path concerning a Latin American country, and surely it will not be the last either. It's revolting in this case, because they are acting against their own interests, but it's not surprising.

"Look friends, strange forces have been acting in the United States since the First World War. Whether these have been carefully planned, or they just constitute the end result of a long series of coincidences, the actual fact is that Soviet Communist Russia emerged in 1918 with the support of the United States. At the conclusion of the Second World War, the communists took over all of Eastern Europe. Country after country was delivered on a silver platter to the Soviet Union by the United States and England. Apparently, the people who dictated that policy are still, more or less, ruling those countries, because the same people also agreed to give China to Mao, by betraying Chiang, who was their friend. The Korean War is another example of the same type of policy. It just seems that the almighty American Army can only fight, and is only allowed to win with the blessing of its Commander-In-Chief, when the fighting helps the Communists. We all know what occurred in Hungary just a couple of years ago. Why are we going to be any different?

"We all know that Castro is a troublemaker with Marxist tendencies. Cuba's just another piece to fit into the global puzzle. We could think that it would be irrational for Eisenhower to want Castro in power, but in reality, it's illogical to reason otherwise. The only thing that concerns me now is what Batista is going to do about it."

"Francisco, you're definitely a clever man. The same arguments have been presented to Batista, who still can't or doesn't want to believe that this is happening to him," said Pepe.

"What does Batista intend to do?" inquired Don Francisco.

"He proposes to hold free elections as planned. He thinks that by inviting the foreign press, U.S. and O.E.A. representatives to inspect the electoral process, any illusion of tampering with the results by his government will be dispelled."

"So the political future of this island is decided by an election, and on the fact that some observers will call it fair and not rigged," Don Francisco said.

"Well, that, and the continuation of military aid that the United States had agreed to give us in previous treaties. That aid in military equipment and weaponry is needed to try to maintain the morale in the Army. God help us if we fail to enact a smooth change of administration," Juan Alberto said.

"God help us, indeed," said Magaly. Suddenly, a voice came from the balcony. Fernando, entering the room, said, "Hey, come on, the race is about to start."

The first few laps went without incident. José Miguel was holding a seventh place position. He wasn't pressing his stand by taking any unnecessary risks. Around 3:00 P.M. he was in third place. His car was averaging 190 km/hr. The straight portion of the intricate path was now in front of him. He then accelerated until the speedometer read 245 km/hr. Now the first wide curve approached him faster than before. It was almost under José María's apartment. His friends were shouting and encouraging him from the balcony, even though they knew he could not see or hear them. The rear end of the car wanted to spin, following the action of the centrifugal force, but he managed to hold it straight on the track. He went on to successfully battle all of the other obstacles along the path of the lap. He raced towards the end of the circuit and executed brilliantly the U-turn that put him in the next lap. He was now moving faster than ever. The car was attaining its maximum speed. He wanted to gain first place, so this time he wasn't going to slow down on the wide curves, he kept his right foot pressed hard on top of the accelerator pedal. The car was responding marvelously, like an obedient but highly spirited Andalusian horse. He passed the southern side of the U.S. Embassy, and was about to maneuver his car through the first wide curve, when the left front tire exploded. Suddenly, the car swerved 90 degrees to the left and proceeded to head, at high speed, in the direction of the media section that was full of spectators. Those who were standing ran in all directions. The most unfortunate were sitting in the wooden bleachers. José Miguel jammed the brakes and rapidly forced the car into first gear, breaking the transmission. It was not enough to stop it in time. Losing complete control of the car, he opened a path of death among a number of people before smashing it, head on, against one of the wooden pillars supporting the bleachers. Human bodies with broken bones and bloody wounds were scattered all over. Several spectators fell on top of the car when the support under them gave way. The wooden column that he hit split in half, and hit him squarely in the head, killing him instantly.

The news on the radio was confusing at first. They gave an account of the accident without broadcasting any details of the number of people injured or killed as a result of the fire after the car exploded under the impact.

Inés was watching the race through the binoculars, when a loud yell came from her mouth, and then she fainted. Her body collapsed on top of Carlos, who was at her side.

Carlos took her in his arms, and moved her to the bedroom, placing her gently on the bed. María Teresa went immediately to take care of her, and Fernando volunteered to go downstairs and try to find out more specific details. He came back half an hour later confirming the death of José Miguel.

CHAPTER TWELVE

The funeral of a prominent figure of Cuban society was always a prolonged social event that was accompanied by specific rituals and ceremonies. José Miguel's wake and procession to the Colón cemetery, at Twelfth Street and Zapata Avenue, where the Font-Vachon family had a mausoleum, was no exception.

Some time after the burial, her deceased husband's family notified Inés that she had to attend the reading of her husband's will. Until that time, she had been living in the house that she had thought belonged to her husband and now to her. During the reading of the will, she found out that despite the fact that her husband had left his entire fortune to her, she would not have any immediate monetary or real assets, because her husband owned nothing. The entire fortune of the family was in the hands of the patriarch, and it would only be partially hers, at the death of the present owners, when it would then pass on to the legitimate heirs. In the meantime, they would only allocate to her a pension of one thousand pesos per month to cover her expenses, and only while she would live alone and not remarry. That was a more than fair amount of money by Cuban standards in 1958.

Inés rented an apartment in the El Vedado section of the city, and with a tremendous emotional effort managed to graduate as an architect in that same year.

Carlos called her on a weekly basis and gave her the comfort that she needed in her life at those difficult times. By late summer, he had convinced her to go out with him. They went to have supper at the Palacio de Cristal restaurant in downtown La Habana.

After dinner, while Carlos was driving Inés back to her apartment, he said, "You know, that black dress that you're wearing is a real knockout. My God, I don't think that I've ever realized how extremely beautiful you really are. Without any makeup and no lipstick, your inner beauty just comes shining through your fair skin."

"You'd better behave. I told you that flattery will get you nowhere with me. Besides, I'll bet that you say the same thing to every woman that you see coming out of the ocean in a brief and scandalous bikini."

"No, you're misjudging me. However, I guarantee you that I've told that to every woman who has woken up next to me at odd hours in the morning. It's a nice compliment to make to someone who has offered you her most precious flower." Inés laughed, and then he continued, "Now, what I've just said might have been a big lie with them. In your case it happens to be the truth."

"I've always said it. You have a one-track mind where women are concerned."

"No, you're mistaken. Not any woman, but you. You've been the only one with whom I've always had that one-track mind that you're referring to. The others have been the result of adventures, while you could be the culmination of idyllic love."

"Carlos, give me more time. I'm trying to start developing my own career and trying to forget the painful and awful experience of losing my husband. I hate his family. I know that they only accepted me because of José Miguel. I really don't care about that, except that now the only income that I have is what they are giving me every month. Surely, I could move back with my parents, but I don't want to. I love my freedom too much."

"I comprehend what you're going through," Carlos said. "I even have my suspicions that you might be being watched by his family. Your mother-in-law would love to prove a scandal in your life, and remove all the support that she legally has to give you."

"I'm glad that you can see this as clearly as I. That's why I don't want you to get mad if I refuse to give you an innocent good-bye kiss when you drop me off at home tonight."

"Don't worry, Inés. I understand. Now, let me tell you that I know a few things about these matters of the heart. I know that you lost José Miguel, whom you loved very much. I also lost my brother, José María. I also went through the motions of finishing the academic year after my brother's death. That mental effort helped remove, from time to time, the image of death from my mind, and the memory of my father crying in church like a young child. And yet, what really relieved my mind of the anguish and sorrow that was crossing through it was a complete change of locale. If you could immerse yourself in a different atmosphere, it would do you a lot of good. I know what some time in Miami did for my sister, as well as for Raúl and me. Even Concha came back acting and feeling like a new person."

"I think that you might be right. I might consider your suggestion and spend some time abroad. I might be able to take a couple of weeks at this time. My new job is not expected to start until three weeks from now."

"Listen, a fantastic idea has just occurred to me. Let's go together, away from it all. Please, spend two weeks in paradise with me. I can assure you that we won't talk of any subject that is not pleasant. We will discuss only silly and trivial matters. We'll just have a glorious and wonderful time together and forget everything else for a while. Let's float in mid-air, you and I, high above any mundane substance, for fourteen delightful days. What do you say?"

"Carlos, you sound better than a travel agent. I think that I might be tempted to do it, but with some conditions. For instance, I don't wish to give you any wrong ideas. We'll stay at the same hotel, but in separate rooms. We'll share our days together, but not the nights. With that said and clarified, I'm willing to go along with the notion of going someplace. Where do you suggest?"

"Acapulco. I know of a terrific Mexican hotel that isn't frequented by the common tourist. It's called Punta Caleta. The view and scenery are fantastic. Is that to your liking?"

"Let me think about it for a couple of days. I'll let you know. Is that okay?"

"That's fine, really fine. I'll leave a day before you, and will be waiting for you at the hotel. You don't know how happy you'll make me feel if you would agree to come."

"All right, but don't get any wrong ideas. Like I said, you get two separate rooms, and we'll have some clean fun together."

"You bet, I'll take a shower every hour on the hour."

"You're always joking."

"You know I only want to make you laugh and forget. Now, let me take you home like a good friend of the family."

A week later they were both in Acapulco. The first few days went by at a tremendous pace. They were having a lot of fun together. Carlos took Inés out every single day. They went horseback riding on the countryside trails, scuba diving in the coral reef, and swimming in the ocean until they were so tired that their arms and legs could barely support them any longer. In the evenings, they ate delicious dinners and drank tequila, listening to beautiful Mexican melodies played by a local mariachi band. Late at night, they went to bed in their separate rooms.

At the end of the first week, Inés was extremely happy and carefree. Nothing was ever mentioned about their lives in Cuba. They were like two simple human beings with all the time in the world on their hands.

Then, on the eighth night, at two o'clock in the morning,

Carlos received a phone call in his room. It was Inés's voice on the other side of the line. "Carlos, you'd better call the doctor. I'm not feeling too well. My right arm and my back hurt a lot, and I feel very hot. I think I'm running a fever."

"Stay calm. I'm on my way to your suite with the hotel doctor. Just give me a few minutes."

Carlos called the main desk, and he was told that they would find a doctor immediately. He then dressed quickly, and went down the hallway to Inés's suite.

When Carlos knocked at her door, she opened it rapidly. She was wearing a long, pink, terrycloth robe. Underneath, she had a sleeveless nightgown that matched the robe. Her right arm was redder than the rest of her body and somewhat inflamed. Her body was hot to the touch.

"You better lie down and try to relax. The doctor is on his way. Tell me what happened to you."

Inés stretched her body on the sofa while Carlos sat at the edge of the same, holding her left hand.

"I don't know. I went to bed fine. Then I woke up all of a sudden, several minutes ago, with a pain in my arm and chills all over my body. It could be something I ate. I don't know but I'm feeling awful. On the other hand, you and I had the same enchiladas for dinner. Maybe the tequila didn't go well with my digestion tonight. In any event, I'm sorry to have woken you, but I didn't want to be alone with the doctor when he arrived."

"Don't be silly. I would've been very angry with you if you wouldn't have told me until tomorrow. Moreover, what other opportunity would I have had to see just how lovely and pretty you looked even when you are sick."

"You really know how to please a woman. Sometimes I wish that you and I were the last two people on this planet, so that I wouldn't have to share you with so many other females."

Carlos brushed his lips on hers in a delicate motion and went to finally kiss her on the cheek. Then, he whispered in her ear, "My divine Inés, my young, exquisite and pretty girl, you wouldn't have to share me with anybody else. Not ever, for I solemnly swear to you, here and now, that there has never been any kiss on my mouth that your lips cannot erase with their mere touch upon mine, and there are no memories of past women's bodies that yours cannot destroy with a mere sign of affection. Get it through that thick skull of yours, I love you."

"Carlos, I . . ." and she could not continue because there was an abrupt knock at the door.

Carlos went to open the door. It was the hotel night manager accompanied by a middle-aged man with metal-rimmed glasses, wearing a typical tropical shirt, who introduced himself as Doctor Suarez. He took Inés into the bedroom and remained there alone with her. Carlos and the manager stayed in the living room, waiting for the results of her examination. The doctor came out some time later.

"Well, I'm happy to report that she's doing much better now. There is really nothing serious to worry about. She has a sore muscle in her right arm. Probably the result of too much exercise or some extra weight that she held on her arm today. As far as the redness of the arm and back is concerned, that is the result of a long exposure to sunlight in the mid-afternoon hours when the sunrays are very strong. That's why she is also running a temperature. I gave her some muscle relaxant, some aspirin for the fever and a sedative so that she would sleep the rest of the night and get the rest her body needs. I also applied some moisturizing lotion to her arm and back, and now she feels more comfortable. I advise that tomorrow she stay in bed most of the day resting, even though she should feel fine when she wakes up. However, if the pain in the arm or the back persists tomorrow, you can call me."

"Thank you very much doctor," said Carlos and he continued, "I'm glad that it's nothing, and I'm sorry to have made you come at this time. By the way, do I pay you now, Doctor Suarez?"

"I normally send the bill to the hotel. You can settle with

them when you check out. And please, don't worry about the time. It's my duty as a doctor to come whenever someone needs me. Go ahead, young man, and get some rest also. Good night."

Carlos escorted both men to the door, and reiterating his gratitude for their prompt response to his request, bid them farewell. Then he went to the bedroom and made sure that Inés was asleep. He noticed that the pink robe was thrown on a side chair and the left string of her nightgown was hanging loose on the side of her upper arm, exposing her left breast. He took a deep breath and carefully placed the string over her shoulder, pulled the white sheet up to cover her up to her neck, and quietly went to the sofa to try to catch some sleep.

The next day he woke up at noontime, when the maid came in to clean the suite and change the bed linen. She was surprised to see Carlos on the sofa and exclaimed, "Oh! I'm sorry, Sir. I didn't know that you were here. I'll come back later."

"No, you don't understand," Carlos started to say, somewhat embarrassed. "The lady got sick last night, and she's resting. Please, don't come back until I call you. Thank you."

Carlos stood up. His body ached slightly from the uncomfortable position he'd slept in on the sofa, but he didn't care. He went to the bedroom and found Inés in the same position and still sleeping. Then he went to the bathroom to wash his face and gargle with mouthwash. After this he grabbed the phone and asked for room service to bring him some orange juice, milk, toast and coffee. While he was talking on the phone, he felt Inés's hand touch his back. "That sounds great. Please ask them to bring enough for two."

"Make that order double, and send it as quickly as possible. Thank you." Looking at Inés, he continued, "Well, well, well, and what does sleeping beauty have to say this morning? How do you feel?"

"Sleeping beauty says that she's feeling very well. I don't know what the doctor gave me, but my pain is gone, and so is the temperature. I only feel sticky from all the sweating that I did while sleeping. If you don't mind, why don't you wait for the food in the living room and let me take a shower."

"Go right ahead. If you need a hand to soap your back, just let me know." Inés laughed loudly. Carlos was very happy to see her well again.

Breakfast came and they both ate at the table on the terrace adjacent to the bedroom. Inés was now wearing a thick, blue terrycloth bathrobe. After breakfast, Carlos lit a cigarette and she held his hand, saying, "You know, I'm glad that you kept me company last night. As a matter of fact, I think I remember that someone told me that he loves me very much."

"Oh! It must have been that fresh Mexican doctor. I think he had you undress also. You must watch out for these guys, because they only have, as you always say, a one-track mind."

"No, I don't think he was the one. He only touched my arm and my back. Somebody else brushed my lips and kissed my face."

"Well, the one who touched your arm and back said that you'd better rest today, and the one who kissed you says that he's going to make sure that you spend most of your time in bed today."

"Alone or with some company?"

"Now, who's teasing whom? Come on, Inés, you have to rest some more."

Carlos stood up from the big chair and with his hands signaled Inés to do likewise. And yet, Inés remained seated and said, "I thought I had to rest my arm and back. There are many things that I can do with the rest of my body, you know."

"My God, I don't know what that doctor gave you last night, but I have to call him before I leave Mexico to ask him for the prescription."

"It's not what he gave me, you fool. It's what you told me and how you said it."

Carlos went to her side, and, approaching her cheek, said, "Let me see, where was I last night? I think I remember that I was kissing you here."

He tenderly kissed her now on both cheeks and then on the tip of her nose. His lips moved slowly to her mouth and by the time they reached it, her lips were wide open, offering him her mouth in the same way that she had two years before. Carlos kissed her long and hard.

She embraced him, and he reached one arm around her back while the other went to hold the back of her knees. Carlos lifted her in one swift motion and kissed her again. Then, he carried her, placing her gently on top of the huge bed. Her robe moved sideways, like the curtain of an elegant opera house, revealing her thighs and legs. Carlos unraveled the big knot at the waist and when the robe was removed he noticed that Inés was not wearing anything else. Her naked body was just lying there under his.

He kissed every single millimeter of her delicious body, while removing his own clothing. She sighed and moaned with every tender caress, every gentle stroke of his hands, lips, tongue or teeth. Her nipples became hard and erect. Her inner fluids moistened the inside of her vagina. She was ready and so was he.

Her legs opened wide and embraced his body. Carlos moved his hand to guide his virile member into her. She arched her body, to allow complete and full penetration. He leaned forward and their mouths engaged in an unstoppable, passionate kiss. Their bodies began moving in rhythm, stroking each other, sometimes very slow and sometimes very fast. In the end, Carlos collapsed panting on top of her. They swore eternal love to each other.

CHAPTER THIRTEEN

Presidential elections were scheduled for the third day of November 1958. Batista himself was not a candidate, following the policy dictated by the Cuban Constitution of 1940. Running for the party in power was Dr. Andrés Rivero Aguero, and against him a well-known political figure by the name of Dr. Carlos Márquez-Sterling. This election was the last try to overcome the ensuing revolutionary crisis through the means of a legitimate political process.

Several hours before the people of Cuba went to the polls, Castro, from his headquarters in the Sierra Maestra mountain range, issued his Revolutionary Law No. 2. This edict stated a number of punishments for any candidate running for public office in that electoral process. They went from barring any candidate to run again for any public office for a period of thirty years, to the death penalty. It was also recommended that people waiting for their respective turn to cast their vote be discouraged to do so by any means. Castro wanted to stop the free elections at any cost. There were bombs planted in many electoral posts and some people were fired at by passengers in cars driving at high speeds through cities and towns. The end result was that a very low percentage of the population voted that day and Dr. Rivero Aguero won by a very narrow margin.

Don Francisco called his friend Pepe on the telephone two days after the election.

"Cuba is lost, I'm afraid to say," Pepe said.

"I suppose I concur with you on that account. I voted for Márquez-Sterling. He was the last solution to this mess we're in now."

"I understand what you're saying, but I doubt it would have helped. In any event, regardless of what we may wish, now is the time to face reality."

"And what's reality for you, Pepe? Do you know anything that I don't know?"

"Well, the only hope we have is that Rivero Aguero gets inaugurated next January as the new constitutional President and the Army can negotiate a truce with Castro. Batista will probably leave the island after the inauguration anyway, and with him out of the way, Castro might be convinced that he can return to normal political life and end the revolution."

"That's wishful thinking. I don't believe that Castro will ever allow that to happen. Our only hope is that the United States won't recognize him, and, as I once said, I'm beginning to have doubts on the clarity of the foreign policy of that country. Sadly, the United States is being governed by politicians with lack of insight on the best interests of that nation. If there are any statesmen left in our neighbor to the north, they aren't in office, and that's for sure."

"There's also truth in what you're saying. Assuming that you're right, then the logical conclusion is that our destiny is to leave this island. The question then is where would we go."

"To the United States, of course. In spite of its politicians, it's the greatest country in this world at the present time. It's without a doubt the last bastion of freedom on this planet, and its people are generous and responsible citizens."

"Well, in that case, I'd better start packing. I'll see you, Francisco. Keep in touch."

"Don't act in haste, Pepe. We still have some time. Give my best to Magaly and the rest of the family. Please, keep me informed of any developments."

"I'll do that. Good-bye for now."

"Good-bye, my dear friend."

María Teresa and Carlos had enrolled once more in the university where classes proceeded as usual. Carlos was seeing Inés on a weekly basis, and in a very discreet fashion. María Teresa kept busy with her studies, and yet, from time to time, she thought of Raúl. Toward the end of November, on one occasion when she was leaving the university, a person that she did not know approached her car and gave her a note. It was written on a dirty piece of paper that had been folded several times and then sealed with scotch tape. She opened it very carefully.

> My dear Mari-Tere:
>
> I only hope that this letter will reach you. I want to be next to you so very, very much, and feel your moist lips on mine. Everybody here thinks very highly of me, and the truth is that I've been victorious in every battle that I've encountered. I never realized that I had such a talent for war tactics, or that I would enjoy what I am doing so much. Menoyo has been a great teacher, and since we have linked with Castro's forces, I am learning more and more about being a good revolutionary. Every day I attend political classes, and I am beginning to understand the true meaning of the revolution and the benefits that it can bring to the poor people of Cuba. As you know, they have always been deprived of economic opportunities by the rich classes. The latter only reaped the fruits of their labor. Now that situation will change, as soon as we obtain power. You will see, at my side, the purity of heart of the people around me, and

you will be a witness to the triumph of good over evil. I wish I had more paper to keep writing, but I am sure that I will see you soon, and we can talk about it then. All my love will be always with you. A big kiss,

Raúl.

December 1958 was an ominous month for the young Republic. On the 17th day, the U.S. Ambassador notified President Batista that his government could not sanction the prolonging of the current state of affairs. Furthermore, Batista was diplomatically asked to leave the country during the next 15 days to avoid any more bloodshed.

Pepe told Don Francisco about the conversation between Ambassador Smith and Batista. Don Francisco decided that he'd better move his family to the United States. He told Fernando, but kept the news from the rest of the family. Everyone else was told that the whole family would go to Miami to spend the Christmas season in that lovely Florida city. Only Concha and the servants remained in the house with the two Chow-Chows. He would send for them later on if it became necessary. They left Cuba on December 21st.

In Miami, while Carlos and María Teresa went to movies and spent time shopping and trying every restaurant in the city, Don Francisco and Fernando started to make the required arrangements with local banks to transfer some of the family funds from Cuban banks to American banks. He also purchased a house on Country Club Prado in Coral Gables and two brand new automobiles, a Buick Roadmaster and a Lincoln limousine. Fernando invested some of the capital in a portfolio of blue chip stocks. In order to make the transactions less obvious, Don Francisco left the sum of approximately one hundred thousand Cuban pesos in Cuban banks. His real estate assets, which included his house in Miramar in La Habana, and a large farm in Las Villas Province as well as his shares in the Bijagua Sugar Mill, also remained intact. Now he was ready to support his family and prepare himself for an indefinite exile.

On December 25th, Don Francisco called Pepe at his home in Cuba. After the formal salutations the conversation continued like this:

"I'm calling you mainly to wish you and your family a very Merry Christmas."

"Thank you very much, Francisco. I'd like to take the opportunity to wish you the same. How's Miami?"

"Everything's fine over here. I'm making some arrangements that are taking a little bit more time than I thought originally. Otherwise things are progressing as planned. By the way, the consensus of opinion of the small Cuban community here, and the overall sentiment of the people in general, is that it's all over. It's finished. What can you tell me?"

"Whoever told you that can match Nostradamus's foresight. Things are looking pretty bad now. The Army is in complete disarray. General Cantillo is negotiating again with Castro to try to find some political solution to the present crisis. The only brilliant page is being written by Captain Abon Ly, who has been holding Camilo Cienfuegos's column at Yaguajay since the 19th of this month, with no supplies and without hope of receiving relief or support from his comrades-in-arms. Batista has reinstated old Pedraza into active duty, and sent him to Las Villas Province with the expectation that he would stop the advance of the revolutionary forces. I think that it is too late. Too late to even contemplate any kind of military miracle at this point."

"Any other news from the U.S. Embassy?"

"None that I know about. I plan to dine today with Juan Alberto and his family. We'll discuss the situation then."

"Why don't you come with your family to Miami as my guests? Invite Juan and his family also."

"It sounds like a good idea. Juan, as far as I know, has been in that country many times, but never in Miami. If I can convince him tonight, I'll call you back tomorrow and let you know.

Magaly will love it; you know how she likes to travel. About the money, don't you worry. We are not as rich as you are, but we are not poor people either. Tell me, where are you staying?"

"At the Fontainebleau Hotel in Miami Beach. You know, Pepe, under the present circumstances this is the best idea I've had today. I hope that all of you can come and, I repeat, as my guests. Save your money here if you want to because I have the premonition that you are going to need it later. I'll be waiting for your call tomorrow."

"Thank you for the invitation. We'll discuss the monetary matter later. It's very generous of you. I'll call one way or the other. So long now."

The three friends were reunited by December 28th and all the members of the large group congregated in the nightclub of the hotel to celebrate the coming of the New Year on December 31st.

At three in the morning, the phone rang in the suite shared by Don Francisco and Fernando. Don Francisco woke up at once and reached the phone before his son. A voice at the other end of the line said, "May I talk to Magistrate Aguirrupe, please? It's urgent."

"This is Aguirrupe speaking. Who's this please, and what can I do for you?"

"This is General Cantillo calling you from Columbia Army Headquarters in La Habana. I'm sorry to call you at this hour, but can you talk to me now, or would you rather have me call you later on? I must tell you that this is very important."

"Go ahead, General, I'm listening."

"I'm calling you under orders given by Batista before he left the country. I can inform you now that Batista and his family are in the Dominican Republic at this time as guests of Trujillo. He left in the presidential plane, shortly after midnight. There is a somewhat chaotic situation at this moment, and I have remained here with the purpose of trying to pacify the entire island and avoid any further carnage."

He was going to continue but Don Francisco interrupted him. "How many people know about this?"

"Not many at this moment, since he only told a few of his closest friends before he was on the way to the airfield and invited them to leave with him. I don't think that it was a spur of the moment decision. He apparently had it on his mind since at least a week ago. In the end, he took a bunch of his friends with him because the plane was full when it departed."

"Can you tell me who left with him?"

"The newly elected president Rivero Aguero, the Vice-President Guás Inclán, his personal secretary, Andrés Domingo, the President of the Senate Anselmo Alliegro, the Chief of Staff in the Army, General Tabernilla and his family, and others. As you can see, I'm now in full command of the Armed Forces and we have no one to take charge of the government. If I were to move into that position, I'm sure that Castro and most of the people would oppose me, and we would only prolong a fight that should be avoided at all cost. With Batista gone, as you know, the next in line to be in charge should be the Vice-President but he has left. Following him, it should be the President of the Senate, but he has also left. We don't even have a duly elected President on hand to swear him into office. Hence, the plan is to follow the Constitution and to swear into office the eldest member of the Supreme Court, who happens to be Magistrate Piedra. I have talked to Piedra already and he is willing to accept the responsibility of his destiny. The only condition that he expressed to me was that all the members of the Supreme Court unanimously swear him into office. He would be the head of an interim government that would give free elections in the next eighteen months, as proclaimed by the Constitution. I'm ready to back him up with the Army, even though I'm praying that it will not become necessary. I hope that Fidel Castro will agree to return to civilian life, where he can satisfy his political aspirations by the vote and will of the people of Cuba."

"General, what you are telling me makes sense, except for

your last statement concerning Fidel Castro. Do you hope, or do you know for a fact that Castro will yield to such plans?"

"To be frank, I honestly think that Fidel is tired of the existing state of affairs as much as we are. Sure, he's winning in the propaganda field, and has even managed to get rid of Batista on those grounds. But he doesn't have a real Army on his side. He has bought most of his victories, and he might really doubt that he can obtain a military win against a unified army front. With the Tabernillas gone, I think that I can present him with that front, but I will need political support. That is, an established form of government to back me up, and the people of Cuba behind that government. So, I don't know it to be a fact, but I sincerely believe that he will agree to our conditions if we present to him a fait accompli before he has a chance to react otherwise. By tomorrow all the news agencies are going to report that Batista is no longer in Cuba, and Castro will know it also. We have to act fast. So, what do you say?"

"You may have a point. I grant you that much, and yet I'm not fully convinced of your overall analysis of the situation. But at the moment, I don't see any other solution. Consequently, without any other idea to offer, I'll ask you, when do you want me over there?"

"Right away. In this case, I must say that the sooner the better. I would like to announce Piedra's interim presidential term no later than by the end of tomorrow."

"I'm sorry, but that's impossible. I'll try to depart the day after tomorrow, and be there by the evening of January 2nd. I'll call from my house as soon as I arrive. Please, try to arrange the meeting at the Palace of Justice for the following day."

"All right. Thank you very much. I knew I could count on you. I'll be waiting for your call."

"You're welcome, General. Good-bye."

Don Francisco called his friends and other members of his family to his suite, and reported the recent events to all of them. Pepe, Juan Alberto, and their respective families were perplexed, but not entirely surprised by the news. They decided to remain in Miami, and delay their return to Cuba until the present situation on the island was clarified. The Aguirrupes agreed with their decision, and Don Francisco offered them his new house in Miami, which was being furnished. María Teresa had been working with some interior designers in Coral Gables, and helping to pick out the furniture, carpets, curtains and other paraphernalia required to make an empty house into suitable living quarters. He told them that they could move in, and share the available space as best they could, until they could make some other definite plans. He also left them the use of his new Buick. Fernando volunteered to make the necessary arrangements for the transfer of their funds to Miami.

On January 2nd, Jaime drove Don Francisco to Key West in the Lincoln and there they both embarked on the ferryboat to La Habana.

The next day, Jaime drove Don Francisco to the Palace of Justice. The people on the streets resembled a wild mob. Men were breaking the parking meters and stealing the coins from them. Men and women were looting stores. Cars were running on the semi-deserted streets with armed people wearing on their arms the red and black insignia of the 26th of July Movement. They were trying to find and murder the last of the people that were in any way involved with Batista's regime. Shots were heard sporadically all over the city. Very few police cars were on the streets. Jaime used only the major avenues, where the speed of the new Lincoln could be an advantage against any other car that might try to stop them. They arrived safely at their destination.

Opinions differed among the Justices. Some of them claimed that they would swear Piedra into office immediately. Others stated that they should proceed with extreme caution. It was Don Francisco's motion that prevailed in the end. He addressed his colleagues in the following manner:

"My dear friends, we have been presented here today with the unique opportunity to make history. Few bodies of law have had a suitable occasion in their lifetime as we now have in our hands. If we swear Magistrate Piedra into office and everything goes well, which is to say that, in due time, and through a harmonious political process, we elect a new President and return our beloved country to a democratic path in accordance with our established Constitution, then we will have succeeded in carving our names in the history of our Republic. It would be indeed a glorious legacy to leave to our children and their descendants.

"On the other hand, if we swear him into office and fail to convince Fidel Castro to lay down his arms and return to civilian life, we would be condemning Piedra to face a firing squad. We wouldn't be the ones pulling the trigger, but we would have to answer to a higher tribunal as those responsible for his death. I believe that I speak for all of us when I say that none of us would enjoy having that burden on his conscience for the rest of his life. Furthermore, if we decide to do nothing now, then we will lose the obvious timing of giving General Cantillo the political solution on which he could act to give democracy a fighting chance.

"So then, what are we to do? The way I see it, and what I recommend to you, is the following:

"We should swear Piedra in as the next interim President of Cuba, if and only if we can secure international recognition of his government. This will be the only way to ensure that Castro does not take revenge against him. It should be noted that this recognition would give the new government the opportunity to sign international treaties and request military support against any outside or inside aggression.

"We would then present to the Revolution a dilemma. They have always claimed that the main objective of their fighting has been to get rid of Batista. Clearly, Batista is out of the picture now, so there should be no need for war. They have always said that they wanted to have a free electoral process with the participation of all political parties. Obviously, since no one can doubt the integrity and the caliber of a man such as Magistrate

Piedra, they would have no reason to say that free elections would not happen in a logical and specified period of time.

"If, in spite of these proceedings, Castro persists in fostering a revolution that no longer has a reason for its existence, then the general public will finally recognize him as a political force that is only interested in gaining power and control. In that case they would lose popular support, and without that they cannot win.

"Now, we can surmise that Cuba's only hope is predicated upon the recognition by the majority of the free nations of this world of our actions at this time. If that is so, what country or countries should we approach to request the international acceptance of our new government? I can think of many, but in reality there is only one that has to be the first. That is the United States of America. If the American Government does it, then the others will follow suit.

"For that reason, I propose that the U.S. Embassy be contacted as soon as possible and informed of our decision. We should request that their State Department issue a prompt answer to our petition. If they answer affirmatively, then we should proceed to swear magistrate Piedra into office without any further delay, and hope for a rapid return to normal living conditions. If their response is negative, then God help us all."

The following day, January 4th, the U.S. Embassy in La Habana sent an emissary to the Palace of Justice to formally inform them of the decision of his government. The United States of America would not recognize any government in Cuba, except that of Fidel Castro.

CHAPTER FOURTEEN

In the meantime, Castro called from his mountain stronghold for a general strike, that took place and opened his route to the capital. He had a total force of approximately two hundred men. Thousands of soldiers surrendered their weapons, and the Army just collapsed by order of General Cantillo, who decided to do so to avoid further encounters.

Camilo Cienfuegos and "Ché" Guevara took possession of the Columbia Army Headquarters and La Cabaña Fortress, without firing a single shot.

When Castro was assured that his men controlled the entire island, and that they were in command of all the main Army posts, he moved to La Habana. He entered the capital city on January 6th, 1959, surrounded by whomever joined him along the way. To each of these men he gave a weapon, and hung a rosary from their necks. When he finally arrived at the outskirts of La Habana, he gave the illusion of being at the front of a large army comprised of simple, religious and devoted men.

The first of Castro's speeches was broadcast on the Cuban television and radio waves. It lasted over five hours. His subsequent tirades were no shorter either. In one of them, Fidel repeated time after time his famous phrase, "Arms, for what reason?" Its main theme was that since the revolution was now triumphant, and peace was maintained all over the island, there was no more need for weapons to be kept in homes. No civilians had any good reason to possess a hunting rifle, or a simple handgun to protect his property. "Arms, for what reason?" With that slogan he issued a law that made it illegal for anybody to have a weapon, under the penalty of death. The authorities collected all sorts of guns in the weeks to come. An entire population was completely disarmed. Then, his government was free to impose its will.

On January 15th, two events occurred that directly affected the lives of the members of the Aguirrupe family. The first one was a revolutionary law that demanded the closing of Villanueva University. The other was an edict that eradicated, once and for all, the entire judicial system in Cuba. From that time on, the only courts would be the revolutionary tribunals, and the only judges would be members of the revolutionary political party.

Villanueva had to be closed down as a punitive measure against the students who were going to classes and advancing their education, while their counterparts at La Habana University were unable to do so. That was the official excuse. The real reason was the fact that Villanueva was an American school, a Catholic university, and a learning center guided by an honorable priest who had always claimed that Castro was nothing else but a Marxist advocate. The Revolutionary Government proclaimed Father John J. Kelly "persona non-grata," and, as such, he had the dubious honor of being the first American priest to be expelled from the country. The Augustinian priests in Cuba usually wore a long white habit with a long black belt. Students from La Habana University, accompanied by Castro's militia men, paraded through the streets of the capital a white goat wearing a black belt, with a sign under its neck which said: "Father Kelly, O.S.A." It was the first time that the new regime contested ideas with mockery and ridicule. It would not be the last.

Castro had to establish a new type of justice on the island to make his wishes come true. To this end, he had to create the revolutionary tribunals, and that could not be done without disbanding the existing judicial system. Don Francisco, along with all of the other members of that system, found himself without a job from one day to the next.

The new trials began as public forums that resembled a Roman Circus. The prosecutor presented his charges, and the accused was then allowed to speak in his defense. After that, and under the shouting of "Paredón" (to the wall), by the people gathered in the arena, the judges would, invariably, condemn the defendant to be executed by the firing squad.

The climax of these legal farces was reached with the case of the People of Cuba versus the pilots from the Cuban Air Force during Batista's ruling period. These men were accused of dropping bombs on peasant villages, near the mountain ranges where Castro was hiding, killing innocent civilians. It was a blatant lie, so poorly fabricated that it could not stand even the loose legal procedures of these trials. The judges had no other recourse but to pronounce the pilots not guilty as charged. In a fit of anger, Castro ordered a second trial. This time, not only were the pilots tried again for the same crime, but the judges that absolved them the first time were also part of the defendant group. This second time, both pilots and judges were found guilty.

Revolutionary laws were enacted almost daily. It was the hour of glory for the people that were now ruling Cuba. Castro was using the human instinct of preservation, and the vice of envy, to achieve his ends. Towards these ends, he would justify any means.

The Urban Reform Law was directed against the landlords who held real estate and collected rents. According to the Revolution, these people had been amassing fortunes by robbing the purses of the People, who had to live some place. From then on, every rent would be reduced to half. Ultimately, the government became the new owner of the property. The populace rejoiced with the new ruling. The rural landowners, industrialists and businessmen in general, as well as the professional classes who did not own any other real estate but their own homes, felt relieved when Castro assured them that they were needed to build the new Cuba.

The Agrarian Reform Law was executed primarily against the rich landowners that were supposed to own vast amounts of non-producing land. This land, according to the Revolution, should be repossessed by the state, and given to the peasants in order to increase agricultural productivity. In reality, the ruling power took possession of all the land and gave none to anybody. The landowners, who lost their property to the avarice of the state, became the targets of the rest of the population, who did not own any farm that could be taken away from them. But again, industrialists, businessmen and professionals fell for the trap. Castro assured them that agriculture was a thing of the past. Industry was the future of the country, and they were its mentors.

Then, the Revolution moved to attack industries and businesses. One by one, beginning with foreign investments and ending with the simple, neighborhood corner store, these were taken over by the insatiable thirst of the new Marxist regime.

Villanueva University put on quite a legal fight, and managed to obtain an official decree reversing the law that had closed its doors earlier in 1959. By May of that same year, it continued its academic year and María Teresa and Carlos, returning to La Habana, managed to finish the academic year by November.

The following month, Don Francisco decided that it was time for him to leave the island for an indefinite period of time. He had lost his job in January, and his farm and his shares in the sugar mill by September of the same year. The only things left which he still possessed in Cuba were his house, his automobiles and his money in the bank.

Under the new laws, he could not take anything of value out of the country, with the exception of his personal belongings. Due to his remarkable foresight in predicting the possibility of such a situation, he had no problem leaving behind whatever property he still had on the island. Another house he already had and the automobiles could be replaced.

María Teresa wanted to remain behind for only an additional eighteen months to complete her studies at the university. Carlos decided to stay with her to keep an eye on her and also to finish his degree. They believed that the situation could not get much worse in that span of time, and that leaving meant starting all over again in an American university.

She did not say it openly, but internally she also thought that she needed more time to convince Raúl to finally leave with her. Don Francisco agreed, reluctantly, in the end.

CHAPTER FIFTEEN

Raúl had last come to see María Teresa on the same night that he had returned to La Habana. It was January 28, 1959. He had called her from his parent's home that afternoon, and told her that he could be at her home by eight that evening, after he had cleaned up and changed his uniform.

He had been left behind, in command of the entire province of Las Villas, after Castro had gone through it. Fidel himself had already heard of his military prowess, and had compensated him by giving him the rank of Commander, the highest position in the new Cuban Revolutionary Army. Raúl knew that the fact that his brother had died for the Revolution had also had a lot to do with his ascension through the ranks. Castro had embraced him on the occasion, and with a sorrowful face, had told him that he and his brother constituted classic examples of the new Cuban youth. These were, according to Castro, young men that were ready to sacrifice their lives for the fatherland.

"Valiant blood runs through your veins," Castro had said while saluting him, "as it did in your brother's. I salute you both."

María Teresa spent hours getting ready. She wanted to look her best for him. She tried on several dresses before deciding on a red and black sleeveless chemise that she had just bought in Miami the month before. It came with a short cape that was supposed to cover the otherwise exposed shoulders. For that particular evening she decided to wear it without the cape. Concha objected vehemently, but María Teresa's will prevailed. She was no longer the little girl that could be told what to do.

When her father saw her at the dinner table wearing the new dress for the first time, he said, "Is that a new dress?"

"Yes, it is. I bought it on the last trip to Miami. Do you like it?"

"Well, I would like it more if it revealed less of the upper part of your body."

"Oh! Father, it's the new style. It comes from France and it's supposed to imitate what women wore during the Napoleonic years of the French Empire."

"My dear, all I can say is that the dress may very well be an authentic depiction of a glorious time in French history; nevertheless, women should not go back in time to find new ways of dressing. Can you imagine what you people might wear if some couturier decided to design his or her new collection of dresses based on the looks of the cave woman?"

"In that case our attire would be a skimpy bear skin and no underwear at all."

"God forbid," interjected Concha.

"According to the latest fashion standards your new dress might be considered provocative but acceptable," said Don Francisco. "I think that Raúl will like it, especially the colors. The red and black combination matches the same colors used by Fidel Castro in his flag, as well as the colors used on the emblems by the Spanish communists during the Spanish Civil War."

"Dad, please, no politics tonight."

"Don't worry, I'll just say hello, politely, and go to the study to read. You can have the rest of the main floor of the house for yourselves."

"I never meant that."

"No, it's okay. I know you didn't."

Raúl showed up right on time. María Teresa ran to the door, stopped for a couple of seconds to catch her breath, and opened the door wide to look at her hero standing on the other side of the front entrance.

At first, she did not recognize him. She was not used to seeing him in full uniform, with military laced boots and a full-grown beard.

"It's me," he said when he looked at her staring at him.

She flung her arms out and jumped the distance that separated them. Her lips came in contact with his. The kiss lasted a few minutes and brought to her mind memories of a warm night in Miami, almost two years ago. She felt the same tingling sensation in her body.

They both marched into her house, and after some brief salutations to her family members, she took him to the outside patio, where they sat on a cozy swing.

Huffing sounds and some subdued barking mixed with growling noises could be heard nearby. They were coming from Samson and Delilah. Raúl looked at the menacing dogs that were now only a few feet away from him and said, "They never liked me before, and they don't seem to accept me now either."

"Oh! Don't be jealous of the dogs."

María Teresa calmed them down, and they approached her side of the swing with caution. They went to lie down next to the edge of the pool sometime thereafter.

"I'm so happy that you came back. I received your note, but you don't have any idea how much I suffered not hearing from you often. I never knew if you were dead or alive, sick or healthy, happy or sad. It's been a terrible year in more ways than one."

"The only thing bad about this whole experience was not having you by my side, not being able to smell the sweet perfume of your body, and not being able to kiss your lips." Raúl pulled her towards him and kissed her hard, long and passionately.

"After I left you, it took me two weeks to reach the mountains south of Santa Clara in Las Villas. I had to hide in several places, sometimes for days, until it was safe for me to continue to the next stop. I was well received by Menoyo and Chomón. Morgan never liked me for one reason or another. The chemistry between us just wasn't there, and the sentiment was mutual. Menoyo took me under his wing, and showed me all he knew about the kind of fighting I was going to encounter. He also opened my eyes to the needs of the poor and destitute people. I learned that the oppressive forces of the bourgeoisie with their capitalistic mentality have been hindering the progress of these people and their deserved freedom. When we joined forces with Castro's platoon, we had intellectual discussions on a daily basis. I then became aware of a lot of philosophical arguments that I'd never heard of before.

"In the battlefields we were invincible. God was with us. I distinguished myself in every single battle in which we participated. We had some casualties from time to time. I also inflicted some on the enemy forces. It wasn't too difficult to win, since after a few quick shots, they would surrender and come to our side. Most of them were young men like me, and also completely ignorant of the realities of life. When we told them that they were fighting for the wrong cause, they didn't believe us at first. After a while, due to my academic background, I was assigned to be a group leader in charge of communicating the revolutionary message to these men, as well as to our new recruits and the farmers in the area. When Castro came through Las Villas, he personally gave me the rank of Commander, and left me in charge of the entire province. I'm now assigned to Columbia Army Headquarters. We can be together again, now and forever."

"I always thought the Revolution meant a simple transitional and political change, just to get rid of Batista and get back to the democratic succession of elected presidents. What's changed?"

"Nothing has changed. That was the main intent, but we have to be sure that the people are fully aware of the errors of the past that lead to Batista. When the poor people, the real people of Cuba, possess the knowledge, they will never be taken for granted again, by anybody."

"I'm not a poor person, and yet I consider myself to be one of the real people of Cuba."

"Of course, Mari-Tere, I wasn't referring to either you or your family. You must realize that I'm talking about the wealthy landowners who exploit the peasants, the rich industrialists who fill their wallets by paying meager wages, the greedy landlords and owners of vast portions of real estate who are squeezing the last pennies from the purses of the needy people, charging exorbitant rents on a market that they monopolize. That situation has to be changed. First, we must pull the poor people from their misery, and then we will pass the government into their hands, where it belongs. We'll never allow it to be in the hands of oppressors where it used to be."

"I wish that you could hear yourself. You haven't realized how mistaken you are in your assertions. Still, this isn't the night for political or socio-economic discussions. Let's leave those topics for another time, and let's talk about us and especially about you. As you probable heard, Villanueva is closed, but we're working diligently to try to reopen it very soon. All sorts of legal recourses are being tried at this time. My father is helping and Attorney Hernandez-Corujo is carrying the day. Can you help us in any way?"

"I won't. I'm not going back to that school. That university has been created by Yankee imperialists, in cahoots with the Catholic Church, to confuse the minds of the spoiled rich brats in Cuba, with the purpose of controlling their actions. I'll complete my studies at La Habana University and that will occur after I finish fulfilling my revolutionary duties."

"Are you serious?"

"Yes, I am."

"How can you be serious about that? You were one of the students at Villanueva. You know very well what was taught inside of their classrooms. Were you then a spoiled rich brat also? Am I one now for wanting to go back, finish my studies and be useful to my country?"

"No, I didn't think that I was one. I'm sorry for what I just said. I didn't mean it the way it came out. In reality I was confused as you probably are now."

"You sound confused to me all right."

"Let's not argue, my love. You'll learn with time," Raúl said in an almost apologetic tone of voice.

"One of us is going to be very much disappointed one day. Tell me one thing though, if you aren't going back to school to complete your studies, then what about us?"

"If you're referring to our wedding, we can get married as soon as you wish. As far as I'm concerned, I'm ready any time."

"You know that what you just said is impossible," María Teresa argued.

Raúl rebutted, "I don't see why we can't get married right away, do you?"

"Raúl, a wedding is not something that one does on the spur of the moment. It isn't planned in one day. That might be the case in Hollywood movies, but not in real life. It's a ceremony that symbolizes a union that is to last until death. I'm looking forward to an experience that I shall remember the rest of my life. Our wedding and our honeymoon should be the most important and memorable events in our lifetime. Don't you agree?"

"Okay. Have it your way, I agree. Let's plan a fantastic wedding for next June."

"June would be fine with me if you were already a lawyer. Please, try to understand my situation. There's been a great change of conditions in this country of ours during this month. My father just lost his lifetime position, and is seriously contemplating leaving Cuba for good. It'd break his heart to see me marrying a Commander of the Army that is supporting the government that shattered his visions."

"What visions are you talking about? I respect your father, but he's living in the past. We represent the future."

"An uncertain future to say the least."

"No, you're mistaken, my love. We will possess a future of hope and revitalization for the people of Cuba. We will set an example for the whole world to watch and emulate."

"Listen, I know that you're full of good ideas. You feel that you've accomplished a great task. You dream of a new Cuba, and you want to be part of that dream. Nonetheless, you have to concede to me that the present state of affairs might lead our beloved nation through dangerous roads, and to a destiny far away from our traditions and expectations. I also desire the best political and economic conditions for the people of Cuba, for you and me, and the future of the children that I want to have with you. Why don't we just wait a while? At least until we know for certain what prospects are coming our way."

"I told you that I wouldn't mind waiting a while. You could also try to enroll in La Habana University and study there in the meantime."

"Did you forget that La Habana University doesn't offer mechanical engineering? However, I would like, at least, to be able to finish my studies. If I decide to go to the United States to complete my education, will you come with me, as my husband, and also complete yours?"

"How can you ask me that? That country supported my enemies for years."

"You're mistaken, Raúl. That country helped you and your cause tremendously."

"Even if it's true, and assuming that I might agree with you, you have to admit that you're asking me to do the impossible. How would we live? What kind of work could I get that would pay me enough to support us and put us through school?"

"I don't think that you'd have to worry about it. My father could help us and support us in the meantime. We could pay him back eventually."

"Oh! No! I'll never allow that."

"All right. I understand. I'm sorry. I didn't mean to offend you. I don't want to hurt your pride. Forget what I just said."

"I know you said it with the best intentions. It's just that I have a lot to accomplish in this revolutionary process. I can't leave my Army position at this time. The country needs me, and I must answer the call of duty."

"I didn't fall in love with a soldier. I fell in love with a good man, who wanted to practice law so that he could gain the reputation of an honorable and brilliant lawyer, and be recognized as such by his peers and fellow men. A revolution borrowed him from me, and I waited patiently for his return for a full year. If that man still wants to stay with the revolution, when do you think I might get him back?"

"Soon. Another year at the most. Please, grant me this time, because what I have to do is very important."

"How important am I to you, Raúl?"

"Also, very important. Can't you see that you're getting jealous of a political situation? Try to see my point of view. I grant you that there are some radical elements within the Revolution. Now, if I, and all the people like me, decide to quickly return to civilian life, we could be opening a clear path to power for these radicals. So you see, we are safeguards. Let me do this until we're sure that the country is again a democracy."

"Are you really sure the radical elements aren't in control already?"

"Look, Mari-Tere, I know that Castro has been accused of being a communist. That's a lie. The Revolution is not red in color, but green as the leaves of the Royal Palm tree in our national emblem. As a matter of fact, as long as Fidel is at the helm, we have the needed insurance to defeat the real communists. Time is the only problem now. Just grant me that time."

"Be careful, Raúl. The green color of the Royal Palm tree could turn red from the blood that is being spilled by so many killings in front of the firing squad. Time might be running short for both of us, due to events that might occur that would be out of our control. However, if it has to be, so be it. I waited for you once, and I shall wait for you once more. Only this time, it'll be more difficult to do so, since before I didn't have you next to me, and now I do. You know that I love you very, very much."

"I love you too. Believe me, Mari-Tere. I love you with all my heart."

Raúl embraced her and started to kiss her on both cheeks and on her mouth. His tongue played a scintillating game with her ears and he bit gently on her lobes. María Teresa emitted a low sound with delicious excitement. He then proceeded to caress her neck and shoulders with his lips. Suddenly, his hand reached over the front of her dress and firmly grabbed one of her breasts. She reacted rapidly, trying to push his hand away, asking him to let her go. Raúl did not move his arm. He kissed her again, with a seductive motion of his tongue upon hers, while his hand commenced to stroke her nipple gently. Her hands let go of his arm, and moved to the back of his neck. She held his head and kissed him back. With a quick motion, Raúl pulled down her dress and bra, completely exposing her breast. He moved his head to reach the breast that his hand held. His lips exerted tender pressure all over her well-developed bosom, ending at the nipple, where the combination of his tongue and teeth created the ecstatic effect that was being revealed on her face.

When Raúl returned to his parents' house, they insisted that he renounce his military career and continue to pursue his education. Luis Mora expressed his desires to Raúl by telling him that he had already given one son to the Revolution, and that he had almost sacrificed his second one by permitting him to play guerrilla warfare in the mountains. Now, he wanted his second and last son back with him.

Raúl did not abide by the pleadings of his father. Instead, he moved into a house on the Army Base, and from then on, he only went to visit his parents on rare occasions. By the middle of the following year, his parents, disillusioned with his behavior, finally left the island and moved to Miami, where they joined the large group of Cuban exiles that were increasing at a great rate. The day that Luis Mora went to the government office to request a permit to leave the country for him and his wife, the bureaucrat who was attending him asked him if he had any children. He briefly responded that he had had two sons, but he had lost them both.

In contrast to the apparent happiness that surrounded María Teresa and Raúl, the relationship between Inés and Carlos turned somber by the end of 1959. These were extremely wicked times for Inés. First of all, the beginning of the year found her working on a project to complete the design of the new Bacardi Rum office building. The great Mies van der Rohe conceived the original drawings and concepts. Inés was thrilled about the idea of working on such a well-known architect's plans. She was living well with her salary and allowance from her former in-laws. Her apartment had all the amenities that she wanted at the time, and she had just purchased a brand new Mercury Turnpike Cruiser. She saw her parents every week, and whenever she could manage to escape discreetly, she was enjoying moments of romantic intimacy with Carlos. In the same manner that a mirror is shattered into a million pieces when it encounters a heavy blow, so did her life shatter in the span of the next eleven months.

By the middle of the year, Bacardi decided to cancel the project, foreseeing the overtaking of the company by the Revolutionary Government. Her father, who worked for the rum manufacturer, had been transferred to Puerto Rico just a couple of months before. Her parents had moved without her. The architecture and engineering firm of Gutierrez y García, who was handling the construction of Bacardi's building, liquidated the business due to lack of private interest in that kind of work. She found herself without a job.

Then, a few months later, the Font-Vachon family left Cuba, after the loss of the majority of the family's fortune. With them, Inés's pension as the widow of the oldest son also disappeared. Carlos offered to help. He asked Inés to marry him, but she refused, claiming that she would agree to that wedding when he had finished his studies and could support them both. She despised the idea of living on his father's money. For some reason, she also refused to take the monetary assistance that Carlos wanted to give her to help make the payments on her apartment, car and other obligations.

She could not find any job suitable to her profession in the private sector, because it did not exist anymore. The only available positions were with the government, and she could not qualify for those. She was refused, time and time again, not because of a lack of knowledge or ability, but due to her previous social and economic background.

A good friend invited her to spend Christmas Eve at her house. She accepted the invitation to have a reason to tell Carlos that she could not go to his house that evening. It was her feeling that since that could be the last Christmas the Aguirrupes would spend in Cuba, she should not intrude. Carlos was disappointed at first, but when she told him that she promised to spend the following day and night with him, he conceded.

At the party, Inés met Dr. Gustavo Albacete, a prominent physician who had inherited a large fortune from his family, on top of the one that he had managed to amass himself. He had given enormous endowments to Castro and his Revolution. Fidel had mentioned him during his first speech, calling him the example of the dedicated professional that had contributed so much toward the liberation of Cuba from its previous tyranny. Several times during that first year of the Revolution, he had gone out fishing with Fidel, his brother Raúl, and other members of the ruling party. Dr. Albacete was married and had three children. The youngest child was already forty years old.

At the dinner table, he sat next to Inés. On various occasions he touched Inés's knee with his hand while addressing her with one question or another. Once, he left his hand on her knee for a longer period of time and moved it up and down her thigh over her evening gown.

He asked Inés to dance with him, and took the opportunity to beg her to go with him on a trip to the countryside the following month. She politely refused.

Every day, for the next thirty days, Inés received five dozen red roses from the friendly doctor, along with a precious piece of jewelry. She kept the flowers but she returned the jewelry. The note was always the same. It read:

> You have come into my heart like a thunderbolt. Would you, please, make this old man happy, and accompany him on his next trip to the countryside? It will only take three days. I am sure that they will be the best of my life and the most promising for yours. With immense love, I am sending you a warm kiss,
> Gustavo.

Gustavo's persistence created a dilemma in her confused mind. She could begin accepting Carlos's help, but she reasoned that Carlos's money was not his. It belonged to his family instead, and the way he was spending it, it would not last for long. She also had to consider that Carlos could not find a suitable job under the current regime any more than she could. Gustavo's offer would make her a highly paid courtesan, but it would also bring her the kind of protection that she needed at that time. Gustavo was the kind of communist that the government considered "useful idiots." But his protection might help her to find a job as an architect and she would then be able to support herself. Also, since Gustavo was a married man with a family, he could not afford to be seen with her in public. She began to realize that she was trying to live under a system that was controlling her life more and more.

In the end, Inés accepted and went with him on his excursion. When they returned, he was extremely cheerful and in good spirits. She was displeased, and mortified with herself. She had received his money and assistance in exchange for her occasional physical favors. For him, she was his mistress. Internally, she felt like a well-paid whore.

When she lay in bed the first time with Gustavo, she insisted he leave the room in complete darkness. He placed her back in front of him and made her kneel down with her face resting on the pillow. He never saw the silent tears that poured from her eyes as he came behind her. To sense him inside her and to feel his hands touching her body were not her worst torment. Her worst torment was the thought that Carlos might find out.

END OF BOOK TWO

BOOK THREE

Güanajay
Prison for Women

CHAPTER ONE

The year 1960 came over the lives of María Teresa and Carlos like a dark cloud, forecasting the stormiest weather of their lives. It was the same kind of prospect for their country.

Fidel Castro was in the process of eliminating anybody that could tarnish his position as the first figure of the Revolution, and question his leadership abilities in becoming the ruler of the nation.

Toward the end of the previous year, Pedro Luis Díaz Lanz, the Commander-in Chief of the new Cuban Revolutionary Air Force, had left the island, defecting to Miami, and had returned to fly over La Habana, dropping pamphlets stating Castro's communist ties. Camilo Cienfuegos, one of his top Commanders in the new Revolutionary Army, had mysteriously disappeared on a routine flight from Camagüey to La Habana. Strong rumors persisted in Cuba that Castro had ordered the single engine plane to be shot down over the ocean. Hubert Matos, the Commander in charge of Camagüey Province, was tried and condemned in a trial that imposed upon him a long-term jail sentence for possible counterrevolutionary activities. In reality, all he had done was express concern for the preponderance given to some well-known communists in the new government.

Most of the civilian figures in Castro's first attempt to create a new government at the beginning of 1959 had either left the country, or they were hiding, trying to conduct clandestine activities against the established ruling elite.

The early part of the month of February saw the visit of Anastas Mikoyan to Cuba. He was heading a Soviet delegation, with the purpose of starting negotiations between the two countries. On the fifth day of that month, Mikoyan went to the Central Park in La Habana to deposit a floral offering at the foot of José Martí's statue. Martí had been one of the heroes of the Cuban Independence War against the Spanish Government at the end of the previous century. Students from La Habana and Villanueva Universities also went to the park that day and destroyed the Soviet offering, substituting the same with their own floral arrangement in the form of the Cuban flag. The police intervened with automatic weapons, but not even the bullets could stop the students from their goal. In the end, several students were admitted to local hospitals, and sixteen of them were sent to jail.

The Association of Economic Corporations of Cuba, presided over by Emeterio T. Padrón, gave Mikoyan, who was accompanied by Vladimir Bigikin, the Soviet Ambassador to Mexico, and members of the Cuban Communist Party, a sumptuous reception and an undeserved welcoming soirée. Before leaving the island, Mikoyan signed a commercial agreement with Cuba in which the Soviet Union would purchase one million tons of sugar from Cuba during the next five years, while at the same time they would open a line of credit for approximately one hundred million dollars for Cuba to spend acquiring Soviet products. As a corollary to the agreement, the Soviet Union would also offer technical assistance to Cuba. With this treaty began Cuba's economic dependence on the Soviets, as well as the infiltration of Soviet agents and other subversive elements into the country.

Another important event occurred during the beginning of the month of March. It was the explosion of the French vessel

"*La Coubre*" that was docked in one of the piers at La Habana harbor. It was loaded with ammunition, grenades, and weapons. The communist propaganda immediately blamed opposition forces, including the possibility of American saboteurs. The explosion killed and maimed many Cubans, and destroyed several piers and their buildings. The entire mess was an embarrassment to the government that was trying to keep from the people the fact that it was acquiring all sorts of armaments.

The United States Government denied any part in the incident, and did so in an official communiqué to the Cuban Government on March 8. However, the straightforward, commercial American propaganda was not up to par with the insidious and deceitful methods of the Cuban communists, and the Cuban people ended up believing their own sources of misinformation. Some Cubans felt sorry for the naiveté of the Americans who gave full credit to Castro's words when in a visit to the United States, some months before, he had told them that he was not a communist, and that he only wanted cooperation from the American Government, and the friendship of the people of that great nation.

Curiously enough, on March 14, the security agent in charge of the investigation of the explosion of "*La Coubre*", Mario Herrera-Rodríguez, died as the result of the explosion of one of the grenades that he was analyzing. Four more policemen were also wounded. The United States was not blamed for this second incident.

In a speech given on March 22, a newspaperman by the name of Dr. Luis Conte-Agüero revealed the existence of a communist conspiracy within the Cuban Government that was trying to take control. This journalist knew Castro from the days when both had been students at La Habana University. They even used to call each other brothers. Just because he dared to speak against communism, he was beaten by a lynch mob that almost killed him. Conte-Agüero managed to seek political asylum in the Embassy of Argentina. On March 30, he left the island that saw him take his first steps. The following day, the Mestre brothers, owners of the radio and television station CMQ, issued a statement that the new government was taking over all means of communication. Both brothers escaped to the United States shortly thereafter.

On April 8, Ambassador Andrés Vargas-Gómez resigned his position in Geneva, and accused Fidel Castro of placing Cuba inside the Iron Curtain. A sick man, Vargas-Gómez was apprehended, tortured and sentenced to a long jail term in a Cuban prison. The road to serfdom was being paved with the blood, anguish and martyrdom of the same men and women that had believed in Fidel only a year before. Gutierrez-Menoyo, the Commander-in-Chief who had opened the second front against Batista in the Escambray Mountains, also went on to become another number in the penal system of the island.

The Soviet Union and Cuba officially established diplomatic relations on May 7. The previous day, Trotsky's assassin, Jacques Monard Mercade, arrived in La Habana, after having been released from jail by the Mexican Government. The International Communist Movement recognized, even at that time, the safety that its hero would enjoy in Cuba, where some of his relatives were living.

From then on, the relationship between the United States and Cuba deteriorated at a very fast pace. The colossus to the north threatened economic sanctions that consisted primarily in halting the purchase of Cuban sugar. Castro retaliated by selling the product to Soviets and asking the Soviets for more military aid. The first Russian technicians arrived on the island, and started to develop the plans for the installation of missile bases throughout the country. The entire countryside was full of large, natural, underground caverns that yielded excellent prospects for the concealment of that type of weaponry.

Open diplomatic hostility increased toward the United States diplomatic corps in Cuba. By September of 1960, the American Ambassador was restrained from traveling throughout the city.

He had to use a particular route, designed by the Cuban Government, in order to move from his residence to the Embassy and back. He was denied access to any other street in the city.

In a speech given by Fidel Castro on January 2, 1961, he demanded that the United States remove their entire diplomatic personnel from Cuba, and gave them forty-eight hours to fulfill his request. Not only Americans attached to the diplomatic mission left the country, but also thousands of their compatriots departed, leaving behind most of their possessions. From that moment on, the Swiss Embassy represented the United States diplomatically in Cuba.

The break in diplomatic relations would culminate some months later in the fiasco of the Bay of Pigs invasion attempted by the Cuban exiled community with the treacherous backing of the United States.

In June of 1961, the priests at Villanueva were told to vacate the school once and for all; they were being expelled from Cuba. The Augustinians from Philadelphia lost their real estate on the island, and left behind a great part of their heart. They were not unique in receiving this kind of treatment. All foreign religious orders were told to close their educational centers, churches, convents, and hospitals. In the final analysis, they were grateful to leave with their lives. Many Cuban and Spanish priests and nuns would pay a higher price by remaining behind, since most of them ended up in the infamous Cuban jails, destined to suffer the most despicable form of psychological and physical tortures.

In July of 1961, Sister Beth was told to depart with the group of Dominican American nuns. She decided to see María Teresa at least one more time.

It was early morning when the car approached the Aguirrupe's house and parked in the driveway. Sister Beth and Sister Cecile knocked at the door.

Concha opened the door.

"May we see María Teresa?" said Sister Beth.

"By all means, Sisters. Please, come in."

María Teresa came running down the stairs, accompanied by her two dogs. While she approached the foyer to embrace and say hello to the two nuns, the dogs stopped at the bottom of the stairway, growling and huffing at the strangers.

"Don't be afraid. They look menacing, but I assure you that they wouldn't hurt anybody. Concha, why don't you take them outside for a while? I'm going to be in my father's study. Please, tell Mirta to send us some coffee and some churros, if she has some already fried. If not, we'll have some toast."

The two Dominicans followed her to the elegant room and waited a few minutes for the food to arrive. They took the opportunity to compliment their hostess on the beauty of the house and its furnishings. When they were alone and María Teresa had closed the doors, Sister Beth said, "I wanted to see you before I depart. We were told to leave the country by Friday. Sister Cecile volunteered to drive me here today. She has my absolute confidence, so please, feel free to say whatever you want in front of her."

"Is the government taking over the school, Sister?" María Teresa said.

"I'm sure that the school will exist no more. What they will do with the buildings is unknown to me. On the other hand, I can assure you that in another two months the private Catholic education system will be completely eradicated from Cuba."

"That's a shame, after all the work and time the Church has invested to bring their religious teaching and their high moral values to the Cuban youth in particular, and to the families in general. Traditionally, we've been a people that have always looked at the Catholic Church with respect. Why are you giving up so easily?"

"What can we do? We could defy Castro and become martyrs, but we have to obey Rome. You have to realize that the Vatican does not want to begin a controversy with a communist country. Not at this time when high voices in our own Church are trying to flirt with atheists. Castro himself is a product of the Jesuits, but he doesn't believe in anything."

"Well, you know what they say about the Jesuits," interjected Sister Cecile. "They either produce saints or demons, but nothing in between."

"You're right, Sister. In this case, they came out with a satanic fiend, all right," María Teresa said.

Sister Beth took another sip of her coffee.

"It's all really very simple. The communists learned from the Spanish Civil War that it's bad propaganda to murder hundreds of priests and nuns. It is better to dispose of them by more practical means. This so-called attempt at an invasion has given them the perfect opportunity to get rid of what they labeled 'undesirable clergy,' and with them, the eradication of religious education. Now, they will have free access to the minds of the children that they want to brainwash with their lies and distortions of human actions. In the long run, we're witnesses of another battle between good and evil, the eternal confrontation of mankind. This time we lost, unfortunately. However, our faith tells us that the victory in the overall war is ours in the end. Let's not forget that truth."

"Amen," said Sister Cecile.

"What are your plans for the near future?" Sister Beth said.

"I really don't know what to do now. The university is closed, and I won't be able to continue my studies at La Habana University, because they don't offer a degree in mechanical engineering. If I think only of my professional life, I think the only avenue left to me would be to go to the United States and finish my education over there. How to leave is another matter. It's easy for you since you've been expelled, but for me, it would be somewhat more difficult."

"Yes, I know, my child, and that's why I wanted to come to see you today. What I wanted to tell you couldn't be said over the telephone. The government is listening to all the lines suspected of carrying counterrevolutionary conversations. I'm sure that if they haven't tapped into our phone system, they probably have yours under surveillance. Now, listen to me carefully. When we leave on Friday, our first stop will be Miami. I'll be there for a couple of days before proceeding to Philadelphia. If you want me to, I'll see your father and tell him that you would like to abandon this place as soon as possible. I'm sure that he can think of something, and make the necessary arrangements."

"I sincerely appreciate the opportunity that you are offering me, and yet, I don't know if I can give you an answer now."

"Is it Raúl?"

"Yes and no. After I left you at the Blanquita Theater, Raúl came to rescue me from that horrid experience. But on that same night he had a quarrel with Carlos, and we ended up having a disastrous argument. Raúl hasn't come to see me since that night. I've telephone him on many occasions, and he hasn't returned any of my calls. Logically, I'm supposed to realize that all is finished between us, but my heart tells me that I still love him very much. Am I stupid for letting my feelings get a hold of my reasoning?"

"No, my sweet angel. You aren't stupid; you are just, as you said, very much in love. Like the French people say, it is an '*affaire de Coeur.*'"

"It's very difficult to go through life always making the right choices and the correct decisions. We all make mistakes from time to time. Now, you have to understand that Raúl could be one of those mistakes. If he's failed to see your love, it's because he doesn't love you anymore, or there is another cause in his life that has become more important to him. Whatever the real reason might be, you can't follow the steps of a man that isn't willing to meet you halfway. In another set of circumstances, you could have had the luxury of waiting, and allowing your heart to fantasize some more about the possibility of living a married life with him. At this time, you must crush your heart with logic, and do what makes sense for you.

"The foremost question should be, should I leave my country or not? All indications point to the fact that to continue living in Cuba will become extremely hard for a person like you, as well as exceedingly dangerous. You might have some money left now, but how long will it last? What will you do when it's all gone? This government will control the means of production. They will become the only source of employment, and you can bet your life that they will not give you or your brother the chance to earn a decent salary. They will probably use you for the most menial tasks. That's really the best that you can hope for, because if you utter any complaint, I'm sure that you'd end your life in a rotten jail. To this extent, your only logical conclusion is to abandon your country and look for opportunities where opportunities lie.

"The next point in this argument is Raúl. If he's intelligent enough, sooner or later he will come to the conclusion that he's made a serious miscalculation of the goals of this revolution, and will find an avenue of escaping from it. If he really loves you, he will find you and come to seek you. Then, you'll live the life of love with him that you so desire. If he doesn't, then believe me, you'll always remember him, but you'll learn to fall in love again with the right man for you. God can make anything happen. If it's part of His design to see you married to Raúl, He will grant it to you. Here or abroad.

"Now, what do you think? Should I see your father when I go to Miami?"

"I don't know what to tell you, Sister. Your intentions are good, no doubt about that. I know that you love me and care for me, and it's very hard for my mind to dispute your reasoning. You're right, and still, I hesitate. Perhaps because not only Raúl worries me, but if I leave, there are also Concha, Carlos, the servants and my faithful dogs. What would I do about all of them?"

"My child, that's no problem. I know that your father would not intend to create any hardship for any member of his household. Please, say yes, and let me talk to him."

"All right, you win. Tell him that I'll leave, provided that all my loved ones depart with me. And also tell him that I haven't heard from him since he talked to me over the telephone last

April. I've tried to call him, but they always say that all circuits are busy. I've mailed him six letters since that time, and gotten no reply to any of them."

Sister Beth and Sister Cecile stood up. Sister Beth embraced Mari-Tere very hard and held her for a few minutes. Before they left the room, she told her to look her up if she ever came to Philadelphia, and when they reached the front door, just before leaving the house, she whispered in María Teresa's ear, "Aequo animo, ex nihilo nihil fit."

CHAPTER TWO

After supper, María Teresa retired to her bedroom with the two dogs. After she changed her clothing and slipped into a comfortable, long robe, she went to Carlos's bedroom and knocked at his door.

"Come in, if you're not decent, because I'm not."

María Teresa smiled and said, "It's Mari-Tere, Carlos. I want to talk to you."

"Wait a minute. I'll open the door as soon as I'm ready."

"Better still, just come to my room. I'll be waiting for you."

Carlos opened the door of María Teresa's bedroom after a single knock and entered quickly. "What's going on, Sis? What do you want?"

María Teresa was sitting on her bed flanked on either side by the Chows-Chows. Carlos sat in the rocking chair facing her.

"Carlos, I have to talk to you seriously. What I want to discuss must remain between you and me. That's why I want to do it behind closed doors."

"Sure. Don't worry about it; my lips are sealed. What's in that pretty head of yours?"

"A couple of days ago, I sent a message to Father in Miami. I wanted him to know that I'm ready, I mean that we're ready, to leave Cuba, and asked him for his help in doing so."

"That's a serious matter, indeed. However, I've been thinking along those same lines myself."

"Have you? I thought that it would be very hard for you to leave Inés."

"Yes, it would be hard, but let me see if I can explain the situation to you. I'm deeply in love with that woman. Our relationship is very passionate and intimate whenever we have the time to be together. I would marry her tomorrow if she would let me, and I would forgive her for what she did. My problem is that her conscience is so burdened that she doesn't believe my heart is capable of pardon. We had a big argument some months ago, and I did something in a moment of rage that I've never done in my life. I slapped her face three times. She came crawling to me and begged me to beat her to death if that's what I wanted. I took her in my arms and kissed her, and then, I realized that I would love her eternally, no matter what she had done, or will do in the future, but she mistook my sentiments for those of only wanting carnal knowledge of her beautiful body. Since then we only talk of funny and silly things. We entertain each other, and never mention her past married life or her present reality. It's like living in a world of fantasy whenever I'm with her. I've tried, on several occasions, to bring our lives into focus but she never lets me do it. She always says that we should enjoy the present moment and never look at our uncertain future. The last time that I tried to put some sense into our situation, she almost came to the point of discussing it. Then, she started to cry and said, 'What's the use? You would always remember my past and never forgive me for what I have become.' I feel so sorry for her that sometimes I feel like crying myself, and only time can heal the scars in her heart. I've wondered if a separation from everything that surrounds her life at the present moment would be best. I might be able to talk her into leaving the country with me, and starting anew in some foreign place. So you see, I have thought of going to the United States and I'm all for it. Besides, there's nothing else for you and me to do here anymore. I'm glad that you told me about your idea of leaving the country soon, because I would never leave without you."

"I'm sorry to hear about Inés, but I also think that we could all rebuild our lives again. We are still very young, and we have the greatest part of our lives before us."

"What prompted you to make that decision?"

"It was Sister Beth. To tell you the truth, I had toyed with the notion of being with Father and Fernando, and yet, I guess I didn't want to be the one to make the decision. When that lovable nun came to see me the other day, she convinced me easily by simply stating what I had already been thinking about, and coming up with the same logical conclusion."

"How do you think we should attempt leaving?"

"I don't know. I'm sure that the government won't give us the necessary permits. Then there are Concha, Mirta, Magda and Esther, Samson and Delilah, the house, our own personal belongings and the money in the bank. Sister Beth is going to tell Father about it, and I'm sure that he'll think of a good plan. In the meantime, we shouldn't tell anyone, and start to get ready for the trip. I don't know how much time we'll have when it happens."

"One thing is certain. Others will enjoy the money in the bank, the house and all the other possessions when we leave. We still have over a hundred thousand pesos in cash. Let's sign a check together and get some of that money out. I would like to buy Inés the biggest and best diamond ring."

"Until we know how we're leaving, we should keep as much money as we can with us. Maybe we'll have to buy our happiness in more than one way. Who knows?"

"If we don't need the money, would you agree to sign with me, so I can make precious use of it?"

"Yes. I'd agree to let you spend it if it would buy you the joy that you deserve."

"How about Raúl? Couldn't he help us obtain the permits and the seats on a plane leaving for Spain or Mexico?"

"I doubt that very much. I haven't talked to Raúl since the last time he set foot in this house."

"Fights are customary in any engagement. I never realized that yours was so serious. Have you tried calling him? Men are usually so stupid that we think that we're going to lose our "macho" image by being the first one to call."

"Yes, I've tried, but he avoids me and never answers any of my calls. Raúl might be a lost cause, and believe me, I love him as much as you love Inés."

"Well, sit tight and keep your chin up. Maybe he'll call you one of these days. Now, I'm going to do some more thinking of my own. Good-night."

"Remember, not a word until we know exactly what to do."

"Don't worry. I repeat, my lips are sealed."

The following morning, Carlos woke up early with his mind made up to assist María Teresa in confronting Raúl at least one more time. He dressed in an impeccably pressed white cotton suit, with a light blue shirt and a slanted striped red and white necktie. He took the Jaguar out of the garage and pointed the ferocious cat emblem on the hood to face the direction of Columbia Army Headquarters.

It took him only twenty minutes to arrive at one of the gates. The sentinel at the post raised his left hand when he saw the approaching automobile. In his right hand he held a Czechoslovakian sub-machine gun.

"What do you want?'"

"I came to see Commander Raúl Mora."

"Do you have an appointment with Commander Mora?"

"Yes, tell him that Carlos Aguirrupe is here at the gate and requests permission to enter the camp to see him."

"One moment."

The sentinel shouted the instructions to the other guards at the entrance shack without removing his eyes from Carlos or the car. One of the guards went to a nearby telephone and started to relay the message. A few minutes later, he told the sentinel that it was all right to let him in. The man changed his attitude almost immediately, and, in a surprisingly pleasant fashion, went on to instruct Carlos on how to reach the main officers' club, where Commander Mora was having breakfast. A few minutes later, Carlos was sitting opposite Raúl.

"What a surprise, Carlos. I never expected to see you in these quarters. I thought that you disliked revolutionary army men. Would you care for some breakfast?"

"You know very well that I don't dislike you, and just to prove the point, I'd be very happy to have some coffee with you."

"Waiter, bring us some more coffee and toast with butter. Now, what brings you here today? Have you come to see one of the leaders of the Revolution in his glory?"

"No, I simply came to have coffee with a friend."

"Is that all? Just a friendly chat for old times' sake?"

"Yes, Raúl. Merely a pleasant conversation with you concerning a person that we both love very much."

"Did Mari-Tere ask you to come?"

"I'm surprised at you. I really thought that you knew my sister better, much better. She is too proud to ask me to do anything like that."

"But not proud enough to avoid calling me over a hundred times and leaving messages all over the place."

Coffee was brought and served in an exquisite set of china.

"Listen, Raúl, I came here today to talk to you about Mari-Tere. Now, let's agree on something first. If you are going to hear what I came to tell you, and you're ready to discuss the issue in an amicable fashion, I'll welcome the opportunity that you are giving me, and I'll continue talking. If, on the other hand, you want to hide yourself under that new superman attitude of yours, and not let the Raúl who told me and swore to me in Miami that he loved my sister ever so much come to the surface, then we have nothing more to talk about. I'll just stand up and say good-bye to you for the last time."

"No, don't leave. I'll listen to you. Now tell me, how is Mari-Tere, and what do you want me to do about her?"

"I only want to ask you for a very simple favor. I want you to go to her and talk to her one more time. If, for whatever reason, the old sparks have faded away, and both of you have nothing in common anymore, then let her go her own way. I know damn well that she still loves you very much, and that it will probably take a long time for her to overcome that sentiment. If it has to be that way, so be it. I'll make sure that she learns to forget you. On the other hand, if you can find the love that once inspired you to become engaged, then I'll do my utmost to see that she's happy at your side. I brought both of you together because I sensed the kind of love that existed between you. Would you allow me the pleasure of doing it for the second time? Would you come to see her again?"

Raúl leaned back in his chair and took a few minutes to respond. Carlos waited patiently for his answer.

"All right. I'll do as you wish. I'll call Mari-Tere today, and tell her that I want to see her, and I'll be at your house next Saturday night."

"Thank you. Now I'll leave you to your duties."

"Wait a minute. Let me also explain something to you. I've always been grateful to you, because, as you said, you did a lot for Mari-Tere and me. I also want you to know that, in my peculiar way, I love her very much. I have tried to go out with other women ever since I left your house a few months ago, but whenever I look in any other woman's eyes, I see your sister; and whenever I do whatever is customary on dates, there is always that small detail that pops out to remind me of her. The differences between Mari-Tere and me aren't personal. We just don't think alike. We see the same things and face the same issues, but from different perspectives. That is what's keeping us apart. I've tried to reason with her, but you know how hard that is to do. I've tried to convince myself that she's right, but to agree with her is to throw overboard everything that I believe in. Even though I might be willing to meet her halfway, I don't think that she's ready to yield an inch. It's a difficult situation, but I promise you that I'll try one more time."

"That's all I'm asking of you. Maybe we can be happy together, again, the three of us. I'll see what I can do to prepare the ground for you before Saturday without alerting the fox that the game is afoot."

Raúl brought a broad smile to his face and stood up to embrace Carlos and wish him farewell. He asked Carlos if he would like to see the rest of the camp. Carlos politely refused, telling him of appointments that in reality he did not have.

Once outside the officer's club, Carlos went directly to his car. Before he could open the door, a Captain getting out of an old battered jeep said to him, "Comrade, from what household did you requisition that car?"

"From a son of a bitch in Miramar. I don't even remember his name. Do you like it?"

"It looks very nice. How does it ride?"

"Watch me and you'll see."

Carlos climbed into the driver's seat and before the officer could blink an eye he was out of sight, speeding like a bullet towards the exit gate.

CHAPTER THREE

María Teresa was surprised when Concha came to tell her that Raúl was on the phone and wanted to talk to her. She was elated when Raúl told her that he wanted to see her again. She immediately accepted and invited Raúl for dinner.

Raúl came for dinner to the Aguirrupe's house. Carlos had managed through Inés's connections to obtain the ingredients for the occasion, since some basic food items were becoming scarce throughout the few markets that still operated in the capital.

After dinner, Raúl, Carlos and María Teresa retired to the study, where Carlos offered some cordials to their guest and then excused himself, politely.

Raúl sat on the sofa next to María Teresa. She looked at him fondly and said, "How've you been? I tried to call you several times, but I was unable to reach you."

"I've been fine. Just working very hard. There are many things to be accomplished, and little time to do it. But I didn't come here tonight to talk about my work. I want to talk to you about us."

"I'm glad that you said that, because I don't want to discuss your work with you anymore. To be quite frank, I've missed you very much. I never want to see you away from me again. I still love you an awful lot."

"You make me very happy when you say that. I also love you immensely, and I confess that in all this time, I was never able to erase you from my mind."

María Teresa moved her hand subtly towards his until they finally touched. Raúl grabbed her hand and started to caress it.

"I'm sorry I threw the engagement ring at you. If you still have it, I'd like to have it back. I assure you that I'll wear it with pride. Tell me, would you marry me?"

"I still have the ring with me, and I'll give it to you gladly. I gave you that ring as a symbol of my love for you. Since that love stills burns in my heart, the ring is yours to keep, for I would never give it to anybody else."

María Teresa put her hand in her bra, and produced the ring that she had kept next to her heart all this time. She placed it, delicately, back on Raúl's finger.

"As far as marrying you is concerned, I'd consider myself extremely blessed to have the opportunity to become your wife. It's just the timing that might be inappropriate."

"The timing? What do you mean by that?"

"Well, when and where do you wish to marry me?"

"Obviously here, and as soon as possible."

"Try to understand. I'd like to marry you in a formal wedding ceremony, with all the members of my family around us, so that they can share our happiness. And I'd like my father to be the person who brings me to the altar and delivers me to you. At this moment, that's impossible. My father and one of my brothers are no longer here. I also know that your parents went to the United States when you no longer wanted to see them, and moved out of their house. As a matter of fact, you don't know this, but your father came to see me to apologize for your behavior and to say good-bye to me."

"Let's leave my parents out of this. They caused me the biggest embarrassment of my life. Could you conceive how I had to face my comrades-in-arms, knowing that they knew my parents had run away? It was disgraceful. Thank God that they never questioned my devotion to the Revolution."

"But Raúl, the fact remains that they're still your parents, and that they're the only family you have."

"No, you're mistaken. My real family is what I now have. But, let's not start quarreling again, not about my parents. Please, continue with your explanation of why we can't get married here and now."

"I told you about the kind of wedding I'd like to have, and since all those members of our families aren't here, I'd like to postpone it until we can be all together again."

"What you're saying is insane. Under those conditions we'd have to wait forever. In other words, we would never get married. Are you implying that you might be willing to live with me as husband and wife without getting married? If that's what you want, I'm all for it."

"How much you want me, and how little you know me! If it all boils down to the matter of having a relationship with you, I want you to know that there is no other man in the world that I would surrender my body to more gladly. I'd let you have your way with me right now, on this sofa, if all that mattered between you and me was to make love to each other. I don't know if you've thought for a moment that I might wish your body on mine more than you ever dreamed of possessing me. But there is a lot more to a marriage than a simple love affair. My upbringing, and the tradition in my family, plus the possibility of doing something that we'd both regret for the rest of our lives, force me to expel those notions from my mind, no matter how pleasant and erotic they might be. It's because of the magnificent way that I love you that I wish to build the kind of eternal relationship that our descendants and we can be proud of, and never have to look back in shame. Now, why can't we have the kind of wedding, and the kind of life afterwards, that we once wanted?"

"All right. If that's what you want, then let's plan a wedding in another two or three months and ask our families to come and join us."

"My God! That's really cute. You know that's impossible. They'd be thrown in jail the moment they set foot in this country."

"That's their problem, not ours."

"No, you're mistaken. That isn't their problem. It's ours."

"In that event, our wedding isn't possible. We'd never be able to meet your conditions."

"Oh yes. It's very feasible."

"I don't see it. I know that you can conjure in that pretty head of yours an answer to almost any given problem, but I really believe that you've overestimated your power of reasoning this time."

"No, I haven't. I concede the point that it's out of the question that they come here. But it's not inconceivable that we go to them."

"What? Are you asking me to betray my fatherland? Are you crazy?"

"No, Raúl, I'm merely asking you to be my husband for the rest of our lives on this planet. Our love should have no boundaries. Besides, what would be our future here? Me, the wife of a soldier whose moments of glory are to persecute, fight and apprehend his own brothers. You, the soldier who would never know when he might fall in disgrace with the leaders that plan to rule over his fatherland with an iron fist. Can't you see, my love? You and I have no real part in this venture. Sooner or later, we'd have no choice but to leave this nightmare behind us. It's better to do it now, when we still have youth and ideals, than after when we are consumed by a political process that could turn us into the cynical and hypocritical inhabitants of a tyrannical regime."

"Speak for yourself, Mari-Tere. You're completely unaware of what's going on and what's at stake in this Revolution. We're in the process of becoming a free and independent country, away from the imperialist domination of the Yankees. We're going to be the first free state of Latin America. And you want me to abandon that, just to follow you?"

"Am I not worthy of the sacrifice?"

"There you go again. You're always entrapping me with the way you talk. If I say yes, then I'm supposed to leave everything and go with you. If I say no, then that could be interpreted as not loving you enough. No matter what I answer, I lose."

"You wouldn't lose if you said that you agreed with me. If you say no, I would never doubt your love for me, only the amount. In other words, is it enough to prompt you to lead me into paradise?"

"I don't know what to say to you anymore. I don't wish to end this conversation with another argument, and yet, I don't know how to proceed. I don't want to leave you, I really love you, but you're demanding too much of my love."

"Let's think about it, and finish this another time. I comprehend that I'm asking you for a lot. Please, I also want you to understand that if I do it, it's only because I'm firmly convinced that it would be for the best for both of us."

"I know. I must be honest with you also, so let me tell you that it'd be difficult for me to change my mind and submit to your request. However, give me time to digest this paradox of yours and maybe I can find an answer that would satisfy you."

"I'll buy that. Just let me ask you one last question. If I were not here with you now, and you found out that I was out of the country—for instance, what if my father had forced me to go with him when he left—would you consider coming after me, or would you give me up forever?"

"You're full of tricky questions tonight. What the hell, it's only a hypothetical situation as you said. In that case, I'd come after you. Yes, that would be my answer. I couldn't conceive of living the rest of my life without you."

"Thank you, Raúl. You don't know how glad I am to hear that."

"And now, I must go. It's getting late, and I have some meetings to attend early in the morning. How about coming with me the week after next to Varadero Beach? We can spend a few days over there and have some fun together. I'd love to go out with you swimming and dancing again."

"That sounds like fun. Thank you for asking me. I'd really like to go, but you must realize that I'd have to bring Concha with me."

"By all means. I understand. Don't worry about it."

Raul's last words sounded meaningless. María Teresa escorted him to the front doors, where Raúl kissed her. Somehow, she did not find the same feeling in his kiss that she had once felt.

CHAPTER FOUR

On August 17, 1961 the Revolutionary Government took another step to ensure complete control over the population. This new measure would eradicate, in one single stroke, all the wealth that remained in the hands of the people. A new currency was issued. The new bills had a different color and format than the old ones. Everyone who had money in the banks, whether it was placed in a checking or savings account, had a short period of time to go and exchange it for the new currency. The catch was that no matter what the amount was in the account, the government would only release a maximum of ten thousand new pesos. The balance, whatever it was, no longer existed. There were no more accumulated fortunes on the island. From that moment on, the ruling political party not only controlled, but also possessed, all the wealth in the nation.

The news came as a shock to María Teresa and Carlos. There were no longer any funds to buy their way out as they had supposed. To complicate matters further, at their rate of expenditure, the amount of money left to them would not last too long, a year at the very best. Luckily, they had some cash money in the safe at the house. And that money was in American dollars. They would have to acquire almost everything through the black market, since ration cards were not enough to survive on, and any kind of work would be refused to them. They had become part of the worthless population, what the government called the dregs of the island. They also realized that when the money was gone, the only other possibility left to them would be to start selling or exchanging the works of art in the house. That could lead them into extremely dangerous situations. The state considered it a counterrevolutionary activity, punishable by several years of imprisonment. The two Aguirrupes decided to hold back as much as possible, and to try to survive for as long as possible, since the government was in control of all the means of production, as well as other institutions. It was the sole employer in Cuba, and subsequently it was utterly impractical to consider the possibility of finding any decent job within their reach.

It was a Wednesday morning when a Mercedes-Benz bearing the red and gold colors of the Spanish flag on either side, came to a full stop in the horseshoe-shaped driveway in front of the Aguirrupe's house. From the front seat of the car, a man emerged wearing a typical oxford gray diplomatic suit, and carrying a fine leather briefcase in his left hand. His right hand was holding a large bouquet of red roses. He was not too tall, but he was fit and had a very pleasant face. When one of the servants answered the doorbell, he said in an impeccable Castilian accent, "May I see Señorita María Teresa Aguirrupe? I came to give her these flowers. You may tell her that Juan Pablo Cortéz from the Spanish Embassy wishes to talk to her."

"Come in, Sir. One moment, please. Just wait here while I look for Señorita María Teresa."

The gentleman in his late thirties waited in the foyer as the maid rushed upstairs to look for María Teresa and deliver the flowers. She was getting dressed when the maid arrived. She took the flowers and read the card inside them.

I have to see you. I have news from your father.
Please, pretend we are old friends when you meet
me, and destroy this card.
Thank you,

Juan Pablo.

María Teresa told Magda to accompany her guest to the library, and ask him to wait for her. She would come down in a few minutes.

A short period of time later, María Teresa opened the doors to the library and said, "Juan Pablo, how nice of you to come to see me. I haven't seen you since the time we met in Florida. Thank you very much for the beautiful flowers. How have you been?"

Without waiting for his reply, she entered the room and closed the doors behind her. She then pointed to one of the chairs in front of her father's desk, and the Spaniard obediently sat on it. She sat on the other chair across from him and said, "Why all the mystery?"

"Señorita, one can't be too careful in these times. I don't know the degree of confidence that you have in your hired help. What I came to see you about is a matter to be kept from the knowledge of anyone that is not directly involved in it."

"Fine, I understand. You said that you have some news from my father."

"Yes, that's true. Now, one thing at a time, please. Let me first introduce myself. My full name is Juan Pablo Cortéz, Count of Querétaro. I'm First Consul attached to the Embassy of Spain in Cuba, and I answer only and directly to the Spanish Ambassador. Your brother Fernando was in Spain two weeks ago. His visit coincided with the Ambassador's scheduled report trip to the motherland. In any event, they met there, and, as a result of that meeting, he brought back a letter from your father to you. I have been instructed to give you that letter to read and then burn afterwards. I'll wait here for your response to the contents of the letter, and, depending upon your answer to it, I'll continue telling you the rest of my instructions."

He opened the briefcase with a key from his vest pocket, and gave a large, sealed, white envelope to María Teresa. She took it with trembling hands and stripped one flap of it with the sharp letter opener that was on top of the desk.

My dear Mari-Tere,

My good and wonderful daughter, I sincerely hope that this letter reaches your hands, and that as you read it, you and all my loved ones over there are at least enjoying good health.

Contemplating all the recent events that have occurred in Cuba, I can't forgive myself for the stupidity of leaving that island without you. Talking to Sister Beth, I've come to know how much I've made you suffer, just by not having you with me at this time. A father, and especially a man with my experience and knowledge, should have known better.

Would you, and could you ever cease to feel resentment for my action? That, we can further discuss when I feel again your loving embrace.

Sister Beth also told me that you want to join me as soon as feasible. She explained everything to me. And now, let me tell you about my plan.

I sent Fernando to Spain to meet the Spanish Ambassador to Cuba, whom I know very well. If this letter reaches your hands that means that he has agreed to help us. In that case, the bearer of this letter is a person of implicit confidence. If you decide to come through this route, and I advise you to take it for I believe it to be the safest, then, put yourself in his hands, and follow the Ambassador's instructions to the letter.

You would know better than me what to do with whatever you have to leave behind. In general,

I would like to offer you some advice to ease the sorrow of departing from that memorabilia.

Leave behind everything that you are not strictly carrying with you. You'll have to leave the house and make whoever is watching believe that you are leaving for a short period of time and everything is remaining just as it was.

Don't be sorry for the house, its contents, the cars, etc. They are only material things. The memories of the good times and the sad times that you have lived in that house are yours to keep forever. No government or ruling party can ever take those away from you. The rest is a pile of building materials that they can enjoy if they want to.

Now, let me tell you what to do about the people with you. I want Carlos to come with you. I don't know how many of these opportunities are going to emerge, so we have to take advantage of this one. Carlos must come with you. You just tell him that from me. Concha is the only one that won't have any problem. Since she is a Spanish citizen, the Ambassador has assured Fernando that he could manage to get her off the island later on, to Spain. From Spain, she can then decide whether to come here to live with us, or to go back to her village. In either case, I'll make sure that she doesn't have to work for the rest of her life.

And now, we come to the cases of Mirta, Magda and Esther. I think that it would be a harsh case of egoism to ask three good and loyal servants to come with us. They have their own families to worry about and we couldn't guarantee the successful departure of all of them. It's also very important that they never suspect that you're planning to leave. Nobody can be or should be trusted at this time with that kind of information. People sometimes with the best of intentions have denounced their own parents under the pain of torture. Remember that the best-kept secret is the one that isn't told. The best thing for you is to dismiss them as soon as possible. Use the excuse that you have no more money to pay them, and don't accept that they continue working for nothing. Get them out of the house. Tell them that you'll manage with Concha and Carlos. I know it's a tough decision, but it's one that has to be made. Give them as much as you can afford as a severance pay.

And now, my daughter, I'll wait for you patiently and eagerly. Till I have you again in my arms, and can kiss your angelical face, you receive my love, as always,

Your father,
Francisco

María Teresa took the marble base lighter that rested on top of the desk, and set the letter on fire. She then looked at the Spaniard and said, "Well, Count, I'm all yours. What's next?"

"I'm so glad that you decided to put yourself and other members of your family in our hands. Please, rest assured that we'll do everything possible to bring you again to the company of your family in the United States.

"Now, first things first. My name is Juan Pablo, never call me Count in front of people. I'm the Spanish diplomat that is courting you for your charms and beauty, even though you are engaged to a Commander in the Army. You are the Cuban that is enjoying my advances in a coquettish fashion, even if only to create the desired jealousy in her fiancé. Very simply, if Commander Mora has been seen with other women in the past months, you have decided to spur his male ego by doing the same with someone that he can't touch. That creates the scenario for my coming here today with the flowers and what is to come in the near future. If you allow me, I'd like you to know that from the moment that I saw your photograph, I have been looking forward to the fulfillment of this task. You, without question, are the most beautiful woman I've ever seen in my life."

"Thank you very much, Señor Cortéz. I mean, Juan Pablo. You are a very gallant man, like most Spaniards."

"No, it's the truth, but, please, let me proceed with my instructions. Take these two envelopes that I brought to you. One contains twenty-five thousand dollars and the other, pesos. Your father was concerned that with the new monetary laws, you might be lacking money. Use it as you see fit.

"Also, please notice as I open my briefcase that it is completely empty. The only things inside it are these two large, black velvet pouches. After today, I'm going to make at least two more trips to this house to see you. I will always carry the same briefcase and it will always be empty as I enter this house. Whatever you want to take safely off the island and cannot carry with you must fit in the confinements of my briefcase at any of those times including today. I would suggest that you start by worrying about all of your personal jewelry, as well as Carlos's. That's why I brought the velvet bags. Whatever you give me will be sent to Spain through the diplomatic mail-pouch. It will be given to your brother Fernando over there.

"The basic plan is well-conceived, and I think it'll work very well because it's simple. It consists of the following steps:

"By the three visits to this house and the three times that I'll come to take you out, we'll establish the smoke screen required to avoid suspicion of your coming to the Embassy Ball on October 12th, when we commemorate the anniversary of Columbus's discovery of America.

"On that occasion I will send the Embassy limousine to collect you and Carlos, and bring you both to the ball. After the party, the Ambassador from Venezuela will supposedly take you and Carlos back home under the pretext of my sudden indisposition to take you home. He'll make a routine stop at the Venezuelan Embassy. Once inside its grounds you'll be safe. Both of you will request political asylum. It'll be automatically granted. I don't know how much time you'll have to be at the Venezuelan Embassy. Maybe one month. Perhaps two at the most. Eventually, both of you will be escorted by the Ambassador to the airport and depart for Caracas. Your father will be there waiting for you when you arrive. He can negotiate visas through the American Embassy in Caracas, and from there you can depart to the United States.

"The day after the ball, I'll personally come for Concha. She'll be offered a job at the Spanish Embassy including room and board. Since she is a Spanish citizen by birth, there will be no problem in creating the position for her. When all the necessary paperwork can be cleared through the bureaucratic red tape, she will be put on an Iberian Airlines plane to Spain."

"The plan seems feasible enough, based on its simplicity. It's logical and presents very few risks. However, it has two big flaws."

"Really? Which ones?"

"Their names are Samson and Delilah."

"Who are they? I was never told of any other people."

"They aren't people. They are my two Chow-Chow dogs. You might consider them something that I can leave behind, but believe me, I can't. If they aren't included in your plans, then I must ask you to forget me also. I'll find my own way."

"That's preposterous! You can't be serious. You don't know the expense and preparation time that this plan has taken. The unofficial communications between the Ambassadors have been most difficult to say the least. Both men are risking a diplomatic career if this ever surfaces, and you are asking me to increase the odds against them by twofold because of two dogs?"

"I'm simply trying to make you understand that those two dogs are very dear to me, and that I won't leave them behind under any circumstances. I'm aware of the degree of personal sacrifices that many important people are making on my behalf at this time, but that won't change my response. If my dogs stay behind, so will I."

"I have heard of Basque stubbornness, and yet I have never seen it materialize in such a lovely girl. I'll see what I can do about them. In the meantime, would you agree to continue with the plan, provided that somehow I include your dogs in it?"

"Yes, I will do as you ask."

"Good. Let's start by calling each other by our first names. From now on I shall be Juan or Juan Pablo to you, and you'll be Mari-Tere to me. Now, please go and bring me back everything that you want me to take at this time. Remember, it has to fit in this briefcase. By the way, could you also bring me the two dogs? If I'm going to risk facing my boss's anger, I would like to meet the two marvels that are the cause of my impending distress."

"Sure, Juan Pablo. The bar is in that corner. There is not too much left, but you're welcome to take whatever you want. Make yourself a drink while you're waiting. I'll be right back."

Juan Pablo was finishing his second drink when María Teresa returned to the room. She was holding a heavy bag in her left hand. Two gorgeous, huge animals, resembling half-lions, half-bears, and proudly showing their blue-black tongues, came running behind her. They sat next to María Teresa, staring intensely at Juan Pablo. Muffled growling sounds came from their mouths sporadically. He looked back at them and began to talk to them in a very smooth and reassuring tone of voice. After a few minutes, he was able to come closer to them. He touched them, and some time afterwards he was back in his chair with the dogs jumping up and playing with him.

María Teresa was astonished. She had never seen the dogs behave that way with a total stranger.

"There is no magic in it, Mari-Tere. I happen to have one Chow of my own, and know how to deal with their aloof and difficult character. Besides, the moment they smelled my dog, they lost all fear of me. After looking at them, I can't blame you for your decision. I wouldn't have had the heart either."

She laughed and helped Juan Pablo to place her mother's jewelry and her father's medals and decorations in the briefcase. She told him that the following time she would give him hers and Carlos's. The last time he would only need to take important papers.

Once outside the house, she accompanied Juan Pablo to the driver's side door of the Mercedes-Benz, and noticed that they were being watched by the militia woman in charge of the Vigilance Committee of the block. Juan Pablo, in a courteous manner, was going to kiss María Teresa's hand, when she suddenly embraced him and deposited a loving kiss on his lips. The Spaniard quickly recovered from the gratifying surprise, and returned María Teresa's kiss with believable passion.

That same afternoon, the same militia woman that had stood across the street from the Aguirrupe's house, next to the parked Army jeep, came to the house to find out what was going on there. María Teresa had no problem in replying to any of the questions with explanations that fully convinced the woman of the possible romance that was springing up between this beautiful girl and the handsome foreigner. Before she left the house, she commented that she was satisfied with the explanation for the time being. She also threatened to return to ask more questions later if it became necessary. "Fatherland or Death. We shall overcome," she said before she disappeared from sight.

Juan Pablo came back three days later to inform María Teresa that the dogs' situation was completely straightened out. They would be admitted into the Spanish Embassy with Concha, when she moved in. Juan Pablo volunteered to take care of the dogs personally until they left with Concha for Spain. María Teresa could go pick them up in Spain afterwards. The entire separation would not be more than two or three months. María Teresa agreed, and all the wheels were set in motion.

The month of September was a busy month for her and

Carlos. The dismissal of the servants was a sad scene, since they had spent many years with the Aguirrupes, especially Mirta, the cook, who had been with them almost since María Teresa was born.

María Teresa started to go out with Juan Pablo. This situation brought the expected reaction of jealousy from Raúl. He accused María Teresa of flirting with the diplomat just to make him feel insecure of her love, and said he was going to retaliate by going out with other women. María Teresa responded that she was just being polite to someone that she had met on her last trip to Florida, and had promised to show him La Habana if he was ever assigned to Cuba.

Carlos employed much of his time trying to see Inés as often as he could. During one of their most idyllic encounters, and in a moment of intimacy, Carlos asked her if she would follow him to Florida, assuming that he managed to reach those shores safely, and arranged her trip from there. Her answer surprised and satisfied Carlos in a most pleasant way. She told him that by now she was sure that she would never love a man in her life in the manner that she loved him, and that she was ready and willing to follow him to the end of the world.

CHAPTER FIVE

October came and all the pieces were in place. On the twelfth of that month, the game began.

María Teresa said good-bye to Concha and the dogs when she left the house. She was wearing a long, black velvet skirt and a sleeveless blouse completely covered with off-white spangles and adorned with pearls all along its collar and waistline. The short blouse hung loosely on top of the skirt. A long, silver fox stole; long, black silk gloves; and plain, high-heeled, black suede shoes completed her outfit. Carlos wore the traditional long-tailed formal attire as he climbed into the rear seat of the Embassy limousine after his sister. Once inside the automobile, he took her hand and winked at her to give her confidence. They looked like a happy couple on a night out.

Juan Pablo greeted them at the front door of the Embassy and introduced them to their hosts. It was exactly eight o'clock in the evening. The typical celebration consisted of a formal dinner that lasted approximately two hours followed by endless hours of dancing and champagne.

Juan Pablo escorted María Teresa at all times. Carlos mingled with the crowd, mainly the young, beautiful girls in their gorgeous gowns.

By midnight the first guests started to make their way out of the party. Juan Pablo approached Carlos at the bar and said, "Carlos, has anyone shown you the rest of the Embassy?"

"No, I haven't had the pleasure of seeing it yet."

"Well, please come with me. I'd be delighted to show you around."

They left together and went to climb the stairs leading to the upper floors. When they reached the hallway on the first floor, Juan Pablo signaled him to enter his office. Inside of the small office Carlos found María Teresa sitting on one of the tall chairs in front of the oak, leather-topped desk.

"I'm sorry, I have bad news for both of you. The Ambassador from Venezuela never showed up tonight. An hour ago I tried to contact him over the telephone and found out that he is bedridden with an illness. However, he indicated that if you could make it inside of his Embassy somehow, he's willing to go along with the original plan. I'd volunteer to drive you over there myself, but if we were caught, Spain would have a lot of explaining to do. It's the kind of diplomatic embarrassment that we can't risk. Franco has forbidden the Ambassador to provoke Castro in any shape or form. After Castro expelled Lojendio, the former Ambassador, in 1960, the relationship between Cuba and Spain has been tense to say the least. If you want to, I can let you borrow my car and you can try it yourselves, or I could drive you home and postpone plans until the next celebration that will take place at Christmas. In that event, tell Concha that she will also have to wait until that time, because bringing her and the dogs to the Embassy tomorrow will give away our position. What do you say?"

Carlos and María Teresa discussed the possibilities for a short while and finally came to the conclusion that they should give it a try that night. Juan Pablo took the telephone on his desk in his hand, and ordered his car to be brought to the main doors. A few minutes laterr he said farewell to his guests and walked slowly back into the Embassy murmuring a prayer for the sake of his friends.

Carlos drove the Mercedes-Benz at a reasonable speed towards their destination. They were now a block away from the Embassy of Venezuela. It was fifteen minutes before one o'clock in the morning and the streets were empty. A smile of triumph started to form on his face.

When he crossed the intersection at the corner of the street, a potent beam of white light shone on the windshield, blinding him temporarily. Instinctively, he brought the car to a quick stop, while covering his eyes with his left forearm.

Soldiers emerged from everywhere surrounding them. He rolled his window down, and said, "What's happening? What's going on?"

The first soldier that approached the standing car ordered them to come out of the automobile. The way they were dressed, and the flags on the hood of the car stating that it was a diplomatic vehicle enjoying immunity, saved the situation.

"I'm sorry, but you can't continue on this street. Please, follow another route to your destination," said the soldier in command.

"We're going to pay our respects to the Venezuelan Ambassador who is sick. We've just come from the Spanish Embassy. You may call the Count of Querétaro if you want to confirm our story," said Carlos using his best imitation of the pure Castilian accent of the typical Spaniard.

"No need to bother anyone at this time. I realize that you people are diplomatic personnel, but this street is closed to all traffic. Only people who can identify themselves as Venezuelan citizens are allowed to use this street as of tonight. I'm sorry for the inconvenience, but those are my orders. You may reach the Venezuela Embassy by phone if you want."

"Thank you very much. We'll return to the Spanish Embassy."

Carlos and María Teresa climbed rapidly into the car again, and, after backing up to the intersection that they had just crossed, he made a right turn and sped the vehicle away from the scene.

They arrived at their house in Miramar shortly after one

o'clock in the morning. Concha was amazed to see them. They explained everything that had happened to them and decided to go to bed and wait until the next day in order to clear their thoughts and see what Juan Pablo might have in mind then.

The next day Juan Pablo came to pick up Concha, but instead he ended up retrieving his car. He guessed that something had gone afoul when the other Embassy vehicle in which he was riding pulled up alongside his own car in the driveway.

He reiterated his plan of repeating the attempt a two and a half months from that date. Reluctantly the Aguirrupes agreed to abide by his plans, since they could not conceive of any other alternative at that time.

Fifteen days later, Inés came through with another possibility of escaping the tyrannical government that was tormenting their lives.

Dr. Gustavo Albacete had just purchased a brand new fishing boat in the Yucatán. Two Chrysler engines that were able to propel it at speeds close to forty knots powered the vessel. The standard Cuban Coast Guard ships were unable to match that speed on the open sea. The boat was being docked at the Biltmore Yacht Club pier, and Gustavo was eager to take the Castro brothers, Fidel and Raúl, in it on a fishing trip. He expected Fidel to be impressed with his new acquisition.

Inés suggested to Carlos that they steal Gustavo's boat, and try to make the trip to Key West in it. It was large enough to accommodate eight people comfortably. There were only two small problems to take care of. One was the amount of fuel that they would need for the trip, and the second was the two soldiers that were always guarding the vessel.

Carlos thought it over, and came to the conclusion that this was their best bet. With his experience in handling boats, they should not encounter any navigational problems. Besides, the vessel was loaded with all kinds of modern equipment and instrumentation. It was also roomy enough to take his sister, Concha and the two dogs. That way, they could all leave at the same time and reach their freedom together. There would be no waiting time for anyone to join them later.

It was during dinner on November 2nd that he explained the next attempt to seek freedom to María Teresa and Concha. There was silence at the table for a few minutes, and then María Teresa said, "When are we leaving?"

"The day after tomorrow."

Concha did not utter a single word. She simply nodded her head.

CHAPTER SIX

Carlos woke up very early the day before the departure. He took the Lincoln out of the garage after having a small cup of freshly brewed Cuban coffee. With a cigarette in his mouth and a million well-organized thoughts in his head, he went to prepare himself for the task that he knew had to be accomplished before the morning of the following day. His first stop was at a small gasoline station, next to the Almendares River. He knew the owner quite well. He asked the attendant to give him the customary ten gallons of gasoline, and to check everything under the hood. He got out of the car and went into the small office to say hello to his old friend.

"Hi, Sergio, how are things with you?"

"Carlos, what a surprise! What the hell are you doing here so early in the morning? Are you going to tell me that you are after the purse of gold that people are supposed to find by waking up early?"

"No," replied Carlos laughing and he continued, "I've always maintained that in order for someone to find that purse, there'd have to be an asshole who woke up even earlier and lost it."

Sergio laughed also, and Carlos said, "Seriously now, I came here at this time because I figured that your station would be almost deserted. I need a favor. I want to buy eighty gallons of gasoline in five gallon cans, and I want you to put those sixteen cans in that limousine."

"You must be out of your fucking mind. You know damn well that I can't sell you any more than what the ration card stipulates. And now you want me to give you eighty gallons of fucking gasoline? Tell me, how many drinks did you have last night?"

"I'm willing to pay well for them, Sergio. I wouldn't be here if it weren't extremely important to me."

"You're a goddamned crazy man. Do you realize what will happen to me if I'm caught?"

"Would five thousand cover the risk?"

"Five thousand pesos? What the hell would I do with another five thousand pesos? I already have ten thousand of those since last August, and there is nothing I can buy with them legally."

"I said five thousand, but not pesos. American dollars. And there is a shit load of things that you can acquire with that money, here and abroad."

"Where the hell do you have five thousand American dollars?"

"Right here in my pocket. The money is listening to our conversation."

Carlos took an envelope from one of the back pockets of his trousers and paraded its contents in front of Sergio's eyes. His friend's face had an expression of great amazement.

"You'd better close your mouth now, Sergio, or you will swallow quite a few flies before the day is over."

"Bring the car inside one of the working bays. I'll give you what you want."

"No questions asked?"

"I don't want to know anything."

From the garage, Carlos went to the Kasalta Market and obtained several cans of different types of food utilizing a similar form of payment. He now had enough food for the trip. The needed water could be taken later on from his house.

He then drove to downtown La Habana where he stopped at a store to buy balloons for a fictitious children's party. Finally, he procured some nylon rope and black paint from a local hardware store.

He went to have lunch at one of the few restaurants that remained open. The variety of dishes offered had diminished considerably from what it had been in the past. The prices were also astronomical. Carlos didn't care. He was going to eat whatever was available and at whatever cost. At the end of the meal, he did what he had wanted to do for quite some time now. He gave a two hundred pesos tip to the waiter, who looked at him completely flabbergasted. Carlos's only comment was, "Not much food, but the service was exquisite."

The rest of the afternoon, he spent at a whorehouse, whose owner he knew very well in more ways than one. He retained the services of two of the youngest and cutest prostitutes for that evening. The agreed upon cost was a thousand pesos each.

It had been a long day for Carlos, who came back to his home in the late afternoon hours to take a short nap and prepare himself for the biggest task of the day.

At seven that same evening, María Teresa woke him up as promised. She helped him to inflate all the balloons with the small air compressor that they had in the garage. When they were all inflated they proceeded to paint them black and attached them to the cans of gasoline and water that were stacked in the limousine. All dressed in black Carlos left the house around nine to pick up the girls he had hired earlier. María Teresa and Concha stayed behind praying for his safe return.

He arrived about an hour later at the Biltmore Yacht Club. The two young girls, very neatly dressed, were dropped near the entrance with fake passes to gain access to the inside of the Club. It was really easier than expected, because the guard at the door looked more at them than at the cards they presented. Then, they made their way, nonchalantly, to the pier where two more guards were on duty keeping an eye on the boats. These were docked in a wide horseshoe-shaped, man-made harbor, with a narrow inlet. Their duty was to pass for two high society girls seeking to have some fun with rugged men. They surpassed their expectations when they convinced the soldiers to escort them to one of the empty boats standing alongside the long pier. Once inside the boat, they undressed and showed them a good time for the next three hours.

Carlos parked the car near the fence surrounding the pier, at the closest point to the water. Dr. Albacete's boat distinguished itself from its peers clearly. It was docked almost at the center of the harbor. "It's really a beauty!" murmured Carlos looking at it through his field glasses.

He opened the trunk of the Lincoln and quickly changed into the black wet suit that he had brought.

The links of the metal fence snapped easily under the pressure of the bolt cutter. He created an opening large enough for him, the cans and the plastic bags that he would have to carry into the water. Silently, he swam under water with his precious cargo until he reached his objective.

The first time that he surfaced, near the rear end of the boat, he stopped for a second to identify it. He had been told that the name of the boat was "Mi Barca".

Sure enough, across the stern of the vessel he could clearly read the words:

MI BARCA
LA HABANA
CUBA
TERRITORIO LIBRE DE AMERICA

"What an asshole," was the first thing that popped into Carlos's mind.

He climbed onto the vessel and started to fill the auxiliary tanks with the fuel. Next, he stashed away all the food and hid the large amount of water that he had brought for the escape. All of the empty cans and containers were filled with ocean water and sunk deep into the harbor.

It took him twenty trips to complete his task, and he was exhausted by the time he'd finished. He lowered the panel of fence links back into its original position and concealed his access to the area as best he could. Lastly, he changed his clothes and started the engine of the car. Without turning on the lights, he drove very slowly towards the highway. Once on it, he pulled the light switch on, and let the big automobile take him back to safer surroundings.

By two in the morning, he was back in his own bed, trying to catch some sleep before the big day that was ahead. Somehow, he could not force himself to do it. His body was resting, but his mind was still traveling at a great speed.

Inés showed up the following morning carrying a large handbag. Once inside the house, she asked María Teresa to let her go to one of the rooms in order to change into the beach outfit that she had brought with her. She emerged from the room wearing a bikini that revealed most of her sensational body. It left very little to the imagination.

Concha made the sign of the cross when she saw her for the first time. Then she said, "Is that all you're going to wear?"

"Concha, I also have a long beach robe to wear on top of this."

"Thank God and all the angels."

Inés laughed and reassured her that the bikini was very fashionable. Moreover, she wanted the men on the pier to pay more attention to her than the people and the animals they were bringing onto the boat. "It's the best and only way that I can think of to distract them," she said at the end.

María Teresa agreed, and, in spite of Concha's protests, wore another provocative bikini that Inés had brought for her.

"I suggest," said Carlos, "that we leave the house laughing and making jokes as we climb into the Lincoln. I want the Block Vigilance Committee to believe that we're going out to have some fun at the beach and nothing else."

They all acted their roles out as planned. When they were all inside the car, including the two Chows, Carlos rolled his window down and shouted to the man standing across the street, "Would you be a good Comrade, and keep an eye on the house? We are going out for a day at the beach, and the house will remain unoccupied for the rest of the day. Thank you very much."

The man never answered. He just looked at them with a scornful smile on his otherwise gloomy expression.

Carlos parked the car right in front of the main entrance to the Club. A parking attendant came out and Carlos said to him in a loud voice, "Please, take good care of the automobile. I'm going to need it back in a couple of hours."

He then slipped a five pesos bill to the young man who was in the process of opening the rear door of the limousine. The guard at the door recognized Inés immediately and said, "Are these your guests, Señora Pidal?"

"Yes, they are. Can you give them a day pass for the Club's facilities?"

"Sure, I'll be happy to do so for your friends, but I'm sorry to say that dogs are not allowed in the Club."

Inés noticed a sudden change of expression on María Teresa's face. She hoped that it would not alert the guard to their real intentions.

"Listen, we aren't going to bring the dogs to any of the rooms, or to swim at the private beach. We're just going to enjoy a short ride in Dr. Albacete's new boat, and I thought that the fresh ocean air would do as well for their lungs as ours. The fact of the matter is that my friend, Mari-Tere, treats them like her own children. For her, they aren't animals, but two small tots."

"I realize what you're saying. The dogs are very nice-looking, and very well-groomed. Understand that I personally have nothing against them, but rules are rules, and I can get into trouble for disobeying them."

"May I say something?" Carlos interjected.

"Go ahead, Sir," the guard replied.

"Since it'd really be an inconvenience for us to go back, drop the dogs off at home, and then return here, how about if you let these good people in through this door and I take the dogs in through the service entrance. Then I could walk them through the grounds and to the pier without molesting any of the other guests or passing through any of the other rooms in the main building."

"Whoever sees the animals inside could come back and blame me for it."

"Not if you say that you don't know how they got inside. Now, if anyone asks me, I can always say that I did it without your consent, and take full responsibility for the action."

"It's possible that you might get away with what you suggest, and believe me, I would do anything to please Señora Pidal. She's a good friend of Dr. Albacete, who at times goes out fishing with Fidel. And yet, the situation could create problems that I don't need."

Carlos came closer to the guard and extracted a bunch of bills from his right side trouser pocket. Unconcerned of surroundings, Carlos placed them inside the guard's breast pocket in a nonchalant manner. He did not know how much money he was giving him. It did not matter.

"Are you trying to bribe me, Sir?" said the guard in a muffled tone of voice.

"No, I would never try to do that. Bribe is a dirty word that I would never dare use with a man of your caliber and understanding. I'm only doing my duty as a friend who wants to help you and your family to obtain some of the necessities of life. Do we understand each other, my friend?"

"Okay, I'll write the one-day passes."

When he gave Carlos the small stamped cards, he added, "There is another guard at the service entrance. I don't know what you plan to do about him and I don't want to know either."

"Thank you very much. Just leave him to me."

Carlos took the two leashes, and guided the dogs to the other side of the building. He never stopped at the service entrance. He eventually reached the section of the fence that he had used the night before to gain access to the harbor. After looking around to make sure no one was watching, he kicked the links to the opening, and quickly went under the fence, pulling Samson and Delilah behind him. Shortly afterwards he approached the pier where Concha, Inés and María Teresa were waiting for him.

The guards looked astonished at the two dogs. Before anybody could say anything, Carlos said, "Hey, is that boat ready? I promised Dr. Albacete that I would take his dogs and friends for a short spin today."

One of the guards told a standing sailor to bring Dr. Albacete's boat immediately for his guests.

Carlos gave the dogs' leashes to María Teresa and jumped into the small boat right after the sailor, offering to give him a hand with the anchor and maneuvering the large vessel. They took the boat to the opposite side of the pier in order to put some gasoline into the supposedly empty tanks. The sailor told Carlos that he could only give him 20 gallons, which should be enough for the short time that they were planning to use it. Carlos consented knowing that the offered amount would fill the tanks to the brim.

Back at the main pier, Carlos docked the boat and helped everybody and the dogs climb onto the boat. He then instructed the guards and the sailor to loosen the ropes and throw them inboard as he intended to pull the boat out of the pier. The two guards looked at him with perplexity, and one of them said, "You don't seem to understand. The sailor can throw us the ropes. We're going with you on this trip."

"What?" said Inés. "This is a private party for me and my friends. I'm sorry but you aren't invited. You've never come when I went out with Gustavo before."

"That's true, Señora, but Dr. Albacete is a special case. Our orders are not to let any boat out on any trip, unless there are at least two guards on board. If you want to go out with your friends, we must go too. I promise that we won't bother you or any of your friends in any way."

Carlos, who was standing in the cabin in front of the controls, called Inés to his side. When she arrived, he whispered to her, "Don't argue. Let it be. I think that it's time for you and María Teresa to take the robes off. Reverse the instructions and tell the guards to loosen the ropes at the boat, and toss them to the sailor standing at the pier. The moment that I start the boat, come to me as fast as you can and grab the wheel. Don't slow down, just point toward that narrow opening, and pray that nothing is coming our way when you cross it. Now, do as I told you."

Inés did exactly what Carlos wanted. She winked an eye at María Teresa who slowly took off her robe and deposited it on top of the side cushions. The two guards were trying to clear the knots in the ropes while watching the two magnificent bodies in front of them. The young sailor on top of the pier also lost all concentration on what he was doing or what he was supposed to do.

Carlos took only a second to respond. The manual throttle was pushed forward in a single swift motion. The two powerful twin engines responded instantaneously, and pushed the vessel forward with a fantastic acceleration. The soldier at the aft did not have time to let go of the rope. The severe pull sprung his body from the ship, and threw him into the water.

The second soldier at starboard lost his balance and fell, rolling towards the rear of the boat. Carlos came rushing to his side. The soldier exclaimed, "Are you crazy man? My buddy fell overboard. What the hell are you trying to do?"

"I'm sorry, but I'm inexperienced with this boat. Here, let me help you stand up."

"Inexperienced my ass. You're a fucking maniac."

Carlos helped the soldier up and then hit him with all his might in the stomach. The soldier went forward gasping for air. The second blow was an uppercut to the chin. This one, in conjunction with a severe push, forced his body out of the boat.

"Yes, I'm just a fucking maniac," yelled Carlos.

He then turned around and almost crawled back to the cabin, where Inés's hands were frozen on the steering wheel. She was at the point of panicking when Carlos placed his hands on the other points of the wheel, and helped her guide the speeding cruiser through the inlet and into the open ocean.

They were in high spirits. Concha felt a little seasick, but decided not to say anything. She just took her rosary out and started praying in silence.

María Teresa took the two Chows into the sleeping birth as soon as they started to behave restless. Inés was in the main cabin, next to Carlos.

The sea started to get rough and Carlos decided to slow down a bit. He told Inés to take over the controls for a while, and took a moment to study the chart, the prevailing winds and the gulf currents in order to set the proper course. After a few minutes he made some corrections in the direction of the boat, and told Inés that if they could hold it properly, they should be in the proximity of Key West by that evening.

María Teresa took the binoculars and started to look around them. Nothing was in sight except the huge body of water. She was beginning to feel relieved and happy. Another half an hour went by and, all of a sudden, María Teresa spotted another vessel at a distance, running a parallel course with their boat. Some time later, she realized that the other ship was turning towards them in a collision course. She alerted Carlos, who told her to keep watching it, and to let him know the moment she could identify it.

Several minutes later, she yelled to Carlos that it was a Cuban gunboat. The sound of two cannons being fired reached their ears almost at the same time as two large splashes of ocean water occurred at starboard. They were too far from them to do any damage to the speeding cruiser. Carlos surmised that they were firing warning shots to make them slow down. He asked the women to go below and to remain calm, while he went ahead to test the real seamanship of his enemies.

He moved the boat a few degrees off course, away from the path of the gunboat, and again pushed the throttle all the way forward. Once more the engines responded with an incredible forward thrust. He was getting away from the gunboat at an increasing rate of velocity. When the boat reached its maximum speed, he yelled, "How do you like this lesson in seafaring, you bastards?"

One Russian Mig-17 jet fighter was dispatched to the area. The Cuban pilot was on his first solo mission and felt like a Buddhist monk in Nirvana. It took him approximately one hour to reach the patrol boat, and another several minutes to sight the stolen vessel. By this time, they were in international waters. That detail never worried or entered the pilot's mind.

Carlos noticed him as he put down the nose of the plane and went straight towards the cruiser.

Concha also saw the incoming jet fighter. She yelled at the top of her lungs to Carlos about the impending danger, and suddenly became hysterical. María Teresa grabbed her by the arms and pushed her inside the cabin where the dogs were barking in frantic excitement.

Carlos told the two women on the cabin with him to brace themselves. He knew he did not have any other alternative but to try to evade the firepower of the plane by moving in an erratic zigzag pattern, although that plan would slow him down somewhat, and give the patrol boat an opportunity to close the gap between them. He decided to do it anyway. He would worry about the other vessel when the time came.

The first burst of firepower came from the machine guns of the plane and started behind the boat. He quickly turned the wheel left and avoided the line of bullets.

For a short while, it was a cat and mouse game between the Mig-17 and the speeding boat below it. Carlos was only winning time. The Cuban pilot fired two of the wing rockets. They missed the target completely and struck the water in front of the boat.

The plane banked on one wing, while firing its machine guns.

Carlos turned the boat once more, trying to avoid the plane's blazing guns. The pilot turned the plane around again and again, until he managed to head in the same direction as the boat. Several bullets impacted across the side of the vessel, from the stern to the bow, ripping and splintering pieces of wood, damaging one of the engines and killing Concha and the two dogs.

María Teresa opened the wrecked door to the sleeping quarters below, and rushed in only to find her loved ones lying in a pool of blood. The rosary was still wrapped in Concha's hands. The two dogs had a terrified look in their eyes. She knelt down and emitted a loud howling sound. Then she brought her head down to touch her thighs and started crying.

Inés had an incredulous look on her face. Carlos yelled at her not to panic. He needed help, and Inés was the only one that could give it to him. He ordered her to check the damage on the engine, and to use one of the fire extinguishers to put out the fire. She replied sobbing that she could not do it. She did not know how.

Carlos left her at the controls once more and went to inspect the boat. He could see that the engine was beyond repair. He had to hope that the other one would be sufficient to get away.

The plane circled the injured vessel several more times. However, the pilot never fired another round. As the gunboat moved closer, the plane backed away and flew in the direction of the island.

Now the Cuban gunboat was gaining ground, and there was nothing that Carlos could do to avoid it. One engine wasn't enough to move the weight of the large cruiser at the required speed. The big bullets from the cannons of the patrol boat were getting closer and closer.

Carlos called María Teresa and Inés, and told them the truth. It was no use to try to evade persecution any longer. The best thing was to surrender, and hope that they would not be killed right then and there. "As long as we are alive we can keep hoping," he told them, even though he knew he did not sound too convincing.

He stopped the engine, and waived a white cushion as a sign of submission. The two young women put the beach robes on, and waited for whatever destiny would now bring into their lives.

A party of four men with rifles and an officer, pistol in hand, jumped onto their boat. The three would-be prisoners raised their hands all at once.

The officer used the butt of his pistol to hit Carlos hard in the kidney. He jerked his body forward under the impact and the pain, but never emitted a single sound. He was told to stay down on the floor. Then one of the soldiers came behind him and knelt on his back. He placed a handcuff on one wrist and swung the arm violently behind his back. He held it there until he placed and locked the other handcuff on his other wrist.

The two girls were also handcuffed. They were not beaten, but instead they were grabbed hard by their hair and pushed forward until they were lying down on their stomachs. Then the officer said, "Who else is on this boat?"

Carlos answered, "A friend by the name of Concha Arostegui. She isn't even a Cuban. She's a Spaniard. And two lovely dogs. They are all dead. By the way, can you tell us where you're taking us?"

"Soldier, search the boat and find out if he's telling the truth," the officer commanded the recruit closest to the controls. Then to another one of his men, he said, "You, go and tie the tow line." Addressing the rest, he continued, "You will remain here, keeping an eye on these miserable sons of bitches until we reach the shore again. If they move or say anything, shoot them. Use one bullet to the back of the head. That's enough for these worms." And then addressing Carlos he finally said, "To answer your question before I leave you, you will be taken to the G-2."

After supervising the towing arrangements, the officer went back to the gunboat and they started the slow trip back to their native land.

Carlos turned his head sideways. He saw María Teresa's face. He tried to smile and give her some sign of encouragement, but she had her eyes closed.

CHAPTER SEVEN

Accompletely enclosed army truck came to the large mansion that now housed the G-2 Branch of the Revolutionary Security Forces. It was located in the Miramar section of La Habana. It was the first stop for anyone being arrested under the suspicion of counterrevolutionary activities or for any other political reason, and consequently, it was the infamous interrogation center where any method was used to extract confessions from the poor souls who wandered into its dungeons.

The rear steel door of the truck was opened from the outside to let Inés, María Teresa and Carlos out. Since the inside of the truck was in complete darkness, the prisoners had to wait a few seconds to accommodate their eyes to the sudden intensity of the Cuban sunlight.

A big mulatto sergeant was shouting at them from outside the truck. Once they came out, he pushed them, one by one, into the building.

They were momentarily separated from each other. Inés and María Teresa ended up in one room together. Carlos was ordered to go into another room. The handcuffs were finally removed from all of them. They were told to strip and then they were searched throughout. Inés tried to resist, and she was roughed up just enough to subdue her. María Teresa had experience with the procedure, and went through it without complaining. At least this time she did not have to put up with a sadistic lesbian.

After the search, they gave the women yellow dresses with short sleeves and buttons along the front. From then on that would be their uniform. In the normal prison, it would clearly distinguish them from the common prisoners. Carlos received a pair of baggy gray trousers with a big black letter "P" on each leg. Again, the color and the letter would later on identify him as separate from the common prisoner, who wore a blue uniform and received better treatment within the Cuban penal system.

Then, they all met again when they sat them on a bench against one of the walls of the next room in the processing line. The big mulatto sergeant was sitting in the only comfortable chair in the whole place, in front of an old wooden table with a typewriter on it. Another old wooden chair was placed beside it. The room had two doors, one through which they had come in, and another leading to another area of the building. There was another soldier in the room with them.

"Prisoners," the sergeant said, "when I call you, I want you to come here and give me all your particulars for the register file. At the end of the questions I will assign you a number. From now on, nobody else in here will address you by name, just by your number. So learn it well, because it will be your only way of communicating with us, which is the only outside world that you will know. While this is taking place, you're to remain silent. I don't want to hear a word from any of you or to see any gesture or sign given to one another. Believe me, you don't want to see me angry. Now, let me start with the blond bitch." Pointing a finger at Inés, he said, "You, come here."

Inés stood up and walked the eight feet to the chair at the side of the table. He started to ask her all the pertinent and routine questions, such as name, address, telephone number, date and place of birth, religion, occupation, parents' names and addresses and relatives' information. While she was talking, he was typing her answers on the beat-up typewriter. When asked why they had been trying to leave the island, Inés answered that they had only been going out for a short boat ride. In the end, the mulatto depressed a white button hidden under the desk. It rang outside the room and gave the signal for two more guards to show up. One took Inés's fingerprints and photograph for the records. The other took her out of the room and escorted her to her cell. Her assigned number was G-3516.

It was María Teresa's turn next. While she was talking to the sergeant, the door that had been used by everybody so far opened, and two soldiers came in dragging a man in a blood-stained army uniform. His face was full of red and blue blotchy patches, an indication of the severe beating he had received. A ghastly wound on the top of his head was spouting blood all over. The soldiers opened the other door in the room, and, raising the wretched man to his feet, pushed him inside. From the noise Carlos concluded that there must have been a staircase leading to some sort of basement behind that door. The wounded man apparently hit every single step as he tumbled his way to the bottom with the two guards walking down behind him. It had only been a glimpse, but that was all that Carlos had needed to recognize the face of that man. He was the same soldier that he had met at the entrance of the Biltmore Yacht Club.

Carlos surmised that the whole scene was supposed to have happened when that particular room was empty, or maybe it had been purposely staged for when they knew that Carlos and María Teresa would be in that room. In any event, the big mulatto stood up, and placing his fingers on the table said, "Has anyone seen anything unusual?" while looking at María Teresa, who was sitting in the chair next to him.

She said, "No, I haven't."

Then, looking in Carlos's direction, he said, "How about you?"

Carlos thought for a second of having a word play with the

ignorant ape. But with his sister in the room, he did not want to risk a scene, so he merely answered negatively. María Teresa's assigned number was G-3517, the year and date of birth of Raúl.

The sergeant called Carlos over, and now that he was alone in the room with the soldiers, he was ready to have a party with them. It was his first opportunity to talk, and his opening words were,"You didn't have to shout for me. I'm the only one here. Who else would you want to interrogate?"

"Sit down, and just answer my questions."

"As clearly as I can. But please, if I'm too fast for your fingers, just ask me again. I don't mind repeating myself. You see, I don't mind repeating myself."

"Name?"

"Carlos Mariano de la Caridad Aguirrupe y Larrazábal."

The sergeant hesitated for a couple of seconds and then he typed, Carlos Aguirrupe.

"No, no, I saw you type Carlos Aguirrupe. My full name is Carlos Mariano de la Caridad Aguirrupe y Larrazábal."

"But there's no more room on the form."

"Well, that's your problem, not mine. I'm willing to wait until the new form is developed, and we can do this all over again. But that's as far as I go. I insist that you take down my full name, since I don't wish to be confused with anybody else."

"You won't be mistaken with anybody else. You'll have a unique number assigned to you."

"A number is a number is a number. Mathematically and numerically I'll be identifiable. But ah! Grammatically speaking only God knows how many Carlos Aguirrupes exist. My ancestors were quite the ladies' men. Do you wish me to tell you the history of my family?"

"No, just answer the questions."

"Please, don't get uptight, my good man. I only want to be of help at this inquiry."

"At this what?"

"Inquiry. A formal investigation into an incident. A process leading to the seeking of information, knowledge and the truth. And, what is most important, what is the truth? The Bible says that the truth shall set us free. Does that mean that if I tell you the truth I will go free?"

"Shut up and just answer the questions."

"Now, I'm confused. Do you want me to keep silent, or do you want me to answer you? Please, could you make up your mind?"

The big mulatto was completely baffled. He banged the table with his fist and warned Carlos to respond briefly to his questions.

Carlos decided to lay off for a while. His next opportunity came when he was asked why was he trying to flee from the island.

"I haven't done any such thing," he replied in the expected brief fashion.

A big smile showed on the sergeant's face. Carlos smiled back at him.

"In view of all the evidence presented in this case, you are going to tell me that you haven't done anything wrong?"

"That's precisely what I'm telling you."

"What were you doing in that boat?"

"I was just taking a friend and some of my relatives for a ride."

"Why did you throw the two soldiers to the water? One of them drowned. You will be accused of murder, as well as of trying to escape from us."

"I didn't throw anyone off the boat. They were just clumsy and fell overboard. If one of them couldn't swim, that isn't my fault. I've never claimed to be a swimming instructor. It's true that I didn't stop to pick them up, but they were never invited in the first place. You see, I was planning to have some fun with the blonde later on in the lower sleeping berth," said Carlos, while winking an eye at the sergeant.

"And your family?"

"Well, I could count on my family's discretion. I wasn't certain about the two soldiers."

"And for that, you sped through the harbor like a maniac."

"I was just trying to show off. You know how it is with women. They usually go for the daring type. You'd have done the same thing, wouldn't you?"

"Don't ask me stupid questions. Why didn't you stop when the patrol boat asked you to?"

"Now, you're the one asking the stupid questions. How the hell did I know that he wanted me to stop? I was being fired upon. Naturally, I tried to get as far away from the cannons as I could. I'm sure that you would've done the same under the circumstances."

"Are you saying that I am stupid?"

"No, God forbid, I'd never say that. You said it, not I."

"I think that you're trying to be cute with me, and I don't like it. You'd better behave and cooperate with us, or you will learn to regret it in the most painful ways."

"I'm sorry if I've troubled you. Believe me, I'd never dare to arouse the anger of any member of the security forces. May I ask you a couple of questions?"

"You're the one being questioned here, not I."

"Yes, I'm the one being thrown in jail and accused of a crime that neither my friend, nor my sister, nor I committed. You aren't."

The sergeant looked at Carlos with disdain. He quickly wrote a few notes on the bottom of the form, and assigned Carlos the number G-7007.

"I'll remember that," Carlos said, as the other soldier fingerprinted him and took his photograph. He then left the room and walked silently to his new fate.

CHAPTER EIGHT

María Teresa and Inés were thrown into the same cell. It was a small, empty space, approximately five feet wide by eight feet long. There was another woman with them, an older one who claimed to have been there for over a week. The solid metal door did not allow too much air to get into the cramped compartment. There were no windows either. A potent light bulb kept the room well lit.

María Teresa sat in one of the corners. Inés came to her side, and was going to start talking to her when María Teresa told her to leave her alone for a while. She wanted to be by herself at that moment. She was also leery of the other inmate in the cell.

Sitting down, with her legs bent up, her feet resting on the floor and her head resting on her knees, she closed her eyes and started crying. It was the first time that she had thought of Concha and her two dogs. Her mind wandered to her father and Fernando. Then, she thought of Carlos, and a guilty feeling took possession of her. She wondered if she was responsible for her brother's predicament, and if it would have been different if she had agreed to leave Cuba when her father had left. She wondered whether she could safely use Raúl's name to receive better treatment, or perhaps even freedom; or if she would incriminate him instead. There were a lot of questions being posed by her mind, and she could not find an adequate answer to any of them.

The older prisoner went to console her, but Inés grabbed her by the arm and told her to leave her alone. She then explained in a low voice that she had lost three dear friends that same day.

Two weeks of intensive interrogation went by. A lieutenant with a pale round face and a small moustache was assigned to question them and find out the truth behind the two women's actions.

The procedures became routine except for the timing. Their numbers were always called from the other side of the metal door. The guard who shouted the number also escorted her prisoner to a small room that contained a table and two chairs, dimly lit by a hanging light bulb. The interrogator was already in the room and signaled the prisoner to occupy the empty chair across from him. The same questions were asked over and over again. The times that the interrogations took place, however, were completely erratic. Sometimes one of the women was called back only two hours after she had been sent back to the cell; sometimes a full day went by. They were called during the day and during the night. The pattern was never the same. They were never allowed to see the outside world, and with the constantly lit cell, it was very difficult for them to measure the time. Food was scarce and also brought to them at irregular hours. After the first two weeks of that kind of treatment, they were completely disoriented.

One day María Teresa was going back to her cell, when the guard opened another door. She protested by saying that she knew that it was not her customary cell. The woman guard pulled her hair backwards and then gave her a terrible kick on her behind. Her body slammed against the back wall of the small cell. The door was closed behind her. She was alone. A few minutes later, without notice, the light went off. She lay on the floor and tried to sleep. Her body could rest on the cool floor, but her mind could not disassociate itself enough from reality to allow her to seek the sustenance of her dreams. She decided to pray. Sometime after, she didn't know how long, her eyes closed, and she slept.

Inés started to become concerned over María Teresa's absence. After a while, she was really worried. The older prisoner in the cell with her noticed the extent of Inés's distress and sat next to her in a consoling manner.

"Come on, my sweet girl, don't worry about your friend. They probably placed her in another cell by mistake. You'll find out tomorrow. You'll see."

"Tomorrow? How would I know when tomorrow is?"

"It's just a saying. I'm sure that you'll see your friend again, and everything will be all right. You are tense and tired. Let me help you relax."

"What do you mean?"

"I mean to lend you a shoulder to cry on. Let all your worries and thoughts out of that pretty head of yours. I understand what happens after weeks of interrogation, when one tries to hide the truth from these bastards. Tell me about it. I must've been here for about a month now, and they are still questioning me regularly. I don't know why, because I've told them all I know. Here, rest your head on my lap, and relax."

The words of the older woman were so reassuring that, without thinking, Inés did as she had been asked to do. The older prisoner then started to caress Inés's head and to brush her hair with her fingers. Two weeks without showering and sweating in that hot cell had made a mess of the beautiful blond hair that adorned Inés's head. The motion of the old woman's fingers through her hair felt like a relaxing massage given in an expensive beauty parlor. Inés began to feel loose and detached from reality.

"Tell me," said the old woman with a velvety voice, "why are you here?"

"I was trying to leave the island on a boat."

"Well, that's not such a big crime. These people make a big

issue of insignificant things like that. But you'll see that at the trial you'll get not more than maybe a couple of years."

"I think that even two years will be too much to bear."

"Well, maybe, if you know someone important who might be willing to vouch for you, you might get much less. Perhaps they'll even let you go free. Who knows? Do you know anyone who could help you?"

"I think so. However, I don't know if he'd be willing to do it. You see I tried to escape in his boat without his consent. He didn't know about it."

"A young man or an older man?"

"An older man. Old enough to be my father."

"In that case, you have nothing to worry about. I can tell you from experience that older men are very apt to forgive a pretty young woman like you. Especially, if you are able to return the favor."

"He knows me very well, and he knows all the ways in which I can return his favors."

"You see, you'll have no problem, then. Maybe you can even save your friends. Wouldn't you like to do that?"

Inés thought of María Teresa and Carlos, especially Carlos. She would gladly do anything to be able to free Carlos.

"What is the name of your important friend?"

"Gustavo. But why do you want to know?"

"Let me tell you something I wouldn't tell anybody in here, except some special people that I can trust. I believe that I can trust you, can't I?"

"Oh yes! You can trust me."

"Listen to me, my dear child. I'm an old woman whose only fault has been to participate in a religious demonstration. They have tried to incriminate me with other transgressions to no avail. Some time ago, they let me receive a visitor from the Curia who told me that the Church would exert all kinds of pressure to seek my release as soon as possible. I know that they'll let me go sometime soon. Maybe that's why I get somewhat better treatment than the other women here. They don't want any signs of physical abuse to show on an old woman when she leaves this place. It would be very bad propaganda. Particularly when members of the Church will be coming for me. Now, if you confide to me the name of this man, I promise you that the minute I get out of here, I'll go to him and fully explain your situation. After that, I'm sure that he'll do almost anything to get you back. So tell me, if you want my help, what's his full name?"

"Dr. Gustavo Albacete."

"You don't say. The man who's so close to Fidel? You're going to have no problems. Hasn't he talked to you about his relationship with Castro?"

"Many times. He even told me about private conversations with both Raúl and Fidel Castro. He had a lot of confidence in me. I just hope that my last act hasn't broken the spell between us."

"No, don't worry. I'm sure that he'll regain his trust in you after I talk to him. Now, why don't you try to get some rest? I'd like to do the same myself. And I repeat, don't you worry! This will be our little secret."

The older woman went to lie on the floor alongside the opposite wall from Inés.

After what seemed like an entire day, a voice was heard in the hallway outside the row of cells. It was the voice of one of the female guards.

"Prisoner G-3516. Prisoner G-3516. Get ready for interrogation."

The door of the cell opened with a loud clanging sound as it hit the outside wall. Inés was already standing up. The older woman looked at her and winked an eye.

Inés marched in front of the guard. From one of the cells a loud shoust was heard.

"I'm here G-3517. I'm here G-3517."

The guard banged at the door with her wooden club and

yelled back, "Shut up in there. Shut up if you don't want me to come back and teach you a few lessons in discipline." They didn't hear the voice again.

Inés smiled, keeping her face from the guard. Now she knew that María Teresa was well. The guard pushed her forward with her club.

"What're you waiting for? Keep walking, you bitch."

Inés continued to the interrogation room that she knew too well. The guard shoved her inside the room, in the usual rough manner, and told her to wait for the lieutenant. This time he took longer than the habitual time.

When he finally showed up, he entered the room with two male guards, and asked Inés, who was already sitting on her chair, "Well, how are you today?"

"I don't think that you want to know."

"You're mistaken. I want to know all there is about you."

"There's not much I can tell you that you don't know already. But if you want me to start anew, I'm ready. My name is Inés Pidal y Aspuru, the widow of José Miguel Font-Vachon."

"Yes. I know all of that. To me you're prisoner number G-3516, and I think that this prisoner has some other information that she has not told me as yet."

"What other information?"

"That's for you to tell me, and for me to verify. Do you see this folder in front of me? Well, this folder has been growing over the past few days. Every time I open it, I'm amazed to find new evidence against you. You worms think we're morons and that we don't know our business. On the contrary, we've investigated your life from the moment that you were born until now. We have questioned your friends, the ones in here and the ones outside, including that old man who has fucked your brains out. What's his name?"

"You talked to him?"

"Sure, his name is Dr. Gustavo Albacete. You see, we know everything. There's nothing new that you can really tell us. Now,

I'm going to make you a proposition. If you show good faith, and cooperate with us by confirming all the information that I have in this folder, you'll be out of here in the next hour, and I'll personally instruct the prosecutor at your trial to beg the tribunal for mercy. On the other hand, if you make me waste my time by extracting from you information that I already know, then I'll demand that you be charged with the maximum sentence for your crimes. What do you say?"

"I don't know what to say. I already told you everything I know."

"You didn't say anything about your amorous relations with Dr. Albacete."

"A lady wouldn't volunteer that kind of information. Besides, you should've known that I knew him since I was able to borrow his boat."

The lieutenant banged the table with his closed fist and said, "You're no lady. You're nothing but a well-paid whore. Now, tell me about your relations with the CIA."

"The CIA? What's that?"

"Don't play the role of the dumb blonde with me. It just doesn't become you. The CIA is the Central Intelligence Agency of the fucking Yankees. Your real boss. The people that you've been working for all this time when you lay in bed with Dr. Albacete. Are you denying that also?"

Inés started to get nervous. She had no idea where this line of questioning was leading, but she did not like it. She commenced to perspire and replied, "It's not a question of denying anything. I tell you that I don't know what you're talking about. Why don't you believe me?"

"Because you're lying, and you know it. This is the last chance that I'm giving you. We know that you started fucking the old man in order to obtain information about Fidel, and pass it along to the CIA through your friends here with you. They were using an attaché from the Spanish Embassy as their contact. You were extracting the information from the repugnant old man and your friends were passing it to the Spaniard between fucks. The reason why you people stole the old man's boat was to ensure that the last pieces of information reached the CIA promptly. The route via Spain to the United States was too long to take this time. I'm going to give you your last chance. Do you understand me, you fucking bitch? Your last chance. Tell me everything that you told the Americans and I'll show you clemency. If you persist in being stubborn, I'll show no mercy whatsoever and in the end I'll get whatever information I want from you. What'll it be?"

"I'd like to get out of here as fast as I can. Unfortunately, I'm no good at inventing situations or creating plots. I can't tell you what I don't know. Please, can't you see that?"

The officer never answered her question. He stood up and said to the two male soldiers in the room, "I'm going to go out for a smoke. This prisoner needs some persuading so that she can see things my way. Please, make her understand. I'll be back in a while."

Inés stood up and tried to get as far away from them as she could. The room was not that big, and the soldiers were on top of her in no time, with their bayonets in their hands.

The first blow struck her shoulder. She felt a sharp pain coming down her arm. She turned around, trying to protect that side of her body, when the second blow hit her squarely on the back, thrusting her body against the wall. In that position she felt an acute pang on her buttocks, where the bayonet hit for the third time. Then, one of the soldiers threw his weapon aside and, using his hands, turned her around sharply. He began to throw punches at her body and her face. Instinctively, she tried to use her arms to cover the ensuing blows. They were too many and too quick for her to parry successfully. She felt blood coming profusely from her nose and her mouth, and then a direct hit to her forehead from the remaining bayonet finally knocked her out.

She fell on the floor, and after a few seconds regained consciousness and realized that she was being kicked furiously. It didn't matter. It didn't hurt anymore.

The soldiers grabbed her and sat her back on the chair. The smell of ammonia under her nose made her come back to her senses completely. The pain all over her body was almost unbearable.

The officer came back with a towel in his hand. He tried to gently wipe the blood from her face, but he could not stop the stream of red liquid pouring out from the ghastly wound in her forehead.

He said to the soldiers, "You imbeciles, I said to persuade her, not to kill her. Get me a medic right away."

A man dressed in a dirty white uniform came with a metal tray, carrying some surgical instruments on it.

"Sew her up and be quick about it," the officer said.

The medic proceeded to clean the wound. Ten stitches later he was all done and he left.

Inés closed her eyes. The lieutenant said, "Don't close your eyes on me yet. I haven't finished with you. I'm sorry that those men screwed up that pretty face of yours. I guess that it won't be that pretty anymore. Please, understand that you've been a very stubborn whore, and I had no choice but to teach you a lesson. And now that you have seen what's good and bad for you, are you ready to confess about your relations with the CIA?"

Inés lifted her head slowly. It caused horrible pain just to move a mere fraction of an inch. When she guessed that her face was in the direction of the officer's face, she let go with the remaining force within her a large blob of saliva and blood that landed on his cheek.

Then, she yelled, "You animals. You fucking animals. I told you I didn't know anything. It was and it is the truth. But after this, even if I knew a lot, I wouldn't tell it to you. Do with me whatever you wish."

"I'm glad you have regained your strength. Let's see if you're going to talk now. I promise you that by the time I finish with you, you'll be inventing lies just to appease me. Now, let me see how tough you are." The officer turned to one of the soldiers and said, "Bring me the electric box. I want to see how this rich bitch dances."

The soldier came back with some belts and a black box containing some wires, a cord and a rheostat. They used the belts to tie Inés's waist, arms and legs to the chair. In the meantime, the officer put the box on top of the table and plugged the cord in a wall outlet.

"Open her uniform and let me see her breasts."

The soldier broke the top buttons of her prisoner's uniform with a single movement. Then, with one hand he yanked her bra downwards exposing her two firm breasts.

"You know, it's a real pity to cause such pain to such beautiful breasts. I'd rather bring some pleasure to them. But, since you insist on pain, then pain it will be, until you decide to tell me what I want to know."

There were two wires coming out of the black box. Each of them ended in an alligator clip. One alligator clip bit mercilessly into Inés's right nipple. The remaining one did the same to her left nipple.

She was now terrified at what was to come, an outcome over which she had no control. Pulling together all the strength remaining in her body, she stubbornly decided to demonstrate to these madmen the valor of a Cuban woman. She looked straight into the interrogator's eyes. Her eyes were full of anger and determination.

"You think you're so brave. You miserable little bastard. This Cuban, who isn't old enough to be your mother, but could easily be your sister or your wife, will show you what real inner strength is. Do as you wish, you son of a bitch. I shall not talk."

"Let her feel some music. I think that she's ready to dance."

The soldier moved the rheostat three notches. The overhead light flickered as Inés's body went into severe convulsions. The pain across her chest banged into her head like a thunderbolt. She could not help emitting a loud scream.

"Enough," said the officer. "Are you ready to talk my sweetheart, or do you want to dance some more?"

"I wish your mother could see you now, if you have one."

"Again." The soldier moved the control knob five notches. Inés jumped up and down, back and forth, and sideways, all at the same time. Her eyes seemed to want to leave their sockets. Her head was continuously pounding inside like a volcano ready to erupt.

"Enough. How about it, my love? Shall we put a stop to all this suffering?"

"I'm ready to meet my Creator. You can go to hell and meet yours."

"Again."

This time, the soldier was looking at Inés with amazement and did not realize that inadvertently he was moving the knob past six notches.

All of a sudden, the volcano inside Inés exploded. A surge of blood came rushing out of her ears and eyes. Her head jumped backwards and then forwards. Then, it did not move anymore.

María Teresa woke up when a guard brought to her cell a tin jar containing a lukewarm liquid that resembled tea. The light in her cell went on again. No sooner had she finished drinking, than she heard a familiar voice:

"Prisoner G-3517, prepare for interrogation. Prisoner G-3517, prepare for interrogation." The door to her cell opened, and she marched in the direction of the interrogation room. Another familiar face was waiting for her at the other side of the desk.

"And how are we feeling today?"

"I can only speak for myself. I'll feel better when I'm out of this nightmare."

"Why do you call it a nightmare? Haven't you been treated well in here? Do you have any complaints?"

"No, I don't have any major complaints. But you have to admit that you've been questioning me repeatedly, and I have told you everything that you wanted to know, over and over again. I don't know what else you want from me?"

The lieutenant leaned back against his chair and said, "Well, relax, I believe that today will be the last day that you'll see me. I'll tell you something. You are the most intelligent woman that I've had the pleasure of interrogating, and perhaps the most beautiful also. You should be proud of your attributes.

"And yet, we must continue trying to learn the whole truth concerning you. I realize that you've been telling me the truth in your own clever way. Today, however, I want you to tell me the whole truth about your activities.

"You see, there's no point in hiding anything from me anymore. I have here in this folder the full confession of prisoner G-3516. You knew her well, and your activities were related to hers. Therefore, in order to make things easier for everybody, why don't you confess also? I'll have the paper signed by you and you can walk out of here and wait for your trial in your own home. Simple enough?"

"Confess to what? I've already told you that my only fault was to be caught while trying to leave this country."

"And why were you in such a hurry to do so?"

"Because every other means had been closed to me. Sure, I could've waited years for a permit that might never have come. You tell me, would you wish to wait years in a place that doesn't like you or want you?"

"You're mistaken, number G-3517. We would have liked it very much if you'd stayed with us forever."

"In that case, why did you close my university? Why did you take my money away from me? Why did you make it so difficult for someone like me to find a job? Why did you insist on removing my liberties, one by one?"

"That's what you were told. We would have given you a job. The kind of work that would have made you a better person, a more useful person for the people that you had robbed before."

"I've never stolen anything from anyone in my entire life."

"That's what you say now. I'm sure that if you spend some

time in one of our rehabilitation centers, you'll learn to see the light."

"Please, don't insult my intelligence. If you want to accuse me of being a criminal for having ideological disagreements with you, that's fine with me. As you said, let me get out of here and face the tribunal that will condemn me on those points. But I haven't committed any other crimes against you or the system that you represent. I won't admit guilt for any other allegations."

"But you forget that I have here the full confession of another prisoner that disagrees with your statement."

"Fine. Then I'll tell you right now that prisoner is lying and what you should do, if you're as just and fair as you claim to be, is to bring that prisoner here to confront me."

"I'd love to do just that, but it's impossible."

An unexpected chill started to permeate through María Teresa's body. "Why?"

"Because that prisoner is no longer with us."

"Where is she?"

"She's dead."

"What? What happened to her?"

"She died of a massive heart attack last night, when she was leaving this room and going back to her cell."

"That's a lie." María Teresa began to get hysterical.

"So you think that we're lying to you. I'll show you. Come with me."

The officer grabbed her by the arm and took her to the cold room that they called the morgue. There were several bodies lying on their respective stretchers. One of them had a tag attached to it. It read G-3516.

The officer held María Teresa by her arms and told the orderly to remove the olive green sheet that was covering the body. A nauseating feeling invaded María Teresa. She turned her head and closed her eyes. The officer standing behind her holding her by the arms shouted in one her ears, "No. Look at her. Look at her and tell me if we're liars like you."

María Teresa looked again. The face was completely deformed by the swelling and the discoloring of the skin. Underneath that mess of dried blood, she recognized the facial features of Inés. Then she noticed the black color of her breasts in contrast with the light tan color of the rest of her body.

"What are those black marks there?" she inquired.

"Those were the spots that the doctor used to apply the electrodes trying to revive her."

María Teresa knew he was lying. Her rudimentary knowledge of anatomy told her so. Her wisdom also advised her to play the game with the officer.

"And what happened to her face, and those black and blue marks on the rest of her body?"

"She fell down the stairs when the heart attack occurred."

"I've seen enough. Please, take me out of here. I believe that you were telling me the truth. I apologize for what I said."

"Well, that's better. We can go back now."

The officer waited for her to start walking and then followed her at a close distance. She said to herself, "My poor dear friend, what have they done to you?" Silently, she offered a prayer for Inés's soul.

María Teresa understood that she would have to deal with her situation very carefully, or she would end up the same way. The interrogator had made his point quite well.

Back in the interrogation room, he said, "I can see that you're somewhat distressed by the loss of your friend. It was really a pity. Such a young woman. I think that we should end this session now, and give you some time to think about everything that you saw today. I wouldn't want the same thing to happen to you. And again, you must remember the old saying, one is here on borrowed time. Go back to your cell, and spend some time straightening out your thoughts. You've found me in a very understanding mood today. I like you, and that's why I must warn you that if you're not willing to sign the confession to all your crimes by the time we meet again, I'll have no choice but to reveal to you my displeasure with your behavior. I'm sure that you wouldn't like to see that, would you?"

"No, I wouldn't."

"Good. Very good. Now, go back to your cell. I have other things to do."

María Teresa walked very slowly. Her mind was in turmoil. "Oh God! Help me find the right avenue out of this labyrinth," she murmured in a very low voice.

She was placed in her original cell this time, but the older woman who had shared it before was not there. She sat on the filthy floor and wanted to cry, but there were no more tears. Half an hour later, the door opened and the older woman prisoner came into the cell.

"What's going on, my dear child? You look distressed."

"My friend is dead. I just saw her."

"What? That nice-looking young woman? How?"

"They said that she had a heart attack."

"Do you believe them?"

"I don't know what to believe anymore."

"I'll lend you my shoulder to cry on, and you can deposit the burden of your grief on it. I'm deeply sorry for what happened to your friend. You know, I liked her a lot also. As a matter of fact, we became very attached to each other the other day when she told me about her relationship with the good doctor, and the adventure that all three of you had together."

Intuition had told María Teresa not to trust that woman. Now, her keen intellect was telling her that she must be an informer.

María Teresa stood up, and said in a jovial manner, "Well, this is the beginning of a beautiful day. Let me start doing my morning exercises."

Without paying attention to the presence of the other prisoner in the cell, she began counting while she did squats. When she reached twenty she stopped, only to start immediately doing jumping jacks. After that she did twenty push-ups.

"If the men can do it, we can do it. It's good for the lungs." Then she sat for a couple of minutes to catch her breath.

The older woman said, "What're you doing?"

"Can't you see? I'm following your instructions. I'm doing my exercises perfectly. Now, what's next? I'm waiting."

"What do you mean?"

"Don't you remember? You're my physical education instructor, aren't you? So, teach me. What are you waiting for? What are we going to do next?"

Then, without waiting for an answer, she simulated that she was carrying a heavy, big ball in her hands, and fictitiously threw it at the astonished older woman.

"Come on. Don't keep it for yourself. Throw it back at me."

The other woman looked at her with amazement and tried to emulate her by throwing the nonexistent ball to María Teresa.

"That's it. Here. Catch it again."

The woman tried to make it to the door. María Teresa caught her when she was half way there and said, "So, you want to try some judo next? I warn you, I have a black belt."

With that said, she twisted the woman's right arm behind her back and pushed her with all her might against the back wall. When she pulled her back, the older woman was bleeding profusely from her nose. María Teresa took hold of her hair, and threw her hard on the floor.

"One fall means one point in my favor. Come on, stand up and let's finish the match."

The woman crawled for the door shouting at the top of her lungs, "Help. Help me. Please, somebody help me. Guards. Guards come quickly."

"We don't have to call anybody. We don't need a referee. I'm a fair judoka." Then, she landed a kick to the woman's stomach, causing her to emit a muffled scream.

"Second fall. I win. Do you want a rematch?" Without waiting for an answer, María Teresa kicked her hard again in the chest, breaking two of her ribs. The woman opened her mouth wide, gasping for air.

Luckily for her, at that moment, the metal door opened and two female guards rushed in and removed the older woman from the cell.

One of them inquired, "What the hell was going on in there?"

"She has gone mad," the older woman said. "Showing her the cadaver of her friend was a mistake. She's gone mad. Take me to the infirmary. I'm badly hurt."

An hour later, the officer in charge of María Teresa's interrogation approached her cell. He found her laughing and pretending to dance with an invisible partner.

"What're you doing?"

"You must be blind or stupid. Can't you see that I'm taking my dancing lessons?"

The lieutenant went back to his office and started to fill out the necessary forms. They indicated that María Teresa and Carlos were guilty of stealing and wrecking an expensive boat. No other faults were found. His orders included the immediate transfer, while waiting for the coming trial, of prisoner number G-3517 to Güanajay Prison for Women, and prisoner G-7007 to La Cabaña Fortress.

CHAPTER NINE

L a Cabaña Fortress was erected by the Spaniards to guard the rear access to El Morro Castle. Carlos Aguirrupe arrived at the dungeons underneath the two-level buildings in the beginning of the month of December 1961. The cells were located somewhat below sea level, and the cement walls were always damp and cold. The standard cell was built to hold approximately a couple of dozen prisoners. These wretched souls were being packed no less than 200 in each cell.

They had to sleep one next to the other, and to defecate into holes in the ground located at the front of the room. A cold-water faucet located high above those holes provided, at times, the only means of cleanliness.

The first day that Carlos entered his assigned quarters he slept standing up. There was no available space, and he did not know anyone. The following morning a man in his late forties approached him. "Hello, my name is Gabriel Salsamendi. What's yours?"

A view of El Morro Castle with the Fortress of La Cabaña behind it

"Carlos Aguirrupe."

"I'm very pleased to meet you, Carlos. Needless to say, it makes me very sad to see another Basque in this rotten hole."

"On the contrary, I'm glad to see you here. You've been the first friendly face that's greeted me."

"I saw you come in yesterday. The people here aren't bad in general. As you can see we're all wearing political uniforms. That means that underneath these clothes, we're all more or less linked together by a common bond. You have to watch out for the common prisoners who work alongside the guards, the ones with the blue uniforms. The guards let them get away with almost anything if their actions are aimed against us."

"I see. How long have you been here?"

"Four months now."

"And how long do you have to go?"

"Who knows? I'm still awaiting trial."

"Do you mean that you've been here four months already without a trial?"

"Sure. I can introduce you to people here who've been waiting eight months."

"Why are you here?"

"I used to work for Crusellas Co. One day I was asked to do guard duty on a weekend. They wanted me to guard the roofs of the buildings against the possibility of an air attack by the imperialist Yankees. I refused, because Fidel said that a task like that was to be performed strictly on a voluntary basis. Can you imagine guarding the building against airplanes with a fucking rifle? These bastards are just insane. Well, the Monday after, when I reported for work, two security officers were waiting for me and took me to the G-2. I was there for three and a half weeks. They gave me shots of I don't know what, and they kept interrogating me, night and day, without sleeping. After a while I confessed to everything they said. I'm being accused of sympathizing with the enemy, being a traitor to the Revolution, and having political views contrary to the will of the people. What about you?"

"I tried to leave in a boat, and was caught."

"Well, we don't have too much to worry about. Maybe three to five years."

"Are you serious?"

"Oh yes! If we're lucky that's all we're going to get. Although there are people here that have been sentenced to twenty years for similar crimes."

"I can't wait that long. I don't think I could bear that."

"Let me tell you one thing, Carlos, for your own good. Learn to accept whatever is given to you as punishment, so that you can live with the hope of leaving this place alive."

"My body might be alive, but after some time in here, my soul will be dead."

"No, it's the other way around. They may mangle, mutilate, or destroy your body. It's your soul that has to remain intact. Think about it."

"Well, I'll see what I can do."

"Now, come with me. I want you to meet some of the other prisoners."

Gabriel introduced Carlos to most of the inmates within that cell. That night, they made room for him on the floor against one of the damp walls. He had to sleep close to the latrine, but it was better than standing up.

In the middle of the night, the latrine hole overflowed, and the nauseating odor reached his nostrils. A feeling of wanting to vomit suddenly overcame him. He stood up quickly, waking up Gabriel who was next to him.

"You'll get used to it eventually. Don't worry, go back to sleep."

Carlos did not reply. He knew, however, that he would never get used to that.

The second time he was awakened was when a sequence of shots were heard. His rapid and uneasy motions in standing up, and the proximity to Gabriel, woke his friend up. Gabriel told him that it was only the execution squad taking care of someone who had been sentenced to death. Carlos said in a low voice, "How often does it happen?"

"It all depends. Sometimes three or four times in a given night. Go back to sleep. There's nothing you can do about it."

The last time that Carlos was suddenly awakened was when he felt something moving along his legs. A large rat was moving across him. This time he did not move. He stayed still, quietly watching the rat move away from him and over the bodies of two other sleeping prisoners.

The following day, they were all taken to a small courtyard to stretch their legs and enjoy the fresh air coming from the nearby ocean. A group of guards came and ordered them to exercise by running in circles. Then, they took their bayonets and started to prod the prisoners to keep them in motion. By the end of the exercise cycle, the floor was partially covered with blood from the wounds made with the tips of the bayonets.

The food received by the political prisoners was not only meager in its quantity, but also extremely bad in quality.

A week passed by, and Carlos realized that he would not be able to endure a long prison term under these conditions. One night, after everybody was asleep, he nudged Gabriel.

"Gabriel, I need to talk to you."

"What is it, Carlos?"

"I won't survive this ordeal. I have to get out of here."

"You must be going crazy as well."

"No, I'm not crazy. Not yet anyway. You must know of some people who've managed to escape. Can you tell me how they did it?"

"If I knew of a way, I would've tried it already. The only sure way out of here is in a coffin."

"What happens if you get sick?"

"They bring what they call a doctor to see you. The guy might give you some medicine, or he might not. In any event, they will bring you back to the cell and let you rot to death. When you die, they'll remove you and thank you for the space that you've created for the next prisoner."

"Will they ever bring you to a hospital?"

"I'd guess that the only time that they'd do something like that would be if your disease threatened to spread to the guards."

"Then, there's one possibility."

"Yes, the possibility of contracting a contagious disease that will kill you in the long run."

"Thank you, Gabriel."

"Don't do anything foolish."

"I won't, my friend."

Carlos waited another month for the right opportunity. In the meantime he had managed to obtain a small plastic bottle of ether from the local infirmary, an empty plastic jar, and a glass sliver from a broken beaker. One of the common prisoners assigned to work in the infirmary had traded the two objects for two packs of cigarettes that another prisoner had given Carlos as a Christmas present.

One night he had a visit from another rat. That was the

moment he had been waiting for. He grabbed the rat by its body, and pushed its nose against a spot on his trouser containing the ether. A few seconds later, the rat did not fight him anymore. It was completely anesthetized. Then, he took the piece of glass and killed the rat by making a large incision along its neck. He cut a piece of flesh off its body, and put it in the plastic jar. He threw what was left of the animal down the latrine hole, along with the evidence of the glass and the plastic ether bottle. A few days later, he retrieved the plastic jar with the now rancid flesh of the rat inside and forced himself to eat it. He swallowed it without chewing, making a supreme effort to keep from vomiting. Then, he waited patiently for nature to take its course.

By the next morning, he was sweating, running a temperature and passing out for no apparent reason. His fellow prisoners started to yell, calling the guards.

As soon as the guards saw the green, pale complexion of Carlos's face and noticed the weakness of his body, they moved him in a stretcher to the infirmary.

There, a doctor examined him and ordered a blood analysis. The analysis revealed a large amount of white blood cells, which indicated a severe infection. The doctor recommended that he be taken to the army hospital, where X-rays could be taken. The doctor diagnosed it as a possible rupture of the appendix. He told the officer in charge that if he could be sure it was only appendicitis, he would let him die in the cell from acute peritonitis. But if it was a severe infection caused by some contagious disease, that malady could spread throughout. Consequently, he wanted him to go to the hospital, where the existing equipment would be able to render a better diagnosis.

CHAPTER TEN

After a detailed examination of the patient, the Army doctor at the hospital decided that Carlos did not have any need for surgical intervention. He diagnosed Carlos as having a bad case of food poisoning, and recommended that his stomach be emptied out with a series of enemas. He also said that Carlos should remain in the hospital for a few days to keep him under observation.

Two days later, due to the care of the male orderly assigned to his case, Carlos started to feel much better. He was only experiencing some dizzy spells from time to time.

The following morning, the orderly came early to take another sample of blood and his blood pressure. When he saw Carlos, he said, "Good morning. You certainly have a better color in your face today. How are you feeling?"

"Much better, thank you."

"Do you feel strong enough to take a shower?"

"I think so, if that's what you want me to do."

"The doctor would approve, and I think that you'll feel like a new man after a shower and a change of clothing. I brought a clean uniform for you to wear."

"Does that mean that I'm getting out of here?"

"That's not for me to decide. I'm sure that you'll be sent back to La Cabaña in the next few days. You have been recuperating nicely from whatever it was that you ate."

"I only ate the food given to me."

"And how come that same food didn't affect the other prisoners?"

"I don't know. I'm not a physician."

"My responsibility is to help you improve your health while you're in my care, and to make sure you don't try to get away. I have a good, clean record, and I want to keep it that way. Please, don't try any funny stuff with me. I'm sure that we'll get along just fine, and to prove to you that I'm on your side, health wise, I'll bring you a good lunch today."

"You've been very good to me. I appreciate it. Don't worry. I won't try anything to damage your reputation."

"Good. I like to hear that. Now, take my arm and walk with me to the showers. Don't rush. Stand up slowly. Are you ready?"

"Yes, I am. Thank you again. Thank you very much."

En route to the shower room, Carlos noticed that a single soldier guarded the entire pavilion. He sat, weapon in hand, in front of a small, metal desk, situated on the far side of the hallway, and next to the only exit. The shower room was small and covered with off-white tiles, except for the opening near the high window, which was used to allow the excess steam to escape. The orderly remained inside the bathroom with Carlos at all times.

"Take your time. I'm not in a hurry," said the orderly with a half smile on his face.

"Do you have any hot water here?"

"Of course, and plenty of it. Just relax and take a good shower. There's soap in the dish on the wall. Use all you want, but let me know if you feel dizzy at any time."

The water did wonders to revitalize Carlos's body and soul. As he was walked back to his bed, he sensed that his mind was getting sharp again. There was a large, round wall clock fixed to the partition across from his bed. It read eight o'clock. Breakfast came punctually about a half an hour later. It consisted only of one piece of bread and a large cup of coffee, but it was the best food he had enjoyed for weeks.

The other prisoners in the same hospital room kept to themselves most of the time. There was very little conversation among them, and they hardly said anything to Carlos.

A man with a rugged, sunburned face, and the calloused hands of a lifelong hard worker, tried to engage in some small talk with Carlos. Carlos apologized, saying he was suddenly overcome with fatigue, and closed his eyes to avoid any more interruptions. He knew the necessity of developing a foolproof plan to escape. Moreover, it would have to be done in the next few hours. He had the feeling that he would be sent back to the prison at any moment.

Carlos pondered the problem, over and over again, throughout the rest of the day. By the time dinner was brought to him, his mind had already come up with several schemes, and he had discarded the risky ones. He was now ready to put into effect the one most likely to succeed.

Carlos had not been a deeply religious man during the past few years of his life. In good faith, he considered it an act of hypocrisy to start praying now. Still, he remembered what he had learned throughout his Catholic upbringing. Phrases and entire passages of the Bible came back into his mind clearly. The words of the "Apostles' Creed" and the "Our Father" were displayed in front of his closed eyes, and he realized how much he could recall. His eyes started to release silent tears as he asked God for forgiveness and assistance in carrying out his plan. A deep sensation of relief and a rich feeling of well-being took possession of his entire body. The sheep of the Good Shepherd may go astray, he thought, and yet, the Good Shepherd has His own way of finding them and caring for them as soon as they seek Him again.

The clock read twenty minutes after ten at night when Carlos opened his eyes. It was time. Without making any perceptible noise, like a big cat ready to pounce on its prey, he approached the door of the room and opened it. Once in the hallway, he turned to the guard who was busy reading the latest edition of the "Gramma" newspaper. The young soldier turned his head and focused his eyes on him.

"What do you want?"

"Just permission to go to the toilet. I have to urinate badly."

"Okay, but don't take too long."

There were no windows in the bathroom. On his way out, while crossing the hallway back to the door leading to the dormitory, he simulated a fainting spell, and dropped to the floor. Instead of calling for help, the guard went instinctively to aid Carlos. It was the chance that Carlos was gambling on, and it paid off.

The inexperienced soldier straddled his legs over Carlos's body to get a better grip on his collar with both hands. Swiftly, Carlos's right leg moved upward and struck the soldier violently in his unguarded testicles. Then, he pushed the soldier's body sideways, and landed a punch, with all his strength, on the soldier's jaw. The blow knocked the guard unconscious. He then grabbed the soldier's revolver, and rushed to check the exit by pressing his ear on the door panel. The lack of noise from the outside indicated that if anyone was there they had not heard anything unusual. He took a quick glimpse of the dormitory. The other patients were all in their respective beds, either sleeping or pretending to be asleep.

To assure that the soldier remained unconscious, Carlos took the revolver and used it to deliver a blow to the base of the soldier's head. He then took off his prisoner's uniform and tossed it into the bathroom. Next, he undressed the soldier and put his uniform on. It did not fit him too well, since the soldier was a little bit shorter and fatter than he was. His feet hurt a bit under the pressure of the smaller boots. He couldn't have cared less.

Carlos opened the window in the shower room and pulled his body upward to take a look at the outside and calculate his drop. It was approximately twelve to fourteen feet to the ground below. He went back into the hallway and took the chair and wastebasket from the desk. Placing one on top of the other gave him enough height to reach one of the pipes near the ceiling. By pulling and swinging his body towards the open window, he managed to push both his feet across it and outside. He let go of the pipe and jerked his body forward until he grabbed the next pipe closer to the window. Then he pushed more of his body outside. He slowly twisted his entire body 180 degrees and climbed down the outside wall until his whole body weight was being held by his two hands on the window ledge. He looked down and made sure that it was all clear below. Then, he let go and pushed his body away from the wall. He bent his knees and allowed his body to roll when he hit the grass below. Quickly, he stood up and pressed his back against the wall of the building he had just left. Everything was dark around him, and the only lights he could see were street lamps on the road about seventy-five yards away. Casually, he headed for the road. He smiled as he thought, "Pity that I couldn't have taken an officer's uniform. It would have made my escape a lot easier."

Carlos started to walk along the road. A few minutes later an Army truck stopped next to him. There were two soldiers in the driving cabin. One of them said, "Hey buddy, are you going to the gate? Jump in and we'll give you a lift."

"No, thank you. I'm just walking to exercise a little bit before retiring for the night."

"All right. As you wish. Have a good night."

"You too, comrade. And thank you again."

Carlos quickly ran behind the accelerating vehicle and silently climbed into it. The truck left the Army camp and made its first stop at a bar in the Jaimanitas beach area. He then descended from the truck with caution. He walked in the opposite direction of the bar until he reached the next corner. There, he waited patiently for the next bus to arrive. He checked his pockets for the first time and noticed that he had 32 pesos and some coins.

CHAPTER ELEVEN

Luckily, he did not have to wait too long for the bus. It was almost empty at that hour of the night.

The bus route took him along Fifth Avenue in Miramar. He decided not to go to his own house, and ordered the conductor to drop him on another corner. Across the street stood the beautiful modern church of Santa Rita. Father Lázaro Fernández, one of the few Cuban Augustinians, was its pastor. Carlos knew him well from his time at Villanueva.

He crossed the median separating the double avenue and approached the rectory building behind the church. He rang the bell several times before a face looked at him through the small security opening in the door that was protected with wrought iron bars.

"Who is it? What do you want?"

"I'm a Catholic student from Villanueva in need of help. Please, open up and let me in."

"You're a soldier. Who are you?"

"I wish to speak to Father Fernández."

"This is Father Fernández."

"Thank God! Lázaro, this is Carlos Aguirrupe. Please, let me in."

The priest unbolted the door and provided enough space to allow Carlos to step inside. He closed and secured the entrance rapidly, and then he turned around to face Carlos.

"Oh my God! It's true. You're Carlos Aguirrupe."

He embraced Carlos happily and then asked what he was doing there.

"I'll tell you the whole story, but first can you give me some water. I'm very thirsty."

"Come in, my son. Come to the kitchen with me. Let me give you some water and some sherry."

Carlos told everything that had happened to him and his family to the good priest, who proved to be an excellent listener. He never interrupted Carlos during the narration of his ordeal. In the end, he said simply, "I'm very sorry to hear about your misery. Now tell me, how can I help?"

"I need to hide for a few days. Can you offer me sanctuary in your church or in another safe place?"

"You know, Carlos, if I'm caught doing this, they won't put me in jail. They'll place me in front of a firing squad."

"Yes, I know, Father. I've come to you in desperation. I have no other place to go, but if you want me to leave right now, I will. I don't wish to endanger your life more than I have already."

"I never said I wouldn't help you. I only mentioned the risk that I'm taking, because I want you to be extremely discrete about it. Yes, you can remain here, since I'm all alone now. The Diocese sends other priests to help me with the masses on weekends. As long as you remain in my own private quarters without making any noise whenever they are here, we'll have no problem. At any other time, you can use the entire rectory as you please. The first thing that you'll have to do is to get rid of that uniform. I'll give you a habit to wear. If anyone should see you by mistake, just tell them that you're a new priest in transit. If that happens, I want you out of here right away."

"Thank you, Father. I knew that you'd come through somehow."

"What made you so sure?"

"Something inside me told me so."

"Do you want to hear a funny one? I thought of you this afternoon. I don't know why, but your image came into my head all of a sudden, and now, here you are. I'll show you to your room after we dispose of your clothing and the gun."

Carlos looked at himself in the mirror in the bedroom and saw a young, handsome priest standing in front of him.

"What do you think? Does the Augustinian black winter habit become you or not?"

"I must admit that I look very good in this robe. Very impressive indeed. Maybe I should consider becoming a priest after all of this is over."

"I wish you were serious about it. The Church needs men like you. But if I know you, you're joking as usual."

"I don't know. Don't be too sure about that. Tell me, Lázaro, may I ask you for another favor?"

"Another one? What is it this time?"

"It concerns my sister. I believe that they sent her to Güanajay Prison. I don't know anything else about her. I have to find out whether she's alive or not, and if she is, I have to find a way to get her out of there."

"Now I can say that you're really insane. Maybe the glasses of sherry went to your head. How do you expect to find out? And furthermore, how do you expect to get her out?"

"I know who can help me do both. Do you remember a student from the Law School by the name of Raúl Mora?"

"Sure, I remember him, and I also know that he's a Commander in this Army of damned men."

"That's true. But what you don't know is that he's madly in love with my sister, and that they were planning to get married some time soon."

"I feel sorry for your sister."

"Come on, Father, where are your Christian beliefs? You're supposed to love your enemies."

"Yes, I'm supposed to forgive them and wish them no harm. But I don't have to enjoy their company."

"All right. I concede the argument. Now, about the favor, would you be willing to call Raúl on the telephone tomorrow and get him to meet me some place?"

"How do you know that Raúl isn't going to turn us in?"

"I don't know. I'm sorry, Father. I'm asking too much. I should know better."

"I understand. I also know María Teresa. Let me sleep on it, and you do the same. We'll discuss it again in the morning. Now, let's get some rest."

"Good night, Father, and thank you so much for your help."

"Don't mention it. I'll pray for both of us before I go to sleep. Good night."

Carlos slept until noon the following day. He went around the house looking for Father Fernández, making as little noise as possible. He found him in the kitchen.

"Are you ready for lunch?"

"Lunch? Whatever happened to breakfast?"

"You slept right through it."

"Is that so? What time is it?"

"Ten past twelve. How are you feeling?"

"Like a millionaire."

"I don't know how millionaires feel, but from the look of your relaxed face, they must live a good life."

Lunch consisted of spaghetti with beaten eggs and anchovies, bread, a slice of mamey and coffee. During lunch, Father Fernández told him that he had been listening to the radio and television during the morning. There was no mention whatsoever of Carlos's escape. He then advised Carlos to be very alert, because that did not mean that they would not be looking for him.

After lunch, they moved into the small living room and sat down across from each other.

"Have you given any more thought to our conversation last night?" Father Fernández said.

"Do you mean about María Teresa?"

"Precisely."

"Well, you know what I'd like to do for her."

"Yes, I know, and I've spent some time thinking about it. I'd really like to find a less complicated way to help her, and not necessarily what you proposed yesterday. Please understand, Carlos, this is a church, and I'm its pastor. We have lost most of the members of the clergy on the island. We now have new priests running the Cuban Church, whose main mission is to try to preserve whatever remains, and build upon it. The direction that they are receiving from the Vatican is one of appeasement and collaboration with the communists. Regardless of my disagreement with said methods of cooperating with the regime, I have no choice but to obey the men to whom I vowed complete and unconditional obedience.

"Now, to call a Commander of the Army, friend or no friend, may be a threat to our lives, and may also endanger the Church's reputation and delicate position. You must understand that I cannot and will not do it. I'm sorry for you and your sister."

"I understand. Don't be too concerned about it, because while I was listening to you, another idea came into my head. Can I borrow a priest's suit and a dark pair of sunglasses?"

"Absolutely. The Americans left behind so much clothing here that I'm sure we can fit you very well. What do you intend to do?"

"Before I tell you, could you lend me some money for a taxi?"

"I can let you have about two hundred pesos, but the taxi is a bad idea. I have a car that I use to go to hospitals and funeral homes when I'm needed. You'll have a much better chance of arriving safely at your destination if you let me drive you."

"Great! Here is my plan. You take me to the Havana Hilton and wait for me. I'll be inside no more than ten minutes. If I'm not out in that time, you go ahead and leave me there. If everything goes well, ten minutes is all the time I'll need to telephone Raúl from the hotel lobby. I'll tell him that the assistant to the nuncio has some delicate points concerning Church and State relations that the diplomatic office of the Church would like to discuss with him before presenting the issues officially to the Cuban Government. I will sweeten the pill by telling him that since he's the only one of Castro's Commanders who has attended Catholic schools and is considered to be knowledgeable in religious matters, he has been chosen to be the one person close to Castro who can best advise the Church. If he agrees, then I'll return to the car, and you can drive me to the nuncio's office and drop me off there. If I'm caught by anyone, I'll say that I stole these garments and that I am acting alone."

"What're you going to do after you have your talk with Raúl?"

"Somehow I'll return here tonight without compromising you and wait for the women."

"Well, it's a long shot that might work. Okay, I'll help you."

"Good! Let's go and get ready."

"Before we go, I'd like to ask you something else. Is María Teresa the only cause for whom you're risking your life at this moment? I'm asking you because I just heard you say women instead of woman."

"I won't lie to you, Father. No, she's not the only reason. There's another woman involved in this. You know her also. Her name is Inés Pidal."

"Yes, I remember her. Is she a friend of yours?"

"More than a friend, Lázaro. She's my lover."

"My son, I don't want to intrude in your private life. I'm sorry I asked you that question. These are difficult times for all of us, and we have to be prepared for the worst to come unexpectedly at any moment. Tell me one thing, would you like me to hear your confession now?"

"I don't know why, but I was expecting that offer from you. I'm going to surprise you by saying yes, and I'll begin by telling you that I haven't confessed my sins to any priest for the past six years. Should we go to the church?"

"No, this room is fine. God will listen to you any place that you request Him to do so. Just empty the burden that you're carrying on your conscience, and let Him infuse His peace unto you, as I give you the absolution in His name."

CHAPTER TWELVE

Two hours later, Carlos was waiting at the front door of the nuncio's office building, in the old section of the city, for Raúl to pick him up. The leather attaché case under his arm, the black suit, the black shirt with the white collar, the round black hat, and the sunglasses, gave him the appearance of an Italian diplomatic envoy. Some of the priests entering or leaving the building glanced at him, but nobody said anything.

Raúl showed up ten minutes later, alone, in a green army sedan. He stopped the car at the front entrance and stepped out looking for the man who had called him without realizing that he was already advancing towards the passenger side door.

"Are you Monsignori Contini?" Raúl asked.

"Si sonno Io. Grazie, Commendatore," said Carlos while climbing to the front seat of the car and closing the door behind him.

Raúl sat back in the driver's seat and for a second looked at his passenger with perplexity.

"Presto. Andiamo presto," said Carlos.

Raúl did not understand Italian, but the inflexion of the man's voice told him that he wanted to depart from that place and start their meeting as they drove through the city. Raúl shifted the car into drive, and a few minutes later he was driving along El Malecón Avenue.

"I hope that you speak Spanish, because I can't speak Italian."

"Don't worry. We can communicate to each other very well in Spanish. Just like old times."

Carlos took off the hat and the glasses, looked him straight in the eye and said, "How've you been, my friend?"

"Carlos? What the hell are you doing in my car dressed like that?"

"I had to see you, Raúl, and this is the best way I could think of."

"This time you've stretched our friendship beyond its limit. You're the prisoner that escaped from the hospital the other day. I read your file. I told you once that I wouldn't tolerate any action against the government. Brace yourself, because I'm taking you back to Columbia with me."

Carlos quickly put his hand into the attaché case and produced the revolver that was hiding in it. He pointed the gun at Raúl and calmly said, "You aren't taking me anywhere. Just keep driving up and down this road. I only want to talk to you."

"You've never fired a gun in your life. Are you going to tell me that you plan to use it against me if I don't comply with your wishes?"

"Believe it, Raúl. I've nothing to lose at this point."

"I see. What do you want?" Raúl started to drive fast along the deserted road.

"First of all, I want you to slow down. This is supposed to be a ride shared by two old friends. Please, don't do anything that would attract the attention of the police. I won't hesitate to use this gun at any moment if I find myself in danger. Do you understand me?"

"Hey! Don't get upset. Yes, I understand. You'd better relax and tell me what's on your mind." Raúl slowed down to sixty-five kilometers per hour and maintained that speed for the rest of the ride.

"Raúl, first of all, let me tell you that I haven't committed any serious crime besides stealing a boat. You can think otherwise if you want to. It's the truth. I don't think that anyone in his right mind would estimate that trying to leave this inferno is a crime. I guarantee you that whoever thinks that it is a crime will become the future fugitive when he realizes the fatal mistake that he has made by complying with a regime that will not rest until it owns everything on this damned island. We're just another example of the fortunate ones who have been able to detect sooner than others the infamy and the lack of respect for human rights of this communist government. We haven't conspired to destroy this brutal ruling power; we only wish to leave it behind, like a bad dream. Now, I'm not going to ask you anything for myself. When I leave you today, I'll walk away from your life forever, if that's what you wish me to do. If I reach safe shores in the future, and you ever need my help, I promise you on my dead mother's name that I will do anything that you ask. Even with all the differences that exist between us, I still consider you the friend I once knew, and who I know still exists under that uniform of yours."

"Do friends point guns at each other?"

"You're right. Tell me that you'll hear me out, and I'll put the gun away."

"In the name of what you call our friendship, I'll listen to you."

Carlos placed the revolver on his lap, as he continued, "Now, listen to me. I need your help once more, because you're the only person that I know who can assist me now. My sister and Inés have been transferred to Güanajay, and I need you to try to get them out of there."

"Wait! What? You must be a goddamned lunatic. I can't do any such thing."

"You're the only person I know that can walk in and out of that jail without major opposition. Please, think of María Teresa and Inés's situation. You know them both, and you know the kind of women they are. They won't be able to survive too long in that environment, and if they do we'll collect two destroyed souls by the time they leave that prison on their own. Is that what you want for a future wife?"

"Don't try to soften me up. Maybe María Teresa never told you, but everything between us ended when she started dating that Spanish Casanova. If she did it to spark my jealousy, she only increased my disdain towards her."

"You're wrong. She only did it with the hope that it would provide us with an opportunity to leave the country. By getting your people used to seeing us at Embassy parties, we expected to go to one and ask for political asylum. She stopped doing it when she felt she was hurting you too much in the process. Then, we considered the alternate method of leaving in the boat. So in a way, if it weren't for her love for you, we wouldn't be in the predicament that we're in now, and she probably wouldn't be in jail. I told you once, and I'm telling you again that María Teresa loves you very much."

"I'd like to believe it, but what you're telling me doesn't make much sense. If she loves me so much, why wouldn't she marry me when I asked her to?"

"Because she doesn't want to be a part of your present life and commitments. She refuses to bring up your children in a world of intellectual bondage. Mari-Tere was hoping you would see the light and come join us. There, in America, not only would you join her, but you would join your own parents as well. You could rest assured that our families would do whatever was necessary to ensure your happiness with her."

"I also love her very much. I'm neither stupid nor blind. But in spite of some of the changes that I've seen in this government, I still believe that Castro's intentions are good, and that this is only a temporary situation to get rid of the past and to build a new Cuba."

"I think you're dead wrong; and yet, I'd be willing to concede to you that you might be partially right. For the sake of argument, let's say that in a few years all is well here. The period of transitory commotion has elapsed, and the people are allowed to own property again. Fidel will pass into history as the true savior of Cuba. I then guarantee that I would return to this island and bring Mari-Tere with me to become your loving wife. On the other hand, if given that same period of time, nothing has improved in Cuba, give me your word of honor that you'll come to us and marry my sister in exile."

"It's a tempting offer, considering that I would marry her in any outcome. Are you serious about it?"

"Yes, I am. I consider it a fair offer, and one upon which I'm willing to give you my word as a Basque."

"Don't be so melodramatic. A simple yes will do."

"No, a simple handshake between friends will do."

Carlos extended his hand to Raúl, who took it in a firm handshake.

"Now, about the women," Carlos said, "I really don't know it for a fact but I strongly believe that they'd be in Güanajay. Would you go to the prison and see what you can do to get them out?"

"That isn't as easy as you think, not even for a Commander in the Army. For a simple criminal or civil transgressor, I could do something. For a political criminal it's extremely difficult to effect any release or commutation of the imposed sentence. I'll try to do something, but I can't promise you success concerning Mari-Tere."

"And Inés? What can you do about her?"

"Nothing. I'm sorry to tell you, Carlos, but Inés is dead. I found out when I read your files, just yesterday. As you can imagine, the names on them interested me, to say the least."

"Oh, my God! When did it happen? How?"

"Calm yourself. Inés died at the G-2 of a heart attack shortly before you were transferred."

"There was nothing wrong with Inés's heart. They killed her."

"I don't think so. The G-2 is only an interrogation center. They don't kill people there."

"How the hell would you know? I was there, on the inside, and I've seen men being beaten and tortured. The sons of bitches murdered her."

"I'm not going to argue with you. Let's assume they did it. There's nothing you or I can do about it now. Regarding Mari-Tere, I'll tell you that you're right in your assumption. She's at Güanajay."

"If it weren't for Mari-Tere," Carlos stopped suddenly when a big knot developed in his throat, and tears began to appear in his eyes. He did not want Raúl to see him crying, and took two big, deep breaths. "I would like you, now more than ever, to get her out of there. During Batista's time, if you had ended up in jail, my father would've done everything possible and even risked his reputation to get you out. I only ask you to do the same for his daughter, my sister and your future wife."

"I'm going to try. That's all I can say for now."

"When?"

"The day after tomorrow. I need some time to think of a plan."

"When you take her out, I'd like you to bring her to me. From then on, I'll take care of her until we fulfill the agreement."

"Where are you going to be? You can't go back to your home. As a matter of fact, there's a minister of the Revolution living in it now."

"I can't tell you where I'll be staying because I'm changing addresses every single day. And I can't tell you to hold Mari-Tere with you until I get in touch with you again, because God knows under what circumstances you'll have to spring her out of prison. The best thing would be for you to deliver her to a safe place where I could pick her up later on."

"Okay, where?"

"I think that probably a Church would be the safest place. Let's try the Church of Santa Rita in Miramar. Father Fernández from Villanueva should be there now. He knows my family well, and I'm sure that he will let her stay there. He also knows you."

"Yes, I remember Father Fernández. Well, it's all set then. Where do you want me to drop you?"

"Do you see that taxi stand on the next corner? You can drop me off there."

"I can take you wherever you want. You don't have to take a taxi."

"Don't you think it would be safer this way? I don't want you to risk anything on my behalf. Mari-Tere is all that is important now, and you must be above suspicion."

"All right. I agree. I'll try to bring her to you shortly. If you don't hear from me, it means that I've failed."

"For God's sake, be careful. I wish you the best of luck."

Carlos got out of the automobile and into one of the taxis. Two taxis and two buses later, he was on his way to the church.

He told everything to Father Fernández, and asked him to pray for the safe return of his sister. He felt very tired and went to bed early that night.

With the picture of Inés in his mind, he lay in bed, covering his eyes with his right forearm. Again, there were tears in his eyes, anguish in his heart and raging anger in his mind.

CHAPTER THIRTEEN

The word Güanajay is not a Spanish word. According to some historians it was derived from the Indian word "guamuhaya." With its adopted name, the town of Güanajay was founded during the 17th century, when the Spanish rulers granted Gaspar Pérez Borroto the rights to own and work the land.

The municipality of Güanajay was located in the eastern province of Pinar del Río, adjacent to La Habana Province.

During the republican years of the history of the town, the national prison for women was erected. María Teresa entered its walls, still feigning her temporary dementia.

Political prisoners occupied several rows of cells. They were separated from the common criminal prisoners, who received better treatment from the guards.

Two different kinds of cells existed to house these women who were dressed in yellow-colored uniforms. The majority of the prisoners were in cells with iron-barred doors and windows. The most reluctant prisoners, who resisted in complying with the rules of the prison system, were placed in cells no larger than three feet wide by six feet long by six feet high, containing no windows and a solid metal door. These were called the "tapiadas" or "walled in" by the other prisoners, and they earned pity and respect for their constant display of stubborn behavior.

The penal system in Cuba also made a distinction between political and common criminals in ways other than the color of their uniforms. The political prisoners received punishment for any infraction no matter how small, on a larger scale than their counterparts. They also received the worst food, and meager rations. The political prisoners were forced to participate in slave labor programs, while the common prisoners were not. There was another major difference between the two distinctive groups. The political prisoners were bound by common beliefs and helped each other as much as they could. They presented a firm and solid philosophical bastion against the brainwashing techniques used by their ideological enemies.

It took María Teresa just a couple of days to realize that in such a precarious situation, there were no class distinctions anymore. She wasn't called a filthy, rich bitch anymore. They were all bound by a common cause now, and that was their hatred of the system that had placed them there together.

María Teresa was thrown into one of the cells containing approximately 30 other women. She did not know what day it was because she had lost all sense of time while at the G-2 center. Without saying a word to anyone, she went to sleep on the floor, and tried to get some rest for her battered mind.

Around two in the morning she woke up. She was cold, and did not have anything to cover her body. Everything was very quiet around her. All of the other prisoners in the cell were sleeping. She turned sideways, and crouched her body in an embryo position, trying to conserve whatever body heat she had. She could not sleep anymore. It was getting too cold.

She started to think about her home, trying to move her mind to other matters. She wondered who might be living in it now, and what other woman might be there enjoying her bed and her clothing.

María Teresa was still resting in that cramped position, when the morning sun began to warm the inside of the cell. Another woman lying next to her, who was covering herself with two pieces of cardboard, opened her eyes and said, "Good morning. I'm number 4004. People here call me "kitty" since that's what my numbers mean in the Chinese numbers game, but my real name is Alicia Ramírez. What's yours?"

"My number is 3517 and my name is María Teresa Aguirrupe. I'm pleased to meet you."

"I'm pleased to meet you too, even though I would've loved it to have been under other circumstances. I didn't want to say anything yesterday. You came in so quietly and then you fell asleep so quickly that I didn't want to disturb you."

Alicia was a woman in her early thirties. She was attractive, and yet her physical features were average and typical of the Cuban woman thrown into that prison. She had been a journalist, working with her husband for a local newspaper, which had since been closed and disbanded by the new government a few months ago. In her spare time, she used to teach catechism to poor children in La Habana. Her crime had been to ask a couple of embarrassing questions at an international press conference given by the Minister of Internal Affairs. Both she and her husband were apprehended shortly thereafter, and accused of being part of a conspiracy against the state inspired by the CIA. They were both sentenced to a term of no less than ten years in jail. Alicia was glad that there had been no children in their young marriage.

"Tell me, were you cold last night?" Alicia said.

"Freezing."

"I'll see if I can find you some newspaper or pieces of cardboard like mine for tonight. They're coming soon to take us outside for work detail. Once outside, the sun will warm you up. Just wait a short while."

"Labor! What labor?"

"Every day we have to go out into the fields and do whatever they want us to do. Normally, we pick all sorts of produce for the government. The bastards must be exporting all of it, because we hear that only a very limited amount reaches the population of the island. By the way, never eat any of it, no matter how hungry you are, if you're caught doing it, they'll punish you severely."

"I'm hungry now. When is breakfast here?"

Alicia laughed out loud. "What they call breakfast is a warm liquid that tastes like something between coffee and tea. Sometimes we're lucky and get a piece of stale bread to go with it. I don't want to talk about the lunch at the fields. I'm going to leave that as a surprise for you."

By seven in the morning, they started to call all the prisoners by their numbers and ask them to form a sort of military formation in the courtyard, with the exception of the "walled in" prisoners. Those were to be kept in confinement.

Two wooden carts with large wooden wheels, pulled by two old mules, entered the courtyard. They were carrying a load of hoes and rakes. Two male soldiers headed the procession to the work fields, followed by the two carts and the line of prisoners. Six female soldiers were guarding the flanks, and two more were at the rear end of the sorrowful parade. One female officer was in charge of the entire operation. She was sitting in the second cart facing the prisoners.

When they finally arrived at their destination, the officer stood up on top of the cart and addressed the entire crowd. "Today, all you worms will have the pleasure and the honor of repaying the People of Cuba for the miseries that you've caused them, by hoeing and raking this field to prepare it for the seeds that you will plant tomorrow. You'll have a fifteen minute break at noon for lunch. When I call your number, come forward and take one of these tools. The guards will assign you rows to work in the field. Now, get to work."

When she called the number 3517, María Teresa approached the car and the officer gave her a hoe and pointed in the direction María Teresa was supposed to go.

"Could someone tell me what to do with this?" María Teresa said. "I've never done this in my life."

The officer was carrying a short horsewhip in her right hand. She jumped down from the cart, and with a swift motion, she struck María Teresa's left hip. Her knees bent under the unexpected blow, and she grabbed the wooden pole of the hoe to prevent the rest of her body from falling to the ground.

"Please, don't hit me. I don't mean to be disrespectful. I only want . . ." The second blow on her left thigh finally sent her to the ground. The officer placed one of her boots on her stomach and pressed hard.

"You're nothing to me except a despicable swine. I can see that you're new here. Listen to me well, you no-good whore. You'll never speak to me again unless I talk to you first. That's lesson number one. If you think that you're going to play games with me, you're mistaken, because if you go crazy on me, I'm going to let the male guards or the common criminals loose on you to do whatever they want. I can promise you that they'll cure you much better than any insane asylum I could send you to. That's lesson number two. If you insist, after that, on giving me any other problems, I'm going to put you in one of those completely enclosed cells, so that you can rot there with the rats for the rest of your life. That's lesson number three. Now, stand up and get to work. If you don't know what to do, just watch the others and do the same."

The officer lifted her foot from María Teresa's body, and, with a terrified look in her eyes, María Teresa picked up the hoe and walked towards the field. None of the other prisoners said anything.

Her leg hurt immensely. She put all her weight on her right leg and proceeded to imitate the others as best she could. The only good thing about it was that Alicia was working next to her. The reassuring eyes of her friend gave her the stamina to proceed.

At noon, several whistles went off. Everybody stopped working and sat down on the ground. A truck arrived with the food. Each of them received a metal bowl containing a whitish blob that was supposed to be boiled rice, moistened with a greenish-brown liquid that was the end result of a meat and cabbage broth, and a tin cup of water. The odor of the food was atrocious, and María Teresa expected the taste to be likewise.

In a low voice she asked Alicia, "How are we supposed to eat this shit?"

"Don't talk now. Just watch me and use your fingers."

She watched Alicia place her lips on the rim of the bowl and stick three of her dirty fingers in the bowl. She then pushed a portion of the food into her mouth.

María Teresa decide to do the same, but as she tried to force herself to eat in that manner, she saw little tiny worms stuck to her fingers, and with repugnance she pushed the bowl away from her. A strong feeling of nausea invaded her body and she moved sideways to vomit whatever little amount of food she had brought inside her. Alicia saw her and said, "Don't do that. You have to force yourself to eat whatever they feed you. Those are only worms from the rice. They're not alive. They're dead and they're protein."

"I'm sorry, I just can't."

A female soldier that watched the incident rushed to where she was sitting. "What the hell is going on here? What's happening to you?"

"I'm sorry. I'm not feeling well. My stomach has been upset for the past few days. It won't happen again."

"I'm sure that it won't happen again, because I'm taking the food that you don't appreciate away from you. We'll see how that delicate stomach of yours behaves tomorrow."

The soldier picked up the bowl where María Teresa had left it, and walked back to her place near the carts. She took some of the food from the bowl in her hand and offered it to one the mules. The animal would not eat it either.

Two days later María Teresa had a lucky break. One of the prisoners in the adjacent cell was allowed to receive a visitor, who brought her some food and crackers.

In that prison there were no precise rules concerning the receiving of visitors, food sent by relatives or friends, or mail. Those things were apparently left to the whimsical desires of the officer in charge. Some of the prisoners said that if the officers let you receive gifts or visitors it was simply because the government was trying to bribe you. Some of these prisoners refused to accept gifts or visitors. They were called the "plantados" in the case of the men, and the "tapiadas" in the case of the women. These recalcitrant humans were placed in isolation and received the worst treatment of all.

Alicia procured an orange and three crackers for María Teresa. They had been her only sustenance for several days, and she ate them very slowly, late at night, enjoying every bite as much as she could.

With the passing weeks, she got used to the daily work routine. At least, she could be outside and breathe the fresh air of the countryside. The camaraderie of her fellow prisoners, and the feeling of unity that had developed among them, also helped tremendously. But she never got used to the abuses and the punishments. The humiliations inflicted upon the prisoners were totally unacceptable to her. There was another thing that she could not force herself to do, even though she tried very hard. She could never eat the entire portion of the meager ration of the putrid food that she normally received. She was losing weight, and there was nothing she could do about it.

One day, the group was sent to a warehouse to repack bananas. There were tons of them lying in a refrigerated room. The boxes were labeled in Russian. Some member of the Politburo is going to eat these, she thought. Why not me? So, she hid a couple of them inside her dress.

Unfortunately, one of the female guards saw her, and reported the incident to the officer who told her not to say anything at the moment. María Teresa returned to her cell and ate them. Alicia promised her that she would dispose of the banana peels the following day.

That night, two female guards approached the door to her cell. "Prisoner number 3517, come forward," one of the guards said.

María Teresa went to the door and one of them took her by her hair and pulled her outside the cell. The other prisoners started screaming and yelling all kinds of obscenities at the guards as they pulled María Teresa by the hair until they disappeared from sight.

They brought her to a small room that she had not seen before. It was in the same corridor where the officer's office was located. The room was empty except for a low wooden table and a chair. The table was around thirty inches wide and fifty inches long. At one of the ends there were some leather straps attached to it. The guards positioned María Teresa in front of the table, facing it. Then, while one of them stood behind her and pushed her head in the direction of the table until her face rested on top of it, the other guard took her hands and tied them to each end of the other side of the table with the straps.

The officer entered the room with a short whip in her hand. Addressing one of the two guards, she said, "You, get on that end of the table and hold her feet down." Then to the other guard, she said, "You, lift her dress up and pull her panties down."

Finally, to María Teresa, she said, "Now I'm going to teach you a lesson on why it's not healthy to steal from the People of Cuba."

She lifted the whip and struck hard on María Teresa's buttocks. María Teresa emitted a loud scream.

"Scream all you want, you filthy bitch, this room is soundproof. Now, I'm going to give you ten more strokes like that one, and you're going to count each one of them. If you faint or miscount, I'm going to start again until you give me the right answer. Understood?" And without waiting for an answer the officer struck again. María Teresa screamed.

"Not just a scream, what's the number?" said the officer.

"One."

"Good. Now let's see if you can continue counting."

María Teresa did not miss a single digit. After she had said the number ten, the officer stopped and the guards loosened the straps and raised her from the table. She was sweating profusely and her whole body started trembling when she tried to stand up again.

"Now, if I ever catch you doing something wrong, or disobeying my orders again, I'm going to give you to the male soldiers. Believe me, they aren't as soft as I am with you bitches."

María Teresa did not respond. She could not make another sound, even if she wanted to. A sudden rise in temperature was invading her entire body and she was going almost into convulsions.

"Take this worm back to her cell."

Two older women and Alicia held her in their arms when the guards pushed her back into the cramped cell. They moved her towards the center of the room, where other prisoners had prepared some sort of bed by using one of the very few thin mattresses that were available. Alicia pulled her underwear down very carefully and saw the red and blue color of her skin. It was also broken in several places and blood was coming out of the wounds. One of the older women started to wipe the sweat from her forehead with her hand and gently commenced to caress her face. She asked the others to give her a moment alone with her. She then whispered in her ear, "Lie there and rest. Don't say anything out loud. Just repeat mentally with me what I'm going to say." After a short pause, she began, "Oh! Bendita Virgen de la Caridad, you who have chosen to appear on this island for the purpose of saving its people, please come here now and listen to the cry of this daughter of yours. This woman needs you now to alleviate her sufferings, and to remove her pain. You who know what sorrow and pain are. You, who have seen the flesh of your flesh experience the pain of carrying all the sins of this world, please help us now. Have mercy on this beautiful daughter of yours. Bring peace and rest to this soul and to this body. Blessed be your name and the name of your Son Jesus Christ, in Whose name we ask you to grant us our wishes. Amen. Now, let's start praying the rosary, you and I."

And the older prisoner started to pray with María Teresa. At the end of the fourth mystery, María Teresa's breathing became more rhythmic, and her eyes closed. She was resting and sleeping. At least for the moment she would not feel any more pain. However, the older prisoner did not stop praying but continued until the last prayer was said.

In the morning, when the same routine of calling the numbers to arrange the prisoners in the outside patio occurred, the older woman remained behind and requested to talk to the officer who served as the warden of that prison.

When the officer came to the cell, the older woman said, "Prisoner 3517 is in no position to report for work duties this morning, as you might have suspected. She is very weak at this point. In all fairness, she should be sent to the infirmary, but I know that you wouldn't approve of that. I would like to ask you, on her behalf, that you let her rest here in my care for one day."

"Don't get cocky with me, Sister. You may have been a nun on the outside, but in here, you're only another prisoner."

"I'm only a servant of the Lord, outside or inside."

The officer had an expression of puzzlement on her face. Something beyond the determination of the older woman's face was pulling her out of there. She did not know what, and could not understand how or why; but she did recognize that it was in her best interests to get the hell out of there fast.

"Well, all right. You can stay with that bitch for today. I'll command the kitchen to bring you some food later."

She rapidly turned around, and left the cellblock at a quick pace.

"God be with you always," murmured the older nun as she went to assist María Teresa.

"How are you feeling, my child?"

"I'm hurt."

"Don't worry too much about it. It's normal after that kind

of beating. You have to drink a lot of fluids today. I'll take care of that, and I know one of the guards who'll bring me some medication from the infirmary. For now, lie quietly on your stomach. I'm going to fetch some water, and I also have a small piece of soap. Let me wash your behind when I return. I'll be very gentle."

"Thank you very much."

"Oh! Don't mention it. I consider it my duty toward mankind."

She came back with two oranges and a pail of water. Carefully she lifted María Teresa's dress until her body was exposed from the waist down. The area below her waist was completely discolored, and had nasty wounds where the whip had cut into the flesh. The soothing fresh water used to cleanse her invigorated María Teresa's senses, and she felt much better. After she ate the two oranges, a guard came, bringing some pills and a large cup of strong tea. She gave them to the older nun, and left.

María Teresa took the medication, and shortly thereafter she started to feel drowsy again. She turned her head to face the other prisoner beside her and said, "Who are you?"

"I'm prisoner number 3344."

"No, I don't mean that. What's your real name?"

"I'm Sister Magdalena."

"My God! You're a nun. What are you doing here?"

"I was brought here shortly after the Bay of Pigs invasion. To make matters even more complicated, I'm not even a Cuban, but a Spaniard."

"Are there other nuns in this prison, Sister?"

"Yes. There are thirty-seven of us in this block of cells. Probably over sixty in the entire prison."

"But, why are you here?"

"The majority of us, especially the ones who aren't Cuban, are waiting for deportation, but only God knows for how long. Some others have been charged with counterrevolutionary activities and sentenced to a prison term. So far, two of the eldest members of our community have died here under the abuses of forced labor. You know how it is in general for these people. We attend to the sick and the poor. Hence, we are competition for this regime that wants the populace to believe that there is no God, and that all the good in this world flows from the omnipotent State. Officially, they wouldn't admit it, but off the record that's the only reason why they're keeping us here. Other nuns on the island who stayed in the convent and only preoccupied themselves with Church affairs inside their cloisters are still free. But nuns like us, that were engaged in bringing God's love and truth to the people through our charitable and educational institutions, had to be expelled from the country, or put in jail, to stop our activities."

"But, Sister, surely the Church knows of your predicament. Why are they doing nothing about it?"

"Some of us believe they are doing something. These matters, unfortunately, have to be addressed through diplomatic channels, and those take a long time to materialize into anything positive. It's also true that the new Vatican envoy is flirting with Castro and the communists, to the point where he's instilling doubtful thoughts in some of us regarding the willingness of the Church to take care of our situation in a prompt manner. I think it's better to leave this kind of affair in God's hands. In the end, it shall be done as God wills."

María Teresa was now having a hard time keeping her eyes open.

"Rest now, my child," Sister Magdalena said. "Close your eyes and rest. I won't leave you today. When you wake up, I'll be at your side."

María Teresa closed her weary eyes, and her mind indulged in one of those fantastic dreams that one brings forward when one wants the body to forget the pain and anguish of a bad experience.

CHAPTER FOURTEEN

Weeks went by and María Teresa recovered fully. She was again doing the regular chores of other the political prisoners. Then, one day, when they had finished the daily work and were going back to the prison, one of the old mules collapsed and died. The sadistic female officer in charge, who was also the warden, decided that instead of waiting there for another animal to be brought to the field, some of the prisoners should take its place. Among the selected prisoners, she chose number 3517.

María Teresa, with a defiant look in her fiery green eyes, said that she was not to be treated like an animal, and refused to pull the cart. The officer moved closer to her, and lifted the arm with the whip, only to find María Teresa's hand seizing her arm with a tremendous grip.

"You can whip me all you want. You can kill me right now, in front of everybody, if it pleases you, but I'm not going to pull that cart. Nothing you can do to me will make me change my mind."

The officer tried to lower her arm. She could not move it a single inch. Other female guards came running, and pulled María Teresa to the ground. The officer fell on top of her, as María

Teresa would not let go of her arm. One of the guards managed to twist María Teresa's other arm until she let go of the officer. Then, both of them quickly stood up.

The other prisoners started shouting all sorts of dirty words, and heading menacingly for the guards. They readied their rifles and turned around to face the incoming crowd. The male soldiers also got their weapons ready and climbed on top of one of the carts.

Then, the officer in charge yelled, "Everybody listen to me. The prisoners will form two parallel lines as usual. We're going back to the prison now. Everybody stay calm." The prisoners stopped momentarily, and she continued. "Prisoner number 3517 is exempted from her present duty. No other prisoner will be called to pull the cart either. The male soldiers will remain behind and they will bring the other cart back when the replacement mule arrives." Seeing that most of the prisoners calmed down, she added, "I don't want to shoot anybody. Let's go back peacefully now." None of the prisoners moved to form the marching line.

The officer yelled louder, "I'm telling all of you to obey now and form two parallel lines. If you force my hand, I'll give orders to open fire. Let me assure you that prisoner 3517 will be the first one to die." She pulled out her pistol and pointed it at María Teresa's head. Then, they all returned without uttering another word.

Once all the prisoners were back in their cells, and the cart in question had returned to the prison, the officer told one of the male soldiers, "Tell Malanga to come see me on the double."

Malanga was the nickname of the person who was in charge of the kitchen. He had been a courier for the 26th of July Movement in La Habana, before he joined Castro in the mountains. There, he had learned how to cook simple dishes, and after the triumph of the revolution, had obtained the rank of sergeant in the Revolutionary Army. There were only six male soldiers assigned to guard duty in Güanajay Prison, and he was in charge of them. In turn he reported to the warden. The kitchen duties permitted him to participate in easy chores on one hand.

On the other, it allowed him to satisfy his ravenous sexual appetite with the common criminals that were serving as assistants to the chef. To them, he gave portions of the better food that was only prepared for the female guards and the male soldiers.

Malanga was a huge mulatto. Every aspect of his physical body was oversized. He had a weird sense of humor. One of his common jokes was to ask any of his female assistants in the kitchen if she wanted to try a bit of his sausage. If she said yes, then he would pull out his genital member and place it inside her mouth, asking her to chew it carefully and not to bite it hard.

When he arrived at the warden's office, she asked him to come in. He remained at attention in front of the officer, and she said, "Malanga, I have a nice task for you. How would you like to teach a lesson to one of the young political inmates?"

"My officer commands and I obey."

"I'm going to assign kitchen duties to one particular prisoner. I want you to have fun with her. She needs to learn to obey without questioning and you can help me break her spirit. Is that understood?"

"You only have to tell me when."

"Tomorrow."

"Is that all?"

"Yes, that's all. Now, go back to the kitchen."

María Teresa reported to the kitchen as ordered, being escorted there by a soldier. Many of her fellow prisoners were completely unaware of the extracurricular activities that took place in that particular area of the prison, since it was available to the common prisoners only. Thinking that the new assignment would provide María Teresa with a lighter duty for that day, plus the opportunity of having a better meal, they all had given her signs of encouragement.

The soldier closed and secured the door behind her as she entered the room.

"Everybody here calls me Malanga. While you're in this room, you can do the same. The first thing that I want you to do is to take a shower. You smell." He pointed to a door at the far end of the kitchen. María Teresa understood by his gestures that some shower facilities were behind it.

"Go ahead. You'll find a piece of soap and a clean towel inside."

"How about my uniform? This is the same one that I've worn since I came here."

"I'll give you another one, a clean one, when you're finished. You can also wash your underwear and wear it again by the end of the day."

"No. Give it to me now, please."

"As you wish." Malanga reached behind him inside of one of the wall cabinets and handed her a blue uniform.

"This isn't my uniform. This is a common prisoner's uniform, and I'm not a common criminal."

"Listen, girl. This is the only one on hand, so wear it while you're in here. You can wash your precious uniform and wear it at the end of the day when you're sent back to your cell. I don't care in the meantime what you have on, and neither should you. Now, do as you're requested to do. You can take all the time you need. I don't want anyone dirty in my kitchen."

When she came back into the kitchen, she found the soldiers talking to each other in an area near the exit door, and Malanga standing in front of the largest pot, dumping pieces of cabbage in a bath of boiling water and salt.

She approached Malanga and said, "I took a shower as you asked me to, and washed my clothing. They should be dry in a few hours. What do I do next?"

Malanga faced her. She then noticed that Malanga's penis was protruding from his open trousers, fully erect. She had never seen anything like that in real life. Pictures in textbooks could only resemble what she was looking at. She started to panic as she heard him say, "Before we do some cooking, I want you to meet this particular friend of mine. As you can see, he's eager and very willing to meet the inside of you. I'm sure that you can accommodate him."

María Teresa ran in the direction of the exit door, with her eyes wide like a frightened animal. One of the soldiers beat her to it. The other soldier came rapidly behind her and between them they held her tightly. She began yelling and screaming, kicking and pushing as much as she could.

"Bring the bitch here. Oh! How I love it when they put up a good fight."

María Teresa had lost quite a number of pounds since the time she had been brought to the interrogation center, and as a result of that, and of her present state of weakness, she did not possess the full strength that she was accustomed to having. Nevertheless, she stood her ground, and the two young men could not force her to move from her position close to the exit door.

"What the hell is wrong with both of you?" yelled the angry sergeant. "One of you grab her arms and the other her legs. Lift her body from the floor and bring her to me."

With great difficulty, the soldiers finally placed her on top of the table. She was swearing at them and spitting in their faces. One of the soldiers, who had received a large glob of saliva in his eye, punched her in the face.

"Don't do that again," Malanga said. "You'll have a chance to get even with the bitch in a short while. I promise you that."

Malanga took some rope and tied her wrists to the rear legs of the table. Then all three men pulled her body along the table until her buttocks were resting at the opposite end. Her ankles were tied with more pieces of rope to the front legs of the table after bending her knees. She was trapped and could not move freely.

"Keep guard at the door. No one is allowed into this room. This beauty is all mine," Malanga said with pleasure in his voice.

He pulled with great force at the sides of her dress which were held together by old buttons that jumped from the restraining threads and scattered all over the floor.

María Teresa tried to move her body sideways, as well as up

and down to try to avoid any kind of penetration. She was determined to fight until the end. Now, in clear desperation of her lost battle to defend and retain her virginity, she was shouting profanities mixed with short inarticulate statements begging for mercy.

The big man calmly dropped down his trousers and underwear. Then, he positioned his huge hands on each one of her knees and pushed them outwardly, completely exposing her vagina. He located his body between her thighs so that she could not close her legs again. The same hands moved to the area where her thighs met her upper body and pressed hard, limiting any further motion.

"I was going to be gentle with you and rub some vegetable oil on before I brought this piece of meat inside of your body. But, you've been such a bitch to all of us, when we are trying to teach you the good manners that your capitalistic parents didn't teach you, that I've decided that you deserve no compassion."

He pointed the end of his penis into her vagina and pressed in. The sudden pain became mixed in her brain with the humiliation of the act and the terror of the unknown. Her brain disengaged in shock. Her eyes remained wide open with a terrified expression on her face. Otherwise, she became completely unaware of what was happening to her.

Malanga had her twice, and afterwards, one at a time, the other soldiers possessed her body, but never her spirit. She was impervious to the rape.

After it was all over, one of the soldiers said, "I don't like this. She looks dead to me."

"No, you stupid asshole, she's not dead. She just fainted," replied the other soldier.

"Have you ever seen someone who fainted with their eyes open like that, and with an expression of panic on their face?" said the first soldier.

"Stop the bullshit, both of you. Now, you, bring me a pitcher of cold water," commanded the sergeant. He took the container and poured its contents over her face and head. The splash of the cold liquid broke the condition of shock, and brought her back to reality. Her first sensation was a feeling of dirtiness all over and inside her. This time, however, she did not have to fake a mental disorder. The experience had left an undeniable and incomprehensible feeling of guilt in her mind. More than hate and anger, she felt repugnance toward the opposite sex, and at the same time, a great fear of men in general started to invade her intellect.

The soldiers removed the ropes from her wrists and ankles. She was free to move at will again. But something very odd happened to her. Even though she wanted to move away from the table, and leave the room, her muscles were resisting any command her brain was issuing, and she remained in the same position.

"Hey, sergeant, I think she really liked it. She's still here with her legs open waiting for more," said one of the soldiers.

Malanga did not like what he was seeing and replied, "I don't know about you, but I've had it for now. That bitch took all I can give her for a while. Besides, I have to start doing some serious cooking soon, or nobody will eat here today. Get her dressed in her yellow uniform and take her back to her cell. Maybe in a couple of days we can bring her back here."

The cell was empty when the soldiers brought her back and bolted the massive iron door behind her. She walked staggeringly to the middle of the cell and collapsed on top of one of the thin mattresses on the floor. There, she started to cry like a child who has been punished for no reason at all. The cry lasted for hours, and it did her a lot of good.

When the other prisoners arrived from their daily chores, she did not say anything. She was gazing at something where there was only the empty prison wall. They did not ask her anything, and let her be for the rest of that night.

CHAPTER FIFTEEN

The following day, almost at dawn, two military jeeps carrying three soldiers each approached the main gate to the prison entrance, behind a black Oldsmobile. At the wheel of the car in front, a bearded young man in a Commander's uniform told the soldier at the main gate, "I'm Commander Mora. Open the gate at once, I want to go in."

"May I see your orders, Commander?"

Raúl pulled out a folded paper from his breast pocket and showed it to the soldier. After a quick glance at the paper that was held in front of his nose, the soldier rushed to open the gate and signaled the vehicles through.

The black car sped to the inside of the prison compound and stopped in front of a small building labeled Administration. Raúl stepped out of the automobile, and walked to the warden's office. Without knocking, he opened the door and went in. The warden was sitting behind her desk. In front of her, there was the list of prisoners that she reviewed every morning in order to assign different groups to the fields. She stood up the moment she saw the higher-ranking officer and saluted him.

"Lieutenant Ruíz at your command, Commander. What can I do for you?"

"To start, you can tell me if you have here a prisoner number 3517," Raúl said with a stern expression on his face.

"Let me check the records." She quickly scanned through the pile of papers.

"Yes, we do have a female prisoner by that number. What do you want with her, if I may ask?"

"You are not allowed to say anything. You only have to obey my orders. Prisoner number 3517 is to be released into my custody as of this very moment. Please, send a guard to bring her at once."

"I'm sorry, Commander, but this is highly irregular. I can't do that without a written order."

"Well, in that case, take a good look at this one."

Raúl produced a military order release form, in which it was stated that the prisoner should be given to Commander Mora for reasons of state security. The approval signature, at the bottom of the document, read Raúl Castro, Fidel's younger brother and the Chief of Staff of the Revolutionary Army. It was a fake, but she wouldn't know the difference. Raúl Mora was counting on that.

"I see. May I keep the order for my records?"

"No, you may look at it, but you can't keep it, for reasons that I'm not allowed to divulge to you. As the order states, you are to release this prisoner to me, and pretend that this incident never happened. I'll take care of straightening your records with the Superior Penal System Bureau. I can assure you that this is a grave matter. The Minister of Internal Affairs needs the prisoner for further questioning. That's all I can tell you at this time. Now, get me the prisoner."

"As you say, Commander."

The warden called a guard on the internal phone system, and told her to bring prisoner 3517 to her office on the double. While they were waiting for María Teresa to show up, she said,

"Commander, I must point out to you that I remember the prisoner in question here, and she acted very strangely when she first arrived. She came somewhat deranged from the G-2, and her condition hasn't improved a hell of a lot. Therefore, I don't know how suitable she would be for questioning, and I don't wish her present condition to be a reflection of my performance at this post."

"Don't worry. I'm not going to render any judgment in this case. I'm sure that we have the necessary medical expertise to bring the prisoner back to her senses if we have to. Just leave that in my hands."

"Well, she might be saying things that in reality never occurred. You know how these crazy people talk and you don't understand . . ."

"Understand? Understand what? What's going on with that prisoner? What've you done to her?"

"Nothing. Nothing, Commander, I swear to you. I just want you and your superiors to note that if she seems to be on cloud nine and she tells strange stories, they are just figments of her imagination."

Raúl had read the file on María Teresa previously, and knew in his heart that she had been pretending to be insane so as to try to get released from the G-2. Now, he was silently laughing at the cunning and histrionic abilities of his love.

A few minutes later, a guard knocked at the door and entered the small office, bringing with her prisoner 3517.

"Prisoner, you are to go with this Commander, and are hereby released from this prison as of now. Please sign this form before you go to attest to the good care and treatment that you've received."

Raúl looked at María Teresa and noticed that she was in a daze. She was not looking back at him, but through him. Her eyes were focused at some point behind his back. He produced a ballpoint pen from his shirt pocket, and took María Teresa's right hand so she could sign the release form in front of her. She removed her hand from his with a fast motion. The guard tried a similar procedure, and this time she signed the form.

Raúl was impressed with her performance. He took one of her arms, and gently proceeded to escort her away from the room. She immediately reacted to his touch and pulled her arm away from him.

"All right, I won't touch you, but you'll have to come with me."

He slowly walked to his car, with María Teresa following him at a very short distance. Once inside the automobile, he left the prison camp followed by the two jeeps and took the highway back to La Habana. He waited for her to say something. She did not utter a single word. Half an hour later, he stopped at a roadside café and told the soldiers to go back to the Army Headquarters without him. Then, finally alone in the car with her, in that semi-deserted place, he said, "Okay, Mari-Tere, you're free now. You can talk to me. I brought you a change of clothing that I bought for you yesterday. I'll pretend to go to the men's room and you can change in the back seat of the car. I'll buy you something to eat in the meantime. What do you want?"

She did not answer. He then realized that she had been sitting in the same position since they had left the prison camp. The same empty stare toward a remote point at the horizon.

"Mari-Tere, it's me, Raúl. You don't have to pretend anymore. We're alone now. Please, talk to me. What do you want?"

Still she said nothing. Raúl finally became aware that María Teresa was not pretending. She was in some kind of shock. He had seen similar conditions with young, inexperienced soldiers in the turmoil of their first battle, and he knew what to do about it. He grabbed her by her shoulders, and turned her upper body until she was facing him. Then, he slapped her in the face three times, and the spell was broken. María Teresa started crying profusely again. This time with her head down almost touching her lap.

He spoke very slowly, and with a soft voice he almost

whispered, "My love, what have they done to you? Please, don't be afraid anymore. I'm here to protect you. What's wrong with you?"

He went to embrace her, but she pushed him away from her. She finally spoke.

"Stay away from me. Please, don't touch me."

"It's me, Raúl. Please, rest your head on my shoulder and let me console your sorrows. You know I love you."

"I don't want the love of any man. Keep away from me."

"But why? What's wrong with you? Aren't you glad to see me again? I came to take you to Carlos."

"Carlos! My brother, Carlos! Where is he?"

"Carlos is safe, Mari-Tere. I just talked to him a few days ago. I'm going to take you to see him and leave you with him as soon as you change your clothing. You can't go around the city with that uniform that you're wearing."

"I'll change in the car. Don't leave me alone now."

"As you wish. Let me park somewhere else. We don't have too much time, but I can bring you something to eat or to drink if you want."

"After I change, I'll hide in the back seat of the car and you can bring me any kind of sandwich and something cold to drink. Please, don't take too long because I might panic." María Teresa found a package in the rear seat containing a new pair of shoes, a pair of wool pants, an off-white cotton blouse and a burgundy sweater. It took her less than five minutes to put on her new clothes. Then, Raúl went inside the small café and came back only a few minutes later with a roast pork sandwich and a bottle of cold beer. María Teresa ate like a lioness that had not been fed for weeks. Raúl had never seen her eat in that fashion before. While she was drinking the beer, he moved the automobile to another spot along the solitary highway, and on a side road that was not being used by almost anybody at that time of the day, he got out of the car. He dug a hole in the ground with a small shovel that he extracted from the trunk of his car. He buried her old uniform and shoes, and covered them as best he could. Some time after he was again on the main road to La Habana at the maximum speed that discretion would allow.

"Are you feeling any better now, Mari-Tere?"

"Yes, I am. Thank you, Raúl. Thank you for rescuing me from that atrocious place."

It was the first time that she had mentioned his name. Raúl estimated correctly that it was a sign of progress.

"I'm very sorry for whatever happened to you," Raúl said. "In a way, I consider it my fault, because I should have kept you with me. I've been thinking, since I saw you this morning, of how wrong I've been with you. I love you very much. Believe me. It's the truth. Maybe I never realized how much until I saw how defenseless you were today. I can only thank God for the high position He has given me, so I could free you from your misery. Your brother will explain the rest to you later. All I want you to know is that I love you, and that I want to be with you for the rest of my life. I know that Carlos is going to try to get you out of the country. Tell him to count on me if I can be of any help, and rest assured that I'll join you as soon as I can. If I'm caught while I try to leave, I'll be shot, and the same fate will be shared by anyone who is with me. That's why it's better that you try it first with him. The moment I know that you're safe and in the company of your family, I'll get to you, one way or another, and then, we'll never be apart again. I want to marry you, and make you very happy. I want you to be the mother of my children. Maybe I should've told you these things before, but it wasn't until now that I saw you so vulnerable that I understood how much you need my protection and how much I desire to give it to you."

Raúl moved one of his hands from the wheel and tried to caress one of her hands. María Teresa pulled her hand away from his again.

"I'm sorry, Raúl. In a way, I also love you, but it's too late for happiness. It's not you. It's simply that I don't think I could be happy next to any man again."

"But why, Mari-Tere?"

"Because of what I've experienced."

"My love, I understand that no prison experience is a gratifying one. I realize that a frail person can suffer a lot in a short time under those conditions. But you have a strong will, and you are a very intelligent woman. There's nothing that they could've done to you that time will not cure. In addition, I'll be with you to provide you with the best medicine that doctors can prescribe, and that's my sincere and everlasting love for you."

"You don't know what you're saying. Yes, there was a time when you and I could've achieved that pinnacle of romance. Unfortunately, not anymore, for this Revolution has taken care of that forever."

"I won't leave you with Carlos until you tell me what they have done to you."

"Do me a favor. Just don't look at me when I tell you. Keep watching the road. I saw the tortured body of Inés, or whatever was left of it. Her face was almost unrecognizable with all the open wounds and dried blood. Her chest was darkened, and her nipples were black. I don't know exactly what happened to her. I think they somehow cooked her alive until she died.

"For stealing a piece of fruit from the hundreds of thousands that they are sending to their Russian friends, when I only wanted to satisfy my hunger, I was beaten with a whip. They made me count, one by one, all the strokes on my naked body. My buttocks bear the scars that might remain with me forever." She paused for a few seconds, and then continued, "The last thing that I'm about to tell you is important to you, Raúl. It is important, because it's the reason why I can't share my life with any man. Their excuse was very simple. I said that I would not take the place of a mule when it died. The following morning I was taken to a kitchen where three men raped me. I don't know how many times it happened. It really doesn't matter. It was the first time that hurt me the most. I'm still bleeding, and I don't know how to stop it. My inside hurts, my pride has been taken away from me, and my old desire to be with the man I love and to be the mother of his children is gone forever."

Feelings, sentiments, emotions, and all sorts of notions ran wildly, in separate directions, inside Raul's mind. His love for that woman, the pity towards an innocent human being found guilty of wanting only to exercise her basic freedom, the betrayal of his once-loved cause, the guilt of having participated in establishing not a system of equality, but a system of terror, were bursting like bubbles from a steaming lava sea, behind his expressionless face at that moment. The sudden mixture of contradictory emotions impaired his clear thinking, and prevented him from organizing his inner thoughts in a logical manner. Utterly bewildered and confused, he only managed to say, "I'm very sorry to hear that. I just don't know what to say."

"Then don't say anything. Just take me to my brother and forget me, Raúl. Erase me from your life as if I had never existed. Be happy with the Revolution that you helped to create, and leave me alone once and for all."

It was close to mid-day when Raúl stopped the Oldsmobile at one side of Santa Rita's Church. He was extremely angry with himself. The last hour of the trip to the church they had not said anything. He knocked at the massive wooden door of the rectory and it opened almost without delay. The youthful face of Father Fernández greeted them.

"Hello, my good friends. Please come in."

"Hello, Father. Please take care of her. Carlos will be coming for her shortly. I can't stay too long. I have a lot of things to do. Do you have a piece of paper so I can leave a note for Carlos?"

"Certainly, my son. Please, go into my private office and use my desk. María Teresa, would you like to have some coffee with me in the meantime?"

"Yes, thank you, Father," said María Teresa following the priest into the kitchen area.

Raúl sat down in the chair behind the priest's desk and, taking some paper and pen, he started to write two short letters.

The first one said:

> My dear friend Carlos:
> I'm leaving with you the only love of my life. Take care of her and do whatever is necessary to bring her to safety. I'm giving you ten thousand pesos so you can try to buy your way out if you have to. Don't worry about returning them to me, because where I'm going, I shall not need them.
> I'm also leaving you another letter in an envelope for Mari-Tere. It contains the ring that she gave me once. Don't give it to her until she's out of this place, and back with her father. You have to do that for me. It'll be the last favor that I shall ask you. Please, don't aggravate Mari-Tere with questions at this time. It's enough for you to know that she has suffered a lot, and she's going to need a lot of care and sympathy from you and the rest of the family in order to eradicate these past experiences from her life. If I ever insulted you with my stupidity, please accept my most sincere and humble apologies.
> Farewell, my good friend. Farewell and good luck.
>
> Raúl.

The second letter was sealed in a separate envelope, and both were given to Father Fernández on Raúl's way out of the rectory.

The moment that Raúl left, Carlos came running from the second floor and embraced his sister. María Teresa remained attached to her brother for a few minutes. When she let him go, he looked at her and said, "Look at you. You must be exhausted. Come upstairs and rest a while. We can talk later."

María Teresa went obediently to the room where her brother took her. She dropped her body on top of the soft bed, and was asleep within seconds.

Carlos went searching for Father Fernández and found him sitting in one of the rocking chairs in the living room.

"Well, Father, is everything ready for tomorrow?"

"Yes, as far as I know it is. María Teresa is finally here and the timing couldn't be any better."

"I'm sure that you'll be very glad to see us go."

"Glad isn't the word. I'll be relieved for now, and happy when I know that the Lord has brought you to safety. By the way, Raúl left these two envelopes for you."

Carlos opened the one addressed to him and placed the second one addressed to his sister in his pocket. He looked very surprised at the amount of money in the envelope, and proceeded to read the contents of the letter.

CHAPTER SIXTEEN

Commander Raúl Mora drove like a madman when he left the rectory. His siren was blasting with its piercing sound all along Fifth Avenue in the direction of Marianao. He was heading straight back to the military camp of Columbia, doing more than ninety miles per hour in the process. He was raging mad, and he picked up the car radio and said in a commanding tone of voice, "This is Commander Mora calling headquarters. Answer at once. Over." The announcement was repeated four times before an answer came.

"This is Banes Number One speaking. Identify yourself and use the proper code name and security clearance password to continue conversation. Over."

"Lieutenant Mendoza, I recognize your voice. Quit the bullshit. I don't have time, at this moment, for the military crap. Now, listen to me and listen well, because I'm only going to give you this order once. This is Commander Mora; I'm heading towards the base, and will be there in no more than ten minutes. I want two helicopters ready to fly with four of my personal guards in each of them by the time I reach the airfield. I will give objective and flying plans when I get there. I want my men and the helicopters fully armed and ready for combat. You can use my special code number MM-PM-00-717 for authorization purposes. Over and out."

Traffic was not what it used to be in La Habana prior to the Revolution. It took him a shorter time than expected to reach the airfield of Columbia.

He stopped the car abruptly a few feet from the two painted circles on the ground where the two helicopters stood. An Air Force officer was waiting for him next to the flying transports where his men were already seated.

"Commander, this is very unusual. What are you trying to do?"

"Captain, let's say that it's an important exercise that we have to perform precisely at this very moment in order to test the degree of preparedness of the men at any given time. Instruct the pilots to take us to Güanajay prison on the double and unannounced. It's a drill intended to test readiness to serve the fatherland."

"I understand, Sir. I'll comply with your request at once. It'll be done as you wish, Sir."

"Thank you, Captain. Now, let's go." Raúl climbed into the small cabin of one of the helicopters. The vehicle lifted off the ground, and turned until they were moving west by southwest at maximum speed.

"I want to be able to communicate with both helicopters' address systems simultaneously, and in complete privacy. Is that possible?" Raúl asked the pilot.

"Sure, Commander." The soldier handed him a microphone after hitting the appropriate buttons.

Raúl picked up the microphone and said, "This is Commander Raúl Mora calling from Falcon I, and these are my orders for this mission. We are going to land unannounced on the internal yards of the prison at Güanajay. I want the entire compound secured and for you to be ready to obey further instructions, from me only, in no more than fifteen minutes. All security and military personnel found on the compound are to be disarmed and placed under temporary arrest. You have permission to shoot but not to kill, if anyone resists. All prisoners are to remain locked in their respective cells, with the exception of the ones working in the fields. You are to divide yourselves in teams of two. Teams A and B will depart from Falcon I, and Team A will secure the common criminal area. Team B will secure the infirmary and the barracks. Teams C and D will depart from Falcon II. Team C will take the main entrance. Team D will take control of the administration building. No communication will be allowed in or out of the prison without my consent. The pilots will remain behind to guard the helicopters. I will be in the kitchen area. All arrested personnel will be locked in one of the regular cells. The majority of the political prisoners might be out working in the fields. If that is the case, Team D will move to reinforce Team C at the gate and arrest all the guards coming from the fields after the political prisoners have been placed back in their cells. Is that understood by everybody?" He waited a minute and when he heard no replies, he added, "Let's go kick some ass today. I have selected you as part of my elite forces. We've been training together for a while now, and everything appears to be satisfactory. At the moment, this is as close as I can bring you to actual combat to test your fighting abilities. I know each of you personally, and I'm proud to serve with you. You're all very good men. Good luck, and act with pride. That's all. From now on, we're to maintain radio silence. Over and out."

When they landed, two soldiers and a guard came running to find out what was going on. They were promptly disarmed and handcuffed. Raúl asked the guard for directions to the kitchen. The rest of the invading party moved swiftly to occupy their positions and achieve their goals. By the time Raúl entered the kitchen, the entire prison was under his command.

Inside the kitchen area, he found Malanga leaning over the stove and stirring what appeared to be a big pot of chicken with rice. Two prisoners were seated at the table, peeling potatoes and plantains that they were placing inside a bucket with cold water and salt.

"You two prisoners, get out of here now. Go back to your cell building on the double."

The cook had his back to Raúl he heard Raul's voice giving the command to his help.

"Who the hell are you?" he said as he turned. The moment he became cognizant of the fact that he was addressing his remark to a Commander of the Army, he speedily moved into full attention.

"Sorry, Commander Mora. I didn't know it was you. Sergeant Valdés at your command."

"So, you know my name, Sergeant?"

"Yes Sir. I recognized you immediately when I saw you."

"Well, at ease, Sergeant Valdés. Sit down in that chair next to the table, and we'll enjoy a nice friendly chat."

"Begging your permission, Sir. I have some cooking to do for the administrative personnel. I'd rather stay here finishing it, if you don't mind."

"The cooking will have to wait. I have to ask you a few questions, and I need your undivided attention. Now, sit over there in front of me."

Malanga obeyed the order.

"Could you tell me, Sir, what's going on here?"

"All in due time, Sergeant. Now tell me, what do you know about me?"

"Not much, Sir, except that you're a true hero of the Revolution."

"Is that all? You seemed to know exactly who I was the moment that you laid eyes on me."

"Well, Sir, your picture has appeared many times on the front page of the newspapers, right next to Fidel. I have also seen you on television several times. And, I also remember you from before."

"From before? Where?"

"You don't remember me at all? I went to your house one

night asking for your brother Manuel, and you answered the door. Then your brother came out and we both left you standing there."

"What was the nature of your business with my brother?"

"I was sent by the 26th of July Movement to deliver to your brother the automatic weapons and the grenades that were used in the attack on the Presidential Palace."

"How interesting! This is indeed a small world. Now, is that the only thing that you know about my life? I mean my private life?"

"Yes, I believe that's all."

"Did you know that I was engaged to be married?"

"No, I didn't know that. May I ask who the lucky lady is?"

"Yes, you certainly may ask that question. Her name is María Teresa Aguirrupe y Larrazábal."

"I've never heard of her, Commander."

"Quite the contrary, Sergeant. I believe you knew her very well."

"Begging your pardon, Sir. I think you're mistaken. I don't know who you are talking about."

"Maybe you'll remember when I tell you that she was also known as prisoner number 3517."

The mulatto's face turned as white as the color of the peeled potatoes floating in the water next to him. His hands had been all this time on top of the table caressing a big cigar that every so often he brought to his mouth. Now, his right hand was moving towards his back trouser pocket. It never reached its goal. It froze in midair the moment his eyes saw the barrel of the Colt .45 held by Commander Mora and aimed between his eyes.

"Don't even think about it, Sergeant. Just put your hands very slowly on top of the table again. Any movement, and I personally guarantee you that you won't have time to make a second motion. Now, just stay there very still and answer the rest of my questions. I'm convinced that you know very well who prisoner 3517 was, so don't insult my intelligence by trying to refute the obvious. What did you do to this prisoner and why?"

"I didn't do anything to her, Sir. She came here for work duties, and helped me one day in the kitchen. That's all."

"It's a real pity that you suffer from memory lapses. Is this something new with you? Now, let me see, how can I help?"

Raúl stood up, throwing his chair backwards against the opposite wall with his left hand. He advanced straight to the Sergeant with the gun in his right hand pointing incessantly at Malanga's head. When he was within range, he dropped his right hand with great force on top of Malanga's hand and hit it with the butt of the pistol, breaking several bones.

Malanga dropped the cigar from his hand and emitted a very loud scream. Instinctively, he tried to use his left hand to cover and protect his right one from further attacks, but again the pistol persuaded him to remain still and withstand the pain.

"Don't you move, you dirty pig. I have more ways to improve the memories of sons of bitches like you. I'll teach you a few more with great pleasure if you want me to. Now, how is your memory working? Is it any better?"

"Yes, I do remember," Malanga said, stammering in pain. "But I want you to know that what I did in this kitchen I did under strict orders. I'm a soldier, like you, and I'm obliged to follow orders, like you." Big droplets of sweat started to accumulate on his forehead.

"What happened here to that prisoner?"

"She was becoming some sort of a rebel, and the warden decided to teach her a lesson in discipline. She asked me to force myself onto the prisoner, and I did."

"How about the other soldiers here?"

"They also had their way with her."

"Who were they?"

"Recruit Gómez and Recruit Domínguez. They also acted under orders."

"Have you studied any history, Sergeant?"

"No, Sir. I haven't. I never finished high school."

"Pity. A real pity. Because recent history tells me that you're using the same excuse for your crime as the one used by Nazi war criminals during the Nuremberg trials. It didn't convince the Allied Judges at that time, and it doesn't convince me now."

"Please, try to understand, Sir. How could I know that the young woman was your fiancée? I'm sorry, Sir. I really am."

"You still don't see the point. Mari-Tere was just the woman in question. In reality, any one of them could have been my fiancée. What you did was wrong, and now it's too late to be sorry. Too late for you as well as for me."

Raúl pulled back on the firing pin of the pistol with his thumb. The big mulatto was sweating profusely, and the broken hand was sending rhythmic and throbbing waves of pain to his brain.

"Prepare yourself to meet, face to face, the demons that possess your body. In the name of the purity of the Revolution that you disgraced with your acts, I condemn you in this military court to . . . ."

"Wait, please, wait a second. Don't send me to hell that fast. First, let me tell you about the purity of your Revolution. I gave the weaponry to your brother to go and kill Batista, acting under orders issued to me by Fidel Castro himself. The guns and the grenades were tampered with to make them defective. It was Castro's intention all along to have the plan fail and the people involved in it to be killed by Batista. He didn't want any competition. And you're talking to me about the purity of the Revolution. You're nothing but an asshole."

"You son of a bitch."

Raúl pulled the trigger and the first bullet hit Malanga in the forehead, pushing him and the chair a few feet back and to the floor. Six more bullets were fired. All of them hit Malanga in the head. His skull broke into several small pieces, tossing parts of his brain all over the blood-stained floor.

Soldiers from Team D rushed in when they heard the shots but found Raúl leaving the room and did not ask any questions.

Raúl went to the yard where the helicopters were and asked the soldiers under his command, "Is everything under control?"

"Yes, Sir. You can be proud of us. Everything went as ordered. All the members of the assigned tasks are at their positions and holding them without any problems."

"Good. Now, Team D will go back to the administration building and bring me the warden and two soldiers by the names of Gómez and Domínguez. On the double."

Commander Mora took the pistol from his holster again and placed a fresh clip in it. Then, he put it back in the belt holster. He went to one of the helicopters and took out a sub-machine gun and four clips.

When his men returned, the warden was protesting loudly.

"What the hell is going on here? Commander Mora, you were here this morning. What's the meaning of this? You might be a Commander, but I'm in charge of this place and I demand to know."

"Handcuff the prisoners and stand aside," Raúl commanded without paying attention to the warden's complaints.

The soldiers obeyed.

"I repeat, what the hell is going on here? Who the hell are you to come to my post and start giving orders like that?"

"You've all been charged with treason, committed by all of you when you abused the power given to you by the Revolution, and disgraced yourselves by committing, allowing and participating in a despicable, immoral act. I find you guilty as charged after the investigation I have conducted in your kitchen with the late Sergeant Valdés.

"In the name of the Revolutionary Justice of the Revolutionary Armed Forces of Cuba, you are hereby sentenced by me to be shot for crimes committed against the Revolution."

While Raúl was speaking, the two soldiers were looking at each other with open mouths and disbelief on their faces.

"Hey, hold on a second!" the warden exclaimed in a loud voice. "I have my rights. Since when is the Revolution so preoccupied with what happened to one of these bitches here? What the hell was she to you and the Minister? What has she told you? I'm sure that they're all lies. I have the right to defend myself."

Raúl opened fire with the automatic weapon. Three bodies fell to the ground full of holes, through which life escaped mercilessly. His own men and the helicopter pilots were astonished, but nobody volunteered a single comment.

"Team D will return to their assigned position in the administration building, and hold it until tomorrow morning. No communication with the outside world is permitted until 9:00 A.M. One of you will make the rounds and inform the other Teams to also remain at their assigned posts. Tomorrow, as soon as the new reinforcements arrive, the members of my special forces will take Falcon II, and return to Columbia where they will report to me. The pilot of Falcon II will remain here until then as part of Team D, and will follow their orders until tomorrow morning. I'm taking Falcon I to report to our glorious leader. Well done, men. Until tomorrow. Fatherland or death. We shall overcome!"

As soon as the vehicle was airborne, Raúl told the pilot to contact Army Headquarters over the radio, and to give him the microphone. After identifying himself and the usual salutations were exchanged, Raúl asked, "Where is Fidel Castro at this time? Over."

"He is at a meeting in the Presidential Palace. Over."

"Get him and tell him that Commander Mora requests an urgent meeting with him. Over."

After a few minutes, a reply came back.

"Meeting granted. Premier Castro wants to know the nature of the meeting and state of urgency before you arrive. Over."

"An attack on the Revolution from within. I know the names of the guilty parties. It is extremely urgent that he knows of the treacherous act. I shall land on the park between the Fine Arts Palace and the Presidential Palace in approximately twenty minutes. Clear me for landing. This is Falcon I. Over."

"Go ahead, Commander. By the time you reach your

destination, everything will be under control. All is clear here. Over and out."

Raúl jumped out of the helicopter before its long metal blades came to a full stop. As soon as his feet hit the ground below, he ran towards the Palace. The soldiers at the south gate were already waiting for him, and signaled him to proceed inside.

Two soldiers were seated next to a desk, located on the second floor landing of the Presidential Palace. One of them moved forward to intercept Raúl as he was climbing the stairs.

"Please, stop, Commander. We've been expecting you, but I must clear you first, before you can proceed."

"Soldier, I'm not in the mood for arguments today. Just get out of my way. Fidel is waiting for me."

The soldier tried to stand in front of Raúl, but the young Commander pushed him aside with such force that he lost his footing and fell on the floor. The other soldier came from behind the desk to help his friend, and pulled out his gun.

"Commander, stop. Stop or I'll shoot. You know the rules. No one is allowed beyond this point with any kind of weapon. Please stop."

Raúl pulled out his pistol, the gun that his brother had given him once; it now seemed like an eternity ago. He turned and fired, hitting the soldier in the chest. He quickly aimed again and fired one more shot. This one found its place in the other soldier's stomach.

There was an instantaneous reaction on the entire second floor. Civilians and soldiers were all coming out of the nearby offices to investigate the cause of the shots. Raúl faced them to say, "All is well. The soldiers were part of a conspiracy, and I had to shoot them. Call the guards. Send for an ambulance." Then, he continued climbing the stairs.

He was now approaching the third floor landing. He made a right turn and walked slowly in the direction of Castro's private offices. When he arrived at his destination, the door in front of him was bolted from the inside. Two soldiers were standing on either side of the door. One of them said, "You have to wait here, Commander, until everything is cleared."

"Let me in, damn it. Let me in. I have to see Fidel now."

"No way, Commander. Our orders are very strict when they concern the safety of our leader. At the first sign of turmoil, this door is closed from the inside and it will not be opened again until the whole situation is cleared. So, please, take it easy, and wait here for the security personnel to arrive."

Raúl took his pistol in his hand and pointed it at the disarmed soldiers.

"Open the door, I'm telling you. Open the goddamned door."

"Take it easy, Commander. We can't do anything from here anyway."

"Then, get away from it."

"Yes, as you wish." The soldiers moved sideways until their backs were against one of the walls of the anteroom.

Raúl banged at the door with the butt of his gun.

"Let me in, Fidel. This is Raúl Mora. I have to see you right away. Open this door and let me in."

"Commander, please put your pistol down on the floor, and we can straighten out the situation. Do it now, please," a voice behind him said.

Raúl turned his head and saw an Army Security Major, backed by four soldiers carrying automatic weapons that were all aimed at him. He unhurriedly put his Colt .45 on the white and gray marble floor, and then kicked it towards the Major.

"Thank you, Commander. What is this anyway?"

"The result of a dirty conspiracy. I came to see Fidel so that he could know about it."

"Sure enough, Sir. Please, just wait a second."

The Major knocked on the door. Three knocks, then two, then three more, followed by a single knock. The door opened, and the Major said, "After you, Commander."

"Thank you," replied Raúl, and walked inside. There were

about eight people in the room. Fidel suddenly appeared from behind the group of visitors.

"Commander Mora, you wished to see me. What news do you bring me?"

"What I have to say to you is a grave matter pertaining to the security of the state. I would like to see you alone."

"You know that it's against my own regulations. The only people that I see alone are the women that I want to fuck." Everybody laughed at the joke. Fidel continued, "Not even my brothers and sisters do I see alone. I'm surrounded by friends here that can be trusted, so tell me, what's on your mind?"

Raúl reached inside his trouser pocket as if he was looking for some piece of paper, and extracted a small pistol. The movement was so swift that Castro did not have a chance to change his stance. The first and second bullets hit him squarely in the chest. The third bullet hit the ceiling, and the fourth was never fired, as Raúl was gunned down from behind by the security Major.

As Raúl lay on his stomach dying, Castro started to remove the bulletproof vest that had saved his life. Bending over the dying man to take a closer look at him, he spat a wad of saliva and tobacco on him and said, "He must've gone crazy or something. What the hell happened to the son of a bitch? Major, I want a full report in 24 hours. Now, have this piece of shit removed from my office. I have affairs of state to take care of."

CHAPTER SEVENTEEN

The next morning, the broadcast on the radio reported the following news:

Yesterday, Commander Raúl Mora behaved in a very strange manner and led some of his elite men on a fictitious takeover of the women's prison facilities at Güanajay. After gaining control of the prison camp, he himself went on a rampage and executed Lieutenant Rosa Ruíz, Sergeant Eusebio Valdés and several recruits. Then, he took an Air Force helicopter and forced the pilot to land it behind the Presidential Palace. Commander Mora entered the Palace under the false pretense of having an important meeting with Premier Castro, and there he wounded two recruits when they tried to block his access to the offices being occupied by our great Leader. In an attempt to put an end to the ensuing danger of having a madman with a gun in his hand shooting crazily in the direction of any moving target, the Maximum Leader of our beloved Revolution decided bravely to face the assailant unarmed and try to convince him to put his weapon down. Commander Raúl Mora in a gesture of the utmost ungratefulness opened fired against Fidel Castro who dodged the bullets and avoided being hit. At last, Major Arias gunned down the attacker, who died from the wounds received.

Before dying, Commander Mora made references to his recent treacherous activities with infiltrated members of the CIA, who had recruited him with the purpose of having someone close to Castro to effect his assassination. They were using hallucinatory drugs on Commander Mora to prepare his mind for this mission. Apparently, an overdose of the drug caused yesterday's reaction on their test subject, and the Commander went berserk.

The Security Forces of the Revolution are on the trail of this subversive group, and promise to bring them to justice very soon. In the meantime, if any of you listeners have any information concerning this incident, we'd appreciate your calling 9-4646. Your call will be handled with strict confidentiality.

Three Cubans listened to the small radio in the living room of the rectory, while having breakfast. María Teresa left her cup of coffee on top of the end table at the side of the sofa where she was sitting, and went silently back to her room. Carlos was going to say something, but Father Fernández grabbed his arm and shook his head.

"Let her be for a while" Father Fernández said. "It will be best for her, after what you told me last night. Poor Raúl. He saw the light when it was too late for him. I don't believe anything they say anyway. To interpret everything backwards is the only way to really know what these people are telling you."

"Yes, poor Raúl. I wonder how the news will reach his parents, who have lost both their sons to this pestilent whirlpool of a revolution."

"Raúl is resting already, Carlos. The big question here is not he, but you and María Teresa. You have to get off of this island today. There isn't a single moment to lose. I don't know if you noticed that they're looking for informants to retrace Raul's steps yesterday. I'm not sure, but someone might have seen him entering or leaving this rectory. If they call the number on the radio, the security forces will be here conducting a search in no time at all."

"I'm very sorry, Father. Now I've put you in serious danger."

"Me? No, don't be a fool. I should have no problem. I can

always say that he came to see me for a private confession. Besides, I can also invite some of the other priests to spend some time with me. I don't think that they would dare interrogate me. Not with another priest in here. The real problem is you and Mari-Tere. If they find you here with me, then God help us all."

"Well, the fishermen that you know are willing to take us, and they are planning to leave tonight. As far as I know, they have bribed the guards at the Miramar Yacht Club, and the boat is hidden nearby. It's being painted black, sail and all. So we shouldn't have any problem getting out of here tonight. The question is what should we do between now and then? I don't want the responsibility of endangering your life, Father. You've done for me and my sister what I'm sure no other person would've done for us."

"That's nonsense. What I did for both of you I would do for any other member of the flock of Christ. Now, let's start to get you and your sister ready for the trip. I'll tell you what I have in mind while you change."

The two men went upstairs searching for María Teresa whom they found in an expectedly sorrowful mood.

"I've decided that now is the time for both of you to get ready for your trip tonight," Father Fernández said to María Teresa, and then he continued, "There's no time to waste. Now, Mari-Tere, you'll wear the same type of clothing that Carlos will wear. I suggest the standard black suit of a priest, and the black shirt minus the white collar. I have different sizes in that cupboard. So, come on, let's get dressed. Mari-Tere, pick out your clothing and go into the next room to change. Come back as soon as you're ready. Come on, hurry up."

"What's the hurry all of a sudden?" María Teresa asked.

"We might be placing Father Fernández in grave danger if we don't comply with his request now. So, don't argue, Mari-Tere. Just do as he says," Carlos said.

They both had their new clothing on in a matter of minutes.

"Here are your black socks and black shoes. Try them on. I

have to tell you that the assortment of shoes isn't as great as the suit sizes."

"Mine are okay," Carlos said.

"These are a little big, but I'll manage," said María Teresa.

"Wait. We used to have a short priest from the Canary Islands. Remember him? Father Perera was his name and he had small feet. Now, let me think where his clothing would be. I'll be right back."

Father Fernández came back with another pair of black shoes that were almost perfect for María Teresa. He also brought some black shoe polish and black electrical tape. He told them that the polish was to cover their hands and faces. The tape should be used to seal the ends of the sleeves of the jacket against their wrists, and the ends of the trousers against their ankles.

"You can do that later when you're ready to go. Now, let me tell you something. Behind the main altar, in the church, there is a secret compartment, large enough to accommodate both of you comfortably until tonight. In the event of impending plundering, we use it to hide those sacred objects that we don't want the mob to desecrate. The only way that anyone is going to find that place is by toppling down the main altar, and with it, the entire building. I'll give you enough food and water for you to take into hiding, and later on, for your trip. If all goes well, I'll come back by 9:00 P.M. to pick you up and take you to your rendezvous. If by 9:15 P.M. I haven't showed up, you must leave and proceed to the boat without me. The church should be all dark. Leave through the side door, and walk to the ocean. God be with you, my children."

"Thank you for everything, Father. I'll always remember your kindness, and I'll repay you someday. For now, please take this money. I have no use for it."

Carlos gave the priest the ten thousand pesos that Raúl had given him the day before. María Teresa gave Father Fernández a big hug, and expressed her gratitude. The good priest urged them to go to the toilet while he gathered the food.

The brother and sister spent the rest of the day trapped in the confined quarters. Once they were in, and the only access door had been closed, María Teresa feared there would not be enough air in the cramped little compartment. The only air came from the space between the bottom of the door and the floor. They both lay down with their mouths and noses as close as possible to the tiny crack, and tried to breathe as best they could. They never changed position or emitted a single sound for the next eight hours.

Every so often, Carlos lit the small flashlight that Father Fernández had given them, and observed the time on his wristwatch. By 9:10 P.M., Carlos started to worry about the friendly priest. He touched María Teresa and in silence pointed to his watch.

Carlos opened the door very slowly after he pulled out the gun he was carrying. He came out from behind the altar. Everything was very quiet and very dark. He motioned to his sister to imitate him, and both of them walked towards the left side door.

He put the gun back in his belt, and little by little opened the outside door. He found the street deserted and noiseless. Then Carlos took his sister's hand and together they walked in the direction of the ocean along the dark sidewalk.

The first corner presented the aggravation of a bright streetlight in front of them. Carlos stopped for a second and hesitated, while trying to decide whether to run to the next block, or to walk across nonchalantly. Unfortunately, they were all in black including their faces and hands. Someone could notice them easily.

A dark gray car was coming and Carlos moved back a couple of steps dragging his sister with him away from the reach of the light. The car stopped in front of them, and a friendly voice said while opening the passenger door, "Quickly, get in. I'll take you to the boat now." It was the voice of Father Fernández.

"Father, what happened?" Carlos said.

"Nothing. That's the good news. I just had to go to a meeting that the Diocese asked me to attend this afternoon. I couldn't say no, and I had to stay for supper. I tried to come as soon as I could. I'm sorry if I worried you."

They reached the boat safely. It looked like a naval engineer's nightmare with a sail on it. Carlos estimated the whole length of the boat to be no more than twenty-six feet. He calculated that it was too small for all six of them, but he could not demand that anyone remain behind.

Carlos was wrong about the safety of the boat. The fishermen knew what they were doing, and the boat soon enough proved to be seaworthy. The night was dark and full of clouds. They tied a piece of black canvas to provide some shelter for the women across the width of the boat. The men congregated towards the stern. One of the fishermen handled the sail and the other the rudder.

It was the first time in months that María Teresa and Carlos felt relaxed. They looked at each other and smiled. Freedom and their family were only ninety nautical miles away.

CHAPTER EIGHTEEN

Dawn found them at open sea, traveling approximately at six knots and on a course north to northwest. The fishermen said they had been looking constantly at the stars during the night, but the night had been so dark that they couldn't see much. However, the next morning they claimed to be on course after some discussions between them and their wives. Carlos looked at María Teresa, shrugged and smiled. Without instruments, he was completely lost, and could only hope that the seafaring expertise of his companions was equal to their talent for arguing. One of the fishermen's wives produced cans of food and crackers from a large brown bag. The other extracted a can opener from a purse and said to María Teresa, "With the rush of leaving last night, and the need to maintain complete silence during the night, I didn't have a chance to introduce myself to you folks. My name is Olga Rangél, and this is my friend Rosita Luaces. The man at the rudder is my husband Benito O'Farrill, and the one at the sail mast is Rosita's husband Cheo Cuervo. Would you care for some breakfast?"

"We're very pleased to meet you. My name is María Teresa Aguirrupe, and this is my brother Carlos. Yes, we would love to share whatever food you may have. My brother and I are extremely grateful to you for your generosity in taking us. You're the difference between a life of freedom and a life of slavery. Thank you very much."

"Don't mention it. We would've done anything for Father Fernández. This is really just a small favor, because we were leaving that atrocious place no matter what."

Rosita opened some cans of tuna and sardines. She served the fish over individual crackers, and passed them along. "Cheo, should we save the boiled eggs for tomorrow?" asked Rosita.

"If everything goes well, we should be in the Florida Keys by some time tonight. Let's have the eggs now. I'm hungry."

Rosita removed six eggs from the bag and gave one to each of the passengers. They tasted delicious. They drank enough water to satisfy their thirst afterwards.

The first few hours of sunlight warmed up the winter day, and removed the chill and dampness of the previous night. Carlos removed his jacket and shirt. Benito and Cheo did likewise. María Teresa moved her hand to reach Carlos and her brother took it between his hands and deposited a tender kiss on it. The thought of getting closer and closer to her family, and the wonderful feeling of being able to breathe clean, fresh air again, gave her a renewed passion for independence that made her mind indulge in notions of liberty. She looked at him and smiled. It was her first smile since Raúl had brought her to the church two days ago.

"Tell me, Rosita, where are you good people from?" Carlos inquired.

"Well, my friend Olga and I were born in Regla. We've known each other since our school days. Benito was born in Guanabo and Cheo in Aguacate. They met each other through us, and for twelve years we lived together in a two-family house in the old section of the city. We used to own four fishing boats, bought with the savings of years of very hard work. The government took three of them, and left us with this one, which was the worst of the bunch. Are you folks from the city?"

"Yes, my sister and I were born and raised in the city. By the way, how did you meet Father Fernández?"

"Well, during the past seven years, our husbands furnished all kinds of seafood to the Augustinians. We remember Father Fernández when he was attached to the university, before they made him pastor of Santa Rita. He was the one who gave us the order for the week, and the one who always paid us. He's always been very good to us, and helped us tremendously with our children."

"Do you have any children?"

"Sure, we have three and Olga has two."

"Where are they? How come you didn't bring them with you?"

"Do you remember when there were some rumors last year about the government wanting to put the children in special schools in order to indoctrinate them? Well, the moment we heard them denying the rumors, we realized it was true and in a panic turned to Father Fernández with our problems. The American priests at the university donated the money to pay for our children's trip to the United States, and they found a parochial school in a place called Pennsylvania where the children have been living, and receiving an education until we could leave the country and join them. It was a very generous act on their part, and we've been extremely grateful to them ever since. That's why when Father Fernández asked us about bringing you along on this trip, we couldn't refuse him."

"But your children couldn't have been very old," María Teresa said.

"Mine are four, six and nine years old. Olga's are five and eight years old. Believe me, the separation has been hard. Not only for us, but mostly for them. They can't fully understand. We've talked to them several times on the phone, and the little ones always end up crying. It breaks our hearts, and yet, we'd rather go through this than see them face a life without real opportunities. We think that the sacrifice will pay off in time."

The wind was steady and in a favorable direction during the rest of the morning and early hours of the afternoon. They did not meet or see any other vessel along the way, and the entire group was in high spirits by mid-afternoon.

The small waves created a slow rocking motion on the small vessel that made everybody sleepy, and they all enjoyed a nice, long siesta with the exception of Benito and Cheo, who took turns at the rudder. Carlos had volunteered for the task, but the more experienced fishermen politely declined his help. Toward the end of the afternoon, Cheo woke everybody up with bad news. The sky in front of them was getting darker and darker. Some dense, black clouds were rolling towards them, and the sea was becoming choppy.

"I'm sorry to say that we have a storm developing just ahead of us, and moving this way at a fast pace. Now, if we decide to head west, the storm could throw us completely off course, and it's very dangerous to try to out-maneuver a storm on the open sea by running a course parallel to it. If we try to go east, then the winds and the Gulf Stream could place us out of reach of the Florida coast. If we then face in a northeast direction we could eventually reach Bermuda, but I'm afraid that we don't have enough water or food for that kind of trip. Going back is out of the question, so we really only have one choice, and that is to proceed and maintain our present course and meet the storm head-on. I have no idea how big it is, but chances are we'll fare well and find land soon after. It's not hurricane season, so it must be just another winter storm. What do you say?"

Everybody turned his or her head to Benito, who sat quietly next to the mast. He looked at Cheo and nodded his head.

"Good," Cheo said. "Now let's get ready. The women will sit at the bottom of the boat toward the bow and grab whatever container they can find to throw the water out. Carlos will help Benito with the sail. When I give you the word, you will go to half sail and then finally to no sail at all. Tie the sail well, or the wind will play some dirty tricks on us. Benito, at that time you can come back here with me and help me with the rudder. It'll become increasingly difficult to guide the boat properly. Carlos you can take care of protecting whatever food and drinking water we have. Whatever happens, don't panic. I've seen worse, and here I am, alive and well to tell you about it. One day, you'll say the same thing to your grandchildren."

Everybody went to their positions and got ready. No one said anything else. The wind rose swiftly, and the waves started to increase in mass and height. In the dusk, lighting illuminated the otherwise black sky. Half an hour later, the rain began to hit the boat and pound against it without mercy. It was very cold water. Cheo gave the first command, and the sail was reduced to half-mast.

The storm grew in size and intensity. The wind picked up velocity and created huge waves that rose menacingly over twelve feet. Cheo gave his second command to remove the sail and secure it. When the boat was riding the crest of the waves, they could see an entire furious ocean around them determined to destroy everything in its path. When the boat was navigating on the bottom of the waves, they could only see walls of threatening water all around them.

Cheo and Benito were trying with all their might to keep the rudder in a steady position. The turbulent sea proved to be a formidable opponent to their efforts and finally broke the rudder. Without it, they were completely at the mercy of the ensuing waves.

A huge wave came crashing onto the boat. The mast became dislodged at its base, and flew into the nearby waters. A second wave hit the boat with such ferocity that it turned it upside down.

When the passengers of the capsized boat hit the water, Carlos pulled María Teresa with great force towards him, and held her tightly with one of his arms. They managed to reach the surface of the ocean. His other arm found the mast and held it. He yelled to María Teresa to grab the mast, and she obeyed him while making a frantic effort to stay above water.

CHAPTER NINETEEN

By the next morning, the sea was completely calm again. There were no signs of the fishermen or their wives. Carlos and María Teresa were glad to be alive and well considering the ordeal that was now behind them. They had no broken bones or any other evident physical damage. They were just exhausted from the constant battle they had fought with the angry ocean.

"How are you?" Carlos said.

"I'm very tired and cold, but otherwise I'm all right."

"I'm tired too, but we can't afford to fall asleep now. I'll tell you what, let me tie you to the mast."

Carlos removed the leather belt from his trousers. He tied it around the pole and one of María Teresa's arms. He then took some pieces of rope that were hanging from the pole at the spot where the sail used to be attached, and used them to tie himself to the same mast.

"Do you have any idea of where we are?"

"Sure, Mari-Tere, we are at a location where a pleasure cruiser will find us soon. Don't worry, dear sister. We'll be drinking champagne and having a good time very shortly. Just keep your chin up now and please try not to fall asleep. If we detect any coastline we should try to swim towards it. Otherwise, don't make too many movements with your legs. I wouldn't like to attract any sharks, and you have very beautiful and tempting legs."

María Teresa always had to laugh with Carlos. Even under these circumstances, her brother could bring some sort of happiness into her battered heart.

"I'll try to keep still, but if I begin to feel some numbness in my legs, I'll have to move them."

"Do what you have to do. I'll be here at your side to protect you like Tarzan. The only thing I don't have is the knife."

"Do you really think that we'll be rescued soon? I'm terribly thirsty."

"Don't think about water or food. Swallow some saliva. It'll help. Now, let's stop the conversation for a while. Save your energy for another occasion."

María Teresa remained calm. Eventually, she fell asleep and so did Carlos. The burning sun in that part of the world and the brine of the surrounding waters started to take its toil on their bodies after a while. A day went by, and their exposed skin turned red in the sun. Nasty blisters began to appear on their lips. The process of dehydration took effect and by the second afternoon they lost consciousness.

Some time later, a young ensign who was on watch on the bridge of the USS-17, a United States Coast Guard boat patrolling the area south of the Florida Keys spotted a black point against the light blue-colored ocean, and reported it to his commanding officer. The officer ordered the ship to change course and head in the direction of the reported spot to investigate.

As soon as the officer realized that they were approaching two survivors of a possible shipwreck that must have occurred during the last storm, he issued orders to rescue them.

Four frogmen swam towards the two survivors and radioed back to the boat that they had found a man and a woman. Both were unconscious. They attached their bodies, one at a time, to a light metal chair that was pulled up to the main deck of the vessel with a winch.

Once Carlos and María Teresa were on the Coast Guard vessel, they were immediately covered with blankets, placed on top of stretchers, and rushed to the ship's infirmary. The same day, a Navy helicopter took them to Jackson Memorial Hospital in Miami, where doctors began the arduous task of trying to bring them back to consciousness.

Forty-eight hours elapsed before Carlos opened his eyes. He found himself in a very pleasant white room. His body had all sorts of plastic tubes connected to it. There was a faint humming sound inside his head. It did not hurt. He turned his head and saw a large window. Beyond the window, there was a green park and palm trees. They were not long, tall, graceful and slender, like the ones in Cuba. They were shorter, but they were beautiful. A voice spoke from the other side of the room and he turned.

"What a pleasant surprise! You have decided to come back to us. That's very nice of you. How are you feeling now?"

The voice belonged to a pretty young nurse with blond hair and the most alluring blue eyes Carlos had ever seen. She spoke in English and Carlos felt relieved to recognize the fact that he must be in the United States.

"I'm feeling much better. I just opened my eyes and found myself in paradise accompanied by angels. Are you for real?"

"I must report to the doctor that you've recovered. Now, lie there quietly and let me take care of you."

"You can do to me anything you want, Miss."

"Miss Kelly. Maureen Kelly."

"Maureen. What a beautiful name for an angel! Tell me, Maureen, how long have I been here?"

"You came a little over two days ago. By the way, what's your name? We went through your clothing and couldn't find any identification. There was only an envelope containing a piece of paper that cannot be read, and a man's wedding ring."

"My name is Carlos Aguirrupe."

"Carlos? That's also a fine name. Are you Cuban, Carlos?"

"Yes, I am, and I have family in Miami. Where am I, by the way?"

"You're in the Jackson Memorial Hospital in Miami. Don't worry. I'll personally notify your family of your presence here. Are you married?"

"No. The ring isn't mine. It belonged to my sister's fiancé. I promised myself, some time ago, that I would only marry a beautiful blonde with exciting blue eyes, and they are very hard to find in Cuba."

A broad smile appeared on Maureen's face revealing two straight rows of pearly white teeth.

"Carlos, do you remember what happened to you?"

"Absolutely. I haven't lost my memory if that's what you wanted to find out. We were in a boat. There were six of us trying to escape from Cuba. We got trapped in a very nasty storm that broke the mast in half and capsized the boat. I don't know what became of the other two couples. We never saw them again. Only my sister and I survived the experience, as far as I know. By the way, how is my sister? Is she also in the same hospital?"

"The woman that the Coast Guard vessel rescued with you died yesterday. I didn't know she was your sister. I'm very, very sorry to have to be the one to bring you this sad news at this time."

The jovial expression on Carlos's face changed to one of immense sadness reflecting the state of his soul. He began to whimper and tears flowed from his eyes and rolled down his cheeks. He tried to get out of bed, ripping some of the connecting tubes in the process.

"Where is she? I want to see my sister. I want to see her."

The nurse rushed towards him and pushed him back. She said in a very persuasive tone of voice, "Please, don't move. You're in no condition to move around yet."

She threw herself on top of him placing her two hands on his shoulders and pressing her face against his. She held the position until Carlos stopped crying. Very slowly, she separated her face from his and whispered in his ear, "Please, be still. I'm going to reconnect the tubes again, and then I'll leave you only for a minute or two, to notify the doctor of your recovery. Don't move and stay as you are while I'm gone. After I return, I'll notify your family of your presence here."

Carlos lay back and remained calm while she fixed the bed and all the vital connections. He looked at her with imploring eyes and said, "Maureen, please, do me a favor."

"Yes, Carlos, anything!"

"My father's name is Francisco Aguirrupe. He lives at the Country Club Prado in Coral Gables. I'm sure that you'll find him in the phone book. Tell him that I'm here and to come to see me as soon as he can, but do not say a word about Mari-Tere, my sister. I want to be the one to break that kind of news to him."

The nurse left the room momentarily. Even though the nature of her work brought her constantly in contact with death, she could not avoid noticing her watery eyes as she went to make the promised phone call, and notify the physician in charge.

Carlos started to prepare himself for what he knew would be the most difficult moment of his life.

THE END